# THE TRUDEAU VECTOR

# THE TRUDE

# AU VECTOR

### A NOVEL

## JURIS JURJEVICS

McArthur & Company
Toronto

First published in Canada in 2005 by
McArthur & Company
322 King St., West, Suite 402
Toronto, Ontario
M5V 1J2
www.mcarthur-co.com

Library and Archives Canada Cataloguing in Publication


Jurjevics, Juris, 1943-
The Trudeau vector : a novel / Juris Jurjevics.


ISBN 1-55278-525-4


I. Title.

PS3610.U74T78 2005        813'.6        C2005-903663-X



Designed by Nancy Resnick

Printed in Canada by Webcom



10 9 8 7 6 5 4 3 2 1

For
Edvards Sudmalis
and
Alexander Nikitin
Grigory Pasko
Igor Sutyagin

*"A word is like a sparrow.
Once set free, you cannot catch it again."*

—Major-General Valentin Yevstigneyev
Deputy Chief of the Defense Ministry
Radiation, Biological and Chemical
Directorate, Moscow

# THE TRUDEAU VECTOR

# 1

The temperature was forty below and dropping. The sun had already set for the winter. It was now no more than a distant pale line between the frozen wastes on which they stood and the flatness above. This late in October, the sun's odd light never rose from below the rim of the earth. The faint silver band barely managed to halo the horizon and blot out the stars these first few Arctic nights, making the purplish black sky a depthless blank. Even that dull streak would recede as winter descended. In another twenty-four hours the sky would be fully dark and the heavens would ignite with constellations and galaxies.

In the beam of Verneau's portable lamp, his driver looked like a psychedelic bird as he trudged. Whenever the light glanced off the white quills of the lumpy extreme environment suit, their fluorescent tips burst into screaming orange. The curved helmet and cowl completed the impression: an outsize version of the penguin costume Verneau's son had worn to the blessing of the animals last St. Francis Day in Montreal. At any other time the memory would have elicited a smile. Not now.

Far overhead, the giant auroral curtain undulated, its gossamer pinks and pale greens billowing along tendrils of magnetic force where the field was particularly concentrated. Verneau found it impossible to bring the blur of colors into focus, to judge whether the aurora was inches or miles from his face. The aurora had appeared earlier like an omen, a rare phenomenon this far north. But a great many things were unusual of late.

Emile Verneau had never before experienced a total communications blackout with field researchers. His greatest fear was that someone had fallen through a fissure in the ice or into the waters of the polynya. But that wouldn't explain the utter radio silence, unless. . . . Unless all four had fallen into the freezing water at once, their wanigan driving through rotted ice or an open lead into the frigid sea. Even the polar suits could not save you then. Verneau muttered a few choice Quebecois epithets at the thought.

His driver paused at the edge of a flat expanse, and beckoned without speaking. They had reached the polynya, a natural opening in the sea ice that defied the cold and stayed open throughout the winter. It smelled of brine and was perfectly still.

The surface of the surrounding ice was well traveled. Several coaxial cables and red tether lines, caked with ice and salt, snaked up to the brink of the polynya. The data drone was no doubt circling like a shark in the water in its programmed elliptical laps.

Verneau's driver shone his light along the water's edge, checking for signs of an accidental plunge. They examined the many footprints, and followed them alongside the cables toward the inflatable shelter thirty yards off, which glowed garnet from the lights within. No human silhouettes, no vehicle outside, neither the large wanigan nor the smaller polecat. *No one home,* just as the initial rescue unit had reported before fanning out to search.

Alex Kossuth, Junzo Ogata, Annie Bascomb, the Russian glaciologist Minskov, and Lidiya Tarakanova. All missing. Tarakanova had been scheduled to leave that morning. The others had come to the campsite to see her off and to conduct the quarterly marine tests and download data from the remote-controlled drone. But they hadn't answered their scheduled base check at noon and couldn't be raised on either their suits' transceivers or their vehicle radios. Now half of Trudeau Station was out searching.

Inside the shelter, the transformer was humming, powered by the string of steadily grinding windmills mounted outside on hollow twelve-foot posts. Two collapsible workstations had been set up, taut canvas strung between telescoping legs. One [illegible] height, an overturned utility crate serving as a chair [illegible] workstation was deployed like a night table: just enc [illegible] quilted floor to allow a scientist access to a laptop con [illegible] sonometer while sitting comfortably on an air bed. A half-eaten foil packet of dehydrated berries lay nearby.

No sign of menace or malfunction. Nothing amiss. Verneau was relieved, he realized, not to find the bloody aftermath of a marauding bear.

Everything was in its characteristic state of neatness in Ogata's area and in complete disarray in Annie Bascomb's. The modesty curtain was drawn across more to hide her messiness than preserve her privacy. Alex Kossuth was halfway through one of his chess games, the board neatly laid out on his air mattress. Minskov's area looked unused, also not surprising. Something about the man was transient. Tarakanova's air bed was deflated, her sleep sack rolled up, her Arctic suit folded up, helmet on top.

On the adjoining bed, atop the sleep sack, he found Junzo Ogata's PDA and scrolled through the project log. The entries appeared completely routine, recording their journey from Arctic Research Station Trudeau to the fieldwork site; their cautious methodology in the demanding polar environment; the dull, exacting procedures of well trained and overeducated minds accruing details, amassing data. Everything about the work was predictable—except the setting.

He reached the last entry, which noted their sleep cycle and set out the morning's agenda. Calculations appeared sidebarred in a yellow window, marginalia that would eventually be incorporated into the database and formal report. Water salinity, upwellings, readings on the earth-tide gravimeter and the automated tide gauge. Verneau cocked his head to read a notation in the awkward scrawl of a stylus on the tablet's screen: *ignis fatuus.* He didn't recognize the term. Or the handwriting—not Ogata's neat geometric print. Kossuth's?

Verneau cursed again. Four scientists could not simply disappear in the middle of this wasteland. The radio in the hut was on and functioning. The equipment was recording its readings.

Could this be a practical joke? Tonight was the annual sundown

.rty, marking the final sunset, such as it was, the official advent of winter. Everyone improvised costumes from station supplies and pulled pranks, a kind of Mardi Gras before the months of arctic Lent. He wished he could believe this was just a sophomoric sundowner prank.

The driver tapped Verneau's arm with an open notebook, which he recognized as Annie's day journal. He took it and read the entry.

> *October 20*
> *We had a small farewell party last night: plum cake and Cointreau with our tea. Lidiya Tarakanova leaves today if the submarine can get through to the polynya. The polynya's opening is drastically, uncharacteristically smaller every day as the light wanes and we are gripped by full Arctic night. This year it must be like finding a puddle in the middle of a desert.*

But they had found it. Dr. Tarakanova had been picked up and rotated out. Annie Bascomb had reported her departure with characteristic glee: *Thank God for small favors, she's gone! Hooray.*

Verneau closed Annie's notebook with a smile. Under any other circumstances, he'd be toasting her departure too. *Das vedanya, Lidiya,* Verneau thought. Good riddance. What a piece of work she was. Demanding, whiny, difficult. She'd been the colleague from hell for a whole year.

A voice panted in his ear over the short-range channel: his driver was summoning him outside.

A beeping tone sounded repeatedly. One of the rescuers was alerting the others with her emergency beacon. A voice reported sighting the wanigan. Station Trudeau, fourteen miles southeast, acknowledged the transmission and asked to be kept advised. Verneau's driver was already consulting his global positioning device and polyethylene chart. The beacon was four hundred yards ahead, coming from the general direction of the nearby rocky outcropping they called Mackenzie's Mount.

"Let's go," Verneau said, climbing up into the high cockpit of the polecat, which started up, swaying along on its wide chassis, the soft oversized tires turning before Verneau had even cinched his safety harness.

*Merde.* Fucking straps. Why did they even need them? The polecat's top cruising speed was only eighteen miles an hour. The electrical motor was sparked by aluminum batteries, easy to start in the frigid conditions, and hydrogen-fueled to make it environmentally faultless, as the Royal Commission insisted. God, he longed for the surge of a combustion engine. A tracked, gasoline-powered snowmobile half the size could accelerate two to three times faster, to hell with the effect on the terrain. He wanted to get to his people. In the Arctic, every minute of exposure was potentially fatal.

"*Hostie,*" Verneau cursed. The swaying was making him nauseous. "This machine is a beach ball."

"Vhat?" The driver half turned, his face invisible behind his helmet's visor.

"Nothing. Go fast," said Verneau. "*Allez, allez. Schnell,* damn it."

It was markedly darker and colder than when they'd arrived at the polynya. Even the waxy red band along the horizon was gone. The digital readout in Verneau's helmet read 1:47 P.M.

A medical unit's tracked catamaran, larger and faster, eased past the polecat like a yacht on a languid cruise. Medical staff, including the station's nurse practitioner and a number of researchers who volunteered as EMTs, were in one wing, their gear in the other, the two halves connected by spars, which flexed as the catamaran skimmed over the ice. The winch, suspended in the middle, clanged against its frame like an alarm bell. Seven pairs of headlights advanced from the other direction, pincering in on the missing scientists. More high-chassied vehicles were approaching across the undulating ice field, lights swaying up and down. First-year ice was smooth and level, but this older pack ice was all hummocks. Verneau's polecat bounded over the rises, swaying side to side.

The tunnels of light converged, the center growing brighter, the surrounding ice flashing blue and green in the combined intensity.

The beams caught three figures supine on the ice.

"*Kurat,*" the driver cursed in Estonian as their vehicle rode up a slight swell and plunged down the other side, sledding. He wrestled the yoke as they skidded sideways and brought the polecat to a stop alongside the larger catamaran.

The trio was clearly visible now, the protruding brims of their helmets glistening like the beaks of felled birds. They seemed to be writhing, but Verneau realized it was only the effect of the quills fluttering in the mild wind. In fact, they were completely still.

Verneau vaulted out and followed the scurrying medical personnel, who shouted to one another over the intercom channel in French and German. Sounds of their heavy breathing filled his headphones.

Two medics hunched over Junzo Ogata, the Japanese geophysicist. Annie Bascomb lay twenty feet farther off, beside Minskov, both of their bodies oddly splayed, arching like circus contortionists, the Russian's legs practically touching the back of his helmet.

The medics knelt down beside Ogata, Bascomb, and Minskov, their lime sashes flashing in the headlights. Verneau and the others paced helplessly.

A medic tossed down an insulated canister of heated oxygen and tore at the feathery outer skin of Ogata's suit, cutting through the slack humidifying layer and the tighter body stocking. The released heat and moisture vaporized instantly, and froze in midair like confetti.

He slapped the leads of a heart monitor against the patch of exposed, steaming chest, instantly gray with frost. The monitor flickered, flashing red numerals and barely wavy lines. Single digits. Minimal cardiac function.

The medic intubated Ogata's airway. Hot, aerosolized oxygen jetted into the lungs at 105 degrees, warming the body from within to counteract the possibly lethal effects of icy blood in the arms and legs surging back toward the heart as the victim revived. Arrhythmia could be catastrophic in this environment.

Verneau hovered anxiously as the medic jabbed an insulated syrette right through the several layers of the shimmering suit, straight into Ogata's thigh, then reached up and lifted an eyelid to check the pupil.

There was none. The medic lifted the other lid. Nothing.

The eyes must have rolled up into his head as he lost consciousness, Verneau thought. The Inuit told tales of hunters whose corneas had frozen white. Verneau knelt down on the hard ice to get a closer look. Ogata's eyes weren't frozen. They were gone. Pupils, irises—gone. Only the white sclera remained.

Emile Verneau looked to the German medic Uli for an explanation, but he was frantically pumping Ogata's chest. "*Komm, komm,*" he chanted impatiently.

The lungs wouldn't deflate, not even as Uli leaned his full weight onto Ogata's torso.

"*Mein Gott.*" He grunted with the effort, made a few more desperate tries, then sat back on his heels, incredulous.

"He cannot be frozen so. His limbs, they are flexible. The faceplate is open, *ja,* so he is a little exposed, but the bodysuit is intact."

Grunts and whispers filled the radio channel. Verneau glanced up at the medics kneeling beside the other two scientists, beseeching them back to life. The intercom clicked as Uli opened his microphone, but he didn't say anything. Verneau touched the mike switch in his own glove. "Uli?"

The young man glanced up, his shield fogged over with moisture from his futile exertion. "They are gone," Uli said in English, then quietly in German: "*Wir konnen nichts machen.*" We can do nothing. He said it calmly and turned back to examine Ogata. "*Zu spät,*" he said, hoarsely. Too late. One of his team members slowly shook his head and covered Minskov's face.

Around the circle, more rescuers were arriving, each adding light as they joined the perimeter, an eccentric gaggle, all straining slightly forward, stunned. A jumble of shouts and moans, cross talk on the audio channel in half a dozen languages. A few were on all fours beside their dead colleagues, disbelieving. "How can that be?" he heard Christian say. More voices crossed on the VHF. "Annie, Annie," someone was repeating softly underneath the multilingual chatter.

Verneau turned away, stepping out of the blinding, shadowless glare. Miles overhead the sheer filaments of the aurora burned white and red, rising like fireworks, exploding with prismatic light across the hollow sky. Each golden streak washed the radios with a wave of static. The wavy lights started sixty miles up, rose a hundred above that, and stretched thousands of miles across the Arctic expanse. Verneau felt infinitesimal looking into that enormous wall of illumination.

The ground creaked loudly, like wooden ships in a storm, as huge segments of ice ground against each other. Never had the sea of ice seemed so desolate. Verneau turned back and stared at Junzo Ogata, Annie Bascomb, Minskov.

Equipment was strewn everywhere. A few of Junzo Ogata's Japanese colleagues had gathered in a semicircle at his feet and were crouching on their haunches, heads bowed.

Verneau didn't know what to do next. He felt numb from the knees down, unbalanced. He tried to force logic to come.

The loudest voices on his headset were the Germans, gibbering at each other excitedly, trying to analyze what had happened. He couldn't follow what they were saying, and at that moment he didn't care. He was shaking.

"*Verdammt! Wo ist Kossuth?*" one of them said.

Everyone who understood German looked up at once. The shock of finding three bodies had made them all forget. They had been searching for four. Where was Alex Kossuth?

Verneau turned slowly, trying to spot color, movement, a light. Nothing.

The scientists' wanigan, he saw, had run into a wall of ice and stopped there, the cockpit lights still on, its headlights jammed into the obstructing ridge. The mild beep of the rescue beacon continued to pulse in his headphones. The sound grew louder in the stunned silence.

Verneau returned to the lighted circle and reached down to Uli, sitting motionless on the ice. He found the pressure switch on his forearm and turned off the keening alarm.


Alex Kossuth heard the excited radio calls, then heard the beacon stop. He slipped off his helmet and the cold instantly bit into his lungs. He shed the other layers one by one, dropping them onto the seat of his polecat. When he had given up all his protection, he stood on the running board, reached in to dim the instrument lights, and set the vehicle in motion. He stepped off and watched it slip away, bouncing across the ice, running free on the hard sea.

In an instant the cat was a shadow, then vanished into the gloom. Watching the spot where it disappeared, he felt as if he had slipped overboard into a frozen ocean. Naked, Kossuth sat down calmly in drifted snow, and contemplated his mind contemplating its options.

With no protective attire and no insulated survival bag, the possibilities were limited. He could perhaps try to hollow out a lair with his hands, but he lacked tools or any heat source other than his unclad body. Snow's insulating effect might reduce the threatening cold, but the delay would be temporary at best. He decided against the effort. He did not want to distract himself with futile actions. He chose to remain aware.

He had expected memories, nostalgia, but his brain was made blank by the burning cold. His face grew stiff with frostbite, his fingers rigid.

His torso and arm muscles, he noticed, were convulsing to increase his metabolism and heat themselves; he was shivering uncontrollably. He breathed as steadily as he could, even as he shook. What message might he leave them before his faculties were gone? Lifting his hand through the loose white flakes, he let the crystals cascade from his numb fingers in a beautiful plume. Sand, he thought, warm sand, urging his body to deny the icy simplicity. But the piercing cold was its own imperative.

The left eyepiece of his spectacles cracked and fell out; the plastic temples collapsed and slipped away.

His nakedness was without color. The blood vessels on the periphery had shut down to conserve heat for the major organs. He concentrated on the brown fat cells between his shoulder blades and around his kidneys, where most body heat was generated, and tried to fix his mind on their activity.

He wished their survival training hadn't been so vivid: the way ice formed in bodily fluids, compressing and dehydrating the cells and destroying the electrolyte balance, ice crushing the walls of cells as it forced its way in. Or out.

Kossuth wanted to brush away the icicles around his mouth but couldn't. His arms clutched his chest and refused to relinquish it. The shivering stopped. His skin was flushed. The blood was surging around in a final effort to escape the invading cold, running for its life through his veins, but falling back. Feebly, he looked skyward and tried to fill himself with the mute beauty of the place.

The photon emissions were wondrous—a pulsating gossamer drape of pink and green and white, a noble winding sheet. Was he hallucinating? They never appeared this far north. Violet threads shot up like lightning. Magnetospheric protons and electrons, striking the upper atmosphere, exciting the gases, turning the nitrogen a glowing blue, the oxygen above it a yellow green. He tried to recall the equation for the particle trajectories at each time step but could not. Whole parts of his consciousness had fallen away.

He felt an immense pain in some part of him he couldn't identify and held his breath, trying to control it. When his temperature dropped sufficiently, perhaps a stroke would spare him further anguish. Hunching forward, he managed to free one foot. Half kneeling, Kossuth tried to rise to his feet.

In that moment he lost sensation and wondered why it had been so sudden. Then it occurred to him. Perhaps, since all the fluids were frozen, by standing he had broken his spine.

# 2

Jessie Hanley shaded her eyes against the hazy California sun and watched her boy run along the beach, shooing sea birds away from his bait bucket with wild Ninja whoops. She rummaged in her bag for a clandestine cigarette, confident that he was too busy doing battle with the gulls to notice. She lit up and exhaled a long lungful of smoke. His delight reminded her of the summer night on his last visit when he had frolicked among the spawning grunion on the beach at Malibu, plunging into the water to scoop up the roiling fish, his hazel eyes alight with wonder.

Looking at Joey, she saw a boy's version of her own face: high cheekbones, deep-set hazel eyes, and a strong chin, the better to bear life's blows. Her nose had once been thin and slightly curved like his, until a surfboard cracked it. The nose the doctors had rebuilt was too perfect, designed for another face entirely, and looked as if it had landed on hers by mistake.

In build, her son was lanky, like her oldest brother and like her, but he'd been spared their straight mouse-brown hair. His was curly and bright red, and he had the freckles to match. She'd loved his hair from the moment he was born. "He looks like an Irish setter who's been out in the rain too long," she'd said, giddy with exhaustion. The labor nurse had laughed, but her ex-husband hadn't. He never had appreciated her off-kilter sense of humor.

Hanley sighed and took a last drag. This long weekend, which had required protracted negotiations with her ex-husband, was not nearly long enough. She had only a few more days to spend with her son and then she wouldn't see him again until Christmas vacation. Damn. Why couldn't they have worked things out, for Joey's sake? But her ex had been perpetually incensed by the disproportionate demands of her job, which he accused her of preferring to family life. He wasn't entirely wrong. The accusation rang truer, certainly, as their marriage came apart.

"Bad enough that your druggie undergraduate years kept you out of med school in the States, bad enough that you paid your way through a second-tier offshore school by working as a mortuary assistant. But now you've got the medical degree. You don't need to do that kind of weird shit anymore." He couldn't understand what she was still doing on her knees in the middle of the Nevada desert, scraping plague fleas from carcasses, or investigating the high incidence of breast cancer among black women in Mississippi, or wading through blue-fly infestations on the Susquehanna River. Never mind that her sheepskin was from a second-rate degree mill, it should have guaranteed a professional's six-figure income, not her paltry public-service salary. "You could be working for Pfizer, traveling first class, and making a killing on Viagra stock."

The litany was endless: it wasn't safe chasing ticks all over the Rockies, or mutated frogs in Minnesota, graveyard fever in Indiana, infected mice on Utah reservations, and crawling around in the air-conditioning vents of Florida hotels looking for God knows what kind of bugs, or digging up ancient cow shit along old cattle trails while searching for anthrax spores some crazy had harvested and sent to the IRS Audit Division—along with the manure.

Their courtship had been loving. He adored her inquisitive—and acquisitive—nature then, and she thought she'd found the guy who could put up with what she wanted to do—to be—who didn't mind the eclectic mess she surrounded herself with. But the novelty wore off fast once they'd married, and vanished entirely after Joey was born. Her husband had gone from drug-loving English major to professorial prude.

"What kind of example is it for Joey to have his forty-two-year-old mother filling the garage with glass-encased colonies of

Australian meat ants, leaf-cutter ants from Costa Rica, honeypot ants from Arizona, prairie dogs, staggering mice, mutated guinea pigs in formaldehyde?" He itemized the countless horrors, living and dead, in their cages, bottles, and boxes.

"I'm afraid to open a drawer. It's not just that she's a terminal slob," he had explained painstakingly, in predivorce mediation. "It's like living with a necrophiliac!"

You should know, she'd thought, listening to the defamation, but deciding to spare the mediator the details of their less-than-inspiring sex life. Wisely, she'd kept her mouth shut for a change.

Years of ranting about her absences and failings embedded the rancor so deeply in their marriage that even their acrimonious divorce had not brought relief. The process merely allowed them to refine their resentments. The one thing they salvaged was Joey. To their credit, they did not use their child as the messenger for their recriminations. Even so, the divorce had set the boy back months in his schoolwork, especially his reading, which had always been a struggle for him. Because of Joey's learning disability, she had agreed to his staying in Berkeley with his father, where the local school offered a special program that worked wonders for kids like him. At least that was how she'd rationalized it and how his dad had sold him on the idea. The truth was more complicated. She loved Joey intensely, but she still doubted she had the internal programming for motherhood. It hadn't been done for her, and she was never quite sure how to do it herself.

Hanley stood up and slapped at the sand on her sweatshirt and shorts, then sauntered into the foam curling up onto the beach. A big wave broke, forcing her to dance backward toward the shore. The taste of ocean made her realize she was hungry.

Far down the beach Joey waved excitedly and called to her. The enormous surf-fishing pole was anchored in the sand and bending in an impressive arc. The boy had a strike! Hanley hooted. She sprinted through the froth at water's edge. By the time she reached him, however, the pole stood straight again. Joey looked chagrined.

"Snapped the line, Mom."

Hanley pulled him close. "Must have been a whale to do that.

Man! No shame in that. It's getting chilly anyway. Whaddaya say we drive to Marina del Rey and have a veggie burger for lunch?"

"Please, please, can't I have a regular hamburger? Those peppers are awful." He made a face.

"Just *awful*," she teased and made a face. "How about a turkey-burger compromise?" No need to scare him with mad cow disease but bovine spongiform encephalopathy wasn't a risk she was willing to take with her own son.

"Yeah, okay. Those are pretty decent."

After the divorce it had taken a lot to console him and for mother and son to recover their closeness. She worried that spoiling Joey every few months was the only way she could ensure that she'd remain in his life.

They gathered up their gear and tackle and trudged to the old truck parked on the shoulder of the Pacific Coast Highway. Last trip they had painted HANLEY & SON on the doors, a job she had concocted to get Joey interested in calligraphy, like the contests she invented to read license plates, bumper stickers, billboards, road signs—anything to help Joey's reading skills in the few weeks a year she had him. Hanley tossed their bag and the rods onto the bed of the truck and got into the cab barefoot. Joey leapt in from the other side and settled alongside his mother.

"Mom, what kind of business can we have with this truck?"

"The world is your oyster." Hanley retrieved her sunglasses from the dash. "Got any ideas?"

The engine turned over and they headed south toward the beachfront community of del Rey.

"Boy, she sure shines for an old heap. What's that stuff we used on it?" Joey squinted against the fall light. "Maybe we could sell that."

"A fancy polish made out of diatoms."

"Di-a what?"

Hanley smiled. "Diatoms. A kind of teensy plant with silica in its cell walls. In this case, fossilized." She pointed at the road. "See that center stripe? The way it glistens?"

"Yeah."

"The paint has them in it too. That's what makes the stripe shine when light hits it at night. That's what diatoms do. Some of them actually create light."

"Like the things you showed me in my chemistry set."

"Right. The fluorescent emulsions. Exactly right." She glanced at her ten-year-old. "You have a good memory."

"Yeah. For everything except spelling." Joey looked downcast.

"We'll have a pity party for you later," Hanley said. The morning haze was burning off. "Listen, baby, you can't let it get to you. It's just a majority thing. Most people's brains organize one way. Yours is much more original. It's wired differently. That's why you're so good at math. But you see things like words in—"

"Different letter sequences."

"That's the story. It doesn't mean you're not smart. Honest. If anyone knows about screwing up in school, it's me. And you're not screwing up. Your grades are fine. It's just that your head isn't in sync with your classmates'. But, hey. You come by it naturally. It's in your genes. And you're bound to hit on a way to match it up eventually." She pushed the hair away from her face. "Lots of people with dyslexia—people who read differently—turn out to be amazing physicists or architects. They can see things in three dimensions in their heads. You listening?"

Joey did not say anything. He was distracted, taking in the shoreline and oil tankers plying the coast.

She reached out and pulled the boy close.


Jessie made a game out of cooking with Joey. He liked the math of converting a recipe for six to serve two, and she would sneak in some reading by asking him to bring her the spices she needed or to read out ingredients. Joey liked her roast "chicken" made out of tofu, and his recipe for banana and pear Jell-O was an unexpected delight. Exhausted by their long day, Joey went to bed early. Hanley was lining up her evening pills and their morning dosages of herbals and vitamins when she got a call from her boss, Lester Munson, summoning her to an emergency consultation.

She hung up and checked her computer to look at the materials Munson had sent out. The three victims were identified only by gender and a letter designation: victims A and C were male, victim B female. The workups of the few remaining red blood cells were extraordinary. About as strange as their lung tissues, though the samples were not easy to decipher on the satellite-relayed transmissions. Still, she could see that passages from the mouth to the respiratory bronchioles had calcified. Normally flexible cartilage had been made brittle. The sacs and alveolar ducts were traumatized, the mucous membranes and respiratory muscles atrophied. This tissue loss alone would have been fatal, especially in the severe climate in which they worked.

Hanley couldn't recall having seen anything quite like it. The condition was devastating—and completely fascinating. An industrial accident? What could they have been working with on the ice floe that would cause this?

Hanley swallowed her portion of pills all at once, downing them with fresh wheatgrass juice, and checked in on Joey.

"I'm afraid they need me at the Center. I called Mrs. Feliz. She's coming over to protect my favorite son."

"Your only son, Mom."

Hanley screwed up her face. "You sure? I keep having these flashbacks. Something about an alien abduction."

Joey howled. He was a great *X-Files* fan, and this was his favorite running gag.

"I'll be back by midnight. You get some sleep."

Joey fondled the laminated ID badge clipped to his mother's work shirt pocket. "Are you and Dr. Ruff still mad at each other?"

"Mad? At Roughage? Nah. We're best friends."

"Really?"

"Not exactly, no, but someday we'll make up." Hanley bent to kiss him goodnight. "Sweet dreams, Wonder Boy."

"Affirmative," he mumbled and turned off his light, his eyes already closed.

# 3

A half-dozen senior staffers were arrayed around a conference table. Around the perimeter of the room, the more junior associates sat in the eclectic collection of thrift-shop couches, armchairs, and scrounged classroom desk chairs that passed for decor at the Infectious Diseases Center. They were there to observe—to keep their mouths shut and learn.

A current of excitement circulated as a stream of images arrived over the satellite computer link to their laptops and to overhead monitors, and other pieces arrived through the door, carried in by assistants and distributed to the assembled staff in sheets. Lester Munson, Director of Communicable Diseases, held up his hands to silence the room.

"Right. Thank you all for coming in on such short notice. Our advice and expertise is being sought, and I'm hopeful we can provide some useful insights. You've had a chance to look at what's come in on these three cases. So far, it looks to me like a one-of-a-kind. Challenging, to put it mildly. We need to pool all our experience on this one. The folks at Trudeau will sleep a lot easier tonight if we can tell them we understand what's going on up there. Anyone? How about some free association? First impressions."

"Hot dog," Hanley murmured to Cybil Weingart, sitting next to her. "It's psychic hotline time. Got a problem? Ask Miss Cleo. The first three-ah minutes of your call-ah are free-ah."

"The most likely cause would be something poisonous,

obviously," said Cybil. "It would explain how they managed to perish so uniformly and so fast. The trauma in the lung field suggests something inhaled rather than ingested."

"Okay," Munson said. "Let's start there."

"The other thing that makes me think inhalation is the contortion of the bodies. They're like nerve-gas victims. They look like the Kurds Saddam freeze-dried with sarin. Nerve gas also goes right for the eyes. That's one of its favorite ways to get in."

"I beg your pardon," Henry Ruff said, his expression disapproving. "Freeze-dried?"

"Yeah." Cybil extended her arms stiffly in front of her in gruesome pantomime. "You know, they were rigid as rock—in spasm."

"Okay, let's work with an inhaled toxin of some kind. Mike, you deal with occupational health," said Munson, chin raised. "Any feeling for what we might be looking at?"

Mike Petterson, his shapely legs propped atop the conference table, was still in his sailing clothes and topsiders, having come straight from his houseboat at the marina. "They might want to look at the station's power plant and portable electrical sources, and vehicles. A station like that must use exotic metals and catalytic agents to produce clean energy, yes?"

"No doubt," said Munson, opening his reading glasses to examine the papers that inventoried the facility. "Silver, cadmium, chromium, mercury."

Petterson nodded. "All lethal. What if the three victims came into contact with one of these metals and, say, vaporized acids?"

"You mean dimethyl sulfide and the like?" Munson said. "In high enough concentrations that would cause severe inflammation and necrosis of the mouth, eyes, pulmonary tract."

Petterson nodded. "Convulsions, delirium, coma."

"Okay," Munson said, signaling to his junior associate, who dutifully wrote *Inhaled poison—chemicals, metals* on the board.

Half turned toward the younger staff at the back, Henry Ruff said, in a lecturing tone, "There may be trace metals in the fingernails if metals are to blame."

Slouched next to Cybil, Hanley eyed Ruff in all his professorial splendor. As always, he was impeccably dressed: a spotless lab coat over a starched white shirt with yellow bow tie and pressed khakis.

"They went down pretty damn fast, Henry. I doubt anything had time to get to their fingernails."

She and Ruff had never gotten along. Ruff clearly didn't approve of her checkered academic career, and she didn't have much use for his superior attitude. She turned her baseball cap frontward, then tugged her braid through the gap above the plastic expansion band so that it stuck out the back. Her faded baseball cap bore an embroidered banana slug, the mascot of her undergraduate alma mater, U.C. Santa Cruz. "The banana slug happens to be the California state mollusk," she would tell anyone who asked. Other than her tan, she wore no makeup and still looked like an adolescent, despite being over forty.

Cybil Weingart blew smoke out of the side of her mouth and looked up from her notes. She and Hanley were the only senior women in the room, and Cybil was the only person able to smoke in Munson's presence and get away with it. She turned to Petterson. "You're saying a very potent chemical reagent triggers the attack on the lungs and eyes and other tissues?"

"Right," Petterson said. "Something may have gone wrong in their vehicle, for instance." He looked down at his notes. "Or in the 'extreme environment suits' they were wearing. A short circuit in the wiring, the heat coils, some kind of smoldering combustion? Obviously I'm guessing, but certainly the speed of this fatal incident suggests a scenario along those lines—a slow chemical reaction that puts out exceptionally caustic fumes."

"Sounds plausible." Munson nodded.

Cybil's body language said she wasn't buying it yet, but she didn't say anything aloud. She squinted at an X-ray just downloaded. "Why do these look funny? Transmission problem?"

Munson said, "Maybe they look odd because they were done with a dental X-ray machine."

"You're kidding."

"No. Their portable unit crapped out, so the station's dentist rigged something quick."

"Smart dentist."

There was a lull in the discussion as another download of material came in and everyone examined it on their laptops or watched on the large monitors mounted along the ceiling at the front of the room. Hanley yawned, tired out by the beach and her son, then scanned the new information.

"Excuse me," she said. "It says here that they were working at a field site near open water. What if they found some shellfish and decided to supplement the freeze-dried camping food? Anybody would—that crap's like eating sawdust mixed with glue. If they did eat shellfish, maybe they were contaminated. *Fusaria?* Some strains of *Fusarium* fungi are fatal in twenty-four hours if you ingest them. And you've definitely got *Fusarium* in the Arctic."

Munson had his assistant write *shellfish* and *Fusaria* on the board. Kim Ishikawa half raised his hand.

"Following up on Jessie's idea, what about paralytic shellfish poisoning? Red tide?" he said. "You can get that from eating Alaskan clams. Saxitoxin. The phytoplankton the clams eat produce it. Isn't that right, Cybil?"

Cybil Weingart nodded. "The latest theory's that saxitoxins are produced by bacteria inside the plankton. Problem is, they can get the bacteria to make the toxin in the lab, but not very much of it. One lab's theorizing that the bacteria developed the toxin, then transferred the ability to make it to the plankton through what they're calling transkingdom sex."

"Transkingdom sex? Holy shit, imagine the porn possibilities!" Hanley said loudly. "Catherine the Great ain't seen nothin' yet!"

The whole room broke up. Munson waved them to quiet down and Cybil was able to continue. "Well, whatever makes the toxins, the mollusks doing the hosting concentrate them; some of them even rearrange the toxins and make them more potent. Not just clams. Lots of bivalves. Mussels, scallops. Any mollusk that filter feeds. The toxins don't hurt them, and the more they feed, the more they absorb. They can house the toxin for years. A great defense against predators. Some bigger shellfish do eat bivalves, toxins and all, without suffering ill effects. If we eat that shellfish, however—bingo.

Numbness, weakness, respiratory paralysis. You get general muscular incoordination in the arms, legs, neck. Dizziness, temporary blindness, incoherent speech, and ever lovin' convulsions. Not usually fatal. But when saxitoxin does kill, it can do it in a couple of hours. The chest muscles get paralyzed and you can't breathe."

"Good call," Munson said. "Fits a lot of what we're seeing here. Saxitoxin. Why does that have such a familiar ring?"

"Because," Cybil said, "saxitoxins used to be high on the bioweapon hit parade. By weight, they're a thousand times more poisonous than cyanide. And they get six times more toxic when they hit acid—like in your stomach. Gary Powers had saxitoxin in his suicide capsules on his U2 spy plane. Nixon claimed we destroyed our stockpile of the stuff. A few years ago CIA admitted they still had some around. Allegedly they distributed cuttings to research centers, so we should be able to get our hands on test samples."

"Good luck," Hanley muttered.

Munson leaned back in his chair. "I'll make some calls."

"You know," said Hanley, "I keep reading that one reason red tide's a growing problem in southern California is the pollutants in the water. Something about the way the pollution slows down reproduction. The critters keep making the toxin, but they don't have any offspring to pass it on to. So each one of them gets more and more poisonous. I wonder if the extreme cold would have the same effect and multiply the potency of the toxin?"

"You mean, raise it to lethal levels. Great question," said Munson. "Kim, could you look into that?"

Ishikawa nodded.

"While we're thinking along the lines of nature's best poisons," Cybil went on, "we should consider tetrodotoxin in blowfish—the stuff the Japanese gourmets are so crazy about." She turned toward Ishikawa. "What's that dish called, Ishi?"

"Fugu."

"Fugu. The Japanese have got special chefs who're licensed to prepare the blowfish with just enough of the toxin left in to give you that little thrill. Of course, every year a couple of big spenders get more than they paid for and check out."

"Symptoms with tetrodotoxin?" Munson said.

"Numbness, weakness, rapid drop in blood pressure, paralysis of the limbs, the chest muscles."

"But are there any tetraodontidae that far north?"

"I'll check on that," Ishikawa said enthusiastically, and made a note.

Ruff turned toward Cybil Weingart. "To test for all of these at Trudeau would require a sample of whatever they ate and a mouse assay. Of course, that method's prone to a lot of false positives, but that's most likely all they'll be able to do with the tools at hand at a research station in the wild."

Hanley shook her head in exasperation. Ruff was showing off, lecturing Cybil in front of the interns as if she didn't know already what he was telling her. He rarely did this to his male colleagues, but did it to her or Cybil at least once in every meeting. From the perspective of age, Cybil just laughed him off, but Hanley didn't share her patience. Henry Ruff might have a collection of Ivy degrees and Phi Beta Kappa cuff links, but she had a hell of a track record and he knew it.

A few years earlier they'd fallen out while searching the Los Angeles police chief's office for contaminants, and their mutual disdain had gone public. Munson had chastised each one privately, and they'd agreed to a grudging truce. Every once in a while he still had to intervene, like the parent of warring siblings on a very long car trip.

Munson raised his chin and *saxitoxin* and *tetrodoxin* were added to the list of possible agents. "Points of entry, people? What if it's not inhaled—or ingested, as Jessie has suggested?"

"Normally I'd look at skin too," said Cybil, "but with those full-body suits and helmets they wear, nothing's exposed, so rule that one out."

Ruff shot his cuffs and assumed a grave tone: "The bodies are certainly compromised in any number of ways," he said. "But I find it hard to see anything enteric." He gave Hanley a satisfied look. "For starters, we've got no vomiting, no diarrhea." He picked something off his sleeve. "Also nothing hemorrhagic. They didn't bleed out. Eliminates a lot right there. I think we can darn well cross off a whole host of culprits that just wouldn't survive in the Arctic." He pressed a finger to his lip. "In point of fact, I am hard pressed to think what *would* survive in such extreme circumstances. And the deformed blood cells," said Ruff, striking his most fatuous pose, fingertips pressed together in front of him. "What are we to make of them?"

"What indeed," Hanley muttered.

Munson's assistant called up a magnification of the blood cells on the large monitors. The few remaining red cells were distorted by whatever had occupied and ruptured them.

Munson squinted. "What are you suggesting, Henry?"

Hanley raised her hand enthusiastically like a schoolgirl, the impression heightened by her grungy sneakers and blue work shirt hanging down over olive green shorts. Munson, brow furrowed, nodded suspiciously in her direction. "Dr. Hanley?"

"One of them is Russian, right? So maybe Dr. Ruff is proposing it's hammer-and-sickle-cell anemia." A groan went around the room; wadded-up paper flew toward her.

"What utter . . . crap!" Ruff exclaimed, vexed.

"Speaking of which," Hanley said, suddenly animated, addressing Ruff. "You know what our state's late, great Nobel laureate Dr. Linus Pauling said on that subject?"

Ruff was indignant. "On what subject?"

"Crap!" Hanley half shouted. "He said that ideas are the shit of science. And you, Dr. Ruff, are certainly full of "—there was a voluble gasp from the junior staff—"ideas."

"Jessie!" Munson exclaimed, exasperated.

"Well, he did. Pauling—"

"Fuck," Munson said, massaging the bridge of his nose.

The juniors snickered. Cybil Weingart rolled her blue eyes at Hanley. "You could use a little colonic irrigation yourself, girl."

Laughter erupted. Hanley feigned mortification but couldn't help laughing too. Cybil was a friend and allowed to tease, even about her weirder health enthusiasms—and contradictions. Cybil liked to call her the nicotine-addicted nature girl. To which Hanley would respond that nicotine had a long and colorful history as a medicinal plant.

"Guys, please," Munson said. "Can we get back to less frivolous pursuits? Two questions." Munson held up fingers in a V. "First, how did they die? Second, since there's no way out of there for the next five months, what's the degree of danger to the several hundred other scientists and staff wintering over?" He scanned the group sitting around the table, eyebrows raised like question marks.

"Have they found the fourth member of the group?" Kim Ishikawa asked. The room quieted down, focusing again on the grim reality that had brought them there.

Munson glanced up at his assistant, who shook his head. "Not that we've heard so far," Munson said, turning back to the table. "Okay. This killing agent took only hours at best. They're alive in the morning, by noon they've gone missing. By early afternoon they're found dead. Three people cut down almost simultaneously. Their eyes destroyed, lung tissue trashed."

Jessie Hanley shook her head soberly. "God, if it's biological, where do you even start to look? From what it says here, this group wasn't working together inside the station. All they have in common is a few days at the work site. If it's exposure to biologicals, the victims' systems wouldn't have had time to make antibodies."

"I don't get something," Petterson said, his white eyelids accentuated by his tanned features. "Why aren't they enlisting Atlanta on this? Isn't this one for the Feds to take a crack at before they subcontract to us?" He crossed his tanned arms. "It's interesting and all, but how can we be consulting on this if they're not on the case yet?"

Lester Munson sniffed. "You're right." He studied the soles of Petterson's deck shoes for a moment. "Centers for Disease Control is the obvious choice to chase this. As I understand it, CDC is unacceptable to the Canadian Royal Commission in charge of Trudeau Station. The U.S. Public Health Service is an arm of our government, don't forget. Part of our military. The Canadians don't want CDC involved in their civilian facility. We're a private nonprofit, as is Arctic Research Station Trudeau, which is why we've been asked by the Royal Commission, not Atlanta."

"Great," Petterson said. "We're just the politically expedient solution?"

"Listen," Munson said. "We've been asked by the NIAID to support the inquiry. The National Institute provides us with assistance—and with stipends—whence our life's work flows. And they want us to do it. End of story."

Henry Ruff wasn't swayed. "This is a Canadian island we're talking about, yes? And apparently they're rather sensitive about it. So let them consult their own perfectly competent health agency. They must be far more familiar with the Arctic than the pack of us sitting in Southern California." He shook his head. "We've gone far afield in the past, but this is unreasonable. We're not Canadian health officials, for goodness' sake, nor are we particularly experienced in northern environs. I'm with Mike on this."

"My dear Henry." Lester Munson sounded conciliatory but everyone in the room felt the tension ratcheting up. "We're not privy to the reasoning. But we've definitely gotten the call. Assistance is what we're expected to provide. We do not want to incur the displeasure of our benefactors, I assure you. Trust me on this one, Henry."

"Don't patronize me, Lester," Ruff said, nettled.

The two of them usually enjoyed one another's rancor, both being combative and fond of confrontation. But this time Munson didn't rise to the bait.

"Be that as it may," Bernard Piker interceded, pointing his pipe stem at Munson for emphasis. "We've gotten a sense of how small a needle we're looking for. Do you have an appreciation, Lester, of the size of this particular haystack?"

Piker looked like a scientist from central casting: eyebrows like a species of caterpillar, unkempt hair, overgrown beard, glasses perched on the tip of his nose. He knitted his considerable brow and went on: "We are not talking a couple of meteorologists playing pinochle in a hut and sending up occasional weather balloons. I've followed Trudeau's projects. That's a billion-dollar facility. Some of the finest scientists on the planet. Geophysics, hydrology"—he counted off on his fingers—"marine biology, glaciology, cryogenics, hydroacoustics, astronomy, meteorology, climatic diagnostics, coronography. Hell, they had their own artist-in-residence last year. Every kind of experiment you can think of is under way up there, running on funding from corporations and governments. ARS Trudeau even has exotic life forms imported for comparative study— swaps with universities and other research shops, from NASA and McGill University to Polz Pharmaceuticals and Moscow University. This is the biggest haystack imaginable."

"So, okay," said Cybil, "maybe they unleashed some new bug in their labs and infected themselves."

"They must all be terrified," Piker said, puffing on his cold pipe. "Justifiably, if you ask me. I mean, imagine if it recurs. Lord. The Feds, the Canadians—everyone has to get involved quick. If they've got something this lethal in their labs or equipment up there, Jesus."

"Good point, Bernie," said Munson, hoping this would get Petterson and Ruff to cut him some slack.

Piker put down his pipe. "At least assure me that our government isn't sponsoring some fancy deadly experiment in that conveniently isolated lab complex."

"Come on, come on," Munson said impatiently. "There's no indication of anything clandestine there. Isolated? Yes. That's actually the good news. The place couldn't be more remote—nowhere near travel routes, resorts, cities. Whatever may be there isn't going anywhere else. In that way at least, we're ahead of the game. This isn't London or Beijing or Toronto. But the catastrophic effect of this thing is pretty impressive. This is one hell of a powerful agent."

"Catch this," Petterson said, scanning the latest handout just being distributed. "I'm looking at page three of this new set. The morning of the incident, a fifth member of the party was picked up by submarine at the opening in the ice where these field people had been camped and collecting data."

"An American sub?" asked Ruff, looking up from his notes.

Petterson shook his head. "No, Russian."

"Well." Munson chewed his lip. "So much for natural isolation from other populations. Still, this fifth guy might supply some valuable details about exactly what his coworkers were doing just before they departed the world."

"The fifth guy's a she," Cybil said.

"Whatever," Munson said. "She then."

Ishikawa tapped out something on his computer. "We're getting a feed of color-enhanced micrographs of the lung tissue taken from two of the victims. The inside of the lung looks like a snowstorm."

Hanley hadn't brought her laptop with her; she got up and stood behind Ishikawa, peering over his shoulder, shading the screen with her baseball cap to reduce the glare. Munson's assistant called up the image on the overhead monitors. Hanley looked back and forth between the image of the lung field and the magnification of the blood samples. Munson saw she was entranced. No one on his staff loved a medical oddity the way Hanley did.

Munson cleared his throat. "Henry," he said, turning his attention to Ruff, "you would agree, would you not, that damage to the central and autonomic nervous system was devastating?"

"Mmm, yes." Ruff fussed with his bow tie, enjoying the solicitation of his opinion. "But we can't really tell why—not yet, not at this distance. We won't know until somebody can take a close-up look or send out specimens."

Munson had been waiting for one of them to amble into it. He looked around at the assembled staff. "You're undoubtedly right, Henry. This does seem to call for a field visit."

A murmur of surprise arose around the perimeter of the room. The junior staff glanced at one another, then focused again on their superiors, who were quiet.

"Come on," Munson said, arms outstretched. "Wouldn't you guys all kill to see what a state-of-the-art Arctic research station looks like up close?"

"Ahhhh," Hanley said, with exaggerated bliss. "A hundred and fifty romantic nights—and nights—in frozen, sunless splendor, far from the madding crowd. You don't even want to know what being so near the magnetic pole might do to your chakras and meridians."

Ruff yanked off his glasses in a practiced gesture. "Are you saying they want more than our thinking on this—that they actually want us to be hands on? I'd have thought there wasn't any more contact with the outside for—what—six months?"

"Five," Munson said. "Out? No, they can't get anyone out. No way while the sun remains down. But in?" He made eye contact with each of his senior people in turn. "The U.S. Air Force and Canadian Coast Guard think it's still early enough to get one of us in."

Piker smiled broadly. "I'll settle for an eight-by-ten glossy in *National Geographic* with circles and arrows and sidebars, thank you very much."

"This is the finest Arctic facility ever conceived." Munson cocked his head toward the blowup of ARS Trudeau taped to the wall. "You folks have got to be a little curious. And what about the chance to pursue unknown agent X in the august company of some of the finest scientific minds?" The group sat silent. "Don't all rush forward at once."

Petterson and Hanley were usually Munson's top candidates for fieldwork. But neither was biting.

"You have got to be kidding," Petterson said. "An Arctic outpost in late October? I thought you said that Russian sub was the last transportation in or out until spring."

Henry Ruff was skeptical. "They couldn't get paramedical personnel to that lady doctor in Antarctica when she diagnosed herself with breast cancer, but they can deliver some lucky epidemiologist from L.A. to the High Arctic in the middle of winter?"

"*Lady* doctor? Please!" exclaimed Hanley. "Geez, how I hate that. Sounds like the name of a bad punk band. How would you like to be called a man doctor?"

"I prefer 'gentleman doctor,'" said Ruff.

"Gentlemen. Ladies. Should I take your silence as serious contemplation of my proposal?"

"*Ladies?*" Henry Ruff exclaimed, turning chivalrous. "Lester Munson, we can't be sending a woman into that wasteland."

"We?" Hanley mimed. Cybil signaled her to be quiet.

"Yeah," Munson said, head down, looking at his hands. "You may be right. This might not be an appropriate work assignment for everyone." He looked meaningfully at Petterson and then at Hanley. "This is a toughie. Just getting there is going to be a challenge."

"What the hell are you talking about?" Hanley sputtered.

Munson considered his words carefully before answering. Hanley was proud of her reputation as the epidemiologist of last resort, but so far she hadn't taken his bait. The Canadian station had to be tempting; she was nothing if not curious. She just needed the right push.

"I just meant . . . this doesn't look like a job for anyone with kids, especially for a single parent. And, yeah, I don't expect every female would feel comfortable with this level of risk." He was being manipulative as hell, but he didn't care: he needed to get one of his best people up there before the flight window closed. If he had to play to her competitive streak, so be it.

Hanley was livid. "The women here haven't done so badly in the past. Getting to the place is going to be a bitch. So what's that got to do with who goes, for God's sake? What nonsense." She leaned toward Cybil Weingart and said, "Can you spare a cigarette?"

"No!" Munson barked, and Hanley looked sheepish. More gently, he said, "You really feel you could commit to a job like this?"

The room went quiet.

Hanley shrugged, feeling both the tug of the chase and a surge of guilt. This was exactly the kind of risky job her ex had said no mother—certainly not the mother of his child—should take. Part of her agreed with him. The thought of not seeing Joey for half a year left her speechless. That's what taking the job would mean. But wasn't it also important for him to see what it meant to care passionately about your work?

"Jessie?"

"I think so," she said, slowly. "This shouldn't be restricted."

"You mean you should have an equal shot at it?"

"Of course."

"What would you need? Hypothetically?"

"Hypothetically . . . I'd need Kim Ishikawa back here, for sure. Constant contact with a couple of data banks. Kim, can you start thinking about what tests to pack?"

Munson looked at Ishikawa. As outwardly dissimilar as he and Hanley were, they had worked well together on their last two assignments. They had a peculiar but effective partnership: Ishikawa, more comfortable with computers than people; Hanley, chain smoking and charming and bullying information from people who didn't even know they had it. Together they were inventive, pressing forward in the odd combination that had become their collaborative style.

Lester Munson looked straight at Hanley. "You sure? Because once you're in, there's no way out."

"How about a month off when I get back?"

"No problem."

She was still for a moment. "Hey, the North Pole was good enough for Superman and Frankenstein," she said, trying to sound cavalier.

"You wanna think about it overnight?" Munson asked.

She looked back at him. He was giving her a face-saving out. She could slip away if she wanted. He was being decent, a worrisome warning in itself.

"If I do, I'll back out." She looked him in the eye. "It's now or never."

Munson shrugged as if giving in, as if *she'd* persuaded *him*. "Okay."

Everyone applauded and spoke at once. Ruff snickered. "At least you won't have to pack your magnetic mattress liner."

Munson actually smiled. The release of tension in the room was palpable. No one had particularly wanted this job, so they were effusive with their well wishes. The few who might have been physically qualified looked perfectly happy to be missing out.

"Okay, folks," Munson said, "it's almost midnight."

"Oh, man!" Hanley exclaimed. "The sitter! Cybil, everybody— mañana." She leaped up, sped to the door, and disappeared.

"Let's put it away until morning," Munson said. "But see you bright and early."

The meeting broke up and Munson returned to his office, relieved Hanley had agreed. This job, he sensed, would call for some unorthodoxy—her forte. For all of Hanley's irritating antics, he was genuinely fond of her. They ran into each other pretty regularly at the Palomino Club and other country-and-western dives patronized by transplanted Southerners in Los Angeles. By odd coincidence, they were both from the Chickahominy River valley in Virginia, although from opposite ends of the economic scale. He came from generations of Virginia tobacco money, a heritage he had challenged by going into public health. Hanley had been the fourth of five kids in a family that couldn't afford one.

Hanley's professional conjectures were as unorthodox as her background. How she arrived at them was hard to fathom. Her insights didn't always seem reasonable. Munson had once presented Hanley with a divining rod after a particularly inspired call. She had solved the deaths of two subway repairmen in Vienna by proposing—and then proving—the crazy idea that the workers had unknowingly unearthed a medieval mass grave right in the center of the city, and breathed in a pocket of toxic gas.

Every epidemiologist took a shot in the dark now and then, but some of Hanley's made no damn sense at all. Yet she would take one, and there the killing agent would be, staring them all in the face: the medieval burial pit in Vienna or the lead from a distant gasoline station's tanks leaching into the well water of an otherwise normal family and driving its members mad. And then the case that had sealed her reputation: three unexplained deaths in a Hispanic community in New York City. As forensic specialists were taking the latest victim's apartment apart, Hanley had looked up from her notebook, taken a drag on her cigarette, and matter-of-factly asked a grieving relative when the deceased had been hexed. Damned if she wasn't right.

Hanley alone was creative but a loose cannon. With Ishikawa watching over her, however, Munson had a dependable duo. Ishikawa was methodical and resourceful, and paced himself sensibly. Although the quieter of the two, he was in some ways more ambitious, the driving force who pushed Hanley to take the leap when the trail of logic ended on a ledge. Yet when Hanley got too wild, he also could hold her back from the brink.

Munson dabbed his brow with a handkerchief as the computer

screen on his desk came alive. Another feed coming in from Trudeau. The high-speed printer churned out the pages. They had found the body of the fourth researcher, a Hungarian meteorologist, Alexander Kossuth, apparently not a victim of whatever had killed the others. For some unknown reason, he had discarded his protective suit and exposed himself to the elements. No visible lung constriction, no eye damage. He appeared healthy, just thoroughly frozen.

Cybil Weingart came by, dressed to leave, holding the same new item on the fourth corpse.

Munson said, "What do you make of this one? Could it possibly be the same exposure, just a different presentation?"

Cybil shook her head. "Hard to believe something would have presented identically in three cases and so differently in the fourth. If you want my expert medical opinion, the man turned himself into a popsicle."

# 4

Trailing its antenna wire, the flotation cone snaked up through the fjord's dark fathoms, stopping just short of the surface. If the Norwegians found the buoy later, they would learn no more than they had from the others they had occasionally netted in their coastal waters, or sometimes discovered floating inside one of their fjords.

Extended to nearly its full length, the wire came alive. One and six-tenths seconds later the transmission was over.

Outside the Norwegian village of Randaberg, miles of receptor cables crisscrossed four hundred hectares of land. This giant net snared the signal, automatically recorded it, and alerted the technician on duty.

In England, the Menwith Hill installation outside the Yorkshire town of Harrogate recorded the same burst at 03:40 Greenwich mean time and immediately conveyed it by landlines to the decryption shop at Bath. Played back at a stepped-down speed, the short radio broadcast was quickly identified by the duty officer as an encoded signal, and fed into the main computer to compare with the other paltry data on the highly evolved Russian naval cipher. Their navy might be falling apart, but there was nothing rusty about their encoding. Still, there was always the chance that this new scrap might be the piece that unlocked the larger puzzle.

After several hours, the officer and his subordinates knew no more than when they had begun. All they could deduce was the probability that a Russian submarine had transmitted a high priority code from a sector inside Norway's territorial waters.

The British liaison captain cocked an eyebrow at his American counterpart.

"Obdurate and unbreached," he said. "Let's hope the Norwegians don't stumble across the grotty thing." The Englishman yawned. "Or we will have to awaken a lot of lads in a lot of time zones."


Admiral Rudenko arrived at the Russian defense minister's anteroom to find the members of the Czech delegation standing dutifully alongside their host, while officers of the various services approached to pay their respects before joining the siege on the vodka and beer.

Most wore civilian attire, the admiral noted, and there were, in fact, a goodly number of civilians among the military men in mufti, including a prominent historian and a weighty art critic. This mixing of worlds was a recent popular innovation intended to enliven social occasions at the Ministry of Defense.

Delicacies adorned the buffet tables. Men were bending their ample girths over the trays of red-and-white-capped mushrooms, lamb meatballs, smoked sturgeon, calamari salad, and asparagus stalks, stabbing awkwardly at the sausages and slices of ham. Their liquor glasses and plates wobbled dangerously as they vied for choice morsels.

The historian and the critic separated themselves from the group, arranged a pair of chairs in love seat fashion, and sat down. They leaned toward one another for a fiercely sincere private exchange so popular with the regime's intellectual pets. The historian, Grementov, appeared almost grief stricken with conscience, pinching his lower lip with thumb and index finger. How did the joke go? *What is the definition of a Russian historian? A man able to predict the past.*

Better sharp steel than these blunt instruments, Rudenko thought. Who would have believed such crushing mediocrities would inherit it all? The terrors of the forties had been unspeakable, and time had (mercifully) dulled his memory of that long, desolate season, but Rudenko could not help wonder if it hadn't been better than this limp emptiness of sycophants rutting after stipends and flashing their credit cards, while the new capitalists and *mafiya* made off with the nation's resources and industries, and government officials skimmed off their billions in bribes.

Tossing back his vodka, he plunked the empty glass on a passing waiter's tray. At an opportune moment he smiled faintly at his host across the room and tapped his watch—pressing business. For once it was the truth. Panov had rung him with a summons. *One of our cousins has been out all night. The family is worried.* They had arranged to meet at the admiral's flat at a quarter to three.

The first minister nodded affably, and the admiral slipped out of the high-ceilinged hall, then up the back staircase to the fourth floor and his borrowed office. His secretary's desk was empty. He collected his overcoat, patting the pockets to check their contents, an aging man's reflex, and called through the open door to his adjutant, instructing him to have the driver pick him up at the *gastronom* in Old Arbat Street.

He left by the broad front stairs, walking down all four flights, donning his uniform cap and gloves before he stepped into the long shadows of afternoon. The chill air was exhilarating. All morning he had sat in overheated rooms listening to the ageless quarrel over whether the navy was finally going to order its very first fixed-wing aircraft carrier. With the Americans about to lay the keel of yet another floating airport, the high command had dusted off the proposal for a Russian counterpart, which had also revived the concomitant bickering over which of the fleets would claim it.

The high latitudes in which the Northern Fleet operated mercifully eliminated Rudenko's old command from contention. The admiral had happily deferred to his comrades. That reduced the contestants to three. The Baltic Fleet's confined sector soon eliminated it as well. That left the commanders of the Pacific Fleet and the shrunken Black Sea Fleet to battle it out. Academic, Rudenko thought, barely listening. The flood of funds after the *Kursk,* a self-inflicted disaster, was temporary and illusory; the last of the allocations would soon be diverted or dry up and vanish in the next accounting cycle. His colleagues were deluding themselves. Their glorious navy was history. Ships were being abandoned dockside because there weren't funds to maintain them, and here these old fools were dreaming of new ones. While their subordinates schemed about selling unwanted submarines to South American drug cartels, the old guard indulged their daydreams of lost glory regained. Ridiculous.

Who needed such difficult runways anyway, when the vertical takeoff jet was in hand? The vanity of the navy and the anxiety of the Duma's bureaucrats defied reason. They were still full of self-importance, going through the motions of restoring the service, even after the fiasco in the Barents Sea and the loss of *Kursk,* their great symbol of parity with the West. After much whining, they had wangled that titanic sub hunter, almost as large as the carrier they panted after. Twenty thousand tons. The creaking ex-Bolsheviks could barely button their flies anymore, yet the specter of the Americans still worked up their juices. Parity! Idiots. Soldiers were begging in the streets and sailors barely had food in their barracks, while their commanders spent their energies fantasizing about their mammoth sailing airfield, complete with nuclear engine. Rudenko gratefully inhaled the biting air.

For fifty years the navy's order of battle had emphasized the submarine. The vast majority of military vessels were still submarines—simple fact. His command alone once boasted its own air force of 450 aircraft and three hundred ships, two-thirds of them undersea boats. Two hundred subs under him alone. Now the entire navy had sixty, only twenty of which were worth anything, and the navy was talking of generating a little cash by renting two of those to India, along with an unfinished old carrier. Yet the chiefs insisted on having at least one strike fleet like the Americans', centered on a new fixed-wing carrier, arguing it would anchor the nation's foreign policies, flex Russian muscle somewhere or other, arouse national pride and, by the way, get the politicians reelected. Sure enough, the blueprints of *Kiev* had risen from the bureaucratic mausoleums.

So why did he stay on?

Rudenko touched his numbed cheek. The temperature was dropping. Another front. The people waiting in trolleybus queues stamped their feet. Beyond the peak of the Foreign Ministry building, clouds rolled past, gray and purple, filled with rain or an early snow. Along the Arbat, Muscovites hunched against the brisk wind. Schoolchildren with rucksacks walked backward into it, bumping into women bundled to the eyes in tightly wound scarves and fur hats. Clusters of newly affluent Muscovites hovered outside every chic shop in the quarter, talking animatedly into cell phones. What was the Western expression? *Shop till you pop*.

The cluster outside the *produkti* parted respectfully for the distinguished-looking admiral in the dark blue greatcoat and brimmed hat. This was one of the few privileges left to officers of his generation, and even this deference was no longer a given. Rudenko promptly collected the waiting packet of caviar and smoked whitefish, added a kilo of kolbasa to his order, teased the attractive new shopgirl with the thick blond braid, and departed. His car was at the curb. The driver bounded out and saluted as he opened the rear door for the admiral. On the front passenger seat, Rudenko saw a huge yellow-and-blue shopping bag from the IKEA furnishings store, the one they'd built at the Kilometer 41 Monument, the once-proud marker of the point at which the advancing German army had been turned back by Russian will and blood. The marker was in the store's parking lot.

The sedan wended its way through the foreign-made cars, taking the circuitous route the admiral favored, past full shops—including one of the McDonald's now pockmarking the capital—then the dilapidated mansions that had sheltered nobility in another age. Today they housed rich entrepreneurs and *mafiya*, small middle-class restaurants, and recently revived businesses. When he was a child, Rudenko's grandfather had taken him through these beautiful streets; the old man had pointed out all the intricately carved facades, the fierce stone eagles and Polovtsian idols that guarded their entrances. Rudenko particularly loved the thick stone sheds that had once housed the tsar's kennels. Like so many of the grand houses, the kennels were torn down after the war to make way for Novy Arbat, six lanes wide, running between the Foreign Ministry and the Kremlin.

The car eased out of Vakhtangov Street onto Novy Arbat, where it picked up speed, momentarily challenging the Audis and BMWs. The challenge was short lived; the imports easily outpaced his old sedan.

Khrushchev had widened Novy Arbat to eight lanes and lined each side with enormous glass-and-concrete towers that challenged, in size and bad taste, the neoclassical monstrosities Stalin had erected. They had been avid to eradicate the vestiges of previous regimes, and to proclaim the new order on an appropriately gargantuan scale. Such waste. To add to the insult, enormous billboards now advertised American sodas and European clothing stores. Rudenko closed his eyes and let the swaying machine lull him, the habit of a lifetime spent at sea.

Perhaps the time had come to stand down. The Naval War College wanted his black sea cap and sealskin jacket to put in a glass display case, like schoolboys' trophies. Should he surrender his mementos? As a submariner, he was entitled to one and a half months' salary for every month served, which would amount to a relatively decent pension for one person with no dependents. Special compensation bestowed by the Committee of Ministers would confer a bit more. He could retire to Sochi and bask on the black-pebbled beaches. Hell, they had probably refrained from retiring him just to save money. He was cheaper to keep on active duty.

The automobile slowed and stopped at the entryway of his residential tower, a huge elegant dowager from another era. Rudenko tucked his package under his arm and glanced at his watch: half past two. The driver let him off, then smartly furled and sheathed the pennant on the right fender as the admiral strode into the gigantic vestibule. Seated at a crude table in the opulent hall was the familiar trio of ladies who were the building's attendants and its first line of defense. One of them manned a heavy black phone to announce visitors. He nodded greeting as he crossed the marble lobby and entered the ornate cage of the elevator. Without speaking, the porter engaged the lift. The platform lumbered upward. Rudenko's four-room flat was halfway up the thirty stories.

Everything about the building was heavy. Constructed of great slabs in the Gothic wedding-cake style favored by Stalin's architects, the tower dwarfed every other structure for blocks around. The old goat had commissioned it himself. Four others just like it had originally been erected to form the five points of the Soviet star: five ramparts occupied by the city's luminaries. Government ministers, actors, NKVD officers, scientists, artists. Rudenko had been among the original tenants. Most were long gone, their flats passed to grandchildren or leased to subtenants. He'd heard a new mogul was building a private pool on his penthouse terrace.

The admiral's immediate neighbors included the pretentious fool who headed the Institute for American Studies, one of the Bolshoi's prima ballerinas and her nineteen-year-old female companion, a nameless mistress of an aging world-class weight lifter, the very social American vice president of a new commercial bank, and upstairs a few senior military men married to their work, like Admiral Rudenko, former commander of the Red Banner Northern Fleet.

Like most men of his age and profession, Rudenko's private life had been irreparably changed by the war. He had been betrothed after the fashion of childhood sweethearts, but that was before the Wehrmacht's glorious march across Russia. His fiancée perished during the Germans' retreat from their hometown of Taganrog on the Sea of Azov, a town built on the bones of an ancient fortress and haunted by violence. The Turks had razed it twice, the Genoese once. Then came Deniken's White traitors during the Revolution, and finally the Germans: once in the first war, twice in the second. Both sisters, three aunts, his maternal grandmother, father, mother—all had died there. He had never gone back. An ill-fated place.

Only his older brother, Alyosha, had survived the war, ironically because he had been safely fighting fascists far from Taganrog; he'd been wounded but survived. Alyosha now scraped by on his compensation and looked after Rudenko's dacha, a modest place south of Moscow, which he had been awarded years earlier by the Sea Forces in recognition of long and loyal service and his extraordinary valor in prosecution of the Great Patriotic War. Never had Rudenko succeeded in coaxing his brother, now in his late eighties, to visit Moscow and his grand apartment overlooking the Yuza River. Aloysha preferred the company of his brown chickens.

The elevator clanked to a halt. The sallow porter hurled open the polished cage doors and the admiral stepped out, pointedly ignoring the man's churlish manner. The Style Moderne door and Deco brass gate crashed shut behind him. One day he would shoot the incorrigible Trotskyite, just not this evening. Rudenko smiled as he shifted the package from hand to hand, searching his greatcoat pockets for his keys to the double-locked door. The door of his oldest neighbor, a film star from the fifties, was open as always; the other two were securely locked and reinforced with metal. Rudenko found his front door unlocked, as was the inner door at the end of the foyer. The immensely high ceiling and the bare parquet floor exaggerated the emptiness, but he immediately sensed that he wasn't alone.

"Georgi Mikhailovich!" The familiar voice of Second Deputy Minister Panov boomed out as the man rose from the shadows of the armchair in front of the decorative hearth and lifted a glass to his old rival.

Rudenko broke into a genuine grin as he slipped off his greatcoat. He strode forward, arms out to embrace his friend.

"Yevgeny Aleksandrovich," he said and clapped Panov on the shoulders, kissing both his cheeks.

"What's this?" Panov feigned shock. "Are you trying to club an old shipmate with a dead fish?" he said, pointing to the package in Rudenko's hand.

Rudenko laughed. Unbuttoning his uniform jacket, he pushed

past into the kitchen. "Have you been waiting long?" he shouted over his shoulder.

"No, no," Panov called back. "I was early. The houseman let me in. I hope you don't mind."

On the edge of the porcelain sink Rudenko unwrapped the smoked fish and emptied the caviar into a proper dish. He put both on a tray, along with the aromatic kilo of kolbasa, hard and speckled with pepper. He took water glasses and plates from the cabinet and returned to the parlor. He placed the crystal caviar dish down, then a plate of bread and butter, and took off his uniform jacket, slipping it across the back of his desk chair.

Panov was still standing. "I confess; I did break into your English scotch to pass the time." He lifted his empty glass sheepishly.

Rudenko waved away the sham apology. "Will you have another, to ease the caviar? Pour us some drink, will you?"

Never one to refuse hospitality, Panov replenished his glass and filled a fresh one for his host. The two had been rivals most of their lives, first as line officers commanding submarines, then as adjutants within the naval ministry, and on up the promotional ladder. But it had gone by so fast. Fate had singled them out as founders of the most critical military arm of the Soviet Union, but age softened their zeal as far younger technocrats swept past them both. Like a pair of war monuments, Comrades Rudenko and Panov dutifully collected their medals at each year's somber commemorations of battles long won (and a few botched) while the paper knights of the *apparat* advanced up the line, sporting their productivity certificates and cellular phones. They downed their drinks.

The admiral poured them each a full glass and eased onto the small sofa facing Panov. The afternoon sun was surrendering and the light glowed in their glasses. They toasted their impromptu reunion. In the past when Panov called on him, it usually meant some wormy, underdeveloped country was yet again in need of a well-spoken, proper-looking naval attaché with a lapel full of medals and an admiral's clothing allowance. Occasionally Rudenko had gotten lucky, like those three exquisite years in Rome as second secretary in the embassy. He had drunk in the West, reveled in his British lover, devoured her beautiful language, breathed in her culture and fragrance. More than his celebrated war record, his facility with languages—especially hers—kept him in demand.

"To the pope," Rudenko said and lifted his drink.

"The pope." Panov's eyes rose with his glass and took in the large oil painting astride the mantelpiece.

"Ah," he said. "More art you've collected."

"Yes. Inga Dobenskaya."

"Not exactly Socialist Realism." Panov chuckled, squinting at the canvas to view it better in the fading light. "A most peculiar landscape, full of scantily clad girls on a what—beach?"

Rudenko shrugged. "She was Molokan. Who could ever fathom the minds of Molokan Christians? A strong painter, nonetheless. Powerful even if you can't comprehend it entirely. Anyway, it reminded me of my youth at the sea's edge. And something else." The thought drifted away.

"Yes, yes. Now I remember it," Panov said. "You introduced me at a party in Leningrad. The night of the admiralty ball in nineteen fifty-something. We were—what?—still in our twenties."

"Yes," Rudenko said. "Fifty-two, I think. There is nothing wrong with your memory." He glanced up at the painting and it held him for a moment. "We were briefly involved."

"Where is she now?"

"Long gone," Rudenko said.

"West?" Panov asked and poured himself another.

Rudenko, taking a swallow, shook his head and pointed up, glass in hand. "Heaven," he said, then leaned back into the sofa's cushions and undid his collar. "And how is your family?"

"Mostly well, thank you for asking. My grandson is just home from his final year of contract work in the Far East. Came back a rich Siberian from the new territory. Out there it's still possible without joining the *mafiya*."

Panov squatted half out of his seat and scooped some black pearls from the crystal dish onto a slice of soft, white buttered bread. He was wearing a decent suit, befitting a deputy minister of the Ministry of Defense. Few, however, would have missed his jaunty military manner and erect bearing. He had always looked so much the warrior: large, brave, flippant in the face of danger. But he had aged, Rudenko saw. The once radiant smile of the boyish naval officer was chalky and translucent, even gray in places where fillings shone through. A gold molar flashed as he laughed. The deep lines around the eyes were not just from squinting against the sea's harsh glare.

"Will you stay for supper?" Rudenko asked. "I can broil us something. And there is a bottle of unblended scotch I had been thinking of sending you on your name day."

Panov, in mid drink, shook his head. "Thank you, Captain," he teased, "but no. And I regret your evening's plans will require some alterations as well. We need to talk."

"Ah, yes? You had better explain yourself."

"A task for my department. It requires a familiarity with certain locales, and maximum knowledge of subsea vessels."

Rudenko sat up and slapped the side of Panov's knee. "Yevgeny Aleksandrovich, I am older even than you. You can't be seriously thinking I can go buccaneering at my age? I can barely push paper."

Panov dismissed the protest with a shake of his head and put his glass alongside the plate of bread. "The North Sea," he said. "We need to determine what has befallen one of our boats. It is missing in an area you know well, or once did."

The sunlight had faded completely, leaching the color from the room. Rudenko rose to turn on the electric lamp on his desk. He wanted to see Panov's face clearly.

"Another boat gone missing? I've heard nothing."

"And you won't. This one can't be a news circus."

Rudenko nodded. "Where exactly has this one been misplaced?"

"In the Sogne Fjord," Panov said. "You remember it?"

The Sogne. Glassy black. When had he last seen it?

"You remember, Georgi Mikhailovich," Panov said, "how we blessed the devil for those ice-free fjords?"

Rudenko smiled. During the war he had played a lethal game of hide-and-seek, slipping in and out of the fjords and coastal island inlets to strike at German convoys plying the Baltic. And to harass the Nazi warships that stalked allied merchant vessels in the open-ocean corridor to Murmansk. Rudenko had humiliated his opponents. Once he'd even torpedoed a U-boat while it dallied on the surface. Only years later did he explain to classes at the war college why the enemy submarine had not dived to escape. The boat had been fatally encumbered by the pod it hauled behind, like a submerged yet buoyant vase. Rudenko would always remember the green opaque eye in a shallow well, a stunning glimpse into the future as prophesied by the Reich's armorers—the nose of a rocket being towed behind.

"The missing submersible—what can you tell me?" he asked Panov.

The deputy minister put down his glass on the low wood table beside his armchair. "*Vladivostok*, K-517, Second Squadron. Akula. She's heavily modified: nuclear-powered, highly maneuverable. Quiet. Loaded with special sonar and monitoring equipment. She carries two SB-4 seabed trawlers for underwater excavation."

"Why the trawlers?"

Panov shrugged. "They had something to bulldoze."

"Armed?"

Panov exhaled. "Nominally. Only torpedoes. No missiles. Conventional ordnance. The crewmen number eighty-nine; the officers, five. Assigned to intelligence work. And there is a civilian aboard. A scientist they picked up from an Arctic station."

"The captain?"

"Rachevsky. You might know him. His home is up near the Kem."

"Yes. A cool commander. Good. He will need his nerve. And the boat is definitely inside Norway's waters?"

Panov nodded. "Her last transmission was yesterday morning and contained no information, no details. Just a compressed, high-speed distress call."

"You brought me a file?" Rudenko said, looking about for a valise.

"Please." Panov forced a light smile. "You are to be briefed at the Naval Ministry this evening. Chernavin is flying in from Petersburg. They will keep any notes for you."

Meaning no record of the incident would exist outside the ministry. Rudenko bent forward a little and took a cigarette from the box lying open between them. "Excuse me. Do you still smoke?" he said and offered the ornate box to his guest. Panov instantly brightened. The smallest gesture of social kindness affected him so.

"She is equipped with a very decent oxygen regeneration system," Panov said, "and can maintain herself for a long period of time. The chief wants the crew rescued—"

"Does he?"

"—but from below the surface."

"From below?" Rudenko said. "It's rarely been successful with operations mounted from the surface. No one has tried it platformed underwater." He inhaled slowly, savoring the smoke. "I don't know."

Years earlier he had joined in a search for an atom-powered submarine missing in the Atlantic. Back then, hulls hadn't been nearly as advanced. There had been no hope at all of rescuing the crew. Not daring to venture below maximum depths, they had trailed magnetometers and television cameras on long cables. With considerable effort and luck, they had found the boat, after a fashion.

Experts had spent weeks deducing how the sub had perished. They concluded, finally, that it had failed to expel its ballast tanks, so the engine simply could not overcome the weight. The press of water above was too great for the propeller to drive through, and so the sub was forced down, stern first. The descent exceeded four times her normal maximum speed; she shot down at two hundred miles per hour. Three hundred meters, four . . . At six hundred the hull imploded, bursting like an eggshell. Everything combustible—paper, film, soap, oil, alcohol—exploded from the heat of the unimaginable pressure. Mercifully, the crew was already dead, every blood vessel ruptured. The debris was scattered across the bottom for several kilometers. Rudenko did not like to dwell on it.

"Georgi—"

Rudenko held up a hand. "Possible—in theory."

Rudenko wanted to know how long *Vladivostok* had been on patrol and was mildly surprised to hear a month. A long voyage for a Russian sub; they had never stayed out for months on end like the Americans. Routes and time at sea had shrunk even further with the crimped budgets. At least, right after the *Kursk* disaster, rescue equipment finally was upgraded to appease the public. If not for that, they wouldn't even be having this conversation.

"Might the trouble be radiation leaking from its engine?"

Panov pursed his lips and made an equivocating motion with his hand. "The Admiralty received two radio reports of minor hair loss the week prior. But that might have been caused just as easily by the stress of prolonged confinement. Radiation levels throughout the ship tested negative."

Rudenko hypothesized the ship might have glanced off the fjord's rock walls, which rose hundreds of meters up out of the water, or struck an unusual formation while maneuvering on the bottom. Or experienced a major mechanical failure. The worst possibility, obviously, was detection and interception.

This seemed unlikely, Panov argued. "No unusual surge of Norwegian military communications or activity has been registered in the hours since *Vladivostok*'s call for help. The Norwegians do not yet know the sub is inside their waters." And *if* the rescue could be effected from below the surface, they would never find out. If accomplished, it would be a first.

Rudenko poured out two half glasses of water and drank his in a single draft. Panov followed suit.

The admiral rose to telephone the Northern Fleet's barracks in Murmansk to have his sea bag packed. From the bathroom he pocketed only his pills. Sailors travel light, he thought, glancing at the sparse array of photographs atop his bedside bureau.

Panov was putting dishes in the kitchen sink when he returned.

The glasses were gone, the whiskey back in the cabinet. His coat was already on.

"Ready, Admiral? Chernavin expects us at seven. We just have time for a quick dinner."

Rudenko nodded.

Panov's ancient Zil and driver carried them to the Hotel Metropol, where they dined on a high floor overlooking the green roofs of the Kremlin, across the river. Its five spindled spires were topped with giant red stars made of glass, which turned in the wind like weather vanes. Except for a party of English tourists and a couple of unsavory types in Italian suits, the restaurant was practically empty, its gilt mirrors exaggerating their solitude.

Panov and Rudenko sat staring at the floodlit citadel and their reflections in the giant windows. The admiral reminded Panov of the winters just after the war, when Galitsin was still alive, living in retirement in a resplendent Kremlin apartment with his wife and their adopted Chinese daughter. They would all gather there at Christmas; none of them had anyone else to go to.

"So long ago," Panov said, wistfully.

The Metropol's menu offerings were grand, but Rudenko did not have much appetite, even though the Admiralty was picking up the tab. He ordered a simple dish of grilled sturgeon. Panov ordered lamb dumplings and baked eggplant stuffed with pine nuts, followed by a generous dessert of apricot and kiwi tarts. When the coffee arrived, the admiral excused himself and went to the washroom.

His hair was entirely white, accentuating his blue eyes; his face had more ripples than the sea. What was someone his age doing even contemplating sea duty? Had Panov and his superiors not considered that?

But of course they had, he realized. If the Baltic Fleet's submarine was inextricable—trapped—who better to do what was necessary than a totally trustworthy flag officer of a different command? One without any personal knowledge of the ship's company. Better a venerable and expendable old man already long past retirement age, than a younger officer with qualms and a career still ahead of him. No, Admiral Rudenko was ideally suited for the cleanup. And the aftermath.

At ten of seven they left the hotel and strolled the long blocks to their destination. From the stanchion above the door flew the flag of the Russian navy.

"Seven, precisely," said Rudenko.

*Vladivostok* had been out of contact for sixteen hours and twenty minutes.

# 5

The notion that Rudenko had some choice in the matter was quickly disposed of. Admiral Vladimir Nikolaievich Chernavin, commander in chief of the Russian navy, personally received them in a modest council chamber. Aside from the perfectly polished art deco conference table big enough to seat twelve, the room's only noteworthy feature was a large display of red ensigns tattered by enemy fusillades, pressed under glass in a black frame.

"Admiral Rudenko. Good of you to respond so promptly," said the commander in chief, and gestured for them to be seated at the walnut conference table. "We have a problem with K-517, as you are perhaps aware." Panov confirmed this with a nod. "*Vladivostok* was on a sensitive mission. I need not explain that the presence of our warship in another nation's sovereign waters naturally requires that we take great care in this matter."

Chernavin had served under Rudenko in the Northern Fleet in the course of his swift ascent to his current rank. Rudenko knew him to be acute, prudent, and completely exacting. Whatever had to be done was done, or else. And done quietly. Which was why the old hands were being rousted for this dance.

Chernavin unfolded a large cross-sectional diagram of *Vladivostok*'s interior. He detailed the modifications to the various compartments and described the officers, ending with Captain Rachevsky.

He stood back from the schematic. "Despite the strong likelihood that the air replenishment system is maintaining the crew, the chance for rescue by a surface ship is nonexistent. The Norwegians would discover such an attempt in an instant. Rescue from beneath the surface by another submarine has never been effected, but one leading proponent of the feasibility of such a procedure is, I understand, an admiral of the Northern Fleet, one G. M. Rudenko."

Panov glanced at Rudenko but said nothing.

Chernavin unrolled a sea chart: the top half, an aerial blue-and-brown rendering of the Sogne Fjord in its entirety—two hundred kilometers long. The bottom portion was a corresponding cross section of the fjord's mid channel.

"The glacial trough of the fjord has few underwater terrain features. Deep, straight, and true. Except for the odd boulder and sandy debris along the bottom, the retreating glacier left little behind. Mostly the channel is flat and very deep." With the tip of his pencil, Chernavin tapped a slight bend in the fjord thirty-eight kilometers in from the coast. "*Vladivostok*'s destination. It was to deploy its SB-4 seabed trawlers and recover equipment of a classified nature from the bottom."

Rudenko nodded. He mostly understood the commander's reference. In the seventies, when land-based missiles had become obsolete given their vulnerability to outright attack, the Americans had considered mounting their missiles on underground tracks so they could be moved around in an absurd game of peekaboo with intercontinental ballistic missiles. Commander Chernavin had formulated the Soviet navy's counteroffensive: a strategic deployment of nuclear missile submarines.

The plan required extensive mapping of the Sea of Okhotsk in the Far East, the jagged coastal terrain of Sweden, and the ice-free Norwegian fjords. This violation of territorial waters was undertaken systematically, first to map the sunken features, and then to select sites for the submarines that followed, each carrying missiles with ample capability to strike targets in North America and Europe with multiple thermonuclear warheads. The criterion for the sites was simple: they had to afford their subs protection from detection. The steep, soaring walls of fjords foiled even the most advanced surveillance. As did the different temperatures and densities of the currents there—some saline, some fresh—which blocked and distorted infrared sensors and even sonar. And they never froze over. Once situated, the submarines lay hidden, the missiles mere minutes from their destinations.

Chernavin's refreshing strategy became the cornerstone of a new doctrine, an ingenious scheme for hiding Soviet missile submarines in nearly unassailable positions. Tests proved the ploy extremely effective. From these firing points, submarine forces could cheaply hold the West's arsenals at bay a while longer. Now even a preemptive strike was possible as the West again ratcheted up the pressure. Strategically the sites were priceless yet cost virtually nothing. What Russian technological production had failed to provide, Chernavin's simple strategy handily accomplished. The Party accelerated his promotion over a good many senior officers, Rudenko included.

Surveying Chernavin's undersea submarine nests had been given the highest priority; the accuracy of a rocket was no greater than the precision with which its launch position was calculated. Two conventionally armed subs of the Strategic Nuclear Forces had taken up the delicate task of pinpointing the sites in Norway and Sweden, and preparing them by dredging and ringing each with passive electronic sentinels that could detect the approach of patrolling vessels. The devices were modeled on Japanese-built sound buoys: self-powered listening mechanisms that relayed all nearby sounds to the attendant submarine. Every submarine was equipped with electronic screening equipment to cull, from the multitude of sea sounds, anything emitted by foreign vessels. Each missile sub would stay on station, nesting for up to twenty days, before the next one rotated in.

Then the giant Akula and Delta I-IV submarines were built, each strong enough to push straight through ten feet of Arctic ice to launch its intercontinental ballistic missiles. These huge subs never went south to the Norwegian Sea, only north. The Barents and the Polar seas became their permanent area of operations.

Rudenko inhaled deeply; it was hot in the council chamber. All that was past, the Cold War over. The illegal sites were nuisances, potential embarrassments to the newly appointed commander in chief of the navy. The admiralty was apparently in the process of cleaning them up, removing all traces. To this day, Rudenko was grateful that the Strategic Nuclear Forces subs stationed with the Northern Fleet had never been under his command.

"Questions, Deputy Minister?" Chernavin said, addressing Panov, then Rudenko: "Admiral?"

Rudenko leaned forward, his forearms coming to rest on the table, hands clasped. "If the Norwegians find *Vladivostok,* or discover us in their front yard, what are my orders?"

Chernavin appraised his former commander with the Asiatic squint that was only one of the reasons his subordinates called him The Tartar.

"Resist them; sink them. Do not surrender your command under any circumstances. You are not to leave *Vladivostok* to their mercy. Its identity and its presence must not be verifiable. That is paramount."

"Yes, sir."

"Get *Vladivostok*'s crew out. The boat is expendable. Destroy it."

"What support from our sister fleet might be available before the rescue? Or afterward?"

Chernavin was silent for a beat. "I'm afraid nothing will be available until you complete your mission and reach the open sea. Several trawlers will happen to be in the vicinity just beyond the territorial limit. The helicopter carrier *Novosibirsk* is exiting the Baltic on maneuvers not far from the mouth of the fjord. Her Yak-36 fighters will go aloft as you exit. Also KA-25 helicopters. Two Sovremenny-class destroyers are with her and will quickly deploy to protect your flanks. Do not communicate with any of them by radio. Signal Peter only. The Admiralty will direct the support elements from there."

Panov sat with his arms folded across his chest. "What about a medical ship in case of serious injuries among the crew?"

Chernavin nodded. "Good. Good point." He called to his aide.

"Get the closest medical ship underway immediately. The admiral will be returning to us by way of the Baltic, so set up the medical ship on a course that will meet with his vessel. Just remember, we don't want too many pieces moving toward Sogne Fjord lest we give the game away before the admiral is out of the channel. Once he is out, they are to churn up the ocean."

The aide spun on his heel and marched off, his heavy step resounding down the empty hall.

"And if the crew cannot be extricated?" Panov inquired.

Chernavin addressed his answer to Admiral Rudenko. "You will do what you have to."

Rudenko and Panov exchanged looks.

Chernavin referred to his notes, massaging the bridge of his nose as he read. "One more item. A priority."

He produced a waterproof yellow case, no bigger than a lunch pail, marked with Roman letters—ARS-T. Panov and Rudenko exchanged glances; neither recognized it, and questions were clearly not going to be entertained. Chernavin set it down in front of them.

"A box like this will be in the captain's personal safe. Find it."

Chernavin picked up an unsealed envelope lying at his elbow. Tilting it, he slid out a key on a long beaded chain. "This is a duplicate of the key to the commanding officer's security safe. There are a half dozen more here for the salvagers." He pushed the envelope across to the admiral. "Should the need arise."

"Yes, sir," Rudenko said.

"So then—" Chernavin rose and shook their hands curtly. "My aide," he said, "will convey your instructions to the secure shipyard at Kem and arrange immediate transport. Please channel all your requests and information through him. Where is the fellow?"

The boyish lieutenant returned with a tray of coffee but only two cups.

"Admiral," Chernavin said, "I will expect you in St. Petersburg at midweek. Don't be late." He gave a tight-lipped smile.

"Yes, sir."

"Good evening." Chernavin signaled his aide.

"Good evening," Panov said, rising. Rudenko rose too.

The lieutenant stood to attention as the commander passed out of the room.

Panov exhaled broadly, slipped off his jacket and draped it over his chair. "And what the hell do we make of that?" he said, waving in the direction of the garish yellow case.

"I haven't the faintest notion," Rudenko said, and turned to the sea chart. "At the moment we have some difficult logistics to weigh and decisions to make."

Panov came around the table to lean over the admiral's shoulder and read the list aloud as Rudenko composed it: "Depth meters, respirators, stretchers, medical supplies, and personnel. What submarine do you have in mind to haul this warehouse to Norway?"

"I was thinking *Rus* might do. Her hull is reinforced and the engines cushioned against sound. She is in port, in Kem, is empty of missiles and has one rescue chamber affixed. A second could be added very fast."

Panov chortled. "*Rus*. I suppose that hooligan of yours still commands."

"Captain Nemerov is an experienced officer," Rudenko said, without looking up from his labors. "Lieutenant!" he called to the aide. "Signal the sub pens at Kem. Have them gut a missile chute on Captain Nemerov's boat and weld a compression chamber and bell lock to it. Inform Captain Nemerov of the situation. Impress upon him that we have hours, not days, to do all this. Have him quietly add two doctors to the roster. Oh, and four qualified divers. Then move the vessel into the enclosed yard. Be discreet, please."

He turned to Panov. "We'll need the extra divers in case *Vladivostok* is down farther than she should be." The lieutenant started down the hall, but Rudenko called him back. "Be sure they know they need to test the rescue submersibles." He looked at Panov. "The Sogne is deep in places. Four thousand feet, as I recall: well over six hundred fathoms. I think I even have a British chart of it somewhere in my quarters at Murmansk."

"Do you wish that chart located, sir?" the lieutenant asked.

Rudenko looked at him quizzically for an instant. "No, no. It's outdated and inadequate. These are much better." He scribbled on a slip of paper and held it out to the aide. "No one is to leave the ship once they report. Here are the coordinates where I will rendezvous with *Rus*. Please convey them to Captain Nemerov along with my order to put to sea the moment the equipment's installed and the men are aboard. He can finish the compression chamber adaptation at sea. *Rus* is to get whatever head start she can."

"Yes, sir," snapped the lieutenant and hurried out.

Rudenko and Panov gathered up the papers and their hats, the admiral working out his itinerary as they walked. Outside, in the night air, Panov motioned away the driver of the waiting sedan, who had leapt out to open the car for them.

"Give us a moment."

The driver nodded.

"Why did it go into Sogne?" Rudenko asked.

"Money is my guess," Panov said. "Or rather the lack of it. The Admiralty is broke. In case you haven't noticed, we are poorer than Thailand. The goddamn baht is worth more than the ruble. Every day a plane from New York brings in one-hundred-dollar bills by the ton so our entrepreneurs and thieves can have real currency to play with. Though these days they prefer euros."

"What does this have to do with the situation?"

"Sorry. They no doubt stretched *Vladivostok*'s use by giving her extra chores. Cleaning up that old nest was the second one."

"What was the first chore?"

Panov said, "A scientific station in the Canadian archipelago— the girl was coming from there."

"On the ice pack?"

"On a small island in the ice field. A model geopolitical venture. Full of science and goodwill. Worse than Soros. Bah! Why do we waste our meager revenues?"

Rudenko jabbed a gloved thumb toward the ministry door. "The coffers are empty and he sends a submarine to fetch this woman?"

Panov's expression revealed nothing. "Apparently, yes."

"And now the vessel is down."

"That's about it," Panov said.

The admiral pulled off his glove and extended his hand, as did Panov. They embraced and held each other's shoulders.

"Godspeed," Panov said. "May the fjords be good to you one more time."

Distracted by details he still needed to take care of in Murmansk, Rudenko slid into the ministry's Mercedes. Panov kept talking as the door closed. The car pulled away from the curb so fast, the admiral barely waved good-bye. Panov had been saying something he'd only half heard; his friend rapidly grew smaller, hand still in the air.

The heavy machine shot down the center lane of the boulevard, reserved for leaders, dignitaries, and emergency vehicles. They were racing for the aerodrome and the plane that would carry him to Kem. Even so, by the time he reached Murmansk, Captain Nemerov and *Rus* would already be out to sea.

# 6

anley dreaded the conversation with her ex-husband. He didn't disappoint.

"You must have known he'd be desolate about missing his next what—three visits? Or is it four? He's going to be heart-broken at the thought of not seeing you for five months."

Hanley sighed with resignation.

"Of course," he said, "you're going anyway. Work is your priority. We all know that. The rest of us have to accept the consequences. You complain about my taking Joey a thousand miles away, but you have to admit, it's damn convenient for you. Leaves you more time for your corpses." He grunted, but Hanley could tell it wasn't a comment on her.

"Are you okay?" she said.

"My stomach."

"Again? Have you tried that seven-day detoxification regimen? Maybe you need to take some antioxidants and chromium and clear your pathways. A little lymph drainage, maybe."

"Why does your advice always sound like lawn care?" he growled.

"At least try a colonic," Hanley said. "That'd solve part of your problem."

"Please," he said, exasperated. "Does somebody pay you to proselytize? Do you get a commission?"

"No, really."

"I'm happy that you've acclimated to California and that you're as self-actualized as you are. I'm delighted that you're living in the moment, attaining self-empowerment and positivity, finding the light centers throughout your being. I am happy that you're clearing your blockages, channels, chakras, marmas, awakening your inner self, or picking suitors using the I Ching. I want you to achieve new energy, synergy, *and* syzygy. I want you to honor your life force and glow like a fucking candle in the night. But I do not wish to try—just once or ever—colonic irrigation. *O-kay?*"

She jerked the phone away from her ear. "Okay."

The line went dead.

"Bye," Hanley said, softly, to herself, "Love you too," and slammed the receiver into the cradle. "Shit." She put on her sunglasses and grabbed the car keys from the counter. Joey was already in the truck when she came out.


A flowery creature blossomed in the tidal pool, its petals tipped with fire-red sensors.

"*Laila cockerelli,*" Hanley said. "And there's a *Peltodoris.*"

"Looks like a potato." Joey was on his hands and knees at the edge of the rocky pond.

"Yep, sure does."

"What do they eat?"

"Sponges."

"Yeah? And what are the orange things for on the other one, over there?" He pointed.

"Ah." Hanley looked happy. "They're its digestive glands. Stomachs, kind of." She looked at her son's intent face and felt a pang.

"And that there," said the boy. "That scummy-looking stuff. What's that?"

Hanley shielded the water with an upraised hand to block the reflection on the surface. "Algae," she said. She scooped up some of the muck.

"Yuck." Joey made a face.

"No, no. It's wonderful. Without algae we wouldn't have hand lotion, petroleum, film, pudding, beer, chocolate milk even."

"Chocolate milk? That stuff's in chocolate milk? Gross!"

Hanley nodded. "Mmm. And they eat sewage. A couple of guys've even coaxed them into nibbling on oil spills. Didn't I ever tell you about the blue-green algae diet?"

"Maybe I should take some on the plane with me," Joey said. "It's gotta be better than that so-called food."

Hanley smiled.

Joey glanced at his mother. "When do you go?"

She put her hands in her pockets. "Late tomorrow. To Edmonton first. That's in Canada. Then Alaska. And then they take us to the research station. It's on an island, surrounded by ice."

"At the North Pole?"

"Almost."

Joey got to his feet. "C'mon, Mom."

Hanley stood and followed her son across the outcropping of rock and onto the beach.

"I'm really sorry that I won't be back in time for Christmas."

"Yeah," Joey said. "But it'll be okay. Dad is taking me to Sea World."

"Listen, we'll e-mail while I'm gone, and next time I have you again, we're going to do an experiment together. A clinic in Berkeley is developing a computer program for you to work with. Someone up there figured out how to program a computer to give a person with dyslexia his own translation of words. It sees how you see. We've sent them some of your homework, and the clinic's been decoding your letter sequences. They're working up a program that can help you read. But you've got to be willing to try. You've got to stay open to it, Joseph Hanley-Brown."

"You're sounding hippie again."

"I am hippie. I plan to have you eating kelp for breakfast by the end of your next visit." She grabbed her son's lapel. "So what about the program?"

"Okay, Ma. I'll try it."

She smiled. "My man."

Joey's eyes fixed on his mother's.

Hanley said, "I'm going to miss you terribly." She reached for his shoulders.

The boy shrugged off her hands and walked away, resentfully. Her heart sank.

"Really, Joe. I will."

The boy stopped and turned—"Me too"—and ran back to embrace her.

# 7

*R**us** sailed out from Kem on the White Sea, bearing north, then eased onto a westerly course, passing from the Barents Sea into the Sea of Norway—submerged all the way to avoid the thick ice floes. Once they reached the Norwegian Current, where the excessive salt levels kept the coastal waters ice free, they slipped into the familiar track that skirted the coast and surfaced to reconfigure the deck.

The instruments in the conn glowed like the dashboard of a car at night, the gauges internally illuminated so as not to impair the night vision of the man at the periscope. Lighting in the room was kept dim, creating an oddly serene mood. The only other source of light was the short vertical tunnel leading up through the conning tower to the outdoor bridge. The tunnel was drafty; the conn was freezing cold.

Captain First Rank Vasily Sergeyevich Nemerov extended his arm into the circle of natural light at the foot of the ladder and checked his watch, an American vintage military-issue timepiece with black face and radium numerals and hands. It was his proudest possession, won years ago in a card game from a colonel of naval infantry.

"Lieutenant," he said to his navigation officer. "I am going upstairs. Watch these fellows while I am out, will you? Cook missed the sailing and Torpedoman Grishov is once more honoring us with his mother's recipes. Make sure no one defects."

The crewmen chuckled without looking away from their instruments and controls. Nemerov mounted the ladder to the open hatch atop the conning tower and climbed up and out onto the tiny cockpit that served as the sub's outdoor bridge.

*Rus* rolled in the swells. For all of her formidable 152-meter keel and great girth, the bridge was little more than a crow's nest, extremely cramped, especially for three men dressed in bulky winter gear. To make room, the captain sent one of the lookouts below, slapping the sailor on the shoulder as he eased past.

Nemerov pulled his peaked hat down tighter and surveyed the sky. The heavens were purplish and dark. A band of ghostly white glare rimmed the horizon. The sea was to his liking, a bit on the fierce side, the waves frothing in the strong wind, the sky threatening snow. Despite the cancellation of a shipboard party to commemorate the third anniversary of his command, Nemerov was quite content to be at sea, away from fleet headquarters at Murmansk and the sub pens at Kem.

Another few miles on the surface and they would have more than stray ice cubes to contend with. Where was the admiral, damn it? *Rus* was nearly in position. Not that anyone could miss her, what with smoke spewing from missile tube 6.

Its hatch was propped open to vent the noxious effluents from the welding going on below. The ballast tanks were partially filled to steady *Rus* for the work under way below decks, and to compensate for the lost weight of the absent missiles. Only air-defense rockets remained, ready to rise from the deck into firing position, a mere six torpedoes, two of them dummies carrying mesmers.

Two cigar-shaped submersibles were fastened onto the stern deck, straddling hatchways to make them accessible from below decks. The rescue craft were viable to a depth of five hundred meters, maneuvered by means of high-velocity jets of water that gave them lateral movement so they could dock with the escape hatches of the disabled sub and extract survivors, ferrying them back to *Rus* and the waiting medical staff.

Nemerov checked his splendid watch and thought about the precious hour and twenty minutes it had taken to hoist the extra submersible into position, to gut four empty rocket chutes to accommodate the pressure chamber and bell lock, then to complete the first welds. Despite it all, in four hours' time preparations were far enough along for *Rus* to cast off. A minor miracle.

He looked skyward. Satellites would have no difficulty detecting *Rus* under these conditions. Infrared sensors could pick out the three heat-radiating points on a polar bear, never mind the steel-melting heat of welding torches and the dense, ozone-laden smoke chuffing from the open missile hatch on the aft deck.

Beneath her keel, planted on the seabed, acoustic tracers were no doubt reporting her engine sounds and the cavitation of water foaming past her hull. On satellites hundreds of miles overhead, other devices were detecting the slight fluctuation in the planet's magnetic field caused by the ship's metal mass. Some damn American had even devised a way to detect the minute aquatic organisms left dead in a submarine's wake, which could be followed like a trail of bread crumbs in the sea. They knew *Rus* was there.

Below decks, the deep-submergence divers were being pressurized in the British compression chamber wedged in the forward area housing the missile chutes. They would have to stay in the chamber for the duration of the operation, living at a pressure equal to the press of water. Divers could go deeper than the submersibles, amazingly enough. But every thirty meters of water required two hours in the twelve-by-eight-foot chamber: sixty-two hours to press the men down to 920 meters, the maximum depth at which they could work in flexible suits.

Once on site, they would pass from the compression room into the bell lock and don their gear. They would close the lock, flood it, and then enter the adjacent flooded missile tube to which the bell was being welded. The divers would swim up the six meters of the silo and out of its hatch, trailing umbilical hoses to sustain them with a helium-rich breathing mixture and a steady flow of reactor-heated water that was circulated into their suits to maintain their core body temperatures in the frigid water.

The rescue submersibles would disembark later, each piloted by one sailor. The deep submergence divers would help position them against *Vladivostok*'s escape hatches and provide assistance as needed.

Until they located the stricken sub, the divers could only sit imprisoned, enduring the tedious process of pressurization, eating snacks and watching the bell lock next door being welded onto the yellow wall of the hollowed-out missile tube that loomed several stories high beside the hard shell of their cluttered hovel.

A large submerged chunk of ice glanced off *Rus*'s bow. The noise reverberated through the ship, like the clapper of a huge bell. The sailor on watch lowered his binoculars at the sound and stared at the white hump as it scraped along the hull. The intercom chimed on the bridge. Nemerov uncradled the microphone and depressed the button. "Nemerov."

"We are at rendezvous, Captain."

"Thank you, Lieutenant. Reduce speed to four knots. Any aircraft on radar or in radio contact?"

A moment passed. "No angels on radar, sir. No aircraft communicating in our vicinity other than civil. The Norwegians at Andoya are chattering away."

"Thank you, Control."

Nemerov replaced the microphone. More ice thudded into the bow plates. The metal hull resonated as the ice raked past. The Norwegian airfields at Trondheim Bodo, Sola, Evenes, and Bardufoss remained quiet. Only their experimental rocket-firing range at Andoya was active. The Norwegians operated a few patrol craft and reconnaissance planes, and had some aging F-16 fighters, P-3Bs, and E-3As. Usually someone came by. This time no one flew out to reconnoiter and observe their passage along the mountainous coast.

The captain took the microphone again. "Reduce speed to two knots. Just enough to keep her trim."

"Yes, sir. Two knots, sir," the deck officer responded from below. "Captain. We have aircraft on radar. One angel from the northwest. Closing."

"How far?"

"Two hundred kilometers."

Nemerov shielded his eyes against the huge flakes of snow that had begun to fall. "I need two men on deck. You have the ship, Lieutenant."

Two seamen responded to the summons almost immediately. Both wore orange life vests and carried two more for the captain and lookout.

Without warning—without a sound—a jet fighter-bomber shot by overhead, afterburners glowing. A terrific boom followed, then fumes from the spirits fueling its engines.

The plane banked sharply, slowing visibly as the pilot eased back on the throttle and arced around in a lazy loop. He decreased speed steadily as he lined up head-on with the sub and made his approach. Seventy-five meters above the prow, he eased to a standstill and began a vertical descent.

"Stop engines," Captain Nemerov ordered. Without engines, the boat was at the mercy of the waves and wind. Nemerov followed two others, sliding down the ladder to the pitching deck. They went forward, past the sail. Ten meters overhead the Jakowlew 38's belly door opened and a pair of legs dangled out into space. Cinched in a harness, his sea bag slung beneath him on a lanyard, the admiral unreeled downward, swaying in the wind like a pendulum.

Nemerov and his men hurried forward, nimbly negotiating the rolling rail-less deck. The down draft of the Jakowlew's whining engines pressed their bulky clothes flat against their bodies. The sailors grabbed the admiral's sea bag as it swung by and brought it to the deck. One of them unhooked it and scrambled back toward the bridge, stooped by the blast of the plane's engines.

The admiral dangled overhead, swinging from port to starboard just out of reach until they managed to catch hold of his line. Nemerov and the mitchman each grabbed an ankle and eased Rudenko down into a sitting posture. Each held him down with one hand, tearing at his harness latches with the other. The deck surged upward on a large wave and the reel line went slack. Then the deck plunged; the rope shot skyward. Reflexively, Nemerov and the mitchman braced themselves and tightened their grip on the admiral. But the harness latches snapped open and the admiral remained sitting between them, smiling.

The Jakowlew rose gently, spinning slowly, and swung away, resuming horizontal flight. Nemerov bent over to lift aside the noise suppressors cupping the admiral's ears.

"*Welcome aboard, sir,*" he shouted. "*Nice of you to drop by.*"

He helped the admiral to his feet, and the mitchman led him back to the bridge, up its short ladder and down the hatch.

Making his way past the sail, Nemerov edged toward missile chute 6, whose hinged hatch stood open like the lid of an old Turkish coffeepot. Acrid smoke streamed out. A pulley straddled the opening; gas cylinders were lashed to the deck with lines running down into the chute. Lying flat, he peered in through the smoky fumes. The arc of the torch was blinding, the flux burning, running off the welding rods, melting the steel to the ship. The work was crude, excessive, but it made him confident the joints would hold. Seeing Nemerov, the engineering officer started climbing the rope ladder up the side of the tube.

"How much longer?" Nemerov shouted.

"Two minutes. No more," the officer yelled back.

Nemerov gave him a hand up. "Well done. Get your men out of there as fast as you can. We've got to get under way."

The welding arc went out. The welder whistled up to the engineer. The job was finished. Nemerov and the officer hauled the gas and oxygen lines onto the deck; the work detail started up the ladder.

"Hurry," Nemerov yelled down, then said to the officer in charge, "Throw the welding equipment over the side. Roll it overboard—the cylinders, everything. Hurry. Then get below. I need her down immediately."

The lieutenant nodded and directed the men coming onto the deck.

Nemerov turned away and loped back to the bridge. He climbed up into the cockpit and clicked the microphone. The hatch came open at his signal. On the forward decks the work detail was closing the hydraulic missile hatch and jettisoning the welding gear. He waited until they had finished and descended through the crew hatchway.

At Nemerov's signal, the cockpit lookout stood down. Nemerov cleared the bridge, clambered down the ladder and pulled the hatch closed, securing it himself. The sealant light went green; they were watertight. Nemerov slid down the steel railings and stood behind the helmsman. The deck officer ordered the vessel pressurized.

*Rus* eased beneath the icy waves at an angle of five degrees. The scraping stopped; all was quiet. It was eleven o'clock in the morning in the Sea of Norway.

Torpedoman Lagir set out tea in the officers' mess, the glasses dark with lumps of strawberry preserves. Admiral Rudenko held the top of the hot glass between two fingers and let the steam warm his hand. Arthritis was gnawing at his knuckles. He stamped his feet unobtrusively to stimulate the circulation in his leg muscles. "Ancient," he said to himself. "Ancient."

At the dining table, Nemerov sat reading the directive from the ministry, which the admiral had delivered personally. Pausing to sip his tea, Rudenko noted the omnipresent hum of the air regeneration machinery and took in the spotless and well-appointed mess. Padded chairs. Apricot walls. Soundproofed. A list of available times for the jogging track in the missile gallery. How different this was from the cramped and leaky iron tubs in which he and his comrades had risked their lives during wartime, the wardroom no bigger than a telephone booth, the hydraulics manually operated by brass wheels at which they slaved. Those were slop buckets compared to the sterile power and great size of a boat such as this. They had lived like rats, ankle deep in water, breathing rank air, alternately boiling and freezing, always scared.

The sailors of *Rus* stood their watch in comfort, enjoyed a hot meal, a film, a warm bunk. No one hunted them or haunted their dreams. Being tracked and targeted was no more real for them than a video game. Their only serious worries were about getting paid.

Rudenko blew on his tea to cool it, and noted the subtle change in Nemerov's expression as he read the mission orders. The jauntiness grew fainter, the body more deliberate in attitude. Every now and then Nemerov consulted the chart enclosed with the papers.

Vasily Sergeyevich Nemerov had been a boy, an ordinary seaman aboard a Northern Fleet cruiser, when the admiral first took note of him and held out the enticing offer of officer's training at the Higher Naval School in Leningrad. As Rudenko had suspected, Nemerov proved a brilliant candidate, graduating first in his class after five long years of study. He still treasured the moment: the two companies of cadets formed up, the colors standard barely moving in the heat, Cadet V. S. Nemerov wearing knee-high boots, dress blue uniform, red piping and lapel plates, a gold belt, his hat balanced in his white-gloved hand, the traditional red carnation in the other. Each graduate in turn laid his flower alongside his classmates' at the sailors' cenotaph as they filed by to honor the Soviet seamen who had preceded them. But Vasily Sergeyevich, the medal winner, the first in his class and thus the last man in the rank, had stepped from the line and slowly marched across the open ground of the square to the reviewing stand filled with guests and faculty. He had presented his flower to Vice Admiral Rudenko, then donned his hat and formally saluted the man who had become more like a father to him than a mentor.

This spirit was the boy's great strength and vulnerability, for the naval apparatus did not countenance deviance, and even with his gold-medal scholarship, it had taken him several extra years to gain admittance to the old Naval Academy on the River Neva for further study. His promotions had come hard, as did his Party membership; the process had tempered him, but it had hardened him as well.

Rudenko quaffed his tea. A sailor entered and silently passed the captain a note. Nemerov acknowledged it and returned to the chart and the directive.

"Admiral," he said, without looking up, and slid the message across to Rudenko.

Rudenko tilted his head back slightly to read it without his glasses. Radar had identified a ship to the stern, another submarine, trailing at thirty-two knots.

Nemerov said, "We will outrun them as we pick up speed, now that we have submerged."

"There will be others," Rudenko said. "They will be waiting for us."

"Yes." Nemerov put aside the chart and looked at the admiral. "I had better inform my officers and senior crewmen." He indicated the charts and orders. "I will send someone back to escort you to your cabin."

Rudenko smiled. "Thank you, yes. I need to put my bones on a horizontal plane for a few hours."

Nemerov nodded and excused himself. Two sailors appeared to fetch Rudenko's sea bag and the tea tray. The cabin they escorted him to was close by—Nemerov's own. As he was now the senior officer aboard, the quarters were his for the duration of his stay.

Like much of the ship's interior, the quarters were painted a mild pastel blue; the tiny water closet, a light green. All the comforts of home. Rudenko slipped off his rubber-soled shoes and shed the harness and the waterproof overalls.

Fatigue and tension were taking their toll. He arched his back against the stiffness knotted deep beneath and tried awkwardly to massage his shoulders. For all his strict regimen of morning swims and massages at the Sanduna bathhouse, no routine of exercise could fully counteract the accumulation of years. Yet he never stopped being surprised at being old, when inside he felt unaged, even young sometimes, the same daredevil who had lived to tell the tales of fourteen war patrols.

For a moment he remembered himself at seventeen, when he'd first gone out as a third-watch midshipman. Every ranking officer on board had perished on deck during an air attack. He assumed command, brought the vessel home, and it had remained his. He had turned eighteen at sea, already a captain by simple virtue of survival.

He unpacked his black sea cap and placed it over the shade of the small desk lamp. How familiar and splendid were the odd sensations of the submarine's passage through the belly of the sea. It had been too long. He sensed his body slowly adjusting to the pressure and the surge.

Rudenko sat down at the tiny desk, wiggling his toes. A miniature nautical chart of the globe and its oceans lay atop the desk as decoration, protected by a thick transparent cover. Rudenko ran a finger over the chart. God had not graced the Red Navy with good strategic bases. The Baltic Fleet, in the event of war, had to pass through the Danish Straits. The Black Sea Fleet was corked by the Dardanelles at the entrance to the Mediterranean and by Gibraltar at the entry to the Atlantic. In the Pacific, even the mighty Asiatic fleet—once 100 nuclear submarines and 830 ships at Vladivostok and Petropavlovsk—was boxed in by the islands of Japan.

At the outbreak of a war, the fleets would be instantly vulnerable, as the Hitlerites had so ably demonstrated. In the summer of 1941 they'd virtually interned the Baltic Fleet in the harbor at Leningrad and kept it bottled up for the duration of the fighting. That same July the Germans had neutralized the Black Sea Fleet by occupying the ports of Sevastopol and Odessa, and all the while the huge Pacific Fleet rode idly at anchor, a noncombatant in the war with Japan. Only the Northern Fleet had sailed out to do battle.

The antidote for this fateful national geography was feeble, and had been for all the many years the policy had been in place. In time of war, the three fleets were to dash for the open ocean through the various gauntlets. Simplicity itself. Also useless. American satellites recorded every square nautical mile of the surface, and everywhere their reconnaissance craft probed Soviet defenses, deliberately provoking alarms to test the electronic reflexes of the fleets and of Russia's air borders. The information they gleaned no doubt helped them plot counterstrategies for jamming shut the gateways of the fleets, just as the Germans had done.

Still, the fleets had endlessly and vainly rehearsed this lone strategy—until Chernavin introduced his ingenious ploy to establish invulnerable firing positions for submarines within and without the confines of the various encumbering seas, and not have the entire subsea force join in the harrowing charge for open water. Submarine missiles rising from friendly locales—like the Sea of Okhotsk and the inlets of Sweden, and the fjords deep inside Norway—such missiles could reach the enemy's homelands easily and were far less likely to be discovered until the first rockets flew. To attack the sequestered subs, the Americans would have to bombard friendly nations. Catastrophic, unthinkable. Even now, the West's technology could not detect submarines hidden in the naturally protected positions Chernavin had identified.

Still, Rudenko was glad he had commanded the one fleet free of such geographic difficulties. The Northern Fleet had no constricting choke points, only sixteen hundred miles of Norway's convoluted coast to negotiate and reach the Atlantic. Or simply go north. This freedom of movement made it Russia's most important naval arm. Without funds, without the Union of Soviet Socialist Republics, this remained true as terrain. Rudenko smiled, remembering an aphorism he'd learned from the real-estate mogul whose campaign contributions had earned him the American ambassadorship to the Vatican: *Location, location, location.*

Rudenko phoned and instructed the officer on duty to wake him at the next change of watch. He felt tired, even a little dizzy. The preparations and the race to the coast had been extremely taxing. He had not slept in many hours. Yet he clung to consciousness as he stretched out, nagged by something he had glimpsed from the cockpit of the Jakowlew jump jet as it swooped in on *Rus,* something he couldn't quite pin down. Yes! It came back to him. The ship's identifying numerals had been crudely painted over. He remembered now what he had only half heard Panov say at their parting on the windy corner in Moscow: "You carry no ensign. You fly no flag."

Melodramatic drivel. If the British or Americans got close enough to see the rescue submersibles on deck, half their navies would turn out. *Sleep,* he ordered himself—*I must sleep.* He eased onto his side, still in his dress uniform. The ornate gold anchors embroidered on his lapels glistened amid the blossoming laurels.

The assistant navigator of the USS *Swordfish* watched the orange blip on the radar screen shrink as the Russian sub lowered its antenna and scope, then disappear as it submerged. He crossed the room to take up his position behind the sonarman to whom the responsibility of surveillance had just passed.

"Target validation," the junior navigator barked.

The sonarman reported the data collected by his passive sound harvesters in the prow: "Target dead ahead. Leveling off toward one five zero feet." He paused, then announced: "Increasing speed."

The assistant navigator grimaced and called up to the executive officer on the outdoor bridge, who initiated diving procedures and turned to the lookouts perched around him on the running boards circling the scope mount.

"Secure bridge and lay below," he shouted above the howling norther, then counted off the seamen as they passed him on the way down. As duty and custom required, he was the last man off the bridge, activating the hatch closure as he went.

"Dog the hatch," he bellowed, and descended to the deck of the conning tower.

The diving officer was already well into the litany of his checklist.

"Pressure."

"Fourteen psi and building," a sailor responded.

"Hatches?"

"Straight board," called another, checking the row of pale green bars indicating that all the ship's apertures were closed and the underwater systems functioning properly.

To match the Russian submarine, the executive officer ordered a lazy angle of descent, hoping to submerge without undue racket. On the surface they had kept their profile low; he was satisfied the Russian radar had not seen them.

It took some minutes to reach the prescribed depth of eighty feet. Finally, with the boat leveled, he allowed the watch to change, the Golds replacing the Blues at their stations. The Blues stood down, already late for chow. In the month they'd been under way, the crew had eaten through half the stores. By noon, fed and fatigued, the Blues would displace the swing shift from their bunks and the Swingers would bathe and shuffle off to breakfast.

Working shift changes, even in the spaciousness of a U.S. nuclear submarine, required a great deal of coordination and strict sleep rotations. The sailors called it hot bunking because the shared beds were still warm from one changeover to the next.

The commander came on duty late, with the Golds, and took the conn. "What's Ivan doing?" he asked the exec.

"Goin' down the alley. The usual, except for the speed, and no evasive maneuvers. No baffle. A Victor class, I would say. A real beauty. Bigger than a football field."

"How fast is she going?"

"Full out. A new course record for the Continental Shelf Speedway."

"What're the numbers?" the commander said.

"Forty-four knots."

"Fifty-five land miles an hour? Sweet baby Jesus."

The exec leaned closer to the sonar screen. "First a fire in a missile tube, followed by an assignation with a jump jet. Now a drag race. This guy's havin' a primo day."

The eighteen-hundred-horsepower turbine of the *Swordfish* would produce no more than thirty knots. The Russian boats were disconcertingly faster, could dive deeper than any American sub, and it rankled the captain. He had no choice, however, but to accept the operational solution that had been ordered by North Atlantic Headquarters in Norfolk as adequate for the moment. The standing order was to hand off surveillance and have another sub take over the duties of tracking the Russians as they outran their American monitors. Privately he wondered what in the hell they could do against the Russian subs if things got out of hand.

The commander pinched the skin on his neck. "Does she know we're here?"

"I don't believe so, sir," the exec said. "They probably don't care, either. They've pinged their sonar only twice since they submerged. Ours has remained in passive mode, and we've kept our bow up her backside, right in her wake. The back scatter should keep us cloaked, sir."

The commander nodded. The Russian's own propeller turbulence would help camouflage *Swordfish*. Unless Ivan made a precautionary baffle swing off course and ran a tight circle to free his own sonar from his wake, the bogie sub would never know they were there.

"Helmsman," said the officer, "keep us on line behind her as long as you can. Tom, raise the radio antenna. Notify me as soon as Fleet Ocean Surveillance takes us off this Russki's case and the *Beaumont* picks her up." Dropping his voice, he said to his exec, "We can't keep up with 'em. It's fucking embarrassing. Don't they know they're bankrupt?"

# 8

**M**unson had instructed Hanley not to communicate anything about her assignment to anyone she met along the
way, "Nothing beyond pleasantries." That was not proving
to be a problem. The only other travelers she'd encountered at the
airport in Edmonton were junketing Japanese doctors and their
wives who had come on direct flights from Tokyo to see the aurora
borealis over the Canadian plains. Each woman deplaned in a full-
length mink, fur hat, and Vuitton handbag.

Hanley was met by a ruggedly dressed alumnus of Trudeau Station who was to brief her and accompany her north.

"Dr. Hanley? How do you do?"

"Jessie, please. Hi," Hanley said, taking in his curly dirty-blond
hair and intelligent brown eyes. He had the smallest scar just under
his left cheek but was otherwise perfect: energetic; well mannered,
with the deep voice of a radio broadcaster; tastefully attired; and
gorgeously cologned. The scent was distracting enough that she
managed to miss his first name, if he'd said it. She did hear the
"Stevenson." She wondered for a moment if Mr. Something Stevenson might appreciate being told how good he smelled.

Hanley and Stevenson barely had time for a hasty snack in the
cafeteria before they were bundled aboard a flight for Anchorage on
a Canadian Air Force plane that had been waiting for them for several hours.

In Anchorage they changed planes again. Each succeeding aircraft was larger yet more crowded. They seemed to be accumulating equipment along the way. Where this flight was taking them, Hanley did not know, and no one was volunteering. Stevenson finally explained why.

"How we deliver you to Trudeau is a slightly dicey issue politically. In the long run, it might be better for you not to know the details of the route. Suffice it to say, we have ten provincial governments. Normally each has to be kept abreast and mollified."

"But *you're* the government," she said.

"It doesn't work like that. We're not like you in the U.S. Quite the opposite. Imagine your South as having won the Civil War; that's sort of where we are. A confederation of strong states with a weak central government. Do you follow?"

"Yeah! Can we send you all our Republicans?"

"I don't believe so." Stevenson smiled. "We have plenty of our own."

"I still don't follow why you're not having a Canadian look into this."

Stevenson puffed out his cheeks like a child. "Simple, really. A computer selected you as most likely to succeed in the circumstances, such as they are. So the Royal Commission on the Arctic extended the invitation."

"Little ole me? Specifically?"

"By name, yes. There were four candidates; you were at the top. Given the parameters, the computer gave you the best odds of finding this thing that's causing such trouble at Trudeau."

"Son of a bitch," Hanley said, chortling. "I wonder what odds they gave Ruff."

"Pardon?"

"Nothing. Go on."

"Anyway, that's our story. Your not being Canadian was coincidental good fortune. Because if the personnel choice were to be Canadian, and subsequently debated in Ottawa—even in council—there'd be dissension and leaks, invariably. The Canadian way."

"Yeah," Hanley said, "it's the same in the States."

The landing gear groaned open.

"We're coming in."

The sky was overcast, the color of gravel, although Hanley calculated it to be only two in the afternoon. The cold was merciless, numbing their legs as they hustled to the air terminal, their breath billowing white.

The simple lunch was devoid of conversation, given their fatigue and the decibel level of the jukebox playing "When It's Springtime in Alaska, It's Forty Below in Nome." Immediately after lunch, Stevenson led her to an empty dressing area in a deserted recreation hall. There he introduced her to her new garments, laid out on a pool table.

"This is an extreme environment suit."

The outfit looked preposterous. The outer body was reflective, made of soft, white quills. The quill tips were iridescent orange.

"Looks like a giant bird."

"As well it might. Birds inspired it: the densely feathered skin of the Emperor Penguin and the eiderdown garments of the Inuit. Forms a perfect exterior insulating layer."

Underneath was a second feathery layer, its pile pointed inward toward a metallicized sheath that formed a third layer.

"That's your vapor barrier." Without it, Stevenson explained, body heat and humidity could not be properly modulated. "Moisture is your enemy. The early explorers thought they could conquer polar temperatures by piling on more and more layers of wool, but they didn't realize that once they began to sweat, the wool had no way of releasing the moisture, which started to freeze. The more wool they put on, the colder they got. Eventually some of them died—wrapped in layers of wool like mummies."

The next layer was a brilliant corset Stevenson called a *gilet*, to cover the torso. Air heated by the body passed through it before being ducted into the helmet. And under it all was a ventile body stocking. Stevenson held it up. "It's an artificial skin, inspired by Inuit garments made from the intestines of sea mammals. Gut's remarkably supple and tough. Allows the humidity of perspiration to escape, but it's waterproof from the outside. And so is this."

Stevenson showed Hanley how the suit went on, a layer at a time, then turned his back to let her try it. She donned the outfit with surprising ease. Hands on hips, he stood back and took stock. "You did that rather ably."

"I've had a lot of practice putting on protective suits," she said. Admiring herself in the full-length mirror by the free weights, Hanley laughed out loud.

"I may audition for *Sesame Street* after this is all over, or maybe as a mascot for the Lakers." She preened her ruff. "Cute." Stevenson bristled at what he mistook as a slight against its engineering. She didn't notice.

"The polar outfit," Stevenson continued coldly, "generates no extra heat. What the suit does—magnificently—is husband the body's own heat source. Its design exploits human physiology. The wearer's own metabolic processes are its thermal engine and its chief regulating system. Before its conception, the simplest outdoor tasks required tremendous effort in the brutal arctic conditions. What might take minutes in a temperate climate, took hours in the Arctic. Just breathing was hard work. To heat air—inhaled at an average of minus forty degrees Fahrenheit and exhaled at ninety-eight point six—was flat-out exhausting," he said. "Every bodily system was overtaxed just to function and support life, much less do anything productive."

The Trudeau suit, she could see, was remarkable. The suit was not an artificial heating plant nor just a protective barrier, but truly an extension of the body's own systems that amplified its inadequate resources, creating a microenvironment that was comfortable even while external conditions were nearly intolerable.

"It's completely ingenious," she said. "The engineering blows me away." He was mollified by her obviously genuine enthusiasm and felt slightly guilty for having misjudged her.

The gloves went on last, heavily insulated yet thin, encased in a mitten that slipped off as needed and held the microphone activator. "The transceivers," Stevenson explained, "are built into the suit behind the right knee joint. Location studies indicated that was the best for sustaining shocks from falls or other accidents. The rescue beacon switch is on the left forearm."

"Just amazing."

"Quite. The suit's microchips and transceivers use the only synthetic energy," Stevenson said, "which comes from tiny batteries located in the armpit to protect them from the cold. Okay, we're up to the helmet." He lifted it from the pool table and handed it to her.

The helmet was black, from the protruding brim over the brow—almost a short beak—to the sides of the pileum. The throat and faceplate were silver. She slipped it on.

"The headgear contains its own humidification apparatus, distress beacon, transmitters, earphones, mike—"

"What, no sports radio?" Hanley said. "I want a refund." This time Stevenson smiled.

Having properly fitted her helmet and sealed the seams underneath the ruff, Stevenson showed Hanley how to engage the systems and adjust the controls in the gloves. A tiny green dot appeared inside the helmet at the periphery of her vision.

"Hey," Hanley called out. "I think my high beams are on."

"No," Stevenson said. "That just means your oil is okay and you're running smoothly. If it goes yellow, you've got a minor problem; red, major malfunction. You've got to cease whatever you're doing and seek shelter."

"Got it," Hanley said. "This is just so great."

"Any questions?" he said, looking pleased.

"What if there is no shelter?"

"Make one," Stevenson said with a wave around him, as though they were already out on the ice. "There's plenty to work with. Lots of ice, a little snow. Snow is preferable. Look."

He tugged on a ring suspended from a grommet in the sleeve. Out came what looked like a loose thread, thin as a hair, and completely retractable.

"Doesn't look like much, but it's an artificial fiber based on the proteins in spider silk, stronger than steel. You can build yourself a hut with this. Carve straight down to make blocks. The material you want is snow. If you can't manage blocks, find snow and burrow in. Don't lie on ice. It's much colder. Not to worry. You'll get several more lessons before anyone lets you outside."

"When do we start the next leg?"

Stevenson hesitated. "The weather is kicking up at the site. We'll dally here till it dies down. We wouldn't want you blown to Siberia. Or hang gliding out onto the Arctic Ocean."

"Thanks," she said, taking off her helmet and admiring herself in the mirror. "My son would love one of these. But the tush could use a tuck, don't you think?" she said, examining her fluffy backside.

"Believe me, you'll be grateful for all the insulation."

"Hey, I'm not complaining. You should see me in a biohazard suit—I look like the love child of Casper the Friendly Ghost and the Michelin Man." Stevenson laughed.

"Exactly how cold is it at Trudeau right now?"

"About minus fifty-two Celsius and—"

"How much is that in Fahrenheit?"

"Around fifty below."

"Ouch," Hanley said. "I am going to freeze my *nalgitas* off."


Stevenson waved to an American Air Force sergeant standing in the doorway by the lockers. "What's our timetable, Chief?"

"Whenever you're ready, sir," the sergeant replied. He zipped up his parka and raised its hood.

Hanley followed Stevenson and the crew chief out onto the tarmac and into the back of a small closed van for the short ride out to their aircraft. Unlike the smaller planes they had been on so far, the C-141 Starlifter was gigantic, with four huge engines mounted two to a wing. They pulled up alongside the gaping cargo hatch in the tail, and the crew chief led the way up into its belly. Comfortable padded seats lined the sides, facing in. The center was dominated by tracks wide enough to accommodate a subway train.

"Jesus," Hanley said, taking in the long, spacious interior. "This isn't a plane. It's a dance hall with wings. You could carry tanks in here."

"Oh, we do, ma'am," said the crew chief.

The huge engines started sequentially, each adding its whine to the growing din until all four were howling. "No commercial flight, this," Stevenson shouted, referring to the obvious lack of sound-proofing. He motioned for Hanley to manipulate the switches in her glove. The third click eliminated most of the outside sound and patched her into the plane's internal communications frequency.

The hydraulic drone of the hatch closing behind them filled the hold cavity. Hanley headed toward the front. She stopped abruptly, taken aback by the sight of an egg-shaped object the size of a dune buggy, sitting on a wheeled skid lashed down on the rollered tracks. "Looks like a space program reject."

"Works about the same way," Stevenson said. "Your personal roller coaster. Keep you safe and snug on the way down. Your air force personnel call it the Commode."

"Charming. Use it often?" Hanley said.

Stevenson made a face. "Once."

Hanley's brow furrowed. "Well, at least we know you survived. How bad was the trip?"

"Oh, no, it wasn't me inside the thing. I was just giving it the push. But we did recover the mannequin unscathed."

"Hey! All right," Hanley said. "I always thought I could be a crash-test dummy if my day job didn't work out."

"Unfortunately, ah, we did experience unfavorable conditions. So it took us a while to chase it down."

"I won't ask."

"Best not to."

Stevenson squinted and rubbed his forehead.

"What's wrong?" she said.

"Headache."

"Stress," Hanley said sympathetically. "I have just the thing for it. A healing energy technique—"

"No thanks," Stevenson said, looking amused. "I've taken aspirin."

"Hey, aspirin is just a fancy concentrate of willow bark. People seem to forget eighty percent of our modern meds started out as plants."

The crew chief signaled for them to take seats on one side and strapped himself in. A headset connected him to the flight deck.

The plane taxied out onto the line, spun its tail into the wind, braked against its revving engines, and held for several minutes. It sounded like Niagara Falls to Hanley. The brakes slowly released and the Starlifter rolled down the runway, building speed. As they lifted off, Hanley caught sight of an illuminated sign at the end of the tarmac.

You are now leaving
Elmendorf Air Force Base
Anchorage, Alaska
Have A Great Day

Hanley closed her eyes and tried to catch up to her present circumstances, but her brain lagged far behind. She replayed putting Joey on the flight for San Francisco and her afternoon at the Center afterward: Munson chattering nervously, the tedious hour with the personnel department moron reviewing her insurance policies and the extra million-dollar rider Munson had added, the quickie physical while dictating a new will to the house counsel, one last telephone skirmish with her ex. All day she'd kept reminding herself to go outside and say good-bye to the sun for the next five months, but by the time she'd had the chance, it was too late, and now here she was, somewhere over the arctic wastes, waiting to be disgorged in an egg by a flying whale thousands of feet above . . . nothing.

She took her laptop out of its case, turned it on, and extended its aerial. Damned if it wasn't downloading satellite-relayed transmissions even here. She pulled off her gloves and checked her mail, reviewing an update from Ishikawa on information that had filtered in from Trudeau Station about anomalies in the pathology workups. The only good news was that so far no one else at Trudeau was showing any symptoms of whatever had killed their three colleagues. She saved an e-mail from her son for last. Hanley smiled to herself, warmed by the contact, and at his generation's completely blasé attitude about technology: Joey was asking for help with his homework as though she were just down the block and not speeding toward the ends of the earth. She tried to write back, but the unit wouldn't transmit. The satellite link was gone.

She looked down at the skin of her hands on the keyboard. Deeply tanned. Wrinkles. Cuticles. Fingerprints. Flesh.

"And I don't want to see any of it falling off," Hanley said to herself, unaware that her mike channel was open.

"No worries," Stevenson said. "Better get some sleep. We've got a long way to go."

"It'd be a lot easier if you'd let me get out of this suit."

"I'd rather you keep it on. It's important to become accustomed to wearing it for prolonged periods." Stevenson was graphic in his attempt to impress her with the lethal hostility of the cold. "At minus twenty-eight degrees and a thirty-mile-per-hour wind, without protective garments you've got forty seconds. Naked flesh freezes solid in under half a minute. At fifty-eight degrees below freezing and no wind at all, ordinary tires shatter, human cells rupture, metal breaks like glass, glass disintegrates like rust. And—"

"I got it, I got it," she said. "Antifreeze turns to concrete."

"Antifreeze, be damned," the chief interjected. "If it gets cold enough at this altitude, by God, our jet fuel'll start turnin' to sludge. Hydraulic fluid'll be clay. Then we're a flyin' boulder. You don't want to be up here when gravity takes a turn. If the temperatures up ahead get too low, we'll turn back."

"You sound like my ex-husband," Hanley said, stretching. "He's an alarmist too. Even I'm beginning to wonder if I couldn't just call this one in."

As the Starlifter roared north, the aurora grew fainter. The wavy splotches of light merged and separated. The green rods, tinged with red, faded. Below was a vast, arid wilderness. Not a tree, not an insect. The weird featureless space gondola seemed an appropriate vehicle for such an alien place, Hanley thought.

"Where are we?" she said.

"Still over Alaska."

"When will we cross the Arctic Circle?"

The chief clicked on his headset, connecting him to the cockpit.

"Sir, our passenger wants to know when we will reach latitude six deuce, three deuce." He paused, listening. "Yes, sir," he said, and turned back to Hanley. "As I suspected, we're already past it, ma'am."

"Past what?" Hanley said.

"The demarcation of the Arctic Circle." The chief pointed his jaw in the direction of the utter blackness outside. "We're there—in the icebox."

"Yeah," she said, turning in her seat and looking out, "and the refrigerator light is definitely not on."

The plane's interior had begun to lose its chill. Hanley took off the helmet and let the roar wash over her.

"I'm going to meditate," Hanley said, closing her eyes.

She tried to empty her mind, but it was hard not to think about Joey, and the truth of her ex-husband's charge of selfishness—that career came first, even before their child. It had been so much harder, but also simpler, when Joey was little. Then all it had taken to make Joey happy was a pocketful of his special valuables. He'd carefully extract them every evening before his clothes went in the wash, and methodically refill his pockets each morning. Rainbow eraser, paper bear, a pompom from a key chain finger puppet, several mysterious stones, "pink money" (pennies), "big money" (a quarter), and a dented compass. She sighed. With a sense of regret she began meditating, imagining her breath steadily inflating and deflating a balloon.

The plane banked slightly, making a course adjustment, and leveled off. Hanley stretched out on the enormous seat, trying to accommodate the bulk of the arctic suit. Stevenson envied his passenger. Hanley looked like a person who could sleep anywhere. A good talent to have where she was going: a world without day or night.

When she awoke several hours later, Stevenson handed her a sandwich and a thermos, then reached into a pocket and pulled out a form and a pen.

"What's that?" Hanley said, and tore open the Saran wrap around her roast beef sandwich.

"Your customs form." He furrowed his brow and read: " 'Are you bringing into Canada food, fruits, vegetables, meats, eggs, dairy products, animals, birds, plant parts, soil, living organisms, vaccines?' " He looked over at the Commode, stocked full of medical equipment and supplies. "Yes, well. I suppose what they don't know can't hurt them," he said, and tossed the form aside.

# 9

The first briefing of *Rus*'s officers went smoothly. The four divers in the pressure chamber participated by means of a television hookup.

The captain outlined the way the rescue would proceed if it proved straightforward and the disabled submarine's crew members were still conscious and able to move unaided: *Rus*'s sailors would pilot the submersibles into place, lock on, evacuate the *Vladivostok*'s crew twenty at a time.

The medical personnel reviewed the steps for handling survivors in the event of radiation leakage from the atomic engine, and the proper way for those boarding her to don protective gear. The small recreational hall next to the sick bay was being fitted out with medical equipment and cots, and an adjacent galley had been converted to a nursing station.

The engineering officer reported the successful testing of the welds in tube 6, and the four divers in the pressure chamber cheered, their voices pitched high by the helium they were breathing. The gathering laughed.

Captain Nemerov asked for questions. On the television monitor one of the divers spoke up. He was a burly man, naked to the waist, wearing the black beret of a naval commando.

"Orlovsky here, Captain." His bulk made the birdlike squeak all the more absurd.

"Yes, Sergeant." They had found him, Nemerov whispered to

Rudenko, at the transients' barracks in Murmansk. A master diver, he'd been commandeered on the spot, and he'd turned out to be a bit of a prankster. Orlovsky had been whiling away the hours in the compression box by tape-recording fairy tales for his nieces and nephews in his falsetto helium voice and singing bawdy ballads for his compatriots, like "When Alaila Dipped Her Feet."

In spite of his squeak, Orlovsky was serious. "If we need additional equipment items, might I suggest that a forward torpedo tube be kept empty for the purpose of passing us such pieces? We could retrieve them once we're outside the hull. It would speed things up."

"Already done," Nemerov said. "Anything else?"

"Well, sir, since you are kind enough to ask." Orlovsky waved a military pamphlet and continued in his cartoon voice. "It is my understanding that when a ship's crew is at rest hours, they have certain recreational privileges. If I am not mistaken."

A few sailors giggled.

"Yes, Sergeant."

"These include radio programs about international issues, the Russian people's labor achievements, cultural expositions, the latest reports of sporting extravaganzas, the new McDonald's opening in St. Petersburg."

"You want CNN piped in, Sergeant?" Nemerov said.

"It also says here that sailors are to be apprised of the different countries they are sailing past—"

The room rocked with laughter. The sergeant continued, deadpan.

"—and perhaps may visit."

The sailors hooted.

"And they are to be provided information concerning the cultural life and sights of those countries in anticipation of shore leave."

His audience laughed and applauded.

Rudenko hid his face in a mug of tea, while Nemerov pretended to cough.

"Sergeant," Nemerov said, as the noise subsided. "How exactly did you wind up aboard *Rus*?"

On screen, Orlovsky took off his beret and scratched his head, thinking deeply. "Well, sir. I remember marching in the military forces parade, through Red Square and on by the embassy of the United States of America—you know, on Sadovoye Koltso—where we stamped our boots a tiny bit harder than usual. Then I was heading back to my base by way of Murmansk. I was, I recall, celebrating before embarking on an icebreaker going east to Kamchatka, in the Pacific region. Then poof. I wake up in this capsule full of debris, sir. I thought they'd relaunched *Mir,* and I was spinning around in space."

The crew howled. Nemerov smiled openly. "We will try to return you to earth soon, Sergeant."

"I thank you, Captain, for relieving my anxieties," Orlovsky chirped. He bowed and everyone roared and applauded.

The meeting ended, followed by a series of quick, small conferences for the specialized personnel, each attended by the captain and the admiral. Detailing all possible scenarios was tedious but necessary if they were to save any of *Vladivostok*'s crew. Survival depended upon anticipating contingencies, and survival was the one kind of success worth anything at sea.


Captain Nemerov ordered the helm to port to ease *Rus* closer to shore. The rocky coastal waters would help impair the efficiency of their pursuers' sonar. When *Rus* was equidistant from the submarine behind it and the boat waiting ahead, Nemerov directed the bow torpedo room to stand ready with the mesmer. Twelve minutes were counted off.

*Rus* eased to starboard. The torpedo was fired, the engines cut and onboard motors muffled. The mesmer erupted with amplified replications of the sounds that normally emanated from *Rus.* Simultaneously the torpedo detected the pursuers' sonar pulses and bounced them back, boosted to a strength that would be perceived as the echo of an object the size of a nuclear sub.

The angle of the mesmer's trajectory carried it farther and farther from shore. If any vessel drew closer to it than two kilometers, it would stop decoying and start jamming their radar and sonar.

While *Rus* hovered above the seabed, her sonorant's passive collecting disks traced the course of the pursuing sub. The Americans' engines passed to port as she valiantly chased the mesmer toward the North Sea. After four minutes, *Rus* resumed a subdued speed toward the coast and the mouth of the Sogne Fjord.

In ancient times, Nemerov mused, mariners deceived pursuers by casting smoldering pitch onto the waves to resemble the distant lights of another ship. This modern equivalent was also effective, but only eleven such mesmers were left in the navy's entire stockpile. Chernavin was sparing nothing on this mission. The captain felt encouraged. He allowed himself a momentary fantasy of the dockside reunions when they brought the submariners home. News blackout and all, the wives would be there.

He surveyed the oncoming undersea terrain on the sonar, then motioned for the periscope. The tube rose, bringing the eyepiece to the level of his chest. He slipped on red-lensed goggles to protect his eyes from the room's illumination.

The coast was a black silhouette of mountaintops. The gap in this towering wall was invisible to the eye. Only instruments could confirm its location. *Rus* made for the opening at seven knots. Nemerov stepped back and the scope slid down.

He paced the bridge very slowly. According to the sonar, they were passing the threshold, crossing the shallow delta. Keel depth, eighty meters. He sent the steward to notify the admiral.


Rudenko rose quickly, smoothed his hair with his hands. His dream had been so vivid, but all he could remember was the woman: Inga Dobenskaya. He hadn't thought of her that way in years. He did not even mind the omen of a dead person in his dream. She had moved him so in life, why not in her afterlife as well? He aged, she didn't—couldn't. He sighed, remembering her sensuousness, but couldn't tell if he was remembering it from their time together or from the dream. How long had it been since they had lain together, coupled in the dark? A lifetime? A night? Had he loved her? Years after she'd died he had realized, yes. Why did his dreams never revisit the wonderful nights in St. Petersburg?

Rudenko donned his cap and followed the corridor to the control room, where he acknowledged the duty officer's nervous greeting with a nod. Nemerov, his eyes still protected by red-lensed goggles, was standing by the ascending periscope. When it had extended enough to break the surface, Nemerov lowered the control arms and peered into the eyepiece. Quickly he swiveled the scope a full turn, checking for vessels, then stepped aside for the admiral.

"Sir."

The admiral reversed his cap and took the control bars in hand.

The wake of the periscope fanned out behind them across the perfectly still surface. The walls of the fjord vaulted straight up out of the water, hundreds of meters high. The breathtaking enormity of the sheer rock faces gave him a momentary twinge. He wanted badly to taste the wintry night in the eerie stillness of those sheltering walls, instead of inhaling the submarine's recirculated air.

He relinquished the scope and stepped back; the deck officer motioned to bring it down. Nemerov removed his red goggles as he and Rudenko retired to the command chairs behind the helmsman, who sat slightly below them with safety cinches around his middle like a seat belt, and serving a similar purpose. At full power, the sub's speed was as high as a car's.

Past the mouth, the fjord's bottom fell away, slanting downward. Nemerov ordered *Rus* deeper. He looked toward the sonarman watching the depth gauge and the computer board above, which gave out the digitized interpretations of the sound waves scouting out the water ahead.

"A clean channel," Nemerov said. "Not an obstruction anywhere. Like a funnel."

"I sincerely hope it's not baited at the other end," Rudenko said.

An hour inched by. The admiral dozed in his chair, while Nemerov watched the helmsman and deck officer maneuver *Rus* along the deep chasm.

"Passive sonar detects no ships' engines, sir," the deck officer announced.

"Switch to active sonar," Nemerov ordered. Risky if anyone was listening for the metronomic pong, but finding *Vladivostok* would be impossible without it.

The first sonar waves returned deformed. The layer of water surrounding *Rus* had distorted the ripple completely. The low salinity had kept it from merging with the deeper layers and skewed the sonar signal. "Take her farther down," Nemerov commanded.

The helmsman acknowledged and *Rus* angled down, gliding out of the layer and into the next. The globes of sound rippled out evenly from the sub and rebounded clearly from the fjord's bottom.

"Depth?"

"Three hundred eighteen meters."

Nemerov flexed his jaw muscles to adjust the pressure in his ears and peered up at a gauge. "Level her out."

The search proceeded. Thirty kilometers into the fjord, the sonar bounded back with greater strength and clarity.

"Contact," the sonarman reported loudly. A large metal object lay somewhere in the depths below them.

"Contact, aye," the first officer repeated.

*Rus* descended in a languid curve to port. The acoustic projector was engaged and a high frequency sound sent out. Back came the reflection forming a signature on the screen.

*Vladivostok.*

Nemerov nudged the admiral. "*Vladivostok* is nestled against the wall of the fjord. Hung up on something. Not quite touching bottom, and slightly tilted."

Rudenko nodded, checking the depth gauge. "Like a dead fish in an aquarium," he said unhappily. "The submersibles will be useless at this depth. Only the divers can reach her."

A sailor sang out the depth every twenty meters as *Rus* descended. When he announced, "Six hundred meters," Nemerov got to his feet.

"Check the descent. Stop engines." He stepped back to view a bank of television monitors overhead. "Switch on the mercury lamps outside."

On the prow two lamps came on, and three low-light television cameras. The admiral craned his neck to see. The images were too murky to be useful.

"Engines on slow," Nemerov said. "Down another hundred."

The helmsman repeated the order and complied. *Rus* carefully descended another hundred meters and there she was, *Vladivostok*, lying helpless, abutting the sunken wall of the fjord.

Two lines stretched up from *Vladivostok*'s hull toward the surface. "The antenna," said the deck officer, pointing out one of the lines on the screen.

"Yes," Nemerov said. "And the other—the thicker one—looks to be the cable for a seabed trawler. But I don't see the SB-4."

"Sir, perhaps the line just came loose and floated up."

Nemerov gave a pessimistic grunt; he suspected otherwise. But the focus of their concern was the inert *Vladivostok* and the sailors who had called out from this glacial trough. Automated and encoded as it had been, the essence of the high-speed transmission was ancient: Save Our Souls.


They attempted radio contact, using the lowest power to avoid detection. The signal was at an extremely low frequency to penetrate the water, and because of the wavelength it took forever.

No response.

The divers were not yet ready to withstand the pressure at that depth. Orlovsky demanded to be allowed to try, but Nemerov refused. It was excruciating to be so close to *Vladivostok* and unable to assist her, but sacrificing his own men would serve no purpose. After an agonizing wait, Nemerov gave the order to initiate the dive. The four divers swam out from the bell lock and up through the well of the flooded missile tube, their life-sustaining hoses uncoiling behind them.

*Rus* stood off a mere forty meters from *Vladivostok,* but perpendicular to it to reduce the impact in the event the stricken ship buckled and exploded. Forty meters was closer than either the admiral or Captain Nemerov wanted to be, but the hoses of the divers kept them on a tight tether. The shorter the distance the four had to swim in the freezing water, the more time they would have aboard *Vladivostok,* and the greater their strength. To conserve their energy further, a motorized sled delivered them to the becalmed vessel.

Lieutenant Nuchin manned the divers' intercom in the crowded cubicle adjacent to the control room, monitoring his men's cardiac rates and body temperatures, closely gauging their pitifully short allotment of time in the water.

The reports from the lead diver were succinct: "Bow planes . . . sheared off. And part of the sail. Hull . . . bowed in places. Oxygen bubbling from seam. Bulkhead and plates are holding . . . at least on the side we can see."

"Radiation readings?"

"Completely normal, sir."

Nuchin directed the second diver, Orlovsky, to investigate the condition of the hull on the starboard flank, the side wedged against the rock wall. Cursing, he squeezed into the space between the huge hull and the rock face of the fjord. He switched on his lamp, flooding the area with two hundred fifty watts of light. With a kick of his flippers, he disappeared entirely from the view of the television monitors as if into a cave.

The captain and the admiral stood in the gangway between the control room and the radio cubicle, listening to Orlovsky's reports as he edged forward. The effect of the helium made him difficult to understand, but the facts were plain enough.

"What I can see of the starboard side . . . is stove in. Probably from collision . . . with the fjord wall. There are gouges and striations . . . in the rock face and the outer hull. I think the collision . . . was at a shallower depth. She slid down after that . . . as she took on water, and landed on a ledge."

Everyone was silent. One of the doctors looked frustrated but said nothing. Orlovsky announced, "I'm pushing under . . . the overhang of the sail. It looks like . . . a broken flipper. Crushed."

For the next several minutes all they heard were the musical sounds of the divers' respirators. Everyone watched the blank screen as if something were actually there. Admiral Rudenko paced, chin down, and stepped close to Nemerov. He spoke in a whisper.

"If survivors can't be transferred to the submersibles, can they be rescued by raising the vessel itself all the way to the surface? Assuming some aboard are still alive?"

"Defy the orders?"

"Orders be damned. So what if we precipitate an incident? *If* we get *Vladivostok* to the surface, and we're fast, we can remove the survivors and scuttle her."

Nemerov shook his head almost imperceptibly. "We could never escape the fjord once we surfaced. They'd be on us."

"Chernavin miscalculated. We'll have to improvise. We can't abandon living men. Nor will I destroy *Vladivostok* with her crew aboard if they can't be rescued."

Nemerov looked shocked. He had never considered such a contingency. Obviously the admiral had feared this possibility from the first.

"I want to speak with all the officers," Rudenko said in a normal voice. Nemerov instructed the watch, who relayed the order.

They assembled immediately and gathered around the admiral. "*Vladivostok* is too deep for use of the rescue chambers," he said. "However, next time out, the deep submergence divers can employ the submersible rescue chambers like flotation devices—to raise the stricken vessel to the surface, where *Rus* will rescue survivors."

Eyes registered surprise but no one said anything. Everyone was excited. The admiral went on.

"We flood our rescue submersibles and bring them to *Vladivostok*'s depth, maneuver them alongside, attach them to the hull, and partially pump out the water with compressed air. The submersibles will rise slowly, like caissons, and the *Vladivostok* with them."

"Divers," the lieutenant announced, "your time is half gone."

The third diver reported that the thick line ascending from the *Vladivostok* originated in the open trawler bay of the aft deck. The bay was empty, which meant the SB-4 seabed trawler was probably somewhere in the dark water overhead. He was following the cable up for fifty meters.

"Number Two," the lieutenant said, "we can't see you. Orlovsky? Report, please."

"Wait . . . I'm crossing. I'm on the conning tower. The watertight door at the bottom is sealed. I'm knocking."

The clang of metal being struck sounded over the speakers in the radio room. He clanked four more times. After a long pause, Orlovsky resumed. Five blows more. The sound had to have carried through the disabled boat if they heard it aboard *Rus*. Some of the men closed their eyes to concentrate, the better to hear the minutest sound.

None came.

Orlovsky muttered a curse.

"Eighteen minutes," the lieutenant intoned.

"Diver Three here. The SB-4 is floating . . . seventy meters up from the deck."

"Diver Two, this is Four, in charge of the hose lines. Orlovsky, there's too much tension on your hoses and cables."

"Divers," Lieutenant Nuchin announced, "return to the sled."

# 10

The crew chief rose to his feet in the severely swaying plane. "Better get situated," he said, pointing to the gondola. "We got about four minutes and it's gonna get a mite rougher when we start our descent." With Stevenson assisting, the chief eased Hanley through the opening and began strapping her in for the parachute ride down. "Just don't be disappointed if we hit phase winds or somethin' and have to turn 'round and take y'all back. Gets breezy up here now and then."

"I won't complain," she said.

"We don't want you gettin' carried off to China."

When Hanley was properly harnessed, head and neck restraints in place, Stevenson and the chief rechecked the safety devices as they reviewed emergency procedures with her. The Canadian emphasized the location of the survival kit; the chief pointed out the ax strapped to the wall: "In case you need to bust outta this egg. And them emergency flashlights? Tell you the truth, they'll only last ten minutes in this cold, so ignite the flares first if you gotta. Here." He handed her a stuffed toy. "A sled dog. From the post exchange in Anchorage. For luck. See?"

Hanley was hardly the stuffed animal type, but she clutched the dog, touched by the gesture.

"Thank you, Chief."

"Going to Trudeau frequency," the pilot broke in.

"Listen up," the chief said. "You do not want any part of water. This tub'll float, but you don't want to go in the drink, no matter what. I mean, how in the hell would they get to you? They don't exactly have boats down there."

"Isn't it frozen solid on the surface?" Hanley asked, chattering slightly as the adrenaline kicked in.

"Supposedly," the chief said, sounding skeptical. "See this here red lever? Immediately after you land, yank it and free the chutes so's you don't turn into a sailboat and get drug for miles along the ice. Also, there's less chance of sinking."

"Sinking?"

"In the unlikely event the ice breaks open on impact and water-logs the canopy, yes, ma'am. By itself, the Commode is a lifeboat—airtight and waterproof. Better than a float suit. But the chute silk will drag you down if it gets wet."

"Yank the red lever," Hanley recited in a tremulous voice, "free the chutes." She found herself longing for her grandmother's red-and-black quilt, the only childhood memento she'd brought with her into her adult life. Joey slept with it when he stayed with her. She wished she were under it right now, hiding.

"And what do I do if there is open water?"

"Ma'am, you yell. Get 'em to you right quick."

The chief hooded his face with a foul-weather mask and cold-weather face mask and goggles. The cockpit radio came on. *"Trudeau Station, Idle Bucket. Please acknowledge."*

*"Idle Bucket, Trudeau."*

The pilot's flat midwestern voice casually reported the final stages of the approach. Winds were nominal. The risk of the gondola blowing off target had diminished. The Starlifter was descending to be in position to eject at three thousand feet.

*"Trudeau, this is Idle Bucket. We are four minutes from drop. Any further instructions? Over."*

*"Idle Bucket, proceed with delivery. Our people are deployed for catch. We have you at three minutes, forty seconds. Mark at three minutes, thirty seconds . . . five seconds, four, three, two, hack."*

"*Thank you, Trudeau. We see your lights. Out.*"

Atop the gondola was a large pack containing the chutes that would open automatically at fifteen hundred feet.

"*Arm the chute,*" the cockpit ordered. "*Release guide wires.*"

"*Roger, Roger,*" the chief replied and scrambled onto the gondola. "Chutes armed and coupled. Wires off. I hope to hell our back door don't freeze in the open position."

"Well, Jessie," Stevenson said, then shook her hand. "It's been fun. We'll have to do it again soon. Oh, here. If you don't mind—" He pulled out a small package and handed it to Hanley. "Please give this to Dee Steensma." Hanley gave a thumbs-up. Stevenson said, "Okay, I'm closing you up."

The hatch was closed and latched. Hanley heard a farewell tap on the fiberglass. The crew chief came on the intercom: "Happy trails, ma'am. Don't drink the water, y'hear."

The plane dropped a hundred feet in the rough air. "Jeez," Hanley said, as her stomach lunged up around her ears.

"*Sixty seconds,*" the pilot announced. The fuselage was dancing side to side. Rear bay doors groaned open. The sudden temperature drop instantly fogged the port.

Hanley exhaled through her mouth and ran her tongue over her lips. She eyed the red release lever by her hand. The harness X-ed her body, a collar and straps holding her head immobile. Packed in all around her were the supplies she had requisitioned: anticonvulsants, metal detoxifiers, antibiotics, fixing solutions, specimen vials, growth medium, sterile petri dishes. Full biohazard gear. Also an album of recent photos of Joey, her Bach Flower Remedies, a kinesiology manual, a tape of the surf at Laguna that Joey had made for her, five meditation CDs, and eight tubes of organic moisturizers.

"*Fifty seconds,*" the cockpit droned. The rocking was so violent it actually broke up the transmission. Hanley was convinced the plane was coming apart.

Stevenson knocked. "Jessie?" The huge jet was pitching violently. "Yeah."

"How did you get talked into this?" Stevenson said cheerfully.

"I don't know. Wanna talk me out of it? Wouldn't take much."

*"Thirty seconds."* It was the copilot's voice. *"Pull chocks."*

It sounded like a metal awning being raised. The engines screamed with raw power and the air howled past outside. Hydraulics whined.

"I hate this," said Hanley. "I want to go home."

The Starlifter nosed skyward and Commode II slid inexorably down the rollered ramp for what seemed like hours, down the middle of the plane toward the open back doors, and then tipped out into infinity.

Sudden silence.

Hanley's stomach was in her throat from the weightless sensation of dropping. She had imagined soaring. Instead she was falling, like a stone.


Orlovsky gave up waiting for a reply to his blows on the bulkhead and swam down toward the gaping hole at the base of the sail. The sub had a double hull; the space between the metal layers was filled with rubber. His hose caught on a jagged lip of rent metal. He gently pried it loose and swam on. At this depth the smallest nick would be fatal. Instead of retracing his route through the narrow space between the rock face and the hull, he moved aft. In the close space, his mercury light shone brilliantly along the boat's flank and the base of the cliff.

In short order, he discovered a second breach, a slightly longer tear than in the sail, yet no wider. He cradled the hose and lines between his thighs to protect them and kicked forward without touching the sharp edges. Inside, he played the light across the dark panels of switches and dials, and stopped at the helm. The helmsman was still strapped in his chair.

He slowly panned the control room with the lamp. Then he focused the lens, and the cone of light became an intense narrow beam that he shone through the hatch leading aft and down the length of the corridor. The hatches were open as far as he could see. Several of the crew floated in the corridor.

Cadavers in the sea were always eerie because the water gave them the impression of movement, but these . . . They weren't right. He shone the light around the control room again, counting. Eleven. He had dived on many wrecks and seen his share of bodies, but never this many or this strange. They were all in queer poses, not at all like drowned men. Instead of floating limply, their limbs were taught, rigid. Some bodies were doubled over, some bent backward in impossible positions.

Something nudged his shoulder. He flinched but knew not to lurch imprudently. It had to be flotsam, or one of the crew. Dead, he told himself. Harmless. He steadied himself and turned. The back of someone's head, the hair swirling blond in the water. The body was suspended above him, upside down. He took hold of its shoulder and turned it gently. The body curled in on itself like an embryo floating in a glass container, its features primordial, eyelids seamless. He had never seen a corpse so white.

The eyes! He pulled the body closer. The eyeballs were not just rolled back in their sockets. The iris and pupils were gone.

"*Yob tvaya mat!*"

Predatory fish? Impossible. Not in these waters, not in this amount of time. A leg floated next to him from a body butting against the ceiling. He grabbed the ankle and pulled the corpse down into his light.

Its hands were tucked between its knees, face contorted, mouth agape. Its eyes were closed. He steeled himself and opened one. White. The colored iris gone, eaten away. Destroyed.

Orlovsky moved his light around the room, seeking out the other corpses' expressions. The eyes he could see were the same. He brushed against a chart floating by.

"Diver Two. You are at the limit. Where are you?"

"I'm in . . . the control room," Orlovsky said, concentrating on his breathing.

There was an excited rumble. The lieutenant spoke again: "What have you found?"

"It's flooded. Eleven dead. More in the corridors. Hatches . . . open . . . between compartments."

The helmsman's extended arms floated under the grips of the helm yoke like a pantomime sleepwalker's.

"Diver Two, you're over the margin. Return to the bell lock."

The lieutenant had to say it twice before Orlovsky acknowledged the order. He eased toward the breach in the hull, then impulsively turned again to the helmsman and unstrapped him from his chair. He wrapped a line around his neck, towed him to the gash in the metal sail, and pushed him out. Protecting his lifeline and hose, Orlovsky followed.

Sergeant Orlovsky squeezed past the hull and up under the sail, his awkward, lifeless burden in tow. The body scraped the wall and thudded against the hull. The man couldn't feel pain, Orlovsky told himself, and kept on swimming. Cold was penetrating the suit despite the hot water circulating in from the hose. His ears were popping; for seconds at a time he heard nothing, then the sound of his respiration returned as they cleared. He felt the body's difficult journey on the line behind him but never looked back. The sled was gone. He would have to cover the distance on his own. His gauge gave him eight minutes more of air mixture, twelve if he conserved.

Much of the sensation in his calf muscles was gone; he fluttered the web fins anyway, trying to increase his pace, moving toward the open hatch of *Rus*'s missile tube 6.

Halfway there he had to pause to massage his calf. Only then did he turn toward the stricken vessel and the burden he towed. His light caught the fjord wall. He followed it up until the light disappeared. In that instant he felt like a mountain climber, a speck confronting that enormity.

# 11

The lieutenant was furious. Orlovsky took the admonishment philosophically, sitting on his hard plastic diving helmet in the equipment-laden compression chamber, staring up at the television camera. Nuchin frothed with barely suppressed rage at the unauthorized action, capped by his dragging aboard a corpse with a noose, like a hangman. "There are proper procedures!"

The admiral calmed him with a word and turned to question Orlovsky himself.

"Tell me, Sergeant, why did you bring the body into the flooded missile well and lash it to the wall?"

Orlovsky's explanation was forthright: "Sir, I worried that no one would believe what I said without seeing it for themselves."

A short while later, Rudenko had the diver repeat everything to Nemerov and the two surgeons on board, then thanked the sergeant and urged him to rest. Orlovsky could barely nod.

Rudenko invited the captain and the medical officers to his cabin to discuss the situation in private.

Sitting on the bunk, one of the medical officers said, "Word has already spread about the corpse floating in tube 6."

Nemerov looked disconcerted. "Despair is washing over the crew. The ship is silent. I wish Sergeant Orlovsky had thought at least to cover the face so the men could have been spared that expression. It's horrible: eyes gouged out, jaw hideously contorted.

The face is floating centimeters from the wide-angle lens of the television camera. It's like a gargoyle."

The admiral said, "The next time they go out, the four divers might improvise a shroud, and shift the body to another empty tube nearby. That way they won't have to pass it each time they exit and reenter the ship. Perhaps it would steady the crew as well. A ghostly submarine is unnerving enough. An unshrouded corpse with a noose around its neck is profoundly disquieting. As for the stricken vessel, I don't see much hope for recovering it or the bodies."

Nemerov nodded. "We can't get them out, can we?" It was a rhetorical question the admiral did not have to answer. The submersibles, the extra personnel, were all useless. *Vladivostok* was as done for as her crew, leaving Rudenko with only three orders—getting the logs and codes, securing Chernavin's yellow container, and covering up the encroachment.

For a moment he wondered how to deal with the divers if they refused to board again, then decided that was Nemerov's problem to contend with if it arose; he, Rudenko, was only a passenger. This was his mission, not his command.

"In ninety minutes," the admiral said.


Kurlak Island was lit up like a Christmas tree. The surrounding vastness glowed in the light of a half dozen aerial flares. Four columns of light shot straight up from intense spotlights near the station's hemispheric domes.

The island was small, no more than two miles long and a mile wide. The ice Hanley had expected to be white and translucent was purple and blue-green in the harsh light of the spotlights.

The gondola teeter-tottered, an erratic pendulum beneath the chute. Below her, atop a ridge, was the station's wind farm, a swarm of huge propellers and curvy parallel walls for funneling wind. The station itself was a cluster of domes and galleries surrounding a larger dome in the center: a working scientific community surviving on an ice-covered island in the middle of a frozen ocean. Shapes flickered as the flares dangled from their chutes. Unlike the spot-lights, the flares bleached the ice. Everything beneath them was pure white or the blackest black.

She had no sense of dimension. In the distorting light, the domes, situated on an elevation below the crest of the ridge, looked two stories high. One of them appeared upside down, like a cup. A radio telescope, she guessed, or maybe a satellite dish.

On the icy plain, a good distance from the compound of round structures, were odd rectangular berms: a long one intersected at hard right angles by shorter ones, like an Orthodox cross. Hanley couldn't imagine what purpose they might serve, but curiosity was beginning to displace her earlier panic.

On a flatter area directly below, Hanley could just make out on the white ice a cleared ribbon of runway, heading away from the island.

*"This is Trudeau Station. Please answer."*

"Ye ye ye yes, thithithi thiss is s s s Dr. Jesssssie Ha . . . nley." Her whole body was shaking from the vibration. "I'yyyyyym here."

*"We have you in sight, Doctor. You are descending with consider-able drift but should be near the mark."*

"Thaaaank yyyou."

*"Our pleasure, Dr. Hanley. You're about to land. Hang on. Trudeau out."*

The gondola hit—and bounced—hard. Twice.

"Lord have mercy," Hanley muttered and yanked the red lever. Nothing.

A component panel popped out of the radio into her lap as the oval Commode rolled onto its side. The hatch fell off; the warm air in the gondola instantly turned to fog. Cold seized her lungs. Like being under water. Freezing water. She couldn't breathe.

In the excitement, Hanley had forgotten to close the visor of her suit. She shut it quickly and checked the light. Blinking red, then a steady green, thank God. But the huge chute hadn't detached and was dragging the gondola across the ice.

"Please, God. No open water."

Voices overlapped on the radio as the Commode thumped along, creaking and shimmying. Picking up speed, she thought. Nylon bags and packing pellets fell around her.

There was an awful metallic noise and something sliced through the skin of the gondola as if it were an onion. A chunk of the shell was gone, sheared away, but the gondola hadn't even slowed. Supplies were shaking out like seasoning, spilling onto the ice.

"I've crashed, I've crashed!" she shouted.

*"Got diced by some sastrugi, Jack. Can you catch it?"* a voice said over the transceiver.

*"Think so. I'm after the chute."*

*"Watch your wheels."*

The gondola shuddered and came to a halt.

*"Are you okay, Dr. Hanley?"* said the radio voice.

Hanley drew a deep breath and closed her eyes and hugged the stuffed toy. "Houston, the beagle has landed."

*"Excuse me?"*

"I'm okay." She was giddy with relief. "I'm okay." She laughed out loud.

A helmeted face appeared in the hatchway over her head, leaning casually on the threshold as if it were a neighbor's windowsill.

"Welcome to the winter wonderland. Doctor Hanley, I presume?" He offered his hand and she extended hers. He clasped it gently, as he might a child's. *"Quel honneur."*

"Please—Jessie."

*"Enchante."* He shook her hand. "How nice of the commission to send you. How brave of you to come."

"My pleasure," Hanley said, pulling at her straps. She was covered with debris, mostly packing chips pouring out of packages jarred open by the landing, and a dozen recent issues of *Alaska Geographic*. "Are you here to take me to your leader?"

"I am your leader, madam. I am Emile Verneau, director of station. Here, allow me to assist."

Verneau gave her a hand as she squirmed out of the gondola.

"Do you play bridge?" he said.

"No. Never learned."

"Oh, well. We are always short good bridge players. But I don't suppose you're going to have much free time anyway."

Two polar-suited figures began removing the supplies and passing them to another pair who loaded a sled hitched behind a garishly striped vehicle nearly nine feet high and sporting bulbous fuchsia tires. It looked like those giant-wheeled trucks she'd seen competing in amphitheaters on cable TV. A dozen such vehicles stood twenty yards off, encircling the Commode. One of them had driven onto the parachute to deflate it. Hanley stopped and pointed. "That what nearly did me in?"

"Sastrugi?" Verneau said and walked over to a fantastically curved keel of ice. Their lights traced its sculpted shape: sleek and twisted. "Whatever you do out here, don't tangle with these. They're extremely dangerous."

The wind picked up and the sastrugi moaned like musical saws. Hanley was amazed. "They're beautiful," she said, admiring the colors in the cone of light from Verneau's lamp.

Verneau said, "These are the hardest ice crystals imaginable. The floe ice out there is chinky and dry, like sandstone. This sastrugi's like sharp metal. Listen."

Verneau undid a slender pole clipped to his wrist. At a touch, spars sprang out into perpendicular position, their sharp metal edges shining in the lamplight. Gently, he leaned down and scraped the deployed ax blade along the length of the torqued sastrugi. It chimed like a tuning fork.

Verneau collapsed the blades and motioned her toward his own outsized vehicle. He pointed out the stirrup indentations and she scaled the side, slid open the passenger door and eased into the ergonomic seat. The radio hissed static and someone said something in French.

One by one, floodlights were extinguished. Verneau responded in French over the radio, and the vehicles formed a caravan heading toward the opaline lights of Trudeau. He counted them off and pulled in behind the last one, bringing up the rear. Only the one caught in the chute remained behind, its driver still tugging at the canopy.

"Who rescued me?" Hanley said, looking toward the vehicle being extricated from the billowing folds.

"The redoubtable Jack Nimit," Verneau said, "Our engineer. Jack puts us all to shame."

A large, boxy buggy, with balloon tires and a flatbed back, passed them going the other way, dispatched, Verneau explained, to collect the gondola and retrieve the trail of scattered supplies.

"It's a slow ride," he said. "Sit back and enjoy the view."

Just as he said it, the last flare sputtered out and the world went dark.

# 12

From a distance, Trudeau appeared to be just another ridge in the terrain, but there was no mistaking the wind propellers gathered along one slope like giant insects, converting the weather's raw energy into electrical power.

"Thermoelectric generators," Verneau said. "We supplement them in summer, using a platinum catalyst with flameless, clean oxidation. And hydrogen cells, like our vehicles use. Also solar panels."

The complex of domes looming over the ice field grew impressively as the procession approached the entrance. A long incline became visible, leading up into a high tunnel.

"Our humble home," Verneau said. "The ramp and the tunnel are like the entrance to the ultimate polar shelter devised many generations ago, the native snow house."

"Igloos?" Hanley said. She had a brief recollection of a grade-school social studies unit on Eskimos.

"Exactly. The incline prevents the lighter warm air in the domes from slipping out through the entry tunnel, while it allows cold air to enter at a languid rate. But we never got the angle exactly right. On rare occasions when the wind picks up, we have to shut the farthest entryway. Otherwise it creates a vacuum effect and sucks the heat right out."

"Our domes," someone else said in accented English over the radio, "are thermal cells, totally insulated. They're completely protected from the environment and the environment from them. The

Arctic is fragile, excruciatingly so—a waterless, frozen desert. It preserves the smallest physical slight and amplifies it."

"Thank you, Koos," Verneau said on the air. "Quite right."

The procession crawled ever so slowly up the incline into the tunnel's mouth. Large icicles threatened overhead.

"This is amazing," Hanley said. She watched the temperature readout gradually rising with their slow ascent.

"The tunnel helps maintain even temperature transition and also helps prevent buildup of the kinds of fog that plague most polar facilities in winter."

"Fog indoors?"

"Yes. Complete with rain. A real pain. Some towns in the Arctic are surrounded by fog—made entirely from the breath of men and beasts."

The incline leveled and opened into an apron. Although still well below freezing, the temperature had to be thirty degrees higher than at the base of the ramp.

The cortege slowed to a stop beneath a long convex window. Heavily insulated charging cables dangled overhead. As each vehicle was shut down, its driver removed a numbered ignition box. These were collected and slotted into a cart. Meanwhile, a man was going around expertly attaching charging cables to each vehicle.

Verneau removed the ignition box and the instrument panel went dark. He pointed to the curved window over the threshold.

"Extern. The department in charge of all our comings and goings, and of making sure as many come back as go out. They also see to it that no polar bears set up housekeeping in the ramp." He waved up at the large window. Someone waved back.

Hanley craned her neck. The roof of the dome was a skylight. "Wow. Catch the special effects." A shooting star arced across the heavens, clearer than any she had ever seen. Then another. "It's so sharp. The optics are incredible."

"Yes," Verneau said. "It's the air. Absolutely dry, undisturbed by convection currents."

Hanley laughed in utter delight like a child. "Awesome," she said, wishing Joey were there to enjoy it with her.

"Come." Verneau held out a hand and led the way into a broad curved hallway. Some yards in, a sign hand-lettered in a dozen languages announced they were required to remove helmets at that point.

"Otherwise we get clouds farther inside," Verneau said and took off his headgear. "All the trapped humidity goes straight to the ceiling." He slipped his arms out of his suit, pushing the plush exterior layer down to his waist. The metallized inner layer flashed like armor. Hanley followed his example.

A woman Hanley guessed to be about her own age or a few years younger, wearing beige overalls and felt clogs, approached them in the passage. Her straight, thick black hair had almost all turned prematurely gray, but on her it looked chic, like burnished steel. Emile Verneau said, "This is Deborah Steensma, our staff dentist. If you'll excuse me, I'll hand you over at this point. I'll see you later."

"Today I'm also the welcoming committee," Steensma said, smiling. "My off-hours job is cruise director. I put together the weekly activities."

"Pleasure to meet you, Deborah."

"Please call me Dee. Everybody does."

"Dee," Hanley said. "I'm Jessie. The dashing Mr. Stevenson gave me a package for you just before he threw me overboard." She produced it from her kit bag.

"My nicotine patches. Thanks. I've been trying to quit smoking."

"Any luck? I've been trying too. For about twenty years." Hanley pushed back her hair. "You know, I have to say you don't seem like a dentist."

Dee laughed. "Yeah, lots of people tell me that. My parents wanted me to have a secure career. 'People always need dentists'—that sort of thing. As long as I agreed to the dental studies, they didn't care what else I took. I snuck in a lot of anthropology. When the dental faculty posted a notice that dentists were needed to practice in underserved native communities in northern Canada, I leapt at the chance. The Inuit used to have really great teeth, you know. Didn't eat a lot of carbohydrates. These days the kids all have terrible teeth, and there's almost no one around trained to take care of them."

"Kids. Here?"

"No, no. This was south of here, in Nunavut, before I came to Trudeau."

"How'd you end up here?" Hanley said.

"The short version? I got involved with an archaeologist who was coming to work at Little Trudeau. We came, he left, I stayed."

"You know," Hanley said, "I've been meaning to have some metal fillings replaced with nontoxic amalgams."

"Not for a while, I'm afraid," Dee said sympathetically. "My practice is oversubscribed. Arctic cold is hell on fillings. The metal contracts, they just fall right out. Be careful if you spend any time outside." She glanced at her watch. "We'd better go." She led the way into the next room, which boasted five concentric rows of walk-in lockers, each with a polar suit on a hook, labeled with its owner's name. Dee led her to the outermost row where a locker had been hastily labeled for her. A barely clad young man passed. Hanley shot Dee a querying look.

Dee smiled. "We're not very modest around here. It takes a little getting used to. The community is pretty liberal, more European than North American in that regard. Are you shy?"

"No, I grew up in a big family. Two parents, five kids, one bathtub. In med school I shared an apartment with two guys, and I thought I'd never had such privacy."

Dee laughed. "I'll wait here while you wash up and change."

Each locker was practically a small room, like the ones professional athletes were always being cornered in by TV reporters. Hanley hung up her helmet and the layers on designated pegs, and finally peeled off her body stocking.

She went to the showers, located in the innermost ring, and peered warily around the curving walls into the asymmetrical cubicles. She chose one, went in, and turned a plastic lever to start the water. A minuscule jet sprayed her with beguiling warmth. She raised her chin. The showerhead emitted only a fine steamy mist, yet managed to be effective, even pleasant. Obviously, it used only a fraction of the water of a conventional shower.

The soap wasn't smooth or bubbly, but granular. It did the job, though. Hanley lingered, humming, face turned upward into the spray. Unbeknownst to her, a diminutive Inuk gentleman with gray-flecked hair appeared, deposited towels and a change of clothes on the bench nearby, and disappeared without so much as a glance or a sound.

"That felt great," Hanley said to herself, pushing back her dripping locks. "Hey! Towels. Thanks," she said, not quite sure who she was thanking. She dried herself off, and examined the quilted camisole, cotton blouse, and trousers. "One size fits most, I guess."

"Are you finished?" Dee called.

"Just about." She slipped on the top. "I feel like a Japanese farmer. Or maybe a martial artist. No underwear, but I'll fake it."

Underneath the bench were soft pale brown boots with stiff soles and high socks. These fit her exactly.

Dee came around the corner. "Looks great on you," she said. "It's a pretty forgiving design, but it definitely looks better on some of us than others."

Emile Verneau rejoined them and led them farther into the complex. "Dee will feed you," he said, "and then I'm afraid, in spite of the long journey you've had, our chairman, Dr. Mackenzie, is expecting you. I apologize for putting you right to work, but I'm sure you can appreciate how eager people here are to hear from you."

"That's fine by me," Hanley said. "I'm much too wound up to sleep anyway."

He glanced at his watch. "See you in an hour, then."

Dee said, "I'm sure you'll be hearing this a lot, but I want you to know how grateful we all are that you were willing to come to our aid. The staff has been trying to keep it together, but rumors—and panic—are rife. I mean, I'm just the dentist, but I've got people lined up at my door worried about this weird symptom or that. We may all be scientists, but folks have been doing some pretty wild speculating. They're really hoping you've got some answers."

"Losing four colleagues in one day would shock anyone. And then not knowing whether you'd been exposed to whatever killed them . . . It would be pretty strange if people weren't anxious."

Dee looked relieved. "Come on. I'll show you around."

Dee led her from the locker area into curving passages along the perimeters of other domes, around bends, up slight slopes that opened into windowed apses overlooking adjacent domes or the starry wilderness, the mere glimpse of which took Hanley's breath away.

Somewhere in every room they passed, Hanley noticed the bright red of the Canadian flag: on stickers, baseball hats, bath towels drying on railings, little pennants adorning tables. Maple leaves even fluttered gently across idle computer screens. The other constant was the official sweatshirt, with a silhouette of the station domes and the inscription:

ARS TRUDEAU
IT'S NOT THE END OF THE WORLD
BUT YOU CAN SURE SEE IT FROM HERE

"The Brits have a couple of raunchier versions," Dee said, "'ARS Trudeau, ARSE End of the World.' You can imagine. Computer geeks with too much time on their hands."

The route to the dining hall was circuitous but could hardly be otherwise. There seemed to be no straight lines anywhere.

"The maze effect is deliberate," Dee explained. "The design minimizes the demands on the central plant, creating climatic pockets that help the computer-managed energy expenditures and heat reclamation. And the overall shape is resistant to the Arctic weather."

"Clever," Hanley said, "but I'm directionally challenged enough as it is. I'll definitely need a map."

"The convoluted spaces have a psychological purpose as well. The irregular patterns are supposed to make areas more intimate and varied. The design helps alleviate the claustrophobic effects—and, frankly, some of the monotony of prolonged confinement. That's also why you'll notice lots of large windows in the public areas. The layout is big—a city block—but you'd be surprised how small that can feel after a while."

Hanley nodded. "On my way down I saw some structures that

definitely weren't curved. More like lines intersecting at right angles. Some distance from the station, in a flat area."

"Little Trudeau. The original station."

"What happens there?"

"Nothing now. There was an archaeological dig near there. An Aleut site: the northernmost place of human occupation in Arctic Canada. That's what brought everyone here in the first place. Quite a find. To shelter everyone working on the dig, they dredged a trench out of the snow maybe four meters deep, another fifteen meters wide. Maybe fifty meters long. Shorter trenches—*allées*—were dug perpendicular to the big one. The tops of the trenches were roofed with corrugated metal and covered over with snow. The roof sticks up a little, which is why you could see it from above. The *allées* held Quonset huts for living quarters and labs and storage. One housed the power plant: gasoline generators. Another was the food hall. What else? An infirmary. A small town under the snow. We lived like moles."

"Anybody still live there?"

"It's abandoned now. There are some emergency food stores down there, and the entrance to the old dig. You can't imagine what it was like to move out of Little Trudeau to this," said Dee. "Like waking up at the Ritz."

They stopped in front of one of the panoramic windows, and Hanley pointed to a light far out, moving laterally on the sea ice. "What's that?"

"Not what. Who. Jack Nimit," Dee said. "Felix Mackenzie dreamed up this place, but Jack's the guy who figured out how to make it happen. Jack's only thirty-four and already an amazing engineer. He's Inuit. He knows the High Arctic better than any of us. Expert at constructing with ice too. It looks like he's about five kilometers out."

"What's he doing out there?"

Dee shrugged. "Don't know. Dealing with it, I guess. These deaths have been a real blow to a lot of people. He and Teddy Zale found Dr. Kossuth—Alex. Jack and Alex were close." The distant light glinted off something with a startling flash.

"Everyone's been trying to cope in their own fashion," said Dee, following the tiny running light. "For Jack it's being out there alone. He's even been going out without a polar suit. He puts on his native furs and leggings. He's got a much higher tolerance for cold than the rest of us. If you ask him why he goes out there, he says he's homesick."

"I'm sorry," Hanley said. Consoling survivors came awkwardly to her, and over the years she'd concluded that the simplest expressions of sympathy were also the best. Anything else came out sounding false.

"Thanks. How about dinner?"

"Great," Hanley said. "I'm starving."

Dee smiled and led her to the spacious main dining hall. Tall boughs of a cherry tree were embedded in an industrial cylinder weighted down with rocks and water, a dramatic centerpiece that dominated the room. The branches were long past blooming but too rare to discard, the only "tree" for thousands of miles.

The range of culinary choices was impressive. The menu was in three panels, like an old-fashioned diner: breakfast, lunch, and dinner available all day and all night. Hanley selected the vegetable soup, a fresh green salad grown hydroponically in the station's horticultural lab, and a plate of peanut butter cookies.

A knot of people passed them, coming in. The singsong language sounded Scandinavian to her. "Swedish?" she guessed.

"Norwegian," Dee corrected. "We have staff from over two dozen countries."

"Where are you from? I can't quite place the accent."

"Holland. But I've been gone a long time. I feel a lot more Canadian than Dutch these days."

The food was excellent and Hanley ate with abandon. Few other tables were occupied. The midnight meal was lunch for the skeletal night crew of scientists, support personnel, and a few lone insomniacs. Across the room, in front of a vaulting window, a group of Japanese men were enjoying an animated discussion about endothelial cells while feasting on turtle eggs and intestines, mango, and wongai plums.

Hanley noticed a miniature rising-sun flag on their table, and a German pennant on the adjoining one, where two Germans scientists were comparing the single-septate lungs of birds to those of reptiles. A poster announced a limited run of a French-Canadian play, *Balconville*, put on by the Polar Cap Players. Another invited everyone to a feline-themed costume party: the Annual Fur Ball.

"They're just finishing their evening libations," Dee said, nodding toward the table of Japanese scientists. "A lot of the staff join them. It's invigorating. Whirlpool, then a swim, hot showers, and sake. Thursdays it's the Swedes: massages and swimming. This coming Sunday the Germans are hosting, although they've gotten very chary with their cache of beer since they hosted the Aussies two weeks ago." She glanced at Hanley. "You've got to work at your social life here to keep going. It's important."

Hanley finished eating just as a demure chime sounded.

"Midnight," Dee said. "We'd better get to Mackenzie's office."

"Right. Before we go, just bring me up to speed. After you brought them in, who performed the autopsies?"

"Dr. Ingrid Kruger. She's a specialist in hypothermia. It was really difficult for her." A sadness crept into her voice, perhaps regret. "If we had known you were coming, she wouldn't have. She and Annie were friends. But she volunteered, after a fashion. She did both autopsies."

"Both? Weren't there four?"

"The Russian contingent received instructions from Moscow that forbade an autopsy on Minskov. And Alex's seemed unnecessary. The cause of death was clearly hypothermia, not whatever killed the others."

"How did the Russian woman happen to leave in the middle of all this?"

"Lidiya? The Russians bring scientists in and out by sub. They had to pick her up before the nearest polynya—a hole in the ice—got too small to find. Definitely the last possible chance for anything to be brought in or anyone to leave. For a while she said she was going to extend her stay, but then she got pretty eager to get out of here. A year is a long time the first time."

"Did Dr. Kruger culture anything after the autopsies?"

"No," said Dee. "She took specimens. I think you got transmissions of the slides. But, no, we didn't culture anything from the fluid or tissue samples. Once Ottawa announced you were coming, we stopped. Truth be told, the more we saw what had happened to them . . . we were petrified."

# 13

After an hour and a half of rest and a ten-minute meeting, the second dive began. Given the difficulty of the job, three divers were sent to cope with the trawler tethered aft, hovering over the boat. The fourth made straight for the reactor.

The trio chained a motorized winch to *Vladivostok*'s deck, then hauled the SB-4 down to the five-hundred-meter level and lashed it securely. Sergeant Orlovsky had never used such an excavation machine himself, although the two engines and two independent screw propellers reminded him of the marines' BMK-150 assault barges.

Swimming up to the SB-4's porthole, he pressed his faceplate against it and held his torch against the pane. A face stared back: another doomed sailor with gutted eyes and tortured features. Orlovsky moaned, but the mask and air bubbles made it sound almost melodic.

That's twice, he thought, struggling to recover the rhythm of his breathing.

After studying the face of the floating corpse in the TV monitor, the senior medical officer had hypothesized that the pressure of water blasting into *Vladivostok* might have damaged the soft tissues of the eyes. "How selective," Orlovsky had remarked, his sarcasm impossible to miss even in his cartoon helium voice. But the SB-4 trawler was intact and the man inside it had suffered the same affliction. Like the *Vladivostok*'s crew, he had been blinded and annihilated. By what?

The divers worked quickly and were now ahead of schedule. Orlovsky and another diver were inside the crippled sub. Diver Four was securing the reactor. Diver One would stay outside and monitor hoses and lines for the other two, keeping them untangled and safe from the sheared metal as his comrades swam through the broken hull and into the bowels of the ship.

Orlovsky steeled himself for the unavoidable reunion with the crew. He was consoled by the thought that his assignment—the captain's quarters—were only a short distance from the control room. Even so, the first sight of the young crewmen caught his heart again. He slid past the bodies, avoiding contact as best he could, hoping the captain's cabin would be empty. At the bulkhead door he stopped and waited for his companion.

From the twitchy motions of the other diver's lamp he could tell the man was as shaken as he had been, and was also trying to avoid touching the floating bodies. Orlovsky pointed to the corridor, gestured his direction and destination, then swam into the passage, counting doors as he went.

At the fourth entryway, he pulled aside the accordion door and shone his light around the compartment. Papers and articles of clothing floated about like flakes in a snow globe.

He pushed through the doorway to the desk on the far side. A heavy silver frame lay facedown on it, anchoring a few papers. Just above the desk was the safe. Mercifully it was open. The key in his leg pouch would have unlocked the safe, but he would have needed a hydraulic press to pry open the door against the water pressure at this depth, making a potential bomb of the watertight compartment. He shone his light inside. Books, nothing else. No yellow container. He removed the captain's log and two codebooks, and stuffed them into a drawstring bag, drew the bag closed, and knotted the top securely. He held his wristwatch in the beam. Seven minutes remained. Diver Four reported that he had shut down the reactor and was exiting the vessel.

From the doorway, the other diver photographed the room with a flash camera and reported their progress to *Rus*. Orlovsky gave him a hand sign and the diver withdrew, swimming back toward the control room, flashes of his camera reflecting like lightning as he went.

The sergeant's hose coiled like a giant snake. He pushed it aside and cinched the bag to his webbing, secured around his thigh. The beam of his headlamp glanced off something on the desk. A *kiot*: a tiny candle in a heavy cup, standing in front of a small ikon. He reached out, took the gold triptych in his gloved hand and folded it shut. He pushed it down into his pouch as he turned to the door.

The retort of the camera flash, somewhere down the hallway, illuminated something above him so briefly that he thought for an instant he might be imagining things. But as he tilted his head back, the beam of his own headlamp exposed it. His throat caught.

She was naked, the breasts buoyant, the aureoles dark circles against the utter whiteness of the body. Her black hair billowed around her shoulders. She was huddled against the ceiling, the face contorted, lips drawn back, exposing the teeth in a leering grimace. The whites of the eyes, like the skin, were almost luminous. She was hunched in that same forlorn pose, as if straining to egest the death in her.

He exhaled sharply. He was afraid of her.

His bubbles rose, large and wobbly, like the soap bubbles he had made with newspaper cones as a child. Why was he thinking of that now?

Orlovsky undid his camera from his chest web and looked away from her to adjust the focal plane and distance. He held the camera up and sighted over the top, then released the motorized shutter for a long series of exposures.

A yellow container floated past the lens: a slim box made of lightweight synthetic material. He unleashed the net drawstring bag strapped to his thigh and swiftly captured the floating object with it, like a butterfly, then retied the bag.

With measured kicks, he glided out of the cabin and turned down the passageway, swimming weightless through the dark hulk. In the control room the third diver's lamp pivoted about the darkness. Orlovsky pointed at his watch; the man needed no further encouragement to quit the vessel. He cleared the jagged hole with little heed for the threatening shards, and slithered away past the rock wall and the hull.

The sergeant made to follow. He held the bag in place with one hand, put his lines outside the hull, and followed them out. Glancing back at the gargoyle figures, more stone than flesh, he crossed himself from right to left as his grandmother had taught him long ago.

# 14

Chairman Felix Mackenzie's office was on the second floor of one of the larger domes. Triangular windowpanes studded the outer wall and ceiling. Mackenzie's desk sat at the curved far end of the long room, surrounded by enormous piles of work. The rest of the room was empty except for a cushioned bench and many stackable folding chairs arrayed in lecture-hall fashion. Mackenzie's assistant entered with a tray of tea and hurried down the center aisle, apologizing as he approached.

"I'm so sorry to keep you waiting, Dr. Hanley, after your long journey. The director is never on time. It's absolutely pathological."

The young man offered them mugs of tea. Dee and Hanley accepted and settled in two spindly modern chairs facing the cluttered desk, an ultramodern oval with a narrow bank of drawers on one side. Two small platforms floated just above it on aluminum shafts, a laptop resting on one, a phone on the other. Compared to the rest of the work area, the desk was relatively clear, an island in the midst of chaos. Precarious columns of papers and books leaned against it; more were stacked almost to eye level along the curve of the wall.

Old copies of the *Daily News-Miner* of Fairbanks and clippings from the *Toronto Globe and Mail* sat atop stacks of geology journals and texts. Core samples of gray stone protruded from the paper. Like a giant paperweight, one cylinder sat atop a mound of papers of all sorts and sizes, from little reminder strips to slabs of newsprint covered with calculations. Books were everywhere, places marked in each with scraps of whatever had been at hand: envelopes, pencils, napkins.

"Mind if I snoop?" said Hanley, sipping her cup.

"Be careful—this place is like a game of pick-up sticks. Move one journal and the whole system collapses."

"There's a system?"

"Mackenzie claims he can put his hand on anything he needs in a matter of seconds. I'm glad I've never had to put it to the test."

"I'll stick to the immovable objects, then." On the wall hung a black-and-white photograph of the director and the late prime minister, the station's namesake, trademark rose in his lapel, taken at the ceremony in Ottawa dedicating the original camp. Hanley studied Mackenzie's face.

Dee said, "You may not have heard of him in the States, but in Canada, Mac's a legend. He's a geologist by training, a pragmatist. But also a dreamer."

Hanley looked at the photo. Sinewy and muscled like a runner, he had the cast of one who had spent a serious part of his life above the Arctic Circle, as if his body had taken on the aspect of the harsh terrain. You might have taken Mackenzie for a fisherman, or a hunter, anything but the urbane director of the lavishly endowed and successful ARS Trudeau.

"He looks as if he'd be more at home in Little Trudeau than here, doesn't he?"

"He's actually quite a genteel man," Dee said. "Considerate almost to a fault. A genuine intellectual. And an old-fashioned generalist—he tries to learn at least something about what everyone is working on. A decade of his life went into designing Trudeau and securing the funds. Not to mention the daunting job of enlisting sponsoring research institutions, luring top scientists away from comfortable stipends to come to this precarious speck in the wilderness. People had to take him on faith. All he had to show them was Little Trudeau and a lot of blueprints. But he made it happen. He brought in Jack Nimit and suddenly Trudeau wasn't a blueprint anymore. It was real: an engineering marvel.

"When the governing board officially named Mackenzie our

first director, he told them he only planned to hold the post for a few years before turning it over to a successor. He was ready to retire, ready to go home to his wife in Vancouver. Then during our third winter here his wife died. Instead of flying out at the end of the season, he flew her ashes in. He scattered them out on the ice floes."

Hanley read from a glossy promotional leaflet on the credenza. " 'Felix Mackenzie, Member of Board of Directors, Canadian Royal Arctic Trust. Wallace Chalmers Harkness Professor of Ocean Sciences, Dalhousie University, Halifax. Associate, Institute of Physics of the Globe, Paris. Visiting Lecturer, Arctic Institute of North America.' "

"Well, rarely visiting," Dee said. "Except for the odd thirty-day furlough, Mac doesn't really leave the station much anymore. Other people—younger people—shoulder the day-to-day administration, but Trudeau is still Mac's baby."

Hanley put the flyer down and continued her stroll. " 'Memorandum and Articles of Association,' " she read from a framed document on the wall.

Alongside it was a beautifully composed black-and-white photograph of an Inuit hunter in heavy furs lying next to a seal on the ice, one arm across its body, the hunter's lips nearly joined to the seal's. A kiss? A puzzling but extraordinary image.

"You must be Dr. Hanley." The voice was soft, the proffered hand leathery like the face. A shock of white hair fell forward toward pale blue eyes, crinkled at their corners by his welcoming expression. "I'm so sorry to press you into service right away. I'm sure you understand our plight. We have a lot of shaky people eager to hear what you have to say. We'll probably have a full house, even at this hour."

Hanley returned the smile. "No problem."

He motioned for Hanley and Dee to sit, and made himself comfortable behind his desk while his assistant brought him tea and carried in more folding chairs.

"Huckleberry," he said proudly. "Used to be a native variety before the change in the island's weather a century ago. This was grown in our horticulture dome." He sipped for a moment. "I'm sorry you're not planning to stay on long enough to experience our warmer seasons. It's damn lovely here in spring and summer. The bird migrations alone are wondrous to behold. Red-throated loons, snow geese, eiders, kittiwakes, terns by the score. And black guillemot, of course."

"What do they live on? How can the island sustain them all?" Hanley said.

"It can't. The ice never really melts, and even in summer the ground is frozen like rock. But we are blessed with a polynya about fourteen miles farther north, and there's a sheltering rocky isle there where they roost."

"Polynya?"

"It's a Russian term for large year-round openings in the ice. Ours is uncharacteristically small and constricted this season, but open nonetheless. In summer, polynyas give the birds and animals access to the rich marine life. Whales, sea lions, bears—it attracts 'em all." He perched the cup on the alluvial fan of papers and interlaced his thick fingers. "I quite identify with the birds. The old ones come first. Around early May. I always go out to greet them."

A man came in and quietly sat down behind them, head buried in a notebook. "Anyway," Mackenzie said, waving hello to the new arrival, "at least you'll get to enjoy our winter residents. Foxes, arctic hares, and, invariably, a polar bear or two."

"My boy will want me to bring home one of each."

"No problem," Mackenzie exclaimed. "How old is he?"

"Nearly eleven," Hanley said. She pointed to two native spears mounted on the wall. "Are those spear points actually cloven hooves?"

"Yes, those spears are twenty centuries old. They're up here on long loan," Mackenzie said. "Our senior anthropologist presented them to me—part of the very first find at the excavation on the southern end of our island. That's where they unearthed the initial evidence of earliest human occupation here, dating back several thousand years. Kurlak was their northernmost settlement. Their successors abandoned Kurlak only at the close of the nineteenth century, following a particularly severe series of winters. A small ice age that marked the permanent return of intensely frigid weather conditions."

"Significant climate changes in that short a time?" said Hanley.

"Yes," Mackenzie nodded, "and they're still under way. Annual temperatures keep rising. The ice pack has lost forty percent of its volume in the last twenty years, I would say. The ice was ten feet thick the first time I ever measured. Eight a few years later. Now it's six. And in summer there's open water at the Pole. Huge changes I never thought I'd see in my lifetime."

Mackenzie excused himself and went to greet more people, and Hanley browsed the shelves. Beside the spears hung a strand of fish hooks made of bone. On a small shelf sat a tattooed doll of an Eskimo woman, what looked to be skinning knives, and an extraordinarily elaborate stone bowl with carved wolves' heads for handles. "Is that Russian on the bowl?" Hanley said.

"Aleut. They never had a written language until their encounters with the Russians. They used Cyrillic characters to make Aleut sounds."

Mackenzie's assistant eased alongside Hanley and whispered:

"If you'd be so kind as to take a seat. It's going to be standing-room only."

# 15

Before he swam back aboard, Orlovsky placed the string bag in an empty forward torpedo tube, where the executive officer recovered it and brought it, personally, to the admiral's quarters.

Rudenko dutifully extracted the yellow waterproof case, codebook, and captain's log. The log fell open but was too sodden to examine further. Stuck to the page was a handwritten notation on a slip of paper. Carefully he peeled away the note, draped it on the translucent lampshade, and turned on the lamp.

The ink had run badly, but the writer's old-fashioned nib had left a sufficient impression for him to discern two sets of numbers and the word *rendezvous*. The numbers, he saw instantly, were coordinates, and he copied them out on the desk pad. Then, violating his orders, he examined the lemon-colored container. It held four saturated sheets of paper, folded. He undid them gently. Tarakanova's report. Chernavin would be disappointed; most of the printing was obliterated. Only a few words remained legible. One he couldn't understand. He sounded it out: *Vasot*. It meant nothing to him. He copied it on another piece of paper, then carefully refolded the wet sheets and placed them in a shallow plastic pan of water from the fjord so the paper wouldn't dry out and perhaps lose the written impressions. He added the log and codebooks to the brew and placed a lid over the container and snapped it shut.

He went back to the word he had copied. Then it struck him.

The script was not Cyrillic at all but Western: *Bacomb*, or perhaps *Bascomb*.

The desk officer called down to notify him that the last dive was under way. Rudenko thanked him, and went forward to the control room to follow the activities in the compression chamber on the closed-circuit monitors.

The divers were donning their heavy rubber suits, helping one another into the hard plastic helmets, checking pressure gauges and hoses, all the while inventorying the hopeless clutter of equipment: special nylon ropes, hydraulic presses, reciprocating saw, salvage drill, explosives. The whole lot would be rent and abandoned. Shredded like so much incriminating paperwork.

The charges would be placed along the entire length of *Vladivostok*'s keel and prow, with special attention to the trawler, and detonated by radio signal when they were nearly out of the fjord. The goal was total destruction.

The divers drew cards to see who would place the charges inside the vessel. The youngest one cursed and threw down the ace of spades.

It rankled Rudenko horribly: the idea of leaving those sailors behind, pulverized beyond recognition. At the very least, the families were owed a body to bury, but their grief would forever be incomplete. At that moment he hated Chernavin. They could not even follow the age-old tradition: make a tomb of the boat, sink the sunken ship, commit the dead to the deep. No. They had to obliterate *Vladivostok* and its crew. The boat would cease to exist, their sacrifice never made. Chernavin's orders.

The divers exited the flooded lock and swam up into the missile silo.

The great distance to the surface would dissipate the noise; seven hundred meters of water would muffle the flesh-rending violence. With luck there would not be anyone on the surface to see the bubbles and churning. Sonar equipment might register the concussion, but *Rus* would be long gone before anyone came to investigate.

The divers swam out. It was nearly over.

Rudenko held his hand to his cheek and observed Captain

Nemerov's preparations for departing the fjord the instant the divers returned. Nemerov looked crestfallen, his search-and-rescue mission turned against his will into search and destroy.

As the divers reported their steady progress, the lieutenant counted off the time and the number of explosives they set. The one who had drawn the unlucky card sounded jittery as he moved among *Vladivostok*'s crew.

Rudenko walked to the chart desk and casually lifted the maps in immediate use to check the larger one beneath. With thumb and forefinger, he intervected the point of the coordinates from Tarakanova's report, confirming what he already knew. They marked a spot the size of a period in the middle of the Arctic Ocean.

# 16

The room was full when Verneau arrived; he tried to close the door behind him, but more late arrivals kept trying to slip in. People congregated in the corridor outside, peering in, chattering nervously to one another.

Mackenzie brought over a few of his colleagues and introduced Hanley. Most were cordial, welcoming. One Russian, Vadim Primakov, was civil but appreciably cool; Simon King, the Canadian director of geothermal research, was openly rude, launching immediately into anti-American polemic.

"What on earth," he asked in a facetious tone, "could have induced our government to import an expert in mayhem all the way from the States?"

"Excuse me?" Hanley said, taken aback.

"Perhaps the promise of a week's cessation of the sulfurous industrial contaminants wafting over the border and destroying our soil and forests? Or is the prime minister to be received in Washington with full honors and party hats and favors—again? Why couldn't medical help have been sent from Winnipeg? Why is it always Aunt Samantha to the rescue?" King said with open contempt.

"I guess we're starting," Mackenzie said.

Hanley turned to whisper to Dee. "Is it me? Or is he always this charming?"

"I wish I could say he grows on you," Dee whispered back. "But I'd be lying."

Over Dee's shoulder, Hanley noted a black-haired, black-eyed Inuk thread past Verneau and slip into the room. He was striking, dressed in a creamy oversized jumper, the sleeves pushed up, and black drawstring pants. Rough hewn, long muscled, high cheek-boned. Asian. She glanced at Dee and asked with a look, *Who*?

Dee casually glanced back and shifted closer to Hanley. "Jack Nimit."

Simon King was still on his feet and on his rant. "How ironic that Annie's death, of all people, should be investigated by Americans, whose superpower culture and environmental flotsam she so abhorred. It shames her memory. Is it really true that we cannot put our own house in order?" he asked facetiously.

"Oh, come now, Simon." Like a parent with a child having a public tantrum, Mackenzie gently chided King for forgetting what Jessie Hanley had risked just to reach Kurlak Island. King reluctantly took his seat.

"We all congratulate you, Dr. Hanley," Mackenzie said, "on your safe arrival, the very first winter visitation—ever. A feat once thought impossible." A number of people applauded, and then the rest of the room joined in. "Could I ask you to give us an idea of your background, and how you plan to proceed?" Mackenzie stood with arm outstretched, inviting her to take the floor.

Hanley rose. She eyed Simon King. Mackenzie would have to deal with him. Her job was alleviating the fear that was palpable in the room.

"Good evening. I'm Dr. Jessica Hanley, an epidemiologist with the Infectious Diseases Center in Los Angeles, part of the State of California's Emergency Medical Services agency. Before that, I worked for the Special Pathogens branch of the U.S. Department of Health."

Simon King shifted impatiently and noisily in his seat, but Hanley pressed on.

"My colleagues and I collaborate with health agencies and institutes everywhere, including"—she looked over at the old Russian, Primakov—"the State Center of Virology and Biotechnology in Novosibirsk. I've been sent to assist numerous countries: Austria, the Philippines, Brazil, England—"

"What are your priorities here at Trudeau?" Mackenzie asked, interrupting.

"My main concern is to prevent recurrence. The sooner we locate the causative agent, the sooner we can keep it from harming anyone else." Hanley could see a number of people exhale deeply, as though they'd been holding their breath since the bodies were discovered. "I can't stress enough how much I need your help. I need to know absolutely everything about the recent activity of the victims. Everything they ate, touched, or did immediately before they went out there. This is a complex facility. I'll need to understand what your friends were involved in professionally . . . privately too, I'm afraid. Unfortunately, in cases like this we can't afford to draw distinctions. Since I don't know what I'm looking for, I need to know everything."

Primakov muttered something in Russian that sounded perturbed, then issued a loud warning in English.

"Will be grave consequences if anything else befalls remaining Russian citizens in my charge." A murmur arose in the room. Mackenzie quickly tried to soothe Primakov.

"Vadim," he said, "everyone's upset by this tragedy. But our friends were scientists and we owe it to their memory to pursue the truth in a rational way. Annie Bascomb, Mr. Ogata, Doctors Minskov and Kossuth all dedicated themselves to the basic principle of the station—cooperative research—and to the condition of trust that implies. Free exchange of information." He repeated this in French, scanning the room to make sure everyone had understood.

Mackenzie rose and stood behind Primakov, who sat near the edge of the room at right angles to the others. He put both his hands on the shoulders of the older man in collegial fashion, and continued to address the gathering as if speaking for both of them.

"Most of you are too young to remember the early days of Arctic science. Here at Trudeau, scientists like Vadim and I—and Alex Kossuth—hoped to pursue research free of borders and private interests—science for its own sake. We determined to guard this undertaking from distorted values and divisive pressures. We keep everyone apprised—daily. Everyone is welcome to contribute and to inquire. We extend this same courtesy to Dr. Hanley."

He looked down at Primakov, who appeared mollified by this acknowledgment of his role as elder statesman.

"Okay, here's a question," said a strapping Australian. "People are afraid to suit up and go out on the pack ice to work. How do we know whether what killed them is still out there?"

All faces turned back to Hanley. "Whatever produced the rapid neuropathological and neurochemical changes in the physiologies of your colleagues is most likely a chemical, an acid, a volatile metal . . . or some unpredictable interaction between them. My first task will be to see if I can find out if something like that poisoned them."

"Poisoned?" the Australian exclaimed.

"Yes. They died so quickly, you see, and nearly at the same moment. That would point toward a simultaneous exposure to something poisonous. Like dimethyl mercury. That would account for the evidence of seizures. Possibly they inhaled something lethal. I understand you use a lot of the latest polymers in your equipment. They can occasionally have very dangerous off-gassing. Even if they seem benign. Nonstick pans, heated to a certain temperature, cause something called polymer fume fever."

"Is that fatal?"

"Not to people. Just feels like a bad case of the flu. Kills a hundred or more pet birds a year, though. My colleague in California is combing the literature and data banks to see if your colleagues' symptoms match any documented toxic exposures. Some saltwater fish absorb dangerous levels of mercury. So we have to take a hard look at any local fish or shellfish they may have eaten. I'll be testing the victims' tissues and effluents to see if any toxins are present. If anything comes up positive, I'll know fairly quickly what we're up against."

"And if it's not anything that straightforward?" King said. "If it's organic?"

"That's a much smaller possibility. The simultaneous deaths make it unlikely. It would require something proceeding at exactly the same rate in each of them. Physiologies differ. The times of death would normally be staggered in people exposed to an organic agent, but I'm not ruling out anything at this point." She paused to see if anyone needed more information.

"Could it be some kind of parasite?"

"Well, yes. All microbes are parasites. We're their food, after all. That's what an infection is: microbes feeding."

At the back of the group a thin woman wearing a tartan scarf tentatively raised her hand and said in an English accent, "Will the autopsy results tell us if a virus is responsible?"

Hanley brushed her hair off her forehead. "Some viruses remain in tissue and fluid samples; some don't. A virus that wreaks havoc in the body may also exhaust itself and collapse into genetic scraps. Other viruses are attacked by enzymes and destroyed. As the body begins to dispose of itself, the viruses are broken up in the decomposition process. There's also a whole class of microbes too small to be detected easily. Mycoplasma doesn't even have cell walls. And there are subviral particles: prions."

"Prions? As in mad cow disease?" A shudder ran through the room. Lots of hands were raised now. Everyone wanted the answer to the questions that had been keeping them awake since their four colleagues had been found dead.

"Exactly, BSE. The prions that cause BSE—mad cow disease—have neither DNA nor RNA, yet they behave like viruses. They recruit existing cells and literally fold them up. The cells die and leave a telltale pattern of holes."

"So if it's a virus or a prion you might not be able to identify it?"

Hanley nodded slowly, looking for some way to reassure the group. "No. But I wouldn't have to as long as I could locate the source—and isolate it. Again, that's not the most likely possibility."

"Dr. Hanley, I don't mean to sound cold-blooded about this, but a lot of us are not convinced that it's safe to have the bodies in the station. Folks are concerned."

"The bodies are in plastic isolation gurneys. Doctors normally use these to transport quarantined patients, but they serve the same purpose in this instance. They confine any contaminants present in the bodies. But let me stress there's no evidence at all of person-to-person transmission."

Someone wept. Hanley realized that what were bodies to her had been friends of people here. She waited a moment, then continued: "If it was a virus, and was still present in the bodies, chances are the autopsies would have released it . . . and the people who performed the procedures wouldn't be here, and we wouldn't be having this conversation. Viruses need living cells to replicate. A single cell might be commandeered a thousand times. Most microbes, even toxin producers, try not to eliminate their hosts, since a dead host is useless to them."

Verneau said, "You almost make it sound like they're sentient beings."

Hanley nodded. "They sort of are. Bacteria and viruses have memory. They feed. They communicate. They scavenge DNA to alter their makeup and circumvent our drugs and bodily defenses. Some bacteria even create enzymes to combat antibiotics. Or jet them out of their cells—flush them away. Some quickly put up a second outer cell wall to absorb the antibiotics. Most microorganisms act very quietly, patiently; a few are quick and violent."

She could feel the tension in the room building again. She raised her hands in a beseeching gesture.

"But so are poisons, which is where I'll be starting the search."

A pink-complexioned man with nearly transparent hair and impossibly blue eyes, dressed in a cardigan and poplin slacks, cleared his throat and leaned forward. "Do excuse me," he said. "I am Hans Lorentz of the Norsk Polar Institute. It is my understanding, as Dr. Mackenzie said, that there is no unshared information here among the denizens of Trudeau. No compartmentalization of research, no projects of which we are unaware, no matter who is the sponsor. Free inquiry and free exchange, as Felix mentioned, they are our cornerstones. Therefore I am compelled to ask our American guest why it is that the special satellite channel, back to her compatriots in America, is apparently set up to convey information in some type of encoded form?"

Lorentz's question caused a stir in the room. Primakov's expression hardened. Simon King looked gleeful, eyes bright.

Hanley nodded. "It's our customary practice to take such measures wherever we're working. For several reasons. We don't want our inquiry inhibited, which means we have to be free to speculate, sometimes wildly, and we emphatically don't want our speculations made public. Panic doesn't help anyone. Not you, and not us. Also, the media is not an ally in our line of work. Misinformation and misinterpreted data can do a lot of harm. Look, I need all the time I can manage. Normally, I'd have a whole team here. Instead, there's just me—and any of you who are willing to help out. Any interference, any damage control with the media, just reduces that supply of hours and takes me away from what I'm here for—to protect you."

Mackenzie was quick to concur. "We have no problem with that, Dr. Hanley. It's only reasonable that premature dissemination would be counterproductive." He looked around the room. "For the time being, we will maintain a quarantine of information. All communications, professional or personal, will have to pass through Teddy Zale before they are transmitted. Our alumni have been told of the deaths, but we have kept details to a minimum."

An angry chorus of protest ran through the room. Simon King gestured broadly and shouted, "That blackout was supposed to be a temporary measure. Surely there's no need for a censor now that Miss Hanley has ridden in on her white horse to save us."

"*Doctor* Hanley, Simon. And however good we are at self-policing, we don't want this picked up by some ham radio operator or hacker. So for the moment Teddy Zale is Big Brother to us all."

"Jessie," Verneau said, steering the conversation away from this inflammatory topic, "what will you need from us?"

"I'll need a free hand and run of the station. I may be coming to your labs and requesting samples of whatever you're working on. I'll be looking at any insects, rodents, mammals, or primates you may be experimenting with. And I need help. Lots of it. I'll need people full time to run tests, three or four volunteers, as soon as I've got the lab set up. At this point, I'll look at anything and every-thing. It hasn't announced itself yet. But rest assured, we'll know it when we see it." She gave it her most charming grin, trying to de-fuse the tension.

"That's the best you can offer, Dr. Hanley? 'I'll know it when I see it?'" Simon King mimicked, his tone churlish and incredulous.

Hanley forced herself to keep smiling, but her eyes turned cold. "Yes, Dr. King. Patterns are revealing. Something will be out of order—it will break a pattern in some way."

King gave a derisive snort.

Hanley exhaled slowly, and said, "Epidemiology is inexact, true. Our objective is to segregate the normal from the abnormal in a given population. Businessmen in Tokyo, for instance, contract stomach cancer at a rate six times greater than businessmen in New York. Why? We look for what's common to a cluster of similarly stricken people, then isolate the factor we think is responsible."

"This is preposterous," King said, scraping back his chair and standing up. "What is common to our former colleagues is that they are dead. What is common to those of us who remain is that we are alive, for the moment. And now we are asked to place our future safety in your hands and your, quote, inexact, unquote, approach." He sat back down.

"I'm sorry. I can't be more specific at this juncture." She could see she wasn't going to win over King and turned to the others. "You're scientists. You know the mix of hard logic and intuition that it takes to find the missing piece of a riddle. One of you may al-ready have the answer to what's happened and not realize it. I've got to get you to share what you know because I'll be pursuing this thing into areas I have little information about and you know inside out. Which is why you must help me . . . for all our sakes."

"Pardon me," said a young woman, "I hadn't planned on an-nouncing it so publicly . . . I'm pregnant. About ten weeks." A murmur arose.

"Oh, my dear," another woman exclaimed warmly, and reached out to touch her forearm. "Congratulations."

Blushing, the young woman turned back to Hanley. "I just

found out, and not knowing what this danger might be is making me anxious as hell. I'm terrified about what I might be exposing the baby to. And then, thinking ahead . . . I mean, usually we'd be heading into four months of isolation. But what if you don't figure it out by spring? That's going to make our journeys home far more complicated. Isn't that true?"

"Well, if it's a chemical toxin, the main thing will be to keep everyone away from the source, but there shouldn't be any problems with travel. If it's biological and transmissible—and I have no reason yet to think that it is—that could be a different story, yes. Then we might need to quarantine some portion of the station."

"Like that apartment block in Hong Kong with SARS? Those hospitals in Beijing? Completely sealed off?"

Verneau rose. "In all candor, *mes amis,* such a circumstance might well make travel impossible if Ottawa invokes a *cordon sanitaire*. After what they've been through with SARS, they're unlikely to take chances. Close medical screenings would be required by the Canadian government; commercial air travel would be out of the question. Even if you manage to satisfy our authorities, some of your home countries might demand you be quarantined upon arrival. For certain, you Brits would be sent off straight to Coppetts Wood." A noisy murmur grew in the group as everyone reacted and spoke at once. "Dr. Hanley is our best chance to avoid this."

"Please," said Mackenzie and rapped on his desk with a rock specimen.

A blonde was on her feet. "Welcome, Jessie, from a fellow American. You mentioned the possibility of poison. What about our provisions? Was it something in the food, do you think? The water?"

Hanley said, "Obviously, I'll be testing both, looking at patterns of diet and talking to your kitchen staff about commonsense precautions."

"If it's bacterial or viral, where could they have contracted it?"

"The usual route is through other species. We call it passaging. The more a bacterium or a virus passes through other life forms, the stronger and more adaptive it becomes. Deadlier too. At some point the emerging virus or bacteria jumps to us humans. Influenza came to us from pigs, measles from dogs, anthrax and smallpox from cattle, leprosy from water buffalo, West Nile from mosquitoes. Emerging viruses often appear where species come into contact with one another that haven't before. In Malaysia a mass burning of fruit trees brought fruit bats closer to human habitation. A virus passed from the fruit bats to domesticated pigs, and from the pigs to humans. Nipah virus. It had a forty percent mortality rate."

"So that's why the SARS docs went rummaging around the livestock markets in Guangdong."

"Exactly. That was the logical place to look—a lot of the first victims worked in restaurants. Sure enough, they found SARS in the civet cats and some other caged wild critters being sold as delicacies in southern China. Which is why I can't rule out any of the animal, marine, or insect research here."

A wave of concern rippled through the group.

"I'm not saying you should be afraid of your lab mice all of a sudden. This was clearly not a routine exposure to something you've all handled in the past. I'm saying be prudent, be cautious. Don't use latex gloves. Put on work gloves. Use common sense."

Hanley paused to gauge her audience, then continued. "I understand that your environment here is undergoing profound changes. Pack ice is melting, some of it centuries old; temperatures are rising; migration patterns changing. Some microbe out there may have come close to humans for the first time. If so, I'll need your help to figure out where and when that contact occurred." She hesitated a moment before speaking again; she knew what she had to say might become awkward. "I'll also need volunteers to work with me in the lab." She enjoyed looking straight at Simon King as she said this, knowing full well that blowhards like him were the last to volunteer for hazardous duty.

Dee Steensma's hand shot up immediately. "I've been about as exposed as a person can get, and I seem to be okay. I'd like to help."

Hanley smiled gratefully. Now that Dee had stepped forward, others would surely follow. Uli Hecht, the cherubic German medical technician who had first worked on the victims, raised his hand. "I too have been exposed. I am very willing."

"Thank you." The next to raise her hand was a beautiful, diligent young Japanese biochemist named Kiyomi Taku.

Finally, Jack Nimit called out. "Think you could use an engineer to configure the lab?"

Hanley nodded. "I'd like to meet with all of you in the morning to start setting up. And, of course, if any more of you find yourselves with extra time on your hands, I can use any help you're willing to give." Once again, she shot a glance at Simon King.

Mackenzie shifted in his chair. "Gentlemen," he said, "and ladies. I think that we can all express our gratitude to our colleagues who have been willing to set aside their own important work to aid Dr. Hanley." He clapped, and gestured for the others to follow suit. "Good. I think that will do for the moment. Let's get some sleep, and then get on with our work, and let Dr. Hanley and her team begin hers. I apologize for the late hour."

He rose and the others did likewise. Chatting, they filed out. Verneau hung back, then came up to Hanley and Mackenzie when the room had cleared.

"Well, you sorted out Simon King," he said, shaking his head. "That prattling windbag. *Tabarnaque*," he cursed. "I can't stand how that whinging fuckwit swans around."

Mackenzie said, "You're being a bit hard on Simon. A lot of Canadians—Annie included—share his politics, if not his manner. For which I apologize, Dr. Hanley."

"Not necessary," Hanley said. "A little anti-Americanism won't kill me. What can you tell me about the three victims? Annie Bascomb?"

Mackenzie looked pained. "Annie. A truly rare individual. Hands down, the most popular person at the station. Certainly the most outspoken."

"And the geophysicist and the Russian glaciologist?"

"Ogata, yes. Competent, accommodating. I thought he had adjusted particularly well to Trudeau. He was enjoying himself. Minskov too." He fixed on her again. "What were you not saying in the meeting? What's your hypothesis?"

"I'm not being evasive, Dr. Mackenzie. It's way too early. The number of tests I have to conduct is pretty staggering. Unless I get lucky early on . . ."

"That's how Ottawa described you—lucky. I pray you are, Jessie Hanley. As you can see, the staff is terribly upset and frightened. No one knows what to do—or not to do, besides staying off the ice. Ah," he said, and extended a hand toward the man approaching them. "Dr. Hanley, I would like you to meet Jack Nimit, the person who oversaw the actual building of Trudeau."

Mackenzie put his arm around the younger man. He was extraordinary looking: Mongolian. He could have just as easily ridden in from the Gobi Desert as from the ice floes.

"Thank you," she said, trying not to stare, "for what you did earlier out there."

"You made a hell of an entrance. I'm glad we could catch up before you flew off in that gadget. I'm only sorry our resident prophet of doom got on your case so soon."

"Please," Mackenzie said, "Simon King has taken up enough of our energy for tonight. Is there anything you especially need, Jessie?"

Hanley paused for a moment. "Yes," she said. "As soon as you can contact the Russian scientist who left on the sub, I need to talk to her. If it was an inhaled poison, I have to assume she wasn't present during the actual exposure, or she wouldn't have made it out. But as an eyewitness to everything they did in the hours before they died, she could be an enormous help. In the meantime, I need to look at everything from the work site."

"Anything else?"

Hanley lowered her voice. "Is there a part of the station you can isolate—completely isolate—if anyone else turns out to be affected?"

Mackenzie looked troubled, but nodded. "The dome where we are keeping the bodies could be sealed off. I suppose we could adapt it for quarantine. Anything else?"

"I need to know what you plan to do if we have to evacuate Trudeau."

# 17

**H**anley circled the gurney. The body was housed in a transparent contamination stretcher. The features were not in repose. The man had died hard, in seizure, the body impossibly contorted and bent back on itself as if broken in half.

Verneau hovered nervously in the doorway. "Poor fellow. He looks so old."

"Dying will do that," Hanley said, securing the surgical mask over her mouth and nose beneath her thick protective goggles. "It can age you something awful." She shivered from the cold as she read the plastic-encased document headed *Verification d'identité*. "How old was Minskov?"

"Fifty-one," Verneau said. Hanley bent down to see through the gossamer fabric cylinder, until her face was even with the ashen profile. The eyes . . . horrible.

Dee said, "I've never seen anyone so pale."

"Yes," Verneau said. "Perhaps the loss of red cells."

"Why did Moscow forbid an autopsy on him?" Hanley said.

Verneau shook his head. "I have no idea. *Nyet* is their automatic response. I don't know. When I spoke to them, they seemed . . . afraid."

Hanley leaned closer to the destroyed man's face. "Why is the face wet?"

Dee stepped closer. "Where?"

"Around the mouth."

"Yes. You're right. How odd. Is it some sort of postmortem seepage?"

Hanley pulled a small vial and a thin eight-inch-long rubber-tipped pipette from her pocket. She bent over the corpse—her face inches from the contorted flesh—and carefully unzipped the protective airtight casing. Dee stepped back instinctively, even though she had assisted in the two autopsies.

"Don't try this at home," Hanley said to Verneau. "And don't touch me under any circumstances if I come in contact with it by mistake."

Hanley pumped the rubber bulb and carefully suctioned a short column of liquid into the pipette. Verneau and Dee held their breath while she transferred the liquid to the vial and stoppered it.

The need to be intimate with the victim was an odd compulsion in Hanley. Too irrational to acknowledge, but real. The proximity did something for her, or to her.

Hanley actually liked corpses: the human mechanism emptied of its animating force. This was not something she volunteered, even to close friends, but she felt comfortable with them, quietly excited by them. Nothing kinky, as she'd hastened to say after foolishly confiding in her husband. They simply represented a riddle, she had told him, trying to recover the situation by steering him away from what she had revealed.

The truer feeling was closer to anticipation. Growing up in rural Virginia, as a child she had already preferred the company of deceased creatures to living ones and collected roadkill to indulge her curiosity. While some kids' backyards were like menageries, hers was a morgue. Others took apart clocks and graduated to car engines. Hanley patiently undid the outerwear of bugs and frogs and birds and advanced to shelter-asphyxiated cats, to see what lay inside them. She was the weird Hanley kid, a woodsy loner into ghoulish pursuits. The other girls mostly ignored her. Boys gave her a wide berth.

A fawn or possum dead by the roadside captivated her imagination, sent her into gleeful overdrive. She learned to hide this passion from others until one day she found herself in a biology lab at college, where she flourished. Mortuary jobs saw her through med school, from which she went into epidemiology and, finally, professional reward.

She had a reputation, she knew, for unusual associative capabilities and impressive retention, an opinion apparently shared by a computer somewhere that had spit out her name. She did not discourage this view, yet she recognized that what really fueled her was her endless fascination with the body emptied of life.

Death left any kind of body profoundly different. The forces that animated and activated were gone, and that tangible absence was intoxicating, even moving on occasion, and completely memorable. That hollowness had contained life. Something even more powerful had driven it out. The palpable vacuity focused her mind and being like nothing else. Her ex frequently accused her of caring more for the dead than the living. "No," she told him, "but I often find them more interesting."

Hanley bit her lip. "Okay. Let's look at the next one."

The second body was Dr. Kossuth's. His colleagues hadn't known what to do with him. Each cell in his body had been destroyed, deformed, and burst open by the expanding ice. He was naked, just as they had found him. His skin was puce; large blotches had turned black.

Kossuth was staring into eternity through cracked eyeglass lenses, the frames barely hanging onto the tip of his nose where they had crumbled and frozen fast. Hanley looked him over quickly, and agreed with the report she'd been given: his cause of death, unlike the other three, was simple hypothermia.

Hanley bent closer, hands on knees. "He's frozen solid," she said, not loud enough to sound disrespectful. "But his lips are moist."

Dee looked more closely. "Beginning to thaw, do you think?" she said, then thought better of it. "Couldn't be. It's much too cold in here."

Hanley took a second vial from her pocket and siphoned another sample before the fluid dried in the cold air.

"No sign of convulsions, and the eyes are intact. All right, we're done here," she said, and turned to Verneau. "I'm about to cause you more political difficulties, but it can't be helped."

"Don't worry about politics," he said. "It is my one real skill. What is it you need?"

"In a few days, after I've checked that we have all the necessary tissue samples, I'll need the isolators holding Annie Bascomb and Mr. Ogata sealed in plastic, then sprayed with hydrochlorate and packed up in fiberboard boxes."

"All right."

"I have biohazard suits, gloves, and full-face masks for whoever handles the gurneys."

"So far it sounds doable," Verneau said.

"In the spring, when we're reconnected to the outside, I'd like them transported to the U.S. Army Medical Research Institute of Infectious Diseases in Frederick, Maryland."

"That's not for months," Dee said.

"Yes, but in the event that I can't track down your bug, that's where you want these bodies going. It's a maximum biohazard containment facility, among other things. I realize there may be objections, given that it's also an American military base that specializes in bioweaponry. I believe there's a secure facility in Winnipeg too, if political considerations preclude USAMRIID."

"*Merde,*" Verneau said, wrapping his arms around his torso for warmth. "Tokyo will go along. Ottawa I'm less certain of. Oh, well. They can thrash it out until spring. It should keep them busy. What about Minskov here, and Alex Kossuth?"

"I suggest you wrap up Minskov's quarantine tent the same way and hold him until spring when the Russians show up to deal with the body. I don't think they would fault you for the precaution."

"I'll see to it," said Verneau.

"But if we find the other bodies are infectious, we will do whatever it takes to decontaminate them all, and the Russians will just have to live with that. Otherwise Minskov's body could infect every person and vehicle it comes into contact with between here and whatever lab they want to take him to. Take precautions with Kossuth, even in this condition."

"Condition?"

"Frozen."

"No autopsy?" said Verneau.

"Other than being dead, he looks healthy. But yes, he should be autopsied too. It's possible he was also exposed and the cold just got him first."

Dee wept soundlessly, gazing quietly at the shrouded corpse of Annie Bascomb lying on the gurney against the curve of the wall, only her head visible. Someone had plaited her long hair in a perfect French braid. She might have been beautiful once. Impossible to say from what remained.

"Come, *ma chère*," said Verneau, guiding Dee with a hand at the small of her back. "This is not a good way for us to remember her."


"I'll show you to your quarters," Dee said. "Would you like to see a bit of the station on the way? It's a selfish request—playing tour guide would be a welcome distraction."

"Sure. I've already got tons of questions. Like what's with the lights in this place?"

"We use full-spectrum fluorescents to conserve energy—and for our health. The lights inside the station—and outside—are programmed in twelve-hour cycles to approximate a normal day at a more southerly latitude. To encourage normalcy. You have to be wary of insomnia," Dee warned. "It's as common around here as the cold. Half our psychologist's business is sleep problems."

"Is there any light at all during the day?" Hanley asked as they stopped by a large window.

Dee was quiet. Her hair shone in the dim light like a polished helmet. Hanley felt Dee sizing her up.

"At this time of year," Dee said, "just the stars and moon. You won't actually see the sun until after February."

"Four months," Hanley said. She stared out at the coastal bluffs above the station, wondering how long it would be before she felt the full brunt of being icebound in the dark. Her body, she realized, was anticipating morning: light. The exterior lights were dim.

Beyond them it was like pitch, yet the stars, reflected in the icy landscape, illuminated the terrain in a way they never would at lower latitudes.

Dee led her past the tool shop, sewage, the nutritionist, laundry and drying cupboard, recreation hall, transport department, even a post office. A hand-lettered sign on its door was dated October eighteenth, the last pickup of the season. It read: BACK IN THE MORNING.

The solar energy department next door was likewise closed for the polar night, but wind energy, across the hall, was crowded and busy.

"We've plenty of amenities to ward off cabin fever," Dee said, opening the door of the reading room. It was a comfortable refuge, with a dozen foam armchairs, green shaded lamps, and writing tables. Fabric-covered concave frames, like sails, partially enclosed the carrels. Even at this hour, several armchairs were occupied. The readers nodded to Dee and discreetly took in the newcomer.

Hanley approached the wall of transparent triangular panes. For the first time she noticed that they reflected no images or lights on the inside, nor were they fogged or iced over. She ran her hand across the clear surface.

"It's not even cold," she said, voice low. "Some super plastic?"

"Closer to glass, actually. Designed for high-altitude military aircraft and adapted for us. Also used in riot shields, but we don't talk about that. A vacuum separates the outer pane and inner pane, and the whole business is set in a special window well. The innermost pane's dusted with a coating devised by an optics firm in Rochester to block internal reflections, so your view is completely undistorted. In the summer months, the coating blocks out the glare of the continuous daylight and also helps capture the solar energy by not reflecting the ultraviolet rays back. In summer the vacuum is filled with water—a little innovation from our resident engineering genius."

"Water?" Hanley said.

Dee looked amused. "Yes. Sunlight warms the water and the solar heat helps warm the facility."

"I'm impressed," Hanley said. "What *about* the cold? The walls, the floor, they don't feel cold. But it's just inches away to the other side."

Dee nodded. "The flooring rests on three separate levels, each independently insulated. Every exterior dome actually fits over a slightly smaller one. A seventeen-inch gap in between the two shells is filled with a new insulation we developed in Edmonton. It keeps the wall thermodynamics neutral."

Before entering the next dome, they stepped into a cylindrical foyer whose curved door Dee slid closed behind them; it had to rotate all the way around to discharge them in the rotunda.

As they entered the second dome, the temperature dropped. Hanley shivered, and the surprising dryness made her salivate.

Dee walked confidently through the dark to a small point of light on a freestanding post. Hanley hesitated, smelling something earthy. A control on the post brought up the lights on an Arctic meadow studded with flora and a rock barren in the center.

"Local plant life. Right now it's buried out there in ice and snow, but this is what you might see in summer." She took a few steps along a path. "Listen. Hear the finches? They're used in hypothermia experiments."

Hanley said, "What are those sorry-looking things?" and pointed at a dry, woolly looking patch of tiny ferns.

"I'm afraid Alaskans call them niggerheads," Dee said. "I don't know the Latin name."

"Sad-looking plants," said Hanley, surveying the collection.

"You better not let our senior botanist hear you. This is all his handiwork. It's a biodiversity repository in case global warming is as devastating to the Arctic as some of our colleagues are predicting. Down below the tree line, most of the major species of Arctic forest are dying off. All sorts of insects can survive there now, and they're having a field day. Come," she said, and walked along a tiny path.

"It's like a miniature moor," said Hanley, following her.

Dee pointed out the low-lying scrub and bare hillock. "Sedges, farbs, rushes, dwarf birches back through there. Tundra." She stopped to survey the tufts of vegetation and reached down. "Green and black lichen, on those rocks. Purple saxifrage—it has lovely blooms in summer."

"You're pretty good at plants for a dentist," Hanley said, standing alongside her on the walkway, looking at the meadow. "Aren't dentists only supposed to like the artificial kind, the waxier the better?"

"Yes. And we only listen to Muzak." Dee smiled. "This is my favorite spot in Trudeau, actually. This habitat may not look like much to you now, but it's the only greenery for a thousand miles. After a few months of nothing but ice and rock, these scruffy plants begin to look like redwoods." She grew serious. "The polar suits will preserve you out there, but we each have to figure out how to keep ourselves going in here, to get along with ourselves. For me, this spot does it."

They followed the path around to the far side of the dome and another cylindrical foyer, which released them back into the station's temperate environment.

"What's that?" Hanley said, looking up at the round convex ceiling that seemed to undulate in shades of blue.

"Mackenzie's Folly. Come on. I'll show you." Dee led Hanley up a spiral staircase made of wood planking. "Even our packing crates were designed to serve," she said. When they reached the top, they paused. "This and the extern," Dee said, "are the highest points on the island."

Hanley barely heard her. She was staring. The translucent blue ceiling turned out to be the bottom of a large round swimming pool crisscrossed by three lanes. Its ceiling was an enormous domed skylight made out of the triangular double-paned Trudeau windows. Hard narrow benches ringed the tiled perimeter; otherwise no other furnishings, not even a diving board or a ladder, interfered with what the designer had intended—a starkly beautiful sculpted space.

"Why put a pool on the roof?"

"Fire," she said. "Our big fear. The only water around us is hard as stone. Melting it takes a huge amount of energy. In case of fire, all this nice warm seawater becomes a reservoir for dousing it.

Gravity delivery in case there's also a power outage." She looked out over the perfectly still surface. "Most everything here has multiple applications."

"Cool. Why saltwater?" Hanley said.

"It doesn't require chlorination. Disposal of chlorinated water would be tricky."

"Do you treat your drinking water at all?" Hanley said.

"No." Dee paused, a look of concern on her face. "Should we?"

"Probably not," Hanley said.

"Come," Dee said, "we're almost finished."

"It's so much larger than I expected," Hanley said.

"It'll shrink pretty rapidly, believe me. The station creates the illusion of spaciousness and freedom of movement. But it doesn't take long to realize how confining it is, and how hostile *that* is." She indicated the terrain beyond the glass wall.

Hanley looked up at the star-studded sky. She felt momentarily disoriented.

"When the sun rises in March, where will it come up?"

"You mean, what direction?"

"Yes," she said, looking out.

"There," Dee said and pointed into the blackness. "South. The sun will rise in the south."

# 18

*Rus* eased out of the fjord. Above the drone of the turbines, the ship was entirely silent. A pall settled over the men, who went about their designated tasks like automatons. Except for the mandatory, ritualized exchanges, no one spoke on watch. Off duty, no one spoke at all.

Rudenko studied the closed-circuit video monitor in the control room, noting the postures of the divers in their pressurized chamber. The young sailor who had set the charges inside *Vladivostok* sat off by himself, knees drawn up, face hidden in his arms. Two others reclined, arms over their eyes to block the incessant overhead light bulbs. Orlovsky sat nearest the camera, either oblivious to its intrusion or not caring. He sat completely still, head bowed, eyes fixed on the middle distance, face lifeless. A drop of water hung at his chin.

Rudenko leaned back against the chart table, gripping an elbow with one hand, his other hand flat against his cheek, thinking. Waiting. The yeoman counted down. The distant detonation reached them as a dull thud, not much more than a pulse, like an irregular beat of their hearts, expected yet surprising. And alarming—a warning of imbalance, a foreboding, so slight they might almost have imagined it, yet frighteningly real. Final.

"Fuck."

Orlovsky's voice on the television monitor was the only human sound in the control room as the ship angled downward, into deeper waters. Behind him, in the corner of their steel cell, the youngest diver wept, arms over his head, head tucked into him, his body a tight ball.

Rudenko held down the intercom switch and spoke quietly to Orlovsky, asking after the boy. Orlovsky looked into the camera lens and pointed to his own temple.

"Something is wrong with his roof. We shouldn't have sent him into the boat. He hasn't stopped shivering since. He keeps saying things; nothing that makes sense. I think he is speaking to his mother. He needs to get out of here, Admiral. All of us do. How many hours before you bring us out of the chamber?"

"Admiral," Nemerov said.

Rudenko eased off the intercom switch. "Yes?"

"I wouldn't encourage them to rush decompression."

"You think it's too dangerous."

"I don't know. But the junior officers tell me we'll have a mutiny if the divers come out. The crew want nothing to do with them."

"The young man needs help."

"My men are afraid the divers were contaminated by their contact with *Vladivostok*."

Rudenko looked at Orlovsky and the others on the screen. "Understandably."

"They want them kept separate. Away."

"It's your ship, Captain. I'm sure you will make the right decision."

Nemerov shook his head. "I can't imagine how." He exhaled slowly through his mouth. "I have never felt ashamed before, commanding a vessel."

"You are lucky," Rudenko said.

"How possibly?"

"The submariners. They were unrescuable. What would we have done if they were trapped like that and alive?"

Nemerov shook his head in disbelief. "Were those his orders?"

Rudenko turned away. "He would never admit to them, but yes."

Orlovsky's face filled the screen, distorted by the fish-eye lens. "Captain! You know standard procedures. We are to return to normal quarters as soon as decompression is over. We've been locked in this can since we sailed."

Nemerov depressed the intercom. "This situation is a little unusual, as I'm sure you understand."

Orlovsky looked distraught. "Sir, it's another—what?—three days at least to St. Petersburg. We'll be pudding brained if we don't get out of this box soon."

"It's not so easy, Sergeant. The men are . . . concerned."

Orlovsky slapped his thigh and looked away. "Ah, of course, of course. I do understand. You're going to keep us penned in here and observe us like monkeys in the zoo."

"That'll be enough!" the lieutenant shouted.

Nemerov raised his hand toward him, signaling for quiet. The sonarman announced the approach of engines: their comrades on the surface, cloaking their departure from Norwegian waters.

"I'm truly sorry, Sergeant," Nemerov said.

"Not as much as we are. Sir."

Nemerov stood silent, ignoring the insubordination.

"Captain," Orlovsky said, on screen.

"Yes, Sergeant?"

"It is my duty to report damaged equipment."

"Yes?" Nemerov said, sounding concerned. "You have some damage to report?"

"Yes," Orlovsky said, "I'm afraid this is broken," and smashed a fist down on the camera lens. The screen went black.

# 19

The scheduled topic of that morning's symposium had been "Periodic Weakenings of the Earth's Magnetic Field." Instead, the audience rose to the Canadian national anthem, during which Felix Mackenzie mounted the platform of the auditorium to face the overflowing hall. Most of them had never seen him in a suit. He had put a flowering sprig of something from the arboretum in his lapel. As the anthem drew to an end, he gestured for the Japanese scientists to come forward.

Dressed in white, their traditional color of mourning, Junzo Ogata's colleagues conducted a short Buddhist ceremony of remembrance. They sounded tiny gongs, burned incense, and prayed. After they returned to their seats, people rose to eulogize their departed friends. First Minskov was briefly memorialized in a stilted, stodgy manner by his Russian comrades. Only one westerner spoke about him, and his remarks were perfunctory.

No one managed to speak about Annie Bascomb without simultaneously smiling and weeping. Annie's rock and roll karaoke nights, her outrageous feminazi costume for the solstice masquerade party, the time she demonstrated to the Aussie gaffer that she could pee in a bottle as well as any man. Verneau took the podium and reminded them of the story Annie herself loved to tell about the young Italian meteorologist who fell hopelessly for her their first year at the station.

"Her poor suitor followed her everywhere, serenaded her every evening. Although he spoke no English and she no Italian, both of them had a smattering of German, but unfortunately not enough for the dashing young man to understand that she was most definitely not interested in him. When he finally did get it, he took it badly. As some of you will recall, he confronted her publicly in the dining hall, shouting, 'Annie Bascomb, *du bist ein Frigidaire*! An ice-a-boxsa!'" Laughter mixed with more tears. "Well, if there's anything Annie wasn't, it was an icebox. We all treasure our memories of her warmth, her passion, her irrepressible spirit."

The hall fell quiet. Verneau left the podium and sat down in the first row. He looked disconsolate.

Last, the older staff remembered Alex Kossuth in hushed, reverent tones. At the very end, Felix Mackenzie rose to speak.

"Dr. Kossuth and I came to the Arctic at the same point in our lives, as young, ambitious scientists eager to make our mark and return to the academic world to reap the rewards of our discoveries. Alex was very idealistic back then. Everything seemed possible and within reach. We thought we could make a great difference where the North was concerned, and we set out to do it." Mackenzie looked away. "He was my oldest friend." He stood silent for a second, collecting himself and looked out at the audience once more. "It wasn't long before the Arctic had seduced us. This place kept drawing us back into its pristine and merciless beauty. We came to see that it was the reward. It became our home." The director looked up from his notes. "Together we conceived of this station and worked to make it a reality. Alex Kossuth loved the North. We spent countless winters together, wonderful summers on the floes. The Arctic was his life's work. Most of all, he loved being one of the tribe at Trudeau. How fitting that he ended his days here, with us, at the high latitudes."

Mackenzie paused to recover himself, then continued:

"While we mourn the terrible manner of his passing, we shall remember him for his selfless contributions to the study and preservation of this unique part of our planet, so little known. Alex . . . was an exceptional scientist. A beloved friend with whom I shared the dream of this station in the wild, and its cooperative undertaking by men and women of science from all the corners of the globe. I already miss him more than I can say."

He stepped down and motioned for Dee and Hanley to stand beside him by the door, like a receiving line. As the group filtered out, Dee and Mackenzie systematically introduced Hanley to everyone, from senior scientists to food servers. Mackenzie deftly managed to impress upon the key department heads and chief researchers the utter need to cooperate with her work, while using the brief encounters to ease their concern. Hanley marveled at Mackenzie's charm and considerable gift for influencing this collection of exceptional and exceptionally difficult men and women. They were almost done with their glad-handing when a beefy Inuit in a loud orange T-shirt ran into the room, scanning the crowd and calling for Jack Nimit. Nimit made his way through the knots of people and listened to what the panting man was reporting. He broke into a run.

"What is it, Jack?" Mackenzie called out to him.

"Courtyard," Nimit shouted back. "Dome Four. Fire."

Hanley was swept along with the rest of them, racing to wherever the fire was. She followed blindly down corridors, up an incline, down three steps and out through a door into the freezing dark.

They were in a courtyard between domes. A polecat was burning fiercely, jetting fire thirty feet high. Two people in environmental suits were wrestling with a pressurized hose, trying to reach the roaring flames. Smoke billowed high overhead, generating a fog up above. The hose began to gush.

"Stop!" Nimit shouted. *"Arrêtez!"*

They couldn't hear him above the noise of the fire. Halfway to the flames, the pressurized liquid turned to flakes, showering the crackling vehicle with what looked like snow. Hands rose to shield faces from the searing heat.

"Don't spray," Nimit yelled, cupping his hands to trumpet the order. "Stop! You're feeding the fire."

Verneau and Mackenzie waved everyone back. As the flames leaped closer to the nearest dome, Hanley ducked reflexively, trying to avoid the blasting heat. She felt a wave of fear: if water couldn't put out the fire, even the reservoir Dee had showed her would be useless. The whole station could go up, leaving them homeless and helpless in this wilderness. If they made it to the abandoned station at Little Trudeau, how long could they last?

Nimit pulled his sleeves over his hands, threw himself at the valve at the coupling, midway to the nozzle, and tried to lever it back. Hanley could see that he was struggling. She ran to the valve, imitated the way Nimit had pulled down his sleeves, and threw her weight against the lever. Even though she was only a few steps farther from the fire, she was instantly aware of the cold knifing through her. She could feel her eyelids frosting over.

The stream of flakes diminished. Nimit ran to the two Japanese who'd been manning the hose. She couldn't hear him, but she could see him gesturing about how to bring the fire under control. Without warning, the burning vehicle exploded, knocking them down, making the rest jump back.

The polecat vaporized, melting to its skeletal frame in a second. A cry went up. The flames glowed blue, then surged into a white fireball. Had the impromptu firefighters been standing closer, they would have been incinerated along with the polecat. As it was, their suits were smoking; the side of the nearest dome was singed black.

"Get everyone out of here." Nimit shouted, scrambling to his feet. "You don't want to be breathing this stuff."

Verneau and Mackenzie herded everyone away from the smoldering wreckage and back into the dome. Nimit and the two shaken Japanese stayed behind, dragging stones into a ring to contain the remaining fire.

Along with the others, Hanley stood at the windowed wall of the dome, watching them work. She tucked her shaking hands into her armpits and jogged in place, trying to regain her circulation. When the trio finally returned to the dome, everyone cheered.

Nimit spotted her. "Thanks for the help with the hose. I can't tell you how many times I've told those guys you can't use water on a chemical fire."

"What the hell happened out there?" she said, her teeth still chattering.

"The fire must have started in the cat's fuel cell. A chemical fire is beyond hot—so hot it breaks down the water into hydrogen and oxygen."

"Into gases?"

"Yep. Then the gases ignited. You saw. That's why the cat blew up like the *Hindenburg*."

"So I was actually watching water burn. Wait till my kid hears about that."

"Yeah, well, it easily could have been everyone's last memory of the place. If the flame had backed up into the hose . . . As it is, the dome where we've got Alex and the others nearly went up with the cat." Her body trembled as he spoke, but not from cold.

"I can't wait to get to work," she said, with forced bravado. "Seems like my job is a hell of a lot safer than yours."


Verneau installed Hanley in a freestanding dome that was normally occupied only in summer. Her quarters were next door to the lab, separated by a short corridor.

"I get the feeling he doesn't want me to waste time commuting," she told Dee. Hanley marked the entrance to the dome with bio-hazard signs, and limited access to everyone except her staff. Jack Nimit began to retrofit the work area. Fortuitously, the space had been designed to be airtight. Nimit rigged a filtered air hood over the lab bench, and an air blower to create negative pressure that would keep any airborne particles in; then he installed two HEPA filters to prevent bacterial and virus-sized particles in the air from getting out.

"One more thing," she told Jack, "I need you to figure out a way to seal off this dome so nothing gets out into the station if anything happens. We'll do our best to decontaminate ourselves, but you'll have to leave us in here and protect the rest of Trudeau." She stared into the black pools of his eyes, unsettled by their odd beauty and softness, so at odds with the hard, angular features.

Nimit, unflappable, assured her he would take care of it.

Hanley dedicated a large, empty area in the dome to the contents of the victims' work site, which a few members of the maintenance staff had grudgingly retrieved, wearing protective gloves and masks beneath their polar suits. They'd demonstrated their displeasure with the assignment by dumping everything unceremoniously into several heaps.

Dressed in Tyvek biohazard suits and full-face respirators, she and Dee created order out of the random piles, making a grid on the floor to separate the items that had belonged to each scientist. Each victim's belongings were placed in the position they'd been in in the shelter, using photographs Verneau supplied.

"Any food you find, Dee, give a shout. I want to test all the food first."

Since Jack Nimit was most familiar with the technical gear, Hanley asked him to catalogue what each item was used for and certainly anything about it that looked unusual. He and Dee painstakingly numbered and tagged each object, creating a log to work from as they began to examine everything the scientists had handled in minute detail.

"The archaeologists' work site at Little Trudeau used to look like this," Dee told Hanley. "This is how they pieced together the lives of the early Kurlak Islanders. It's so strange to be doing this to . . ."

"I know," said Hanley, giving Dee's arm a quick squeeze. She stared at the objects and back at the corresponding list in her hand. She was reconstructing the catastrophe, minus the essential actors— the scientists who had last used the objects and occupied the dwelling.

Hanley drained the Cointreau bottle into a vial and designated every morsel of remaining food for culture. She even scrutinized the victims' biodegrading plastic toilet buckets, but their wastes had long been reduced to nothing by the powdered enzymes used both in the station and out on the ice to render human waste harmless to the ecosystem. If the scientists had feasted on local fish or crustaceans, no trace of them was left.

"Okay, I'm taking these to the lab. Lock this all up when you're done and bring me the key."

"Lock?" Dee said. "We haven't got a lot of locks at Trudeau."

"Ask Nimit to make some quick. I want this all secured."

Returning to the lab area next door, Hanley and her volunteer staff, moving awkwardly in the unaccustomed bulk of the biohazard gear, cleared a work space among all the unopened boxes she had brought in on the Commode.

"Let's take a really good look at these suits," said Hanley. "Every inch of 'em."

"What do we look for?" Kiyomi said, peering into a helmet with a penlight.

"The clues are usually in things that break the usual pattern, but really there are no rules. I'll settle for spots, stains, burns, corrosion, odd smells, anything that shouldn't be there. Something like a flame retardant might be the culprit—harmless in itself, then rendered toxic in the presence of some other substance or process."

"Like what?"

"Something catalytic might have caused a gaseous emission that discharged into the suits."

After examining the exterior and interior surfaces, they cut open the quills of the outer layer and the sluice vests through which the air had traveled.

"There goes thirty thousand dollars, Canadian," Uli said as the X-Acto knives ripped through each elaborately constructed outfit. He tore out a handful of translucent quills. "Here, Kiyomi. Grab some straws from the haystack."

Hanley examined the bald patch Uli had left behind. To her surprise, the fabric beneath the quills was black.

"Like polar bear," Kiyomi explained. "Black skin to absorb sunlight. Bear fur is transparent. Only looks white because it reflects light."

"So these outfits are kind of a weird bear-bird hybrid," said Hanley, teasing apart the layers of one of the vests.

"The outer layer, yes," Dee said. "Trudeau's just been granted a patent in Canada and is applying in the States. All the major sporting-goods firms are jockeying to license the technology."

Hanley, half listening, was intent on looking for any abnormalities or discolorations in the various layers. Anything at all. Nothing obvious turned up. She sent Uli to the herbarium to get a pair of finches.

"Kiyomi, please collect every liquid and aerosol they had with them at the work site. Make a chart: I want you to test every layer of the suit with each potential catalyst in turn. If you reproduce what happened, the finches will tell us soon enough. They'll be our canaries in the coal mine."

She showed Kiyomi and Uli how to put on the respirators with independent air supply packs, and sent them, the birds, and the suits to a sealed area next door.

Consummate professionals, her volunteer staff made not the slightest murmur about the risks. They already had a tacit understanding that no matter what their concerns, no matter what Hanley seemed to be looking for, they would do what she asked. Outside the lab, they spoke little of their work, determined to spare the rest of Trudeau more anxiety.

Jack Nimit came in from the corridor. He was wearing a native jacket of Arctic fox, its collar trimmed in white and carrying a zero-residue portable incinerator. He'd stripped it out of the scientists' wanigan; it hadn't been listed in the inventory. Hanley uttered an expletive and rushed to swab its surfaces.

"What are you after?" he said.

"There's a possibility the incinerator converted something contaminated or infected into nearly microscopic particles they all inhaled."

But the device lived up to its reputation and was completely clean. Nothing showed up under the microscope; she set a few swabs to culture, but without any expectations.

Next, she and Dee went to the labs of the four members of the field team. Ogata's surveying tools and Kossuth's meteorological equipment suggested nothing. Annie Bascomb's research as an environmental biochemist studying the effect of organochlorines on Arctic wildlife suggested lots of possibilities, but Hanley didn't know where to start. In a neighboring lab, she interviewed Bascomb's coworkers about the chemical pollutants she'd discovered in the field. Hanley took everything even remotely appearing guilty for testing. Although she worried about the psychological effect, she sealed Bascomb's lab, over Simon King's loud protests, putting it off limits.

In Minskov's lab, Hanley bagged the plastic tubes of ice core samples taken on that last field trip. "What exactly are these things, Dee?"

"From what I understand, they take a core sample in the ice, bring it back and thaw it out. They examine nutrients, microbes, whatever species of algae might be in it. I think it's pretty routine stuff. I'm sure you'll find Minskov's records on his computer."

Hanley took the backup disks, and gave them to Kiyomi to analyze. The ice samples seemed promising. If the three had bumped into anything deadly in the ice, this was a likely point of contact. According to Minskov's colleagues, the ice he'd been sampling could be as much as a million years old. Maybe he'd uncovered something to which humans had never been exposed, for which they had no defenses. Hanley felt a ripple of excitement and fear.

Working beside Kiyomi, Hanley started culturing each of the ice samples, and then resealed them in airtight canisters. "Where did you work at Trudeau before you signed up for this?" she asked.

"In the hibernaculum."

"Sounds nice. What exactly is a hibernaculum?"

"A NASA-sponsored project on hibernation. We're studying why Arctic animals can put bodies on hold—not eat for seven months and yet remain in good condition. NASA wants hibernation hormones for experiments. Canadian, American, and German pharmaceutical companies are involved as well. They want to know about animals' cholesterol levels, which are twice as high in winter as in summer, yet they suffer no hardening of their arteries. Bears build protein even though they aren't eating; they don't accumulate toxic waste products, and use up only fat. Bile fluid of theirs, when administered to humans, dissolves gallstones. No surgery."

"I can imagine what the drug companies would pay for that."

Kiyomi nodded. "It covers half our budget."

Hanley put her hand on Kiyomi's shoulder. "Thank you for volunteering. It's really above and beyond the call—"

Kiyomi said softly, "Junzo, Annie, Dr. Minskov, Alex. They were our friends."


After a two-hour sleep break, Hanley and Dee arranged to interview the medical personnel who had responded to the distress call, double-checking their official reports. The individual versions of events varied slightly; the facts didn't. Two of the victims, Bascomb and Ogata, had been technically alive, each with a thready pulse, no appreciable blood pressure, lungs resistant to deflation, bodies pale as ice. The third—Minskov—had no vital signs.

"We tried resuscitation anyway," the nurse practitioner said.

"*Ja,*" Uli agreed.

"But nothing."

"*Nichts.*"

Hanley thanked them and asked them to send in Annie Bascomb's boss in the environment division, Simon King.

"Did Annie Bascomb behave in an unusual way before departing for the work site?"

"No."

Did she have any pets at the station?"

"No."

"Had she sustained an injury in the lab recently?"

"No."

"Any bites from test animals?"

"No."

"Did she often come in contact with birds? Perhaps as part of her environmental investigations?"

"No."

"Was her gait abnormal?"

"No."

"Did she have any contact with hides?"

"No."

"Bristles?"

"No."

"Mercuric compounds?"

"No."

"Sulfur?"

"No."

"Fungicides?"

"No."

"Did she like shellfish?"

"No."

"Eggs?"

"No. Will that be all?"

"Does he ever say yes?" Hanley said after he left.

"No." Dee and Hanley broke out laughing.

Back in the lab dome, Hanley donned protective gear and discreetly checked the heated oxygen the medical techs had administered, testing the canisters for residue of ethylene glycol, chromium, methyl mercury . . . to no avail.

She hadn't really expected anything: too many witnesses had seen the wracked condition of the bodies before the oxygen had been administered.

Kiyomi came over from her bench station and handed her the results on the liquid Hanley had harvested from the two corpses. The clear liquid around their mouths was water. Simple fresh water, with a minuscule complement of benign oral bacteria.

"Goddamn it."

Hanley balled up the report and tossed it in the direction of the wastebasket. Nothing.

Hanley asked Jack Nimit to show her the wanigan that had been the scientists' primary vehicle. Together, they examined it for any malfunctions that might have produced something toxic. He worked with complete concentration. She bent close, staring at him—his small hands, the Asiatic planes of his face.

Nimit was expert in dismantling the machine, checking the tiniest components. It was spotless. No signs of corrosion or chemical activity. Certainly no fire. Not even rust in the Arctic dryness.

"Damn," she muttered. She had been counting on some kind of trail, some evidence of physical cause and effect.

They went to the second, smaller vehicle, the polecat Kossuth had driven, and repeated the procedure. Nothing.

"I can't believe it," Hanley said.

"What?"

"No residue, no sign of chemical reaction. These machines are spotless."

"Thank you."

"You're not welcome. You haven't cleaned them or anything?"

"No one's been near them since this happened. Believe me, no one's wanted to."


The lab log was filling up with negative results: Kiyomi had found nothing on Minskov's disks; so far, the ice core samples had cultured nothing of interest. Neither had the leftover food they had found at the work site. Ishikawa had done an exhaustive OSHA search on the list of chemicals and compounds she'd sent him from the campsite and from Annie Bascomb's lab. He'd found plenty of toxics, but none that caused these symptoms and none that vanished after death without a trace. He'd combed the pharmaceutical directory for contraindications of all their medications, looking for accidental combinations that could be fatal.

"*We're starting to lose the satellite,*" Ishikawa said, static in the audio. Tiny cameras atop their laptop monitors allowed Ishikawa and Hanley to see one another.

"My kid send me any e-mail?" she asked.

"*Yeah, I'm forwarding it.*" Ishikawa looked away. "*Okay, it should be there now.*"

"Thanks."

"*From here on you can communicate with Joey directly, by the way. We cleared it with the chief.*"

She barely got to sign off before the satellite cut out. Hanley quickly opened her three messages from Joey, devouring the details of his daily life a million light-years away in a sunlit part of the planet.

The last e-mail was a plea. Joey had been touting his mom's northern adventure to his science class. He begged her for a live session with her and his classmates. Shit, she couldn't exactly broadcast what she was doing up there to a class of ten-year-olds. But it couldn't hurt to show them the wonders of Trudeau Station, might even turn a few of them on to science.

"That's more like it," Dee said, walking over.

Hanley looked up, startled. "What?"

"You're smiling. Haven't seen that lately." Dee tossed the report next to the keyboard. "Kiyomi found kainic acid in the brain tissue."

"Kainic acid."

"That's what she said."

Hanley had to wait a few minutes before she could reestablish contact with L.A.

"Kainic acid. What's the symptomology, Ishi?" said Hanley.

Ishikawa did a quick database search. *"Affects nerve cells. You get irritability, shakiness, neurological disorders."* He looked up from his keyboard. *"But what's it doing in the brain?"*

"Good question," Hanley said, tossing a pencil aside and leaning back away from the monitor.

*"Listen, Cybil's here, and she says to tell you that kainic acid is closely related to domoic acid, which is the culprit in a lot of Canadian shellfish-poisoning cases. Domoic acid binds to glutamate receptors in the brain. It makes the nerve cells transmit continuously until they die. Overloaded circuits."*

"Shellfish," Hanley said to herself. "Thanks, Ishi—catch you later."

Leaving Dee in charge of the lab, Hanley grabbed a specimen container and went to interview the nervous kitchen workers who had prepared and packed the food taken by the field team.

The head cook said, "There's a pretty standard set of meals we make for the folks going out on the ice. Lots of extra calories to keep them going."

"Anything else . . . not on this list? Maybe a special food request from one of them?"

A few of the staff exchanged glances.

"Look," the cook said, "we could get in trouble with Fisheries and Oceans Canada, but we do harvest some live whelks in the summer. Not everybody likes the chewiness. But that Russian lady was really partial to 'em. She came in here and kind of insisted we throw in a few for her going-away party."

"You have them here?"

"We keep them here in saltwater tanks until we're ready to cook them." Hanley could feel her adrenaline surging. Their toxins were so potent, even cooking didn't destroy them. Nothing in the stomach contents had suggested toxins, according to Ingrid Kruger's autopsy report, but saxitoxin, one of the shellfish poisons Cybil had suggested, generally left the gastrointestinal tract unaffected. And if they were an acquired taste, Kossuth might not have eaten them. Slow down, she told herself. Take it one step at a time.

"Are you absolutely sure? We didn't find any shells at the work site."

"No, they'd just toss the shells back in the polynya. Okay ecologically and less for them to carry back to the station."

"Right. I'm going to have to confiscate the rest."

"Oh, God. You think that's what killed them?" One of the cooks started to cry. Hanley stared in disbelief into the aluminum tank they showed her. "You really eat those . . . things? They're as big as conchs."

She collected the remaining whelks from the kitchen's tank and sealed them in a heavy plastic crate marked with biohazard warnings. If the culprit was saxitoxin, or something close, they'd find it in the tissue samples, and in at least some of the whelks.

Hanley raced down the corridors to her lab dome, cursing when she took a wrong turn and had to double back.

"Kiyomi! Uli!" she shouted at the door. "Give me a hand." She quickly explained what she'd discovered.

"You really think you might have found it?" Uli asked.

For the first time, she was feeling confident, but she knew better than to promise a quick solution. Even with her staff, she was diplomatic and noncommittal.

"I'm certainly less and less convinced we're looking at something inorganic." She looked at Kiyomi and Uli, wondering how honest she should be with them—or anyone at Trudeau—about the narrowing possibilities. "The good news is, if it's the whelks, it's not contagious, and completely preventable."

She logged on and sent Ishikawa a quick memo, asking him to do some background searches on whelks and saxitoxins.

"Uli, I need you to count the whelks and then scrounge up three mice for every whelk. Beg, borrow, steal. I don't care what you have to do. Just get healthy mice that weigh between eighteen and twenty grams apiece. Take a few from each lab so you don't clean anybody out. On second thought, if there's any way you can take them all from Simon King and ruin one of his experiments, do that."

Uli laughed and headed out the door.

"Okay, Kiyomi, when Uli gets back from his hunt, you're going to do the mouse assay. Glove up. You're going to take tissue from each whelk, and inject it into three mice. Mark each shell and each mouse so we know which ones we're testing with what. Note the precise time of the injection. We'll need to take shifts and monitor them round the clock, because if they die—and I sure hope they do—we need to know exactly when."

# 20

The dacha, a short distance from St. Petersburg, was unusually grand, built of stone. Panov had borrowed it for the weekend to celebrate his wife's name day with a group of old friends. He received Rudenko in the yard with boyish boisterousness.

"Welcome back to dry land!" he shouted. Rudenko smiled and they embraced.

Rudenko did not know the Panovs' circle, a dozen St. Petersburg couples, but the evening passed pleasantly. By midnight all but one of the women had retired to the several guest rooms at the nearby cottage, leaving the men to drink and gossip over billiards and exchange the latest irreverent jokes from Moscow.

The minister of munitions was the first to pass out, and a goodly number of celebrants followed suit within the hour. The remaining handful stayed up singing bawdy peasant songs and barracks ballads, their faces flushed, eyes misted with spirits and sentiment. By four A.M. one lone woman and somebody else's husband were left, both slumped on the floor, leaning on one another and the couch, snoring.

Panov and Rudenko took large towels from the linen cupboard and trudged through the snow to the *banya*. Stripping in the chilly vestibule of the low birch hut, they ducked their heads to enter the innermost room and quickly stoked the fire under the dry baking rocks that encased the woodstove. In seconds the room was solid with dry heat. Rudenko cupped his nose to protect his lungs; Panov appeared completely unaffected. He busied himself pouring water, scalding the stones, laughing boisterously each time a splash sizzled and thickened the atmosphere. The temperature soared.

After nearly a quarter hour of basting themselves and beating one another with cut birch branches soaked in warm water, Panov led the way outside, his body steaming. Taking up an ax, he hopped through the snow, stark naked, trailing vapors, and yelping like a fox. Rudenko, light-headed, trotted after, his body pale as the drifts and feeling white hot. At the frozen pond, Panov skittered to a stop, padded onto the icy surface, then reared back and smashed down with the blunt ax head. Rudenko danced up and down beside him, hopping from foot to foot, his genitals shriveled by the cold he could not yet feel.

Although it was an old break Panov toiled at, the ice had healed hard. It took four sharp blows to crack; the fifth smashed through. Ax and axman plunged straight down in a great spray of water and icy debris, but Panov instantly bobbed back to the surface, laughing uncontrollably.

Panov pulled Rudenko in after him, and their shrieks echoed across the pond and the morning stillness as if they were young men again. After romping in the ice water, the two climbed out and padded back to the bathhouse red as beets, giggling like boys.


At eleven on Sunday morning, it finally grew light and the guests began to stir. Madame Panova cooked them all *blini* for their midday meal. It was a slow process, and they lingered for hours in the huge kitchen, waiting for their second and third helpings, coating the delicate crepes with sugar and apricot jam, rolling them into tubes, and eating them with their hands, like children. When everyone else had been served, Panov tilted his head back and lowered a drizzling pancake into his mouth like a sword swallower. By early afternoon it was getting dark. The guests left in a small caravan of sedans, Madame Panova with them, gaily going off to spend the evening with her sister in the city.

Panov and Rudenko settled themselves at the birch table to

finish their tea and the last of the vodka. The rest of the evening they dozed by the fire. Too sated to consume anything more, Rudenko eventually bedded down and slid into the deepest sleep: a blank, dreamless floating.

In the morning, after a late and lazy breakfast, they headed toward St. Petersburg, Panov at the wheel chattering like a bird, while Rudenko, only half listening, thought about his appointment in town.

Some miles from the outskirts they passed Tsarskoye Selo. Did the admiral know, Panov asked, that Tsar Nikolai and his family were detained there in anticipation of their exile in England? Panov's lecture raced on, covering the monarchy's last days at the palatial retreat—how the tsar had occupied himself in quarantine studying maps of London, reading Conan Doyle aloud to his children, worrying how soon his brood might be well enough to undertake their voyage into exile.

"Measles!" Panov exclaimed, and shook his head at the wonder of it. "Isn't it odd how history pivots on small things?" Rudenko grew impatient for his old friend's lecture to wind down. Panov was ever drawn by ironies, and also given to prattling incessantly when he was anxious.

"To think, had it not been for that bit of bad luck, the tsar and tsarina and all their little tsarevitches would soon have been taking tea with their cousins in London. Ha!"

Rudenko grunted, examining his friend's intent profile: the flitting eyes, chin thrust forward over the steering wheel, which he clenched with both hands. We all learned to drive so late in life, he thought. The admiral closed his eyes. The drone of his old friend's voice became a nearly physical pleasure, lulling him into slumber.

Sometime later he awoke with a start as Panov eased the car into the long avenue running beside the frozen Neva.

Rudenko remained slouched in his sleeping position, his eyes almost level with the bonnet, watching varied tops of the palaces flanking the quays. Yawning, he sat up. They were approaching the Peter and Paul Fortress.

"That's where it all started," Panov declared. "Hanged him at nineteen—Lenin's older brother. Did they ever think what they were unleashing? Nothing like executing one's nearest and dearest to light a fuse, eh? Did you know General Giap's wife died under a French guillotine and her sister in a French prison in Indochina? Ho Chi Minh was in love with the sister." Panov had unearthed this particular irony of history while posted in Hanoi.

The antique cannon on the fortress parapet clacked and boomed, announcing the noon hour. Another thirty minutes, Rudenko thought. Panov, he realized, was now driving just to drive, aimlessly traversing the snow-covered streets by the embankments.

They rolled past the Naval Museum and the university, the sphinxes flanking the stairs that led down to the river's edge by the Academy of Arts, and crossed Nikolayevsky Bridge to the Admiralty, with its huge, narrow gold spire. How many evenings he had walked those painfully beautiful streets with Vasily when the boy was still a cadet.

Rudenko took off his military cap, wedged it between the windscreen and dashboard, and stared at the badge: a gold anchor on an enameled button, enveloped by gold laurels. Above it, the double-headed Russian eagle. Once the uniform had been like a grail to him, the subject of dreams and ambitions, the symbol of fulfillment. Today it felt like a burden.

Panov maneuvered the car along the canals and river segments, past birch and lime trees, and buildings centuries old. The sun was finally showing itself. The old Singer Sewing Machine building sped by, then a string of other cathedrals now being reclaimed by the faithful, including the former Museum of Atheism.

The massive gilded dome of St. Isaac's Cathedral was ablaze. A funny place, Rudenko remembered. From the cupola inside St. Isaacs, a pendulum had hung three hundred and twenty feet down, onto a blanket of sand. Its motion demonstrated the gyroscopic movement of the earth in the perfect elliptical patterns it etched into the sand. One spring afternoon he had taken Cadet Nemerov there and explained the principles of inertial navigation systems as used in modern submarines. Afterward they'd retired to the Hotel Astoria for coffee, and Vasily told him about his girl. The waitress took them for father and son. It was one of Rudenko's happiest memories.

Ahead, at the top of Nevsky Prospect, dwarfed by St. Isaac's behind it, was the Romanesque structure of the Admiralty fronting the River Neva.

"We have a few minutes, Georgi Mikhailovich," Panov said. "Perhaps we should speak." He eased the car to the side of the road and stopped. Rudenko turned to him. Panov sighed. "Whatever Chernavin wants from you, try to get out of it."

"What will he want?" Rudenko said.

"What he always wants," Panov said. "Control."

"But what exactly?"

Panov shook his jowls. "I don't know for certain. His superiors are squeezing our Tartar friend. The exalted ones expect their golden warrior to continue spinning new strategies to circumvent our woeful financial and technological inadequacies. They want gizmos that cost nothing and work miracles." He snorted. "For years they embraced his rocket schemes and advanced him over many others. And why not? He kept a good number of them from being called to account. Until recently. Now their eyes are vacant when he's mentioned, as if they weren't intimately involved with his rise and station. Soon they may be wagging their fingers to admonish those who were responsible for promoting the interests of this upstart. Audacity, they will say, is no substitute for moderation and loyalty. The genius will burn like a meteor and fall unnoticed and unsung."

"Maybe," Rudenko said.

Panov nodded, sighing. "Maybe not."

"What do you think of him?"

"Ach," Panov said, irritably. "I don't. I don't like to think about him. The man is smart, no doubt, but he has never been bloodied in a real battle. His innovations are pretty but not ultimately trustworthy. The real thing is not neat, as these paper fighters like to picture it, everything moving smoothly, the opposition deploying as anticipated. To them, fighting is not a goddamned shitty mess, as it was for us. It is precise application of overwhelming force to antiseptic tactical problems. Everything is contingencies. Bah!" Panov gave a dismissive wave.

The pale light angled through the windscreen, bleaching his face. "Our satellite detectors, they are good to a depth of one hundred feet and no more. The orbits of the satellites are discontinuous and entirely predictable. The other stuff, the fancy sound equipment, can't tell the difference between a torpedo being fired and a whale farting. Who knows if the Americans' toys are any better." Rudenko could hear the irritation in his old friend's voice. "Games. Silly games. Chernavin promotes his glib schemes to the Kremlin like a flesh peddler. Since they will never be really tested, he can postulate anything."

Panov hesitated. After a few moments, he spoke again.

"As your recent assignment demonstrated, his old schemes are coming back to haunt: the business of Strategic Forces hiding rocket submarines in fjords. He has more strategies. In my official capacity I do not know anything, but devices have been boasted about in my presence over the years." Panov turned to Rudenko. Rudenko said nothing, wondering how much more his old friend was willing to divulge.

"What do our submariners call the thin, weaker places in pack ice?" Panov said. "The places where the floes are translucent, they are so thin."

"Skylights," Rudenko said.

"Yes, that's it. Such weak ice areas are not predictable. Back then, a boat might or might not break through to launch. We did not have the capacity the Americans developed of blasting right through with their special rockets."

"Until our Akulas and Deltas," said Rudenko.

"Indeed. But before we had subs that could reliably punch through the ice, we had to rely on luck. And luck was not a policy our betters trusted. Chernavin proposed a refinement of his fjord scheme that would give us a completely reliable series of Arctic firing posts. His scheme involved the natural openings in the sea ice. Up in the Arctic polynyas appear in exact locations at exact times, even in the dead of winter. These holes and their locations were of great interest to Chernavin; he communicated that interest to our own Arctic Research Institute here in Leningrad. Conveniently enough, the openings were comprehensively mapped by the Canadians. Our naval genius devised the stratagem to position submarines in the waters beneath these openings and use them like open windows to shoot through, should the need ever arise. Mercifully, it never did—and never will, now. But they served his purpose at the time. The covering of the Arctic ice cloaked our missile boats from detection. And they were within easy range of valuable targets in the Western Hemisphere, much closer than the fjords of Norway."

Panov peered into the distance. "Absurdly simple again. Absurdly cheap. First the fjords, then polynya. Hell, it was masterful. The Americans spent millions on a submarine rocket that could blast its way up through the polar cap, and on satellite antimissile systems that never went anywhere. This man"—Panov snorted—"this man arrives at the same end result thanks to Mother Nature, without having to invent or produce much of anything."

Rudenko was shocked, and embarrassed, not to have known, even though he had never commanded nuclear missile forces. "How long did this go on? And why the undersea trawlers?"

Panov shrugged. "No idea. It all remains closely guarded, even from the rest of the naval service. And was, into the eighties, certainly." Panov looked over at his passenger for a moment, and back to the windshield. "Then came the great Soviet collapse. Still, Chernavin was already on his pedestal, launched, on the way. What did he care about a few pieces of left luggage? But recently something's gone wrong. Something to do with the research place in the Arctic. *Vladivostok* was bringing a civilian back from there to report to him."

"Civilian? The woman?"

Panov nodded. He had turned off the engine and it was growing chilly in the car.

Rudenko pushed his hands deep into his coat pockets. "What happened?"

"Who knows? Some emergency. Ninety-four Russian sailors

are dead, she is dead, the sub is lost, and Chernavin is unsure of everything." He slapped his thigh. "It shouldn't even matter. Firing positions be damned. We can hardly feed the sailors we have—or house their dependents or pay their paltry salaries augmented with food chits. We are lucky to get any boats out at all, much less attack anyone. Chernavin's clever schemes are history, a footnote. There's only trouble. It needs to be cleaned up, the trash collected."

"Have they discovered how the sailors died?" Rudenko said. "The ship's radiation levels were normal."

Panov turned the key in the ignition. "They rushed the body you brought back to the Institute of Microbiology and Virology. Carved it up instantly and tested it every way conceivable. Nothing. They flew it to the biological weapons facility at Sergiev Posad. More nothing. They know nothing." Panov was flushed. "They flew experts in from Koltsova to advise. They had no answer either. Meanwhile the poor divers who retrieved the corpse are still rotting in quarantine somewhere. The doctors are terrified."

"Yevgeny Aleksandrovich, what is it you want to say to me?"

Panov stared across the water. "Chernavin is trying to contain this little disaster of his. He's involving as few people outside his reach as possible. And stupidly refusing help from other sections, even though the situation is out of hand." He turned back to Rudenko. "Don't agree to anything you don't have to. Stay out of this mess. Chernavin kept it all from us for years. Let him clean his own barn. Don't get involved."

Rudenko pushed up the sleeve of his coat and checked his watch. "I will try," he said.

A three-car tram crossed the intersection, the rails screeching. Rudenko smelled ozone.

"Tell me one thing, Georgi Mikhailovich," Panov said. "The corpses. Their faces. Was it as bad as they say?"

Rudenko nodded grimly. "Yes. The whites of eyes floating out in strands. Bodies horribly twisted. No one slept all the way back. I will spare you the photographs."

Panov whistled through clenched teeth as he glanced in his side-view mirror and pulled out into the traffic, almost running over a giant dog and his New Russian master, both bedecked in black Italian leather. *Asshole,* mouthed the man.

"Fuck your mother," Panov cursed under his breath.

# 21

"Sabotage." Chernavin said it in a somewhat distracted tone, and stared out of the high windows in his office as though studying the vehicular traffic along the Neva.

Behind him, against the incline of the immense stone embankment on the far side of the river, Rudenko could see a row of semi-reclining citizens sunning themselves. Beneath their long winter coats, they had stripped down to their shoes and undergarments. They held their overcoats open to the pale light like exhibitionists.

*Sabotage*. Chernavin had returned to his desk and to his theme. "A distressing but inescapable conclusion, given the evidence *Rus* brought back. Especially the corpse."

"Is the naval bureau planning a commemorative ceremony?"

"No. I think not. Security precludes it at this time," he said, leaving Rudenko to surmise the unspoken: there would never be a memorial for *Vladivostok*, or even an announcement of her loss. She would simply be decommissioned. No doubt individual notices were even now being quietly delivered to next of kin, the language dry but conciliatory, and vague as to the circumstances that had claimed son, brother, husband, father. "Regrettable . . . lost at sea."

Rudenko nodded. How little this deskbound mariner understood of servicemen's lives or their families' grief. Directly or indirectly, Chernavin had killed *Vladivostok*'s crew.

Chernavin held his glasses to his nose to scan the report lying open on his desk. With studied detachment, he highlighted its contents.

"The chief of pathology of the IMV reports that in the view of her department the cadaver submitted to their examination had succumbed to a lethal neurotoxin, most probably in gaseous form. The gaseous substance—of unknown nature—lowered the level of cholinesterase, a chemical in red blood cells that controls muscular action. The red blood cells were few and highly distorted. Whatever the substance, it is efficient and caustic, and extremely destructive of bronchial and ocular tissues." He tossed the paper onto his desk. "Not pretty."

"No," Rudenko said, reaching into his breast pocket for the photo, which he placed on top of the dossier. "As this will bear witness."

Not a flicker of discomfort marred Chernavin's demeanor as he examined the image. "Where was this taken?" he said.

"In the captain's cabin."

"I see."

"One wonders about the woman's condition."

"Yes," Chernavin said, "as well one might."

"I hope you will not disapprove of my having carried this to you personally, but I thought it best kept close."

"Not at all, admiral. In fact, I commend you for performing your duties so well, and so discreetly. Your men acquitted themselves in a most responsible and selfless manner, for which you must be given appropriate credit." He smiled. "You should know, too, that your name has come up as a candidate for the Naval Committee. Congratulations."

"Thank you, sir. I trust my recommendations of citations for various members of the *Rus* crew will be favorably received."

"Without saying."

Chernavin abandoned his desk and led the admiral to a settee by the fireplace. He wondered aloud if the admiral would consider another undertaking. Rudenko kept silent, as if, unanswered, the question would remain abstract. He hoped some excuse would occur to him, but the man simply pressed forward, taking his silence for a kind of assent.

"Time is of the essence. We need a reliable man to backtrack the *Vladivostok* and safeguard the well-being of the other Russian nationals at the station from which the woman was transported. If necessary, to evacuate them, winter or no."

A knock at the door announced a tall blond man in an elegant dark suit. The commander rose and introduced Pyotr Stepanovich Koyt, of the State Research Center of Virology and Biotechnology, once the Siberian center for biological weapons, and rumored to be active again. A lab fatality had been widely reported: an accidental exposure to Ebola that no one was even aware they had. The man took the seat beside Rudenko. Quite casually Chernavin asked Koyt to look at the photo Rudenko had brought. The man gave it a cursory glance. He adjusted his French cuffs and passed it back.

"It is our Dr. Tarakanova. She does not look well."

Koyt's features were a mixture of dark and light: the black eyes of a Russian father, the pale hair of a Scandinavian mother, Rudenko guessed. There was no mistaking his true calling. He was the requisite type: suave and well traveled.

"We understand," Chernavin said, "that three other members of the Canadian scientific collegium died similarly. A Russian among them." He glanced at Koyt, who supplied the name.

"Minskov."

"No satisfactory explanation for these fatalities has been forthcoming from Ottawa. It is in the vital interests of the nation that you confirm the safety of our citizens at the Arctic installation."

Chernavin's sudden patriotic fervor embarrassed Rudenko. It was a sham display for Koyt's benefit. Koyt, however, only half listened while toying with the wooden egret on the low table beside his chair, gold cuff links flashing. Just waiting for the pro forma presentation to end, Rudenko thought. He already knows all this. Chernavin's briefing was only for show.

"No doubt you are eager to redeem the recent sacrifice of your comrades, Admiral," Chernavin said.

"No doubt," Koyt echoed, thrumming the arm of his chair. "Such a waste."

"As an expert in some medical areas," Chernavin said, "Koyt here will accompany you. He can liaise with whatever Canadian agencies are at work at the station. What do you say, Admiral?"

Rudenko noted the knitted brow of his superior and wondered. "If there is a green flag in this," he said, referring to the old maritime ensign of the KGB, "then I must know it. Now." He looked to Koyt. "And it must be clear that such a pennant shall fly below the flag of the fleet commander."

Chernavin was visibly taken aback by Rudenko's directness and fumbled for a moment, undoubtedly considering whether to address the insolence and the insinuation. Koyt interrupted.

"Admiral," Koyt said, lighting a cigarette. "There is no question"—the smoke streamed out as he spoke—"of your authority in this matter. The Ministry of Defense bestows your orders and your authority. My orders from the Center are to protect our interests and our people at Trudeau, and find out what happened. You have only to take me there and bring us all safely back when I am done."

"There!" Admiral of the Fleet Chernavin smiled benevolently at Fleet Admiral Rudenko and rose to conclude the meeting. "You see? It's settled."

# 22

News of Hanley's racewalk from the kitchen to the lab had traveled fast. Now everyone at the station wanted an update on the mice. Whenever she broke for a meal, Hanley could barely get a bite to her lips before someone stopped by her table, nominally to wish her well, but desperate to hear something definitive and reassuring.

She had nothing to tell them. She and her staff monitored the mice round the clock, periodically examining each mouse for signs of disease, but in spite of the lumps under their fur where the whelk tissue had been injected, the mice continued to behave normally: sniffing, burrowing, eating, scratching, sleeping. Finding it difficult to sleep herself, Hanley took the overnight shifts, glad to be able to give her volunteer staff a break. She sat huddled in her extra-large L.A. Morgue sleep shirt (OUR DAY BEGINS WHEN YOURS ENDS), chain-smoking and staring at the mice for hours at a time, almost willing them to die. At first, their every twitch had seemed like the beginning of a spasm, but after four days, the mice injected with whelk tissue remained infuriatingly healthy. "Goddamn it!" Hanley exploded. "No way our toxin could take this long. Scratch the whelks. Kiyomi, how many chemicals from the site do you and Uli have left to test?"

"Almost finished. We are finding nothing."

Hanley asked Ishi to summon the Center's senior staff for an online brainstorming session.

Her colleagues met around a table on the patio in the California sunshine: Lester Munson; Cybil Weingart next to him, smoking; Petterson in nearly opaque sunglasses and white pants; Bernard Piker with his meerschaum pipe, and bow-tied Henry Ruff, sitting cross-legged on an ottoman like a caliph, shading his eyes with one hand. Hanley was in attendance via videocam, on a portable monitor. A towel tented over the screen cut the glare. An assistant had laden the table with binders of materials about the casualties at Trudeau.

"Everyone here?" Munson said. "Right. Jessie, can you hear us?"

"*Loud and clear, Chief.*"

"Folks, Dr. Hanley has been unable to find evidence of an inorganic chemical gaseous agent. No evidence of noxious gases. No pollutant. No poison. At this point, she thinks the agent is probably organic, and she intends to shift the emphasis of her investigation. Her only concrete lead in that department has come up negative, so we need some other avenues to explore." He turned to his assistant at the whiteboard. The assistant wrote *Bugs* in red on the whiteboard, denoting the possible agents, then *Vectors* for the possible carriers. Munson faced the others. "Anyone with a useful observation to make here, jump right in. Speak."

"Plague's out," said Cybil, brushing ash from her blouse. "Takes too damn long. They would have known they were sick, called for help. Even with simultaneous exposure, plague would have incubated at different rates in three different people."

"Let's broaden our thinking," said Ishikawa. "A new form of coronavirus? Faster than SARS? That baby can mutate fast, but it's a tortoise compared to this bunny. This didn't take days to develop. Hours at best."

Cybil said, "Ishi's got a point. If it's a microorganism, it's virulent as hell. Breeds like a bioreactor." Cybil blew a plume of smoke at the screen. "Here's another big difference. Most of the microbe villains we're used to basically drown their victims. Ebola, Legionnaire's." She took a drag. "They bleed out, drown in their own fluids. These people's lungs turned to gravel."

"Fibers," Ishikawa corrected.

"Okay," said Munson. "Let's ponder lungs for a minute."

"Actually," said Petterson, "mycoplasma comes to mind. Hasn't got a cell wall, hides between the cells, hardly looks like an organism at all—more like a fiber, in fact. And a mycoplasma outbreak looks like a snowstorm on X-ray, like this thing."

"Yep," said Bernard Piker, cleaning his glasses on his tie. "It's been implicated in all sorts of odd conditions—chronic fatigue, Gulf War syndrome. It can certainly cause acute respiratory distress. It's rarely quick, though. Certainly not taking down three out of three in one exposure. Unless this is some hyped-up variety we haven't seen before."

"Okay, so mycoplasma's a possible." Munson glanced around. "Any more thoughts about lungs?"

Hanley said, "*What about one of the Actinomycetales, like nocardia? Could they have been near contaminated soil and inhaled it?*"

"Possible," Ishikawa said. "In a bad case of nocardiosis you'd have coma, seizures, permanent brain damage. The corpses *were* contorted, seemingly by seizures. So maybe, yes."

Ruff was making a disparaging face. "That's all very well, but the lung damage in nocardiosis is progressive, not instantaneous. Not fatal unless you're immunocompromised. These folks were healthy. Besides, is there any soil up there that's not frozen? Where would they have encountered the stuff?"

Despite Ruff's counterarguments, Munson signaled his assistant to add *Actinomycetales* to the bug column.

Ruff swept off his glasses for effect and gestured with them toward the screen as he spoke: "This agent was fiendishly quick in killing three people. How could it *possibly* be a microorganism?"

"*Dr. Ruff,*" Hanley said on screen, "*bacteria produce a new generation in twenty minutes, viruses even faster, and they replicate exponentially. That seems quick enough to me. The 1918 flu killed in forty-eight hours, so why couldn't this bug kill in four? Just because we haven't clocked any bug that fast doesn't mean there isn't one out there. May I remind you that we have identified less than two percent of the planet's microbes?*"

Ruff scowled. "Then you're suggesting the three cases are

sentinels in—what—an outbreak of a new plague? That a never-before-identified microbe killed them?" He shook his head. "It seems a bit grandiose. I simply can't concur with your speculation. It's just not logical."

"*Henry,*" she said, "*the clock is running on me. I've got two hundred people here essentially quarantined until the first week in March. Then they're going to want out. Some want out already. They're not without influence. It's going to get noisy after that. We have to find it before then and we don't have much time. If it is microbial, we've also got to worry about the Russian woman who left. If she's a carrier, we have no idea where she may have carried it to. God forbid it decides to put in a second appearance halfway around the world: somewhere populated.*"

"I still don't—"

"*Look,*" said Hanley, "*I agree. Nothing but poison or a weapon kills three out of three. But if by some miracle it is a microbe, it's a monster.*"

Ruff drew himself up. "Dr. Hanley—"

"*Henry, I'm invoking a SWAG.*"

"Swag?"

"*Yeah. A Scientific Wild-Ass Guess. I'm not ruling out poisons and inorganics. But it's time to go after biological bugs too. I need to find where this thing vectored in, seal it off from Trudeau, and keep it from traveling.*"

Petterson slipped off his loafers and propped his bare feet on the back of a chair. "I'm with Jessie. I don't think it's a variation on an old theme. This could well be right out of the box—something new we haven't run into before."

Ruff backhanded a dismissive motion toward the monitor. "What you're proposing is pretty extreme—to go after an alleged Level-four bug with barely Level-two equipment and safeties."

"*I haven't much choice,*" she said, "*unless you want to drop by with an inflatable Level-four facility.*"

"Well," Munson said, "Consider the bright side, Jess. If it *is* a new bug, with a mystery vector, nab it and you get to name it. You'll be famous."

"If they let you publish anything about this," Petterson muttered, "except maybe name it after you. Posthumously."

"Okay, folks." Munson raised his palms. "Jessie said the magic word: *weapon*. With something this potent, we have to consider a biological that's been weaponized. Cybil, you're the WMD expert. Can you run down the bioweapons hit parade?"

"Sure. Everybody's got a different top-ten list of designer bugs. Everyone agrees anthrax is number one, of course. Popular because it's hardy. Lots of others die in the sunlight. Anthrax spores live on and on in all kinds of environments. In some ways, this almost looks like anthrax. Pulmonary anthrax is rare outside industrial settings, so if these scientists had it, someone exposed them to it. And if it is anthrax, it's a juiced-up variety that works faster than anything nature invented. As soon as the techs at Trudeau get those cultures under way, we'll know soon enough. But, I tell ya, these lung X-rays we've got here just don't do it for me," Cybil said. "I've never seen an anthrax X-ray without extremely enlarged mediastinal lymph nodes. That's the classic sign." She tapped the binder of materials on the victims. "It's not here."

"Okay," said Munson, rapping on the patio table. "So what else?"

"I hate to say this"—she blew smoke at the sky—"the likeliest suspects are standards in bioweapon arsenals: botulinum and tetanus. They both can live in extreme environments, and they've both got some pretty devastating neurologic effects. Granted, they've got some symptoms we're not seeing here—vomiting, involuntary defecation—but I wonder if we're not looking at a relative."

"Natural relative or manufactured?" asked Piker.

"Grim question," said Cybil. "Unnaturally inspired pathogen? I don't know." She ran her fingers through her gray hair. "Viruses are damn hard to cultivate and keep alive outside a host. Hard to control. Bacteria and fungi are cheap and easy. Cook up a slurry for them to live on and you've got yourself a toxin factory. You don't have to calculate your intended victim's body weight or anything. The pathogens just multiply inside the host until they hit the fatal dose level. Then boom. You don't need much equipment or even a high school diploma. If you can brew beer, you can brew bioweapons." She paused to light a cigarette with the stub of another.

"Excuse me," interrupted Ruff, "but don't bioterrorists aim for bigger targets? Cities, tribes, transportation systems, national institutions, international symbols? Three Arctic scientists at a field site hardly seem enough of a prize. And how on earth would terrorists get there?"

"Actually," said Cybil, in her monotone, "bioterrorists like out-of-town tryouts before they take the show downtown. They want to be sure in advance that what they've got works. Nothing better than some lonely spot. In the trade they call it a demonstration attack. In his own excessive way, that's part of what Saddam was doing gassing the Kurds."

Hanley said, "*If this is a demonstration attack, I don't want to be around for the real thing.*"

"Henry has a good point," said Munson. "How would terrorists have gotten up there?"

Cybil shrugged. "I suppose they'd have to be there from the get-go."

"How likely is that?"

On screen, Hanley locked her hands behind her head, and grinned mischievously. "*Yeah, Cyb. You think Santa's been up here subcontracting his workshop in the off-season to terrorist elves?*"

Cybil closed one eye against the smoke of her cigarette. "The research station's got scientists from how many countries? Why couldn't one of them be the wrong sort of scientist? Or do we think we're *all* holy?"

Munson turned to his assistant at the board and said, "Mad scientist," which the assistant dutifully wrote in marker on the white board, adding *Religious zealot*?

"*Cybil, can you put together a list of the labs you think are even close to genetically engineering something that would do this? Maybe one of them has somebody up here on a sabbatical. Any chance Tarakanova was fooling around in a lab here, playing Supreme Force of the Universe?*"

"The odds are just as good," Petterson said, "that it's naturally occurring and has been there all the time, quietly waiting for a host."

Cybil picked up the autopsy picture of Annie Bascomb. "Looks like patience paid off."

"*Okay,*" said Hanley, "*I've got to set up a hot lab and start combing Trudeau for possible hosts, preferably ones that haven't had human contact in the past. I think most of the rare species are in— hang on—*" she looked through her notes, "*Dr. Skudra's lab.*"

"Jess," Cybil said to the screen. "You be careful."

"Gentlemen, gentle ladies, thank you," said Munson. "I think we've got a lot of ideas to pursue. We're adjourned."

Ishi took the monitor off line; the meeting broke up. Back inside, Munson gestured Cybil into his office and motioned for her to close the door. He plopped down in his chair and swiveled nervously back and forth. Cybil shaded her eyes against the light streaming in and turned the venetian blinds to diffuse the light.

"What do you think?" Munson said. He seemed worried.

"I think what you think. If it's biological and that efficient, she's in trouble. They all are."

"Yeah." Munson nodded repeatedly. "And so are the rest of us if it gets out of there. Two million people a day cross borders. All you need is one person carrying it out."

T he sign over the inner door proclaimed HOT LAB—NO UNAU-
THORIZED ENTRANCE. ONLY LAB SUITS BEYOND THIS POINT.
BIOSAFETY LEVEL 3. Nimit rigged a portable shower tent to
douse entrants with bleach on the way in and out, then rinse them
off with water. Hanley and her staff stripped to their underwear, put
on scrubs and surgical gloves, got into their full biohazard suits,
taped shut a second pair of outer gloves, strapped on their portable
oxygen supplies and tested airflow. They pressed shut the seals on
the suits and, one by one, stepped under the sterilizing shower,
doused themselves, rinsed off with water, and entered the lab beyond the second door. A Level-4 facility wasn't possible; this "baby
hot lab" would have to do.

Equipment was limited. Much of it Nimit cadged from other
labs at Trudeau, supplemented by the tools and gear Hanley had
brought with her. They had an autoclave, sterile dishes, culture
nutrients, reagents, beakers, slides, a borrowed centrifuge, a spec-
troscope, two Zeiss microscopes with video camera ports and flat-
screen monitors, four shockproof crates of fertilized hens' eggs
brought in on the Commode, and human O cells in a growth
medium on which viral cultures could be coaxed into the open.
Hanley had managed to augment her small supply of rabbit blood
with a cache volunteered by the cryogenics lab. Though the setup
wasn't ideal, she had worked in worse circumstances.

The pair of youngsters, Uli Hecht and the severely beautiful

Kiyomi Taku, were diligent workers, sampling and examining tissue from each organ and recording their findings. Uli recorded specimens on swabs from the mouths, lungs, and intestines that Kiyomi had started to colonize in flasks of monkey kidney cells.

"Keep checking those," Hanley instructed him. "If clear zones form, we'll know a virus is starting to kill the kidney cells. Unfortunately for us, this killer bug proceeded too fast for antibodies to form, so that search route's closed. But we've still got plenty of trails to follow. Kiyomi, Uli, let's get the bloodwork started. Ideally we'd have blood from all three victims, but the Russians have put Minskov off limits, so we're restricted to two. Once Kossuth's been autopsied, we should run all these tests on him too, even though he wasn't symptomatic, just to cover all the bases.

"Okay, guys, you want to start by adding blood samples from the victims to the rabbit blood. If the virus is hiding in the specimen, its protein coating will cling to the rabbit blood cells. After a while you'll see it. They'll clump together and settle to the bottom of the vial. Only Kiyomi touches anything: she's used to lab procedures. Uli, I want you to record every step. Kiyomi will double-check the log daily."

Kiyomi gave a nod.

"While you work on the autopsy specimens, I'm going to start collecting specimens from around Trudeau so we can run tests on them."

"What will you be looking for?" said Kiyomi.

"Well, for starters, anything that has the same effect on blood in a test tube that our bug had on blood in a living body." She pointed to the blood-sample vials on the counter. Stripped of its red blood cells and hemoglobin, the blood was barely pink.

Hanley looked into their faces. "You've all got to be careful. We have no idea where this thing may be hiding. If you break, bump open, crack, or otherwise compromise a specimen dish that's being tested"—she pointed to a bright red container standing just away from the worktable about midway—"get it into the dunk bin fast. It's full of sterilizing agents."

Her staff nodded earnestly.

"And yell for me or Dee. One of us will always be here. Okay, Kiyomi will label everything and number each egg's shell. I want you to take the tissue specimens from the autopsies and inject them into the chicken eggs."

"To culture for virus," Uli said.

"No," Kiyomi said. "Bacteria may be cultured. Virus cannot. Virus will only transfer—incubate. It wants live tissue."

"Yours preferably," Hanley added. "So stay out of its way. Remember, viruses can't really die. They're not alive; they can't reproduce unless they have living cells to hijack and turn into virus factories. But toss the pieces of a virus in a test tube with living cells and it recombines, self-assembles, resurrects."

Uli seemed puzzled. "Are microorganisms that 'smart'?" Hanley was instantly reminded of Joey's disarming queries.

"They seem to be. In a matter of months, SARS went from infecting three percent of the people who came into contact with it to seventy percent. It takes us sixteen, seventeen years to develop an antibiotic. Bacteria work up defenses against it in minutes. Bacteria and viruses will defend themselves by changing their chemical composition so as not to be identified and targeted."

"How?"

"They'll scrounge DNA from cell debris and swap genetic materials with other microorganisms to disguise themselves and acquire traits they might need against hostile antibiotics or extreme temperatures, acids, light, whatever."

"Clever beasts," Uli said.

"Seriously . . ." Hanley eyed them. "Be careful. If you have a lab accident with a bacillus, we have some defense to offer you—antibiotics." She held up a large syrette. "But antibiotics don't work on viruses. Our three victims appear to be the first humans to contract this new bug. So we have no immunity. We're in the same position as the Inuit and Indians were when they came into contact for the first time with European diseases—and as Europeans were with native illnesses at first contact."

"Defenseless," Uli said.

Hanley nodded. "Pretty much. Smallpox burned through the

New World; syphilis burned through the old. Our bug would love to take on the planet, so we must be careful."

Kiyomi said, "You do not think the Russian submarine brought it? Or that we ourselves brought it to the Arctic?"

"We don't know yet," Hanley said. "So far, however, it doesn't behave like anything we've seen in other parts of the world. Most likely, we came to it and not the other way around. The climate here is changing. The permafrost melts more than normal in the light months, likely freeing up a lot of nourishing organic matter, spurring reproduction of a lot of microorganisms and carriers. Humans disturb it, it strikes. That's why I'll be starting with organisms that you lot at Trudeau have been the first to study."

"How will we know if we find it?" Uli said.

"If the bug is bacterial, we'll be able to see the colony in the growth medium in the petri dishes. It will look like mold, like mildew. Like pressed flowers."

"And if it's a virus?"

"It'll look like a bright mosaic. Don't worry. It's pretty dramatic. It will fluoresce. You won't miss it."

"If they had personalities," Uli said, "how would you describe them?"

Hanley had to laugh. It could have been Joey asking. "Bacteria are like . . . a rock and roll band, always improvising. A virus, more like a classical organist."

"Because it mimics other instruments."

"Exactly. Kiyomi?"

Kiyomi bowed respectfully to Hanley and addressed Uli. "I will handle actual bodily specimens. Dr. Hanley will prepare growth media and cell tissues. Uli, please make a chart for each of the deceased. Note every specimen, every test. We have mucous, spinal fluid, stools, liver tissues, spleen muscle, lung, pancreas, cervix, and so on. Many to prepare, but we must still work with care. Diligent record keeping is essential for success."

Hanley looked at them in turn. "If you have an accident in the hot lab while you're suited up, do not leave the dome. Hit any of the red buttons you see all around the lab. Keep the lab door closed.

Shower yourself down, suit and all. Stay put. Stay in the suit. Don't go farther than the outer lab. You don't want to be carrying it into the rest of the station."

"*Wieviel?*" Uli said. "Ah . . . how long do we have if we have a lab accident and it is the organism? If we are infected?"

Hanley stood quietly for a moment. "To live, you mean? Four hours, I think. You'd have four hours."

# 24

D r. Cecil Skudra was a small man with a plain face and a blazing gold incisor. He had an absent air about him, at once focused and distracted. While Hanley plied him with questions about the unusual life forms in his charge, he stared at the swarm of insects buzzing silently in a large glass box. Insect life was Dr. Skudra's life, as far as Hanley could make out. He was a thoughtful sociobiologist from Riga, quietly studying how societies evolved to fit in with their environments, and was silent until you raised the subject of the biological basis for social action in Arctic mosquitoes, whereupon he could hold forth for hours.

"Female mosquitoes," the doctor was saying, "are drawn to certain bands of temperature and humidity. They're especially attracted to carbon dioxide. Hence, anything exhaling it will drive them into rapturous frenzy. That's why they have a preference for our heads, you see." He glanced sideways at his visitor and continued. "Hemoglobin and some amino acids draw them as well. Like those in perspiration. They want your protein for their babies."

"Blood-crazed mosquitoes?" Hanley said.

The doctor nodded, absently; he was thinking about something else. "The Arctic mosquito is exceptionally avid in this regard. She will pounce on warm-blooded animals with ferocity and remove four times her body weight. Caribou have been known to lose a quart of blood a day to them. An undefended individual would be emptied of blood in a few hours," Skudra said. "Native tribes sometimes executed a man in this manner. There are accounts, as well, of large animals and people being driven completely mad by them. Fascinating creatures."

Hanley's eyes never left the swarm. "Indeed," she said. "But how do these insects"—she pointed to a female that had landed on the glass—"how do they manage to survive in this climate?"

"Their eggs can endure subfreezing temperatures quite easily. An evolutionary adaptation. Also, it doesn't hurt that they are mindlessly ruthless. They will eat anything to survive—detritus, algae, bacteria. Even each other."

"Their own kind?" Hanley said, impressed.

"Exactly, exactly," Skudra said proudly. "The Arctic variety will eat its siblings. Scarcity of prey is a strong factor here. They are like army ants that way: they attack en masse."

"Have you ever known any to appear in winter?" Hanley said.

"Under laboratory conditions? Of course. In nature? Never."

"Any other insect colonies in the facility?"

"Yellow jackets."

"Wasps?" she said in a surprised voice.

"Oh, yes." Skudra nodded vigorously. "A study in survival," he said, his voice breathy. "The workers and drones all perish, of course, every thirty days or so. Only the queen goes on. Come winter, the workers aren't renewed and the queen seeks shelter. It can be minus forty outside, and yet it never falls below fifteen degrees in the queen's chamber. Also, the queen somehow lowers her own body temperature below freezing. Yet ice crystals do not form in her cells—unlike what happened to poor Alex. She is in a kind of suspended animation: mummified, yet alive. If we can figure out the processes . . . The study is being conducted in conjunction with McGill University. Another experiment is examining the cellular antifreeze that fish and beetles seem to manufacture. Fascinating data."

"I can see that," Hanley said. "Are there ticks up here, in summer?"

"Yes, myriad. Do you suspect a tick-borne disease?"

"I have to consider insect carriers," Hanley said. "Especially in conjunction with birds. Some insect-borne agents, like equine piroplasmosis, do go after red blood cells, but only in horses and mules."

"Not people?"

"Not so far. Still, diseases behave differently in different parts of the world, and differently in different species. I may be looking for something that behaves differently here than anywhere else in the world."

Skudra was pensive. "I am not envious of your task, madam."

"Me either," said Hanley. "I need a sample of everything you've got that lives in—or near—the polynya." She consulted her list. "Sea lice, any birds trapped within the last year, crustaceans. Particularly any species unknown outside the Arctic."

"We've got some very unusual toadstools. One fires its spore cap like a cannon. Another snares microscopic worms."

"Any of them psychedelics? I could use some of those right about now."


Skudra steered Hanley to an overheated lab from which emanated an overpowering sulfurous stench. Inside it was dark as night and warm. She reached out timidly in front of her, like a blind person. Skudra guided her by the elbow. "Put the goggles on. There's no light in here. We try to recreate the habitats familiar to our guests. They are creatures who live without light."

Hanley put on the night-vision goggles. A cylindrical tank glowed with hazy green water so hot it bubbled. Hanley peered in at long amorphous shapes that wriggled like snakes.

"Those are mad ugly, as my son would say. And mad smelly."

"Aren't they just," Skudra said fondly. "Sea worms. First discovered in 1977. These were found in hydrothermal springs in the Pacific. Hence the apparatus you see here. They require a high temperature, of course."

The sight of a worm slithering past in an endless loop distracted Hanley. "How big would these worms be if you laid them out?"

"Four to five feet," Skudra said casually, apparently oblivious to the pervasive smell. "Careful. The water's blazing hot."

Hanley sneezed. "I've never seen anything like them." She held her nose.

"Not surprising," Skudra said "They are a different family of animal, an entirely other order of life, these worms. The bacteria within them obtain energy not from oxygen but from sulfurous compounds that are poisonous to most organisms, but not to them or their hosts. This worm incorporates the sulfur directly into its muscles. An incredible creature. Metabolizes sulfide. I mean, sulfide is many times more deadly than cyanide. Universally toxic, yet these fellows thrive on it."

"That's a handy skill," Hanley said, wiping her nose. "It's a wonder they don't perish from the smell alone."

"Yes. They're quite new to us, but actually they're very ancient. They're soft bodied, so they've left no fossil traces, other than tracks in some of the oldest sedimentary samples."

"What are you doing with these hot environment creatures here in the Arctic?"

"Oh, these are local."

Hanley looked up sharply. "Local?"

"Most certainly. They're right out of an underwater volcano on the Gakkel Ridge. A test rig brought up these giant worms from three miles down in the Arctic Ocean." Skudra surveyed the specimens with evident pride. "This is life not driven by sunlight, but by thermal energy."

She hunched forward, hands on knees, to get a closer view. "They're very odd."

"Most of what endures beneath the ice is," he said, sounding almost worshipful.

"You really love it here," Hanley said.

"Yes. This is a wondrous place Mackenzie conceived. We sit on the edge of creation. To study our planet from this vantage point is truly special. Amazing no one thought of it sooner. It would be a pity if this calamity closed the station. Well . . . I'll take whatever tissue sample you need of the worms."

"My God." Hanley was startled by an apparition in another tank, like a disembodied arm at a séance. Perfectly white. But it wasn't an amputated limb, she realized, examining it more closely.

Skudra saw what had caught her attention.

"Ah," he said. "A rare appearance."

"What is it?"

"Beautiful, isn't he? A saltwater fish, Doctor, that lives at great depths. Far down, without light, in seawater that is below the freezing point yet liquid."

"I couldn't have even imagined such a creature."

"No," Skudra agreed. "It's unique. Only a handful of us have ever been privileged to see it. Another kind of organism entirely. Produces its own defense against freezing, which we are studying."

"How can it be so . . . white?"

"Its blood is white," Skudra said, pushing his goggles up. "A bit like your victims'."

# 25

Hanley and Dee began logging in the organisms and tissue samples Skudra had sent over; her team finally broke for dinner around eight.

"God, what a menagerie. I think I need to lie down," Hanley said, and retreated to her quarters. Yet when Dee came in an hour later with more test results, Hanley was up and on the laptop, networked with L.A. Ishikawa came up online with her.

"*Hey, Jess,*" he said, "*I've been on the database at Scripps, trying to make sense of the scientists' notes from the work site. Everything's straightforward, except for that one odd note—Ignis fatuus—scrawled in Ogata's log. I ran it through. Check out what I got.*"

Glowing lines scrolled up the screen, depositing information on the blue field in a spray of electrons.

" 'Will o' the wisp,' " Hanley read aloud. " 'The Will who bears the wispy fire/To trail the swains among the mire.' What the hell is that, Ishi? *'Ignis fatuus?'*"

"*Swamp gas, apparently.*"

"Swamp gas? F-ing swamp gas, out on the Arctic pack ice? You think they were hallucinating before they died? Damn. We need someone who saw what happened out there. Where is Miss Lidiya?"

"*Munson's doing the diplomatic channels thing through D.C., trying to chase her down, but he hasn't been able to get a straight answer out of the Russians. The sub's not on anybody's radar screen, so to speak.*"

"What's up?" Hanley turned to Dee.

Dee helped herself to Hanley's burning cigarette and took a long drag. "We found butyric acid," Dee read, smoke punctuating her words.

Hanley looked up. "What part of the body?"

"Spine."

"Yeah, okay. It's normal to find it in the cerebrospinal fluid that cushions the spinal cord and the brain. Let's see." She took Kiyomi's meticulous chart from Dee.

"This level's well over normal. Ishi, can you run these numbers? What do you make of them?"

*"Some diseases elevate the butyric levels,"* he said. *"Tetanus for one. I should check with Cybil on that."* Ishikawa was in shirt-sleeves. She could see sunlight streaming through the window behind him.

"Yeah." Hanley took the next report from Dee and scanned the data. "Please. Tell her we've got abnormal levels with no sign of what might have caused them."

*"I'll get right on it,"* Ishikawa said, leaning in, his face taking up most of the small video box in the corner of her screen. *"What else?"*

"Damned if I know," Hanley said. "That's it from me."

They signed off. Dee went to her quarters to rest. Hanley looked at her notes and puzzled over the swamp gas. Was the Arctic desert prone to mirages, like the deserts of California? She tried to remember what caused them—wasn't it heat? So maybe one or more of them was hallucinating. She went to find Ned Gibson, the staff psychologist, to run it past him.

A note taped to Gibson's door said that if anyone needed him, they could find him at Mackenzie's Folly. Hands in pockets, shoulders slumped, she meandered past the health complex, its glass-backed squash court—empty and dark—the eggshell-white aerobics area, the teal weight room, past black exercise machines sitting idle, and finally found herself in the oval of the pool atrium. It smelled of the sea.

A woman was lying faceup on one of the hardwood benches,

naked. Hanley recognized her: Dr. Kruger, the German surgeon whose autopsies she had been studying on discs. Like most of the Europeans, she seemed not to have the slightest qualm about appearing nude in front of strangers, male or female.

Maybe I wouldn't either, Hanley thought, if I looked like that.

Ingrid Kruger was perfectly proportioned. Her evenly tanned skin shone over smooth muscles. Downy hair glistened across her mons. Only the soles of her feet and the palms of her hands were white, and the faint rings around her eyes where she had protected herself against ultraviolet light.

Dr. Kruger opened her eyes but remained supine on the hard bench alongside the pool. She shielded her face from the light overhead and stared up at Hanley. The straight brown hair in a single braid and aquiline nose framed startling eyes that blurted everything the rest of her face wouldn't even intimate. An odd countenance as faces went.

"If you are uncomfortable," she said, with the slightest German accent, "you will avert away, yes?"

Hanley smiled wanly. "Sorry. I didn't mean to intrude." She stepped back and averted her eyes. Kruger rose in a fluid motion and launched herself easily out over the water, her body flashing its reflection across the surface just as she shattered it, knifing in. Wound tight, Hanley thought.

A male swimmer, equally naked, was negotiating the turn in the second lane. With an expert kick, he cleared the far wall and shot back toward her underwater. The man broke the surface just in front of Hanley.

"Dr. Hanley," he said, hailing her. He lifted himself out, streaming water, and picked up a towel. He held out his free hand in greeting. Hanley hesitated for a moment. She couldn't remember ever shaking hands with a naked man before. The hand was warm and wet.

"Ned Gibson," he said. "Oh, sorry," and offered a corner of the towel for her to dry her hand, exposing himself again.

"No, no," Hanley said, "It's . . . uh." She wiped her hand on her pants. "Pleasure to meet you."

Ingrid Kruger began a speedy backstroke, the water streaming along the bared shapes of her breasts and pelvis, her arms pinwheeling, legs fluttering with impressive synchronicity. She was a strong athlete.

"Well, then," Ned Gibson said, "I'll finish drying off and slip something on."

Hanley stood gazing out over the water while he toweled his russet hair and raised a terrycloth robe around his shoulders, eased each arm into it and belted the front. "I'm sorry we haven't had a chance to speak sooner." He dabbed at his eyes with the wide lapel.

"Dr. Gibson—"

"Ned, please." Gibson put his hands on his hips.

"Ned. I could use some help."

"Of course. Getting cabin fever already?" He leaned toward her, concerned. He smelled of a sweet aperitif.

"Probably. But that's not why I wanted to talk to you. I need information about the four people who died out there—their psychological condition."

Gibson gazed down at his bare feet. "There are ethics involved here. My patients' confidentiality."

"Yes. I realize."

A young couple appeared at the far end of the pool, tossed aside their robes and sat down on the tiled edge to ease themselves in. Their pale nakedness clashed with the deep green of the water. Dr. Kruger had switched to a breaststroke, her long chestnut braid trailing behind her in the water.

"Let's discuss this in private," Gibson said.


Gibson spoke from his tiny water closet as he dressed for bed: "Arctic duty is amazingly intimate," he said. "People bond intensely. The staff becomes a clan. For many it's the defining experience of their lives." He came out dressed in pajamas and a thin Japanese robe. "Posts in the High Arctic were always pretty crude. Zero privacy. People squabbled, became delusional, even cracked—violently sometimes. That's why we pay so much attention to needs and comforts here. Even so, winter's a challenge. The loneliness. No rain, no natural light. Disturbed time sense."

"I know," Hanley said. "I think I'm experiencing it."

"Yes. I've been monitoring your regimen."

Hanley was taken aback, unused to being the subject of such scrutiny, except from her ex-husband.

"Mac asked me to keep an eye on you."

A huge yawn came over Hanley that she couldn't stifle. "Sorry. I haven't been sleeping much since I got here."

"You and half the station," Gibson said. "Understandable, given what's happened."

"No, this is normal for Arctic life. Some of the staff don't sleep for months. Maybe a few hours a night. The deaths of our colleagues have just exacerbated that. Are you dreaming in colors when you do sleep?"

"Yes," Hanley said, "spectacular ones. How did you know?"

"It's a symptom. What's happening is that you're cycling."

"Meaning?" she said.

"That the few hours you sleep are rarely the same hours night after night. You're slipping into a thirty-five-hour day."

"I see," she said.

"What day of the week is it, Jessie?"

She shook her head. "I don't know."

"It's Tuesday. You've been with us eight days, and you're already losing your bearings. Partly because of the nature of your mission here but mostly because of the circadian rhythm you're establishing. You seem to be a bit of a loner, which is fine, but not when it comes to this. You need to maintain at least minimal social contact."

"I don't think people would appreciate seeing me shooting pool when I ought to be figuring out how to protect them. They're worried." She lightened her voice. "Hey, I'm fine. My schedule gets thrown off whenever I'm in the field. I never sleep much. And I'm doing my twenty minutes of meditation every day." She wondered if he could tell she was lying—she hadn't been able to relax enough to meditate since she'd arrived. Enough of this, she decided: let him answer the questions. She steered the subject back to her investigation: "Do people in the Arctic often hallucinate?"

"It's not uncommon. Not the typical Arctic experience, but certainly not unheard of."

"What is the typical Arctic experience?" she said.

"Arctic stations are usually pretty crude. Like Little Trudeau. Maybe a dozen people occupying one room in a plywood shelter. Toilet facility in an open corner, no walls. Kerosene stoves, few women to talk to. Thirty degrees around your ankles, eighty-five at the tip of your nose. I made some great friends at Little Trudeau, but there was also a lot of backbiting and paranoia the deeper we got into winter. Small conflicts blown out of all proportion. Insidious gossip. Seething feuds, open hostility—fights. Everyone sullen or distant after a while."

"Did you worry about suicides?"

"All the time. The suicide rate above the Arctic Circle is twenty times greater than in the rest of the world. Seasonal depression is a given. Inuit call it *perlerorneq*—'winter sadness.' Claustrophobia is major too. We're surrounded by vastness, yet we're essentially confined. You can really feel it now that folks are scared to venture outside the station."

"But before all this happened?"

"We tried to put mechanisms in place for venting emotions. We articulate everything. Nothing is considered rude or invasive. No stigma is attached to anything, whether it's coed bathing, or being with someone—or not—or exercising or meditating, or joining a discussion group, so long as it relieves the monotony and isolation. Which is why we emphasize the weekly events—they may seem a little too cruise-ship or retirement-village, but they're essential. People participate in things they wouldn't have imagined doing in the world. Talent nights, open mikes, swim teams, eating societies, poetry slams, Inuit drumming, ballroom dancing. Some winters we've had a drama society. Anything goes."

"Sounds healthy."

"We thought so. We thought we'd dodged a lot of the more debilitating tensions associated with duty above the Circle."

"But apparently not all."

"No," he said, "admittedly not. But Trudeau has made prolonged participation nearly normal in a way it never was before. Few lasted for more than a season at a time in the old habitats. Now there's a group for whom it's basically home."

"Mackenzie, Primakov?"

"Yes, and others: Teddy Zale, Simon King, Cecil Skudra. Alex."

He rose and puttered at the kitchenette counter, snapping on the electric kettle and dropping a pair of tea bags into a dark blue pot. He spooned some honey into his mug. "I'm going to have my evening tea. Herbal. May I offer you some?"

"Thank you, yes," Hanley said.

His furniture was minimal: a freestanding lamp with a green shade and a bench improvised from driftwood. A tiny ledge served as a night table. The wall housed a television, video player, headphones, and satellite phone. Not a sentimental object in view. The curved interior wall was clear and glassy and faced out onto a walkway a few steps down. Another clear wall beyond gave onto inky blackness. In summer he would have quite a view, Hanley thought. Gibson drew a blackout curtain across the clear wall. Instantly the room grew smaller and more intimate.

Hanley pictured the sunlight and the endless ocean she had left behind in California, and the months before she would see them again. The electric kettle whistled. Gibson poured the boiling water into the teapot and brought it to the narrow, low bench to steep.

"So if Alex Kossuth was so at home here, what happened?"

"Alex," he said, and sighed. "Alex developed insomnia. And a degree of disorientation, something like the psychoses you find in prisoners."

"Hallucination could have been part of that?"

He paused, gathering his thoughts. "Working in perpetual darkness like this is unnatural. It takes its toll. Some people zone out, go zombie."

"Zombie?"

"Local slang. They stop sleeping. They slow down mentally, fixate on whatever's in front of them and just stare. They lose all sense of time. Develop a shuffling gait, like they're wearing slippers. Walk away in the middle of conversations."

"Alex Kossuth was 'going zombie'?"

"Yes." He picked up a cup and poured out the tea. "It was more severe than I'd thought. There's a more violent form, an Arctic hysteria that looks like road rage. People scream, rant, wave knives around, run naked onto the ice. Alex wasn't the knife-waving type. Benign withdrawal and depression, bickering, flare-ups, acrimony over trivia—that was Alex's pattern. But common enough that it didn't raise any red flags."

"Did Kossuth drink? Take pills?" she said.

"He drank." Gibson sounded slightly uncomfortable.

"Was he melancholy when he drank?"

"At times."

"Lately?"

"Yes. He would say things to people that didn't quite make sense. Mutter, talk to himself."

She clasped her hands. "What would he talk about when he'd had a few?"

"About *Nastrond*."

"Excuse me?"

Gibson appeared thoughtful and uncomfortable both. "Scandinavian mythology. He knew a lot about it."

"*Nastrond?*" Hanley asked.

"The Shore of Corpses. In Nordic cultures the far North represented the hereafter, the place dead Vikings sailed to when they crossed over. The boats they put their dead into and set adrift? This is where they were being sent."

"Like the River Styx," Hanley said.

"Yes, only it's an ocean."

"Pretty dramatic. But you still didn't think he was a danger to himself?"

Gibson shook his head ruefully. "No."

"Was he unwell physically?"

"Not that I'm aware of."

"You tried approaching him?"

"Twice. He wouldn't accept therapy." Gibson's brow seemed lined. "He wouldn't say much. I thought he was going through a depression. Maybe age. Or his feelings for Annie."

"Excuse me?"

"She was pretty exceptional, even for this crowd, and extremely popular. She would have made a terrific politician. Half the station was infatuated with her."

"Including Kossuth?"

"Alex didn't hide his feelings."

"What did she think of him?"

"They'd always had a bond, just not the kind he wanted. He had recruited her to Trudeau, and she was grateful to him for that. She was genuinely fond of him. But that's as far as it went. The Inuit have a word for it that I won't embarrass myself by trying to pronounce. It translates roughly as, 'She is kindly disposed to him after having not loved him.'"

"Could the rejection have pushed him far enough to want to harm Annie?"

"God, no. He always knew it was impossible. For starters, he was twice her age—more than twice. He was wry about it—ironic. Besides, he knew Annie was gay."

"Gay?"

"Openly."

"So she wouldn't have been involved with any man at the site."

"No."

"Was she with anyone at the station?"

"Yes. Ingrid Kruger."

"The German doc? But she did the autopsy."

"Yes. We had no idea you—or anyone from the world outside— might be coming to investigate. We thought we were on our own. Felix Mackenzie made a lame attempt to talk her out of it, even though no one else was nearly as qualified. She insisted she could do it, more likely to be exact if she did. And she didn't want anyone else to touch her."

"What did you think, professionally?"

"A bad situation with no good options. As it was, the station's dentist had to assist. She had more surgical experience than our nurse practitioner. And please, if Ingrid's at all hostile, don't take it personally. I think she blames herself for not protecting Annie."

Hanley was quiet for a minute, absorbing the idea of Dr. Kruger forced to autopsy her lover's body.

"Alex Kossuth . . . did he leave a note?"

"No note."

"So you'd say his killing himself was spontaneous?"

"Apparently. But Alex was yearning for solace. Something was troubling him. He wouldn't say what. I really did try."

"I believe you."

"I guess I'm trying to justify—to myself as much as anyone— why I didn't intervene more aggressively with Alex. What he had was, for better or worse, normal for the Arctic."

"I'm sorry to push you about this. I'm not just being nosy. Suicidal people can be reckless—guy decides to total his car, he doesn't always care who else on the highway he takes with him. Maybe Alex took some unnecessary risk, exposed himself and the others to something he knew was dangerous. If that happened, I have to keep that exposure from being repeated. Aside from Annie, what were his relationships with the other researchers out there?"

Gibson shook his head. "No suspicion I was aware of, nor paranoia either. Ogata's party, they were well acquainted—friends even."

"And the fifth person in the group? She wasn't very well liked, I gather."

"Lidiya Tarakanova could be difficult, yes, but she was rotating out. People were pretty tolerant because they didn't have much longer to put up with her. She was just along for the ride because they were going to the pickup site anyway. Not an emergency evacuation, just the last boat home."

"Excuse me," Hanley said, rubbing her face and eyes. "I'm crashing fast."

"I can see that," Gibson said. "Please think over what I said about giving over to the station and the people here. We're social creatures, Doctor. You're allowed to have needs."

"Yeah. I'll think about it."

Hanley bid goodnight and left. The corridors were dim.

"What the hell," she said to herself.

She made her way through the quiet to the fourth domicile dome and knocked lightly on room 1103A. After a moment, the door slid open.

"Dr. Hanley," he said, startled, his face shadowed.

"You're up."

"Yeah, a troubled mind." Jack Nimit stepped aside to let her pass. *"Itirut,"* he said. "Enter." He stood in a lone circle of light. His black hair was drawn tightly back from his face and cinched at the nape of his neck. A slight fan of hair descended over his shoulders. She tried consciously not to think of the difference in their ages as she stepped toward him. He tensed.

"Can I be of help?"

"I hope so," she said.

She turned the light out, raised her arms and pulled off her top, drawing with it the camisole underneath. It crackled and burst into light with static electricity. Her torso shone in the glow.

She took the bottom of his pullover and pulled it up. He lifted his arms to accommodate her. The garment sparked. Half naked, they stood mutely staring at one another, bare silhouettes in the room.

She touched his hairless chest and he touched her back, hearts racing. She smiled, enjoying the effect she was having, and his effect on her. His hand slid along the underside of her breast and she gasped lightly, the smile giving way to surprised delight.

They kissed. The sensation of her flesh on his chest was ineffable. Her nipples engorged. Her work pants slid down around her ankles, coiled around her feet. She stepped out of them.

He ran his hand along her neck and across her shoulder, his other hand supporting her breast like something he had been awarded. As he bent to kiss her neck, he reached down and lightly touched her sex with the palm of his hand. Her arms closed around him, her body urging him toward her as she touched him in kind.

She ached for him to caress her, to feel his body joined to hers. With the gentlest motion, she swayed against him, raising her knee, her leg curling around—opening to him. He eased her back. They were already leaning against his bed in the narrow room. He slid down alongside her, kissing her, caressing. Holding him close, she rolled onto her back, carrying him with her onto the narrow bunk.

She guided him and he slid easily into her. Nothing was as insistent as the sensation they shared at that moment.

He was moving in the most measured way: slowly, slowly. Just like riding a bicycle, she thought, and smiled to herself. They gasped out brief expulsions of breath with each movement, as they touched tenderly, tongues moistening each other's lips, mouths, chins, cheeks, their breath catching at each withdrawal and thrust. Her eyes were adjusting to the dark—seeing him.

Her legs encircled his buttocks; her arms embraced his neck. Small cries came from her with their motion. It became more insistent. She slid her hand between them, touched him where they met. He had no body hair. He shuddered as she moved against him, flexing and unflexing, separate beings exquisitely joined, clutching one another, fucking in the dark, with eyes and bodies open.

shikawa had given up trying to get home to Sherman Oaks. The Center assigned him two more assistants and brought in a couch large enough to stretch out on and catnap. Throughout the day and into the evening, the junior staff working for him came and went without knocking, taping the results of their searches on whatever object was handiest, including Ishikawa himself if he was asleep.

Rising to an office papered with notes, Ishikawa had the momentary impression of being back in his room at his parents' house, the ceiling adorned with Shinto paper ornaments—votive offerings for protection and success. Except the notes stuck to his office walls were of irregular sizes and myriad colors and shapes. They were written on fancy stationery; torn scraps; index cards; envelopes; bookmarks; official memo forms; looseleaf pages; notepaper; matchbook covers; even a parking ticket, on which someone had scrawled

*Oxygen—12% in tissues and organs,*
*13% in muscles, 34% in lungs, 41% in blood.*

He had pinned, stapled, clipped, and taped the notes to his walls by category, so that at a glance one could tell what the most fruitful lines of thinking were at that particular moment. A mild offshore breeze fluttered the notes. An oddly pleasing noise, a gentle rustling.

First light. Ishikawa checked his watch. No one around yet. He hoped Hanley was still unconscious. Guiltily, he rolled over, facing the wall, and cleared his mind enough to slip back to sleep.

Vasily Sergeyevich Nemerov eased his wife aside, using his own larger body as counterweight. She did not resist. The woman was exhausted. He marveled at her. How lucky he was to have succumbed to such a magnificent seductress. She was always particularly ardent and uninhibited just before he put to sea and immediately upon his return. Sonja's French blood no doubt accounted for her physicality. Her grandmother was a caustic Parisian relic. Two letters arrived from her each year: one on Sonja's birthday and the other on the anniversary of Sonja's mother's passing.

Grandfather had been a French naval officer who had perished at sea. His sacrifice for France had entitled Sonja's mother to wed in the great hall of Napoleon's tomb, given away by the proud nation, as it were; a singular honor. The daughter of the republic had married a Russian exile who brought her back to Mother Russia shortly before the Great Patriotic War. Some years later his rehabilitation had been brought into question, and he died in front of a firing squad, a patriotic oath on his lips. Typhoid claimed Sonja's mother not long after.

Vasily had met Sonja in Leningrad during his cadet days, and they'd pledged their troth upon his graduation. At first everything went wrong that could. They argued endlessly. Yet, ill suited as their ambitions and natures seemed to be, when they came together as man and wife, all else retreated. They restored one another; they always had.

He yawned and lay back on the pillow. She had nearly repaired him again, after the harrowing maneuvers in the fjord. The elements of the Baltic Fleet had rendezvoused prematurely, creating havoc on the surface. He had eluded these bunglers as well as several British and Norwegian vessels, using the cacophony of their engines and competing sonars to cloak *Rus*'s withdrawal.

He looked at Sonja, and touched a strand of hair at the nape of her neck. She was a bit heavier since the birth of their younger daughter, but she was exquisite. Realizing he was now hopelessly awake, he covered her and put on his pajamas in the dark, then eased the door of their bedroom closed and shuffled into the kitchen in his English slippers. Lightning branched across the sky and he glanced out onto the square. A thunderous roar followed. Nemerov put up water for tea and went to check on his daughters.

The elder was deep in sleep. Tiptoeing to the younger one's crib, he stooped and peered in through the bars. The scant light was reflected back by a pair of eyes. A thinker, this one, calm and reflective from her first day. In the dark of winter mornings she would lie quietly keeping her own counsel, only her eyes moving. He reached into her crib, one finger extended. She wrapped her small hand around it.

"Is it time to get up?" she whispered.

"No, it's terribly early. Close your eyes and try to sleep."

Her lids closed obediently. Nemerov tucked in her blanket and rose; he shuffled to the bathroom, peed, shaved, washed, and returned to the kitchen to fix himself a boiled egg. He brushed some baby cockroaches into the sink and flushed them away. Plate in hand, he settled in a chair by the kitchen window and rubbed a large circle of moisture from the pane with the heel of his hand.

Kirov Square was perfectly white. The sodium street lamps made black sockets of the side streets and flattened everything so that nothing cast a shadow. No one was abroad. At the end of winter, Murmansk would come alive with celebrations. The workers would fill the squares and avenues, their pockets heavy with extra rubles earned as compensation for laboring in the harsh North. They would flock down to the stores along the docks and buy up the Japanese DVD players and German cameras sold on the cheap by merchant seamen newly returned from foreign ports.

"Papa."

His little one stood in the doorway, rubbing her eyes, her complexion slightly ruddy from the sunlamps at school. Sun treatments, extra milk, and carrots were among the benefits mandated by local ordinance for Murmansk schoolchildren throughout the winter.

"Go back to bed, Natashenka. It is too early to be up."

"I can't," she said. "What were you and mama fighting about last night?"

"You are so nosy," he said. "Your mother wants me to quit the navy and take work at a new shipping company. How about some warm milk?"

She shook her head. "Would you still wear your uniform?"

"Yes."

"Papa?"

"What?"

"A story," she said and wedged herself between his knees.

"Ah," Nemerov said. He enfolded her and raised her up to sit on his thigh, which she did as naturally as a bird. "And which story do you wish?" This was entirely pro forma; she'd had the same favorite story for months now.

"River Princess," she said right away.

"Done."

Holding her against his chest, her head tucked under his chin, Nemerov unwound the tale of the handsome mandolin player who loved the river Volkhov and cast gifts into the water as tributes to her beauty, and finally plunged in himself when he could no longer bear the pain of people rejecting his music.

"Water creatures brought him before the Sea Tsar for punishment, to his castle built of . . ." Nemerov waited for Natasha to finish the sentence.

"Green wood from the timbers of lost ships," she said.

"The tsar was crowned with . . ."

"Gold from treasure cargo."

"And covered with . . ."

"Scales."

"Blue hair flowed down to his waist and waves rippled out from him in all directions whenever he moved. It turned out the river Volkhov was . . ."

"His youngest and most beautiful daughter." This was her favorite line, and she said it emphatically.

"The troubadour was enraptured, but he couldn't live under the sea with her, nor could she ever leave it. Miserable and heartbroken, he fell asleep in her arms, only to awaken back on dry land, a strange sensation in his fingertips. He was lying on the riverbank next to her, his hand touching the gentle current, and on his finger was a magnificent . . ."

Nemerov waited, but Natasha was asleep, her hand in his. A noise outside made Nemerov glance over his shoulder out the window. In the frozen morning a lone man marched across the square, insignia glinting in the sodium lights. He recognized the figure from the gait alone. If most of mankind had descended from the ape, there were those odd few who seemed more likely cousins to the wolf. Admiral Rudenko had that lupine grace and leanness. Despite his protests of rheumatism, he was as limber as a yogi.

Rudenko was wearing his ceremonial greatcoat, the shoulder boards and cuffs flashing—he had come straight from his condolence call upon the widow of *Vladivostok*'s captain. Had he sat up with her the whole night after delivering the ikon?

"Is he coming to take you to the bottom of the sea?" his daughter said.

Nemerov turned back and clutched her to his chest.

"Don't go, Papa. You haven't been home even a week."

Nemerov fervently wished he could give back all his years of training and sailing. Changes in the northern year-round ice were opening channels across the top of Russia, saving thousands of miles by eliminating the need to circle around the Horn of Africa to reach the South China Sea and beyond. Ships' masters experienced in navigating icy sea-lanes were in high demand. A single trip would pay as much as he could earn in a year as a naval officer—not that the paymaster had been seen since June. After what he had witnessed in the fjord, he knew he would resign soon and take a civilian command on one of Sovkomflot's cargo vessels plying the new route. But how to tell Rudenko?

The captain carried his child back to the crib. "Please don't go back," he heard her mumble. He settled her in and went to the front door of the flat. He knotted the drawstrings of his pajamas and was assailed by images of that body, tethered as if by a hangman, its skin like a miscarried fetus—translucent, white—and that agonized leer on its face.

He badly wanted nothing further to do with anything or anyone involved with that doomed ship. He would tell Rudenko right off: he was finished with the navy. What need was there for either of them anymore? What future? Were they just hanging on? Had his ambitions died in the fjord with those sailors? He stepped out onto the dark landing. A pensioner had pilfered the lightbulb again.

Footsteps echoed in the flaking stairwell. All his instincts urged flight, yet he knew he could not flee. Whatever other compunctions he might brush aside, what about the admiral? Leaning over the rail, Nemerov could dimly make out a gloved hand on the banister.

"Admiral," he called down with what lightheartedness he could muster. "You are just in time to take breakfast with your goddaughter."

# 27

"Where are you from?" Nimit asked.

"Before California? Virginia. Wrong side of the Chickahominy River."

"Meaning?"

"Poor. Our parents were pretty overwhelmed. We kind of had to look after ourselves. Every kid was responsible for the one younger. Mom died when I was in college, Dad remarried, the family sort of broke up. A couple of us stay in touch, but we're not the kind of family that has occasions where we all get together. And the two of us—the two girls, as it happens—who actually made it to college have a hard time communicating with our brothers. Not that either of us is all that social to begin with. But mostly my brothers like to drink whiskey, hunt wild turkey or deer, watch the ball game on television. My sister and I are not included. Women are essentially there to cater." She propped herself up and lit a cigarette.

"What were you like as a kid?" he said.

"Odd. A loner."

"Boyfriends?"

"Nearly none."

"Why not?"

"Scared them off. I collected roadkill, bugs, rats. Plus I was flat chested."

"At least you got that part straightened out," he said, reaching for her. She laughed and turned to face him.

"And where is home for you, Mr. Nimit?"

"Here"—Nimit nodded at the black-and-white plain outside—"but if you mean where did I grow up, I was raised on Ellesmere Island, way south of here."

"Miss it terribly?"

"Not for a minute. I hated it. Couldn't wait to leave."

Hanley didn't hide her surprise. "Really?"

"Yeah," he said, "not an approved attitude for an Inuk. It's the truth, though. I was miserable. We weren't exactly the nomadic noble savages, leading hard yet perfectly balanced lives in the unforgiving, beautiful Arctic. The government had moved our families there decades earlier. Not precisely consensual. Farther north than we'd ever wanted to be. But the farther north you have inhabitants, the more territory you can claim. Not pretty but there you are. Everyone was on the dole and living in plywood houses. Kids sniffing glue and whiffing gasoline out of plastic garbage bags, getting stoned, setting fire to themselves. Nobody under forty could even speak Inuktitut anymore. Nothing was ever thrown away. Everyone had broken refrigerators and junked snowmobiles in their yards. A garbage bag in a honey bucket in the house held the household sewage. The slop bags got hauled out on the tundra and piled up. They'd freeze solid. Same with laundry detergent. Plastic cracks in the intense cold. By summer it all turns into a giant septic pond. The stench was humiliating." He glanced over. "Get the picture?"

"Vividly."

"It's getting better now that Canada's returned some of our territory. Of course a lot of it's a load of crap. They've got an Inuit superhero on TV to get the kids interested in Inuktitut. But I'm really hoping what we develop at Trudeau will help. I'd like to see Inuit using Arctic suits, and living in Trudeau domes, for instance, instead of wooden box houses with peaked roofs and Formica and linoleum. I don't know, it might seem more like a natural progression instead of that borrowed architecture. I mean, the dome design is basically the Inuit igloo. We just modernized it."

"How did you wind up at Trudeau?"

"In a word: Mackenzie. I first met him when I was in college.

I made sure I did well in school as a kid and got scholarshipped out of there. Went south, studied engineering at Dalhousie, and determined to avoid the high latitudes. But gradually I gravitated north like an iron filing. Before long I was erecting ice platforms for oil rigs just above the Arctic Circle when Mackenzie landed on me, said he had a lot of the items for the station in place, that he had the dream but needed someone special to build it. Gave me a free hand. I can't tell you how exhilarating that was.

"Mac, he gave me back the Arctic. I worked for him at Little Trudeau for two summers drawing up the plans. Nobody'd ever built anything like this."

She felt envious. "You're lucky you had him as a mentor."

"Mentor? More like lifesaver. You ever have someone like that change your life?"

She shook her head. "No. I like my boss fine, but nobody like that. Nobody guided me for a second, which is why I suppose I have a little trouble playing well with others. I had to scrap."

"You seem to play pretty well one on one." He drew her into a kiss.

"And you seem to relish a challenge."

"You mean personally or as an engineer?"

"Both, but I meant as an engineer."

"Sure. And there's more than a little ethnic pride mixed up in there too. People always expect the station's engineer to be a German or a Dane."

"Yeah, folks don't expect much from a hillbilly chick, either."

Nimit laughed.

"What was the toughest part of putting all this together?"

"Maybe the three domes on the end. They sit on stilts I set into the tundra. That prevents drifts from building up and keeps the heat from the domes from melting the permafrost. Permafrost is just what it sounds like—frozen year-round—even in the constant sunlight, so I borrowed a technique from Siberian builders. You heat steel pipe until it's red-hot, then drive it into the frozen ground. When you draw it out, the pipe extracts a core of tundra. Then you push the empty pipe back down and fill it with concrete. Kind of invasive ecologically, but the government was more lenient in the building stage about unavoidable damage. They're a lot less understanding now about our activities out on the sea ice, especially in the summer months when the tundra's exposed and vulnerable, and the slightest bruise grows into a gully, fast.

"Anyway, we built like mad all summer putting up Big Trudeau. I had two crews working round the clock like a relay race. We put the domes together about four hundred miles south of here, then stacked 'em one atop the other, and flew 'em in by heavy-duty helicopters, like bell jars slung underneath giant mosquitoes. The staff all came out and cheered us coming in. My crew had practiced assembling them down south. We planned and rehearsed it down to the last rivet. The big helos craned the domes into place and we put it all together like an erector set. By the time winter set in, I knew I was back north for good."

"I'm glad you came back," she said, a little hoarsely, surprised by how deeply he moved her.

"You'd better get some sleep," he said, kissing her.

"I've forgotten how."

"Just close your eyes. I'll do the rest."


The wind was at seven knots from the north. The clouds, low and turbulent. Visibility was under four kilometers. The moment to sail.

An American submarine, hunter variety, was reported on station just outside territorial waters, facing the pens at Kem. The cowboys would not have long to wait, Nemerov thought. He ordered the lines cast off, and coaxed the boat from its berth and out through the gaping doors. Immediately it slid under the surface, staying at periscope depth in the channel maintained by the icebreakers.

Except for Rudenko and the civilian Koyt, the crew was Nemerov's own: Chernavin had insisted on it. The boat was new: *Arkangel*. There had not even been time to commission her. She was a sub hunter too, eight knots faster than missile submarines like *Rus*, and quieter. Unlike the steel alloys used in other boats, the titanium hull would give no magnetic clues to its presence.

The representative from the yard at Severodvinsk had boasted of her capabilities and design. "See how the sail is no more than a bulge, like the hump of a whale, which she most resembles. She moves through the water with such grace. There will not be another boat like her in my lifetime."

Nemerov did not share the boat builder's enthusiasm. In her modern lines he found not grace but an atavistic menace. This was a boat that stalked other U-boats to kill them. But clearly Chernavin had given them the best the navy had. It added to his unease as *Arkangel* put to sea.

Forty minutes out, the American sub slipped behind Nemerov's new boat and paced it at a leisurely distance, until a second submarine of the Russian Northern Fleet rose from the sea bottom and began scissoring *Arkangel*'s wake, hopelessly confusing the pursuer's sonar.

First Captain Nemerov followed the periscope slowly around on its quadrant. The wave troughs were high. He ordered a sharp dive. *Arkangel* plunged down into the colder layers and, beneath the ice, turned her prow north.

# 28

Hanley suited up for the baby hot lab. Inside, she prepared a series of cultures on the worm specimens from Skudra's lab. In the outer room, Uli was examining the shelves of flasks and petri dishes, checking the status of each culture from the Ogata autopsy.

"Sample one-oh-three, negative. One-oh-four, negative. One-oh-five, negative."

Uli looked up from his notes and called into the hot lab. "Jessie, I have no toxic bacteria in any of the samples."

"I know," she called back. "It's so damn frustrating."

"But could you come? I have a question as I look further."

"Be right out." Hanley finished the culture she was working on, retreated into the detox shower, and emerged into the outer lab. She removed her helmet and approached the workbench where Uli had laid out lab sheets containing results of dozens of attempts to culture bacteria from Ogata's tissue samples.

"What's your question?"

"I am thinking perhaps I am doing the cultures wrong. Is it okay that every culture is 'Result: negative'?"

"Well, if there's nothing there, there's nothing there."

She scanned the long row of results, turned back one page, then another. "Whoa," said Hanley, and read through the sheets again. "They're *all* negative."

"Entirely," Uli said. *"Alles."*

"And Bascomb's labs?" said Hanley, exiting the rest of her suit in record time. Uli skimmed the printouts and nodded. *"Null.* This is important?"

Hanley grabbed the printouts and ran straight to the laptop. The network link to California was active. Hanley turned up the volume and shouted. "Ishi?"

*"Yeah. You've got something?"*

"More like nothing, actually. But so much nothing it seems like something. Just the weirdest finding. Uli is with me." She indicated the screen while glancing back at her colleague. "Talk to him."

Uli said, "Yes, here are too many negative—eh, how do you say?—*resultats,* yes?—in the bacterial cultures."

"Ishi," said Hanley. "The growth media showed no signs of bacteria at all. You hear that, Ishi? Not just no toxic bacteria. Not just no potential pathogens. No benign bacteria. No bacteria whatsoever."

*"You're serious?"*

"You heard me," Hanley said. "The bodies are entirely devoid of bacteria. All the normal flora are missing. It's like Ogata and Bascomb were swept clean by whatever destroyed the respiratory system and blood cells."

*"That's pretty damn remarkable. I'll check for precedents, but offhand I'd say we aren't going to find any."*

Hanley leaned back, half sitting on the lab stool. "How do we even begin to think about this? You've normally got—what?—about ten to a hundred million bacteria in every gram of your tissue between your stomach and your rectum. Every time you go to the bathroom, you shed a hundred billion bacteria. In your mouth, gums, teeth, you've got another—" She shouted to Dee for help. "How many bacteria in the human mouth?"

"Ten billion, they taught us in dental school. Something like two hundred species."

"Okay. Another ten billion," Hanley repeated. "More elsewhere. A hundred trillion altogether. That's fourteen zeros. We're talking a solid pound of microscopic critters. These cadavers haven't a single bacterium. Zero. Zip."

*"I've never encountered anything even remotely comparable,"* Ishikawa said.

Hanley said. "Uli, can you bring all the results to me so I can send them on to Ishi?" Uli nodded and left hurriedly.

"Well, Ishi, consider the upside. I think we've just ruled out a bacterial culprit." She sat down. "That narrows it down. On the other hand, the antibiotics I brought will be useless if there's another outbreak. And this thing acts so fast I can't imagine any of the current antivirals would have a chance."

Hanley closed her eyes and tried to impose order on the rush of conjecture streaming through her brain. On the screen the small image of Ishikawa moved in herky-jerky fashion, like a silent movie actor.

"Okay. Now we know we're after a virus," Hanley said. "Maybe a prion. Maybe mycoplasma. But botulinum is out. Tetanus too. And all their sisters and their cousins and their aunts." She kneaded her shoulder. "Normally, a bacteriophage virus has one species of bacteria it stalks and preys on. As soon as that host's depleted, the virus burns out. What we've got here is like the mother of all bacteriophages. The all-you-can-eat virus. Instead of just killing off one strain, this sucker kills them all, and doesn't stop until every damn one is gone. Man, it seems impossible."

*"A virus like that would have changed the course of evolution,"* Ishi said. *"I think you need to run all the same tests on Kossuth, just to double-check yourself. And Jess? You alone?"*

"Yeah, Ishi?" she said, turning down his volume.

*"Even if it's not bacterial, I don't think we can rule out bioengineering. Cybil says the only guys, aside from our own, who've been working on souped-up pathogens are a lot of the old Soviets. They aren't affiliated with labs anymore. They're freelancing. A few for the French, a few in the Middle East. She knows where most of them are and what they're up to. A couple unaccounted for, no doubt following the money. The rest are probably driving taxis somewhere, but who knows? Tarakanova's not on the list. For what it's worth,*

*Cybil says Tarakanova seems to have gone walkabout once she got back to Russia. She's trying to see if any of the known bioweapons guys crossed paths recently with any of your folks up at Trudeau, maybe talked them into a little off-the-books research."* Ishikawa rummaged through a stalagmite of paper. *"For the moment, let's say it's nature, not nurture. So what are the possible natural vectors for our bacteria eater?"*

"The Arctic is a hotbed of migration in summer, right? High animal population—narwhal, walrus, seal, cod, bear, fox. Birds, lots of birds. Always good suspects."

*"You mean like that weird lung thing in Cleveland, or avian flu in Asia? So the portal of entry would be respiratory . . . ?"*

"Right. They don't notice the droppings when they set up camp, and the next day, boom. The Arctic isn't like other places. Creatures up here can suspend their metabolism. Not just mammals like bears. Bacteria, yeast, fungi just stop living until conditions become hospitable again. One of them is sitting out there waiting, and these poor bastards come along and bump into it."

*"I'm getting the picture. You know what this means, right?"*

"Yeah. Time for me to go on a wild-goose-shit chase." She lit a cigarette. "Some desert Munson sent me to. A sterile wilderness, I thought. A couple of species, a dozen max. Right. Turns out the Arctic is about as empty as Sausalito on a Saturday." Hanley closed her eyes and tilted her head back. "You have no idea how much I miss the ocean. And the sun. Hell, even a crappy, rainy day at the beach would feel like a sunbath right now."

*"Jess, I'm a little worried about you. Any chance you could get some more help? Maybe the doc who did the autopsies could lend a hand. We can't afford to miss some key fact because you're dangerously sleep deprived."*

"I know, I know." Hanley peered at his image in the corner of her computer screen. "You're lookin' a little worn yourself. You okay?"

*"Yeah, just tapped out."*

"Sorry to load more work on you, but any chance you could track down Tarakanova? Ishi, I've got to know what she saw before she left. And what if she was exposed?"

*"I'll get on it, Jess."*

"Fuck the diplomatic channels, Ishi. If you have to find her yourself . . ."

*"I hear you, Jess.* Sayonara."

*"Arigato,* Kim." His image receded from the screen.

Hanley took a deep breath and resisted the temptation to view again the color photographs from the autopsies. She exhaled slowly and focused on her hands, willing the muscles to relax, then shifted her concentration to her arms, her shoulders, keeping her breathing deep and steady. The thoughts slowed to a trickle, but continued like an annoying drip. No bacteria. How long could a body survive with no bacteria? Breathing. Lungs. Hydrogen sulfide traces in the lung field. Where the hell did that come from? Exhaling a deep lungful of air, she sat up straight and stood up with a groan.

She stared out into the Arctic darkness, illuminated only by stars and the ring of subdued lights around the station's perimeter. Hanley felt dizzy. From sleeplessness, she hoped. Had Bascomb and the others felt this way in the hours before they died? Was it an early symptom of something more than fatigue? Hanley took her pulse. Normal.

Everyone at the station was jumpy. Dee had told her people were coming to the infirmary at three times the normal rate. Maybe she should too, just to check out the headache. She felt muzzy with fatigue. Maybe she should lie down for a few minutes. Hanley consulted the Dr. Bach's chart and selected Elm, for those *overwhelmed by responsibility,* lay down, and did a deep-breathing meditation, pulling her buckwheat-hull eyeshade over her eyes. Shit, maybe if she had a cigarette, or a joint. She was bone tired. She dozed for a few minutes, wakened by a familiar cramping in her abdomen. Well, look at the upside, she thought. At least you're not pregnant. The pain jolted her into a sitting position, and had her hunched around the deep ache. When it subsided temporarily, Hanley staggered to the toilet and sat. Nothing.

She hauled herself up. Something in the white toilet bowl caught her eye. At the bottom of the water was a cloudy pool of dense, red blood. Hers. Hanley doubled over with pain, squatting next to the bowl. She wrapped her arms around her midsection, shivering.

"Damn," she groaned. The blood in the water was perfectly still, oddly beautiful.

The body is process, she thought, trying to distract herself from the pain. The body is cells. One trillion cells. A quarter of them blood.

Three people had perished horribly, their red cells split open, the contents spilled out. Some unknown agent, overwhelmingly toxic and blindingly fast, had blocked the lungs and stopped the three-quarters-of-a-second transfer of oxygen to the red blood cells. In a matter of minutes they were rendered voiceless, sightless, unable to breathe.

The cramps backed off a little. She rose, shuffled to the bed, and eased herself back down. Her menstrual cycle was completely off, her body was out of sync, unable to adjust to a lightless Arctic schedule. Exhausted, hurting, and horny for Jack—what a combination, she thought.

She turned on her side and studied the room, trying to steady herself. The color schemes were soft combinations of warm colors, like the ob-gyn's office she'd gone to for Lamaze classes when she was pregnant with Joey. Clearly designed to minimize anxiety. The cramping was letting up, but she felt hollow and queasy.

Dee called to her from the doorway.

"Got any lipstick? I'm running out already and the season's not a month old."

"Boy, did you come to the wrong person. I don't think I've worn makeup since high school."

"You might consider it," Dee said with a knowing smile. "You never know who might like it."

Hanley was startled. The walls here really were made of glass. She wasn't sure what to make of what had just happened with Jack, or the depth of feeling he evoked in her. She certainly wasn't ready for it to be a matter of public speculation, even with Dee. Dee examined herself in the bathroom mirror. "I'm really getting that polar pallor. White as a sheet." Dee made a face at herself. "Are the nicotine patches working for you?"

"Not that I've noticed," Hanley said, reaching on the bedside table for a cigarette and lighting up. "But the extra nicotine jolt is always welcome."

Dee came back into the living area. She said, "I was trying to look at least passably human for the sardine party in the Germans' quarters. You coming?"

"Sardines?" Hanley made a face. "Never liked them. Anchovies either."

Dee laughed. "The reference is to the size of the quarters—as in packed together like—no one's going to make you eat any itty-bitty fishes."

"Thanks, but I'll pass. I'm not sure I could switch into party gear right now." After Dee left, Hanley rummaged through her stock of CDs and cassettes, pulling out Joey's recording of coastal surf. She put on a headset and listened once more to the waves breaking on Laguna Beach.

After ten minutes she gave up and ran the DVD of the two autopsies. Kruger's autopsy reports were on Hanley's laptop, and she referred to them each step of the way through the procedure.

For the dozenth time, she watched as Dr. Kruger sectioned the liver and kidneys. She took a portion of body fat, weighed it, and dropped it into formalin, then directed Dee in extracting the various fluids. Intestinal samples were next. The inevitable dehydration of the corpse made their work difficult. They were acquitting themselves well, but the strain of the unfamiliar tasks and unaccustomed proximity to their dead friend—and Kruger's lover—was evident in the silence. Their few exchanges were entirely clinical, punctuated only by sounds of instruments and equipment as they examined and sampled muscle, the anterior abdominal wall, the pancreas, spleen, a section of the cervical cord, the aorta, the ovaries, a piece of cerebral cortex.

None of the fluids that drained from the body were red. In life Annie Bascomb had been a tawny beauty; in death she could have been an albino. Her body, drained of color, was rendered translucent, so pale you nearly expected to see through it.

Toward the end, Dee removed the modest cloth covering Annie Bascomb's face. There was a voluble gasp from someone off camera.

Dee glanced up, but Hanley couldn't make out her expression through the plastic face shield and surgical mask. The deceased had been a friend and a familiar colleague. Her rictus leer would have unnerved any one of them. The eyeballs—what was left of them—had sunk and flattened, giving the face the most peculiar aspect. It was chilling, even on film, even to a stranger.

The gowned figures on the screen stood silent and the only sounds were the shutter clicking and the motorized rewinding of the 35-millimeter still camera.

Hanley froze the frame, and retrieved one of the still photographs taken at the end of the procedure. She compared the two.

Neither showed any moisture around the lips.

Hanley walked to the rounded window in her quarters and leaned her head against it, almost wishing she could feel the Arctic cold against the skin. In the lights of the station complex, the ice plain below shone like the cracked glaze of old china.

Hanley's computer chimed. When she logged on, Joey was on the videophone.

"Mom!"

"Darling," she exclaimed. "How did you ever—"

"Dr. Ishikawa sent me a tiny camera and told Dad how to connect it to the computer. I can see you, I can see you!" He waved enthusiastically.

"Sweetie, it's wonderful to see you too. Oh, how I wish—"

"What's it like, Mom? Is it exciting? What's it feel like being there?"

"Weird. Like another planet. People are training for a trip to Mars above the Arctic Circle because it's the closest place on Earth to what Mars must be like."

"Wow! Is it really dark?"

"Yeah, but you could read a newspaper by the starlight. The stars never set. And when there's a moon, things actually cast a shadow it's so bright."

"Are you cold all the time?"

"No, the station is pretty cozy. Outside it's so cold they say it burns, but if you wear your Arctic suit, you're okay. You're not allowed to wear earrings, though, or rings. Or that nose ring I hear you're thinking of getting."

"Mom!"

"Gotcha! It's very exciting. Kind of intimidating too."

"Mom, Mom. I almost forgot. The whole class went to the aquarium at Monterrey, and we had workshops and I got to dissect a tiny shark's head. It was so cool."

"Get out."

"No, really. It was awesome. Everyone brought theirs back to school packed in dry ice, and we worked on them some more and wrote it all up."

"You too?"

"Yeah." He nodded vehemently. "On my laptop. I do everything on my laptop now. Even math."

"Is it helping?"

"Lots, Mom."

"That's great, hon."

"Have you found the superbug yet?"

"No."

"How about the vector?"

She laughed. "Not yet. I didn't know you knew what that meant."

"Of course," he said huffily. "Are the dead people infected?"

"No."

"You sure?"

"Pretty much. We've got them in isolators, just in case."

"Quarantine bags."

"Yeah," she said, surprised again. "You've got big ears."

"What about the other dead people? Could my class look at them online?"

"What other dead people?"

"The ones in the tomb."

"What are you talking about? Have you been watching bad late-night TV again?"

"No, no. See," he said. He retracted into a box in the corner of the screen. The rest filled with a description of Little Trudeau, then pictures of archaeological finds: bone knives, stone chopping tools, knotted cord, a carved walrus tusk. "It's an excav . . . excav—"

"Excavation," his mother pronounced. She shook her head with pride. "You've been researching."

"Yeah." He turned shy. "Kinda. The whole class worked on the web site with our computer teacher."

"Well, I'm deeply impressed."

"Really?"

"Totally."

"Mom, could you get me pictures of the mummies? We couldn't get any, and I kinda promised the guys you would."

"Sure, sweetie. But listen, hon, there's no need to tell your dad we've been talking about dead people and shark heads. You know he doesn't like it."

"Sure, Mom. He just gets upset." There was commotion off-screen. "Gotta go. Love you."

"Love you, guy."

The screen blanked. She was instantly alone in the world.

# 29

Early Saturday, while the rest of her team was still at breakfast, Hanley eased out of her bed next to Nimit and read the overnights online from L.A. Then she padded quietly to the lab. She'd been there nearly two weeks, and so far the bug wasn't showing itself in any of the human tissue, or any of Skudra's specimens. Nothing had fluoresced, no sign of a positive reaction. The vials of rabbit blood still glistened like dark rubies; none was stripped to the victims' pale pink.

She'd done what she could inside Trudeau itself. Time to get out on the ice and investigate the place they'd fallen ill and died.

And now she'd promised Joey photos from Little Trudeau too. He was being so good about her absence; keeping him well stocked with bragging rights at school was the least she could do for him.

She walked into her bathroom and consulted the chart of her Bach's Flower Remedies. A toss-up: did she need Aspen, *for fear of unknown things,* or Hornbeam *for procrastination, tiredness just at the thought of doing something?* "What the hell." She took a few drops of each, dressed silently without waking Jack, and set off for her appointment with Dr. Kruger. In the corridors, she passed two staff members wearing surgical masks. Had they actually stepped out of the way to avoid her, or were they just being polite?

Hanley found Ingrid Kruger sitting on the floor of the squash court, back against the wall. Kruger was reading what Hanley recognized as Annie Bascomb's journal from the work site. Hanley greeted the doctor and sat down alongside her.

"Find anything?" she said, indicating the journal.

Kruger flipped to a marked page and pointed to an entry.

*Holy fucking hell! What could they have been thinking. It's outrageous. And so damn dangerous.*

Hanley leaned back from the entry. "Is that recent? Do you know what she's talking about?"

"No on both counts. She wrote it this past summer. And I have no idea what it means."

"You were Annie Bascomb's closest friend at the station?"

"Yes."

"But you don't know what she was talking about—"

"Listen," Kruger interrupted. "I loved her. We were lovers. She had a personality everyone was drawn to. I am difficult and not amusing. She was difficult but just such fun. An activist in all the best and worst ways. An absolutist about the things she believed in. Annie just insisted that you like her, whether you agreed with her or not. You should have heard her carry on when the report came that Inuit have twice the dioxin in their bodies as other Canadians. She wasn't at all surprised to learn it came from factories in the U.S. Thanks to the weather patterns, the Arctic is the lucky recipient of all that poison. The stuff blows up here and makes its way right up the food chain. Dioxin loves fat—as do the Inuit. Every time they catch a seal, they're eating the American toxins along with it. If she could, I think Annie would have built a wall the length of the border. She'd have enlisted a lot of volunteers. She meant a lot to the people here. To me most of all."

"How are you holding up?"

She took in Hanley with a long stare. "I'm not. I haven't dealt well with patients since Annie died. I don't think I will ever be able to again. Not here. My usefulness at Trudeau is at an end. If there were a road out, I'd already be gone. Come spring, I will be. Ned Gibson too. People are packing it in. They are showing a brave face, yes, but they are terribly frightened. In the meantime, I am hanging on—just. So if you want to know something, you had better ask it more directly than you're doing, yes? I am not in any shape to deal with nuance. What is it you want?"

"I have a favor to ask. We've come up with a bizarre result in the cultures of two victims,"—she avoided mentioning Annie by name—"a complete lack of bacteria. It's so bizarre that we really should run all the same tests on Alex Kossuth, just to be sure our findings are definitive. My colleagues are already working double shifts, and I need to get out to the polynya. Is there any chance you could take the samples from Kossuth?"

Kruger took a slow, deep breath before answering. "I can tell you Alex exhibits all the classic signs of extreme hypothermia, but if it will help you find out what happened, I suppose I could manage an uncomplicated autopsy. Perhaps concrete work will be a relief. I may need a day or two to nerve myself."

"No problem. Take your time. And thank you. It will be a huge help. And I'm sorry if I seem to be prying, but may I ask you a few more questions about Annie?"

"Ask."

"You talked about the dioxin. I know part of her work involved tracking the movements of pollutants. Clearly, she was upset over the summer. I wonder if she'd recently confided any new worries."

Kruger appeared agitated by the question. "New worries?"

"Yes. Perhaps something she'd been working on before she went out to the polynya? Some contaminant that was particularly toxic, maybe something she was afraid to handle? Maybe that's what she meant by that—" She pointed toward the journal.

Kruger thought for a moment. "Annie was a little less enthusiastic about her work the past few months, but many of us were grateful for the break from her enthusiasms." Kruger smiled at some private memory. "I thought she was harboring something, a dalliance with someone else perhaps. She never told me. I concluded workplace politics were bothering her, or a tryst she was feeling guilty about. That's all."

"You weren't jealous?"

She smiled sadly. "No, I expected her to be interested in her peers and they in her. Only natural. I didn't own her. The first time I felt jealousy was after she was gone. I keep turning the last few months over in my mind, wondering what she wasn't saying. Now I'll never have the chance to ask. I keep wanting to poke around her office, but I've been waiting for you to unseal the room."

"I'm sorry. I didn't realize you wanted to get in there. Nothing turned up in the specimens we took from her lab, so I really should have taken the tape down. Feel free to go in there whenever you like. One last question," Hanley said. Kruger was already on her feet; Hanley got to hers too. "Did you apply water to her lips and Ogata's in the course of handling the bodies? Or to Kossuth's?"

She seemed puzzled. "Water? I don't think so. I can't think why we would have done that."

"I couldn't either." Hanley extended her hand. "Thank you. I'm very sorry for your loss."

Ingrid Kruger bit her lip. "Everyone's loss. Everyone's. If you'll excuse me, I will collect your samples, but right now I am going for a swim. I'm up to four a day. By spring I'll be fit enough to swim back to Munich." She turned away. "The water is the only place I do not think about it."


"Kim Ishikawa!" the stranger called out, striding across the parking lot, hand outstretched.

Ishikawa extended his hand reflexively, trying to place him. They shook hands. The man pushed his aviator sunglasses to the top of his head, exposing eyes as gray as the stone wall behind him. The face was smiling, the eyes not.

"Have we met?" Ishikawa said.

"Ah." The man's ebullience ebbed. "No, unfortunately not." He tried his best winning expression: happy sincerity.

"Walter Payne, *Times*, L.A.," he said, holding out a card.

Ishikawa accepted it, feeling the embossed lettering with his thumb. He said nothing, and locked his Toyota with a button on his remote.

"I was wondering," the reporter continued quickly, "if you had a moment to comment on the progress your colleague is making at the Trudeau research station?"

"Trudeau?"

"Please, Kim. I know you know. And now you know I know."

"Know what?"

"Sure. Turn the tables. Wouldn't you rather tell me directly than have me get it wrong? Or misattribute something to you?"

"I'm afraid I can't help you."

"Can't or won't?"

"Have you tried our press office?" Ishikawa said, pointing toward the building. Payne fell in step.

"Yeah, yeah. Mrs. G. and I just went a couple of rounds and called it a draw."

"Which is why you're hitting on me in the parking lot?"

The reporter tried looking disingenuous. "I need confirmation, is all, of what's happening up there. Just a nod, a wink, a raised eyebrow, a fucking erection."

Ishikawa couldn't help smiling. "How about a shake of the head no?"

Payne laughed mirthlessly. "Not quite what my editor had in mind."

"Sorry."

"No problem. I'll nail it down yet. All those unexplained deaths in the frozen wastes—too good a story to give up on. Not to mention the, quote, 'Unprecedented midwinter insertion,' unquote."

"Have you tried the Canadians? Isn't Trudeau their facility?"

Payne smirked. "So you've heard of Trudeau, then. Sure, our bureau in Ottawa is in discussions with the Canadian government's various spokespersons. So far they're incredulous—surprised that we're asking, referring it up the line, looking into it, waiting for clarification, and offering a lot of free tea."

"Sounds frustrating."

"Yeah."

"Well." Ishikawa held up the business card. "I'll be in touch if anything comes up."

"I'll be waiting by the phone," Payne said. "Anxiously." He

pulled his sunglasses back down over his eyes. They had reached the automatic doors, beyond which Payne could not follow. Ishikawa strode into the restricted corridors of the Center, past the guard.

He clipped on his ID badge and went straight to Munson's office to tell him the press was on to them. Munson called security to close off the grounds and man the parking-lot entrance booth.

"You got any files or disks or anything on your hard drive at home?" he asked.

"No," Ishikawa said. "It's all here."

"Good," Munson said, "then we still have a chance of corking this a while longer."

"Les?"

"Yeah?"

"Jess wants me to find the Russian woman from the sub."

Munson hesitated. "She's right. I'll catch hell for it, but that's the boss's job, right?" Munson pivoted in his office chair. "Okay. Get on it. And while you're at it, see if anyone on this list of Trudeau alumni can tell you anything that might help Jess. Seems one of the victims," he rummaged on his desk for the e-mail from Jessie, "Bascomb, was real worried about something, but even her girlfriend has no idea what." He tossed Ishikawa a printout the size of a small-town phonebook. "Cybil can cover you on the link to Trudeau. Who else is wired into the daily downloads from Jessie?"

"National Institutes of Health, the Antiviral Substance Program at the Scripps Clinic, the Agency for Toxic Substances and Disease Registry. I'm not sure who else is monitoring. Centers for Disease Control, certainly."

"Unhook 'em. Let's try to buy her a little more time."

# 30

Hanley listened politely while Felix Mackenzie insisted there hadn't been any real archaeology in Canada to speak of back before they'd found the Aleut campsites on the island. "And, speaking of the Aleut site, I've been thinking about what you said concerning evacuation. We've maintained Little Trudeau for years as our lifeboat, in case of disaster or fire. We always thought of it as a temporary shelter, but perhaps I should have Jack check the generators, even lay in more food."

"If there's a way to do it without alarming anyone, I would."

"Jack's outside a lot, so it shouldn't draw much attention." Mackenzie rubbed his face. "What are your next steps?"

"I need to get Alex Kossuth autopsied. I can barely spare the manpower, but Dr. Kruger said she's willing to lend a hand."

"That's fine. I'm worried about her. She's very worked up about what killed Annie and the others."

"Understandably. I also need to inspect the work site at the polynya, but I get the impression I may have trouble getting anyone to take me, except maybe Jack. He's the only one who doesn't seem to be afraid to go outside these days. Can you spare him for a few days?"

"Yes, yes. I'll see to that," Mackenzie said. "Jack will do it. You're right. He's never been afraid. I'll be happy to arrange it. Jack'll get you kitted out and prepped."

"Good," she said, pleased that he'd agreed to let Jack help her. She blushed slightly, and quickly turned back to her notes.

"Dr. Mackenzie, I know this is a long shot, but were any of the three—or anyone here—ever involved in the recovery of viral fragments from corpses buried in the permafrost?"

"You mean like the Hultin Expedition, the folks who exhumed victims of the 1918 influenza epidemic and extracted tissue samples?"

"Exactly."

"We all followed their work with great interest, but no. We've done nothing like that at Trudeau."

"But you do have a cemetery here."

"Cemetery? Ah, you mean the native burial site at Little Trudeau. That's been sealed for some time. We had objections from Inuit groups about our disturbing sacred remains. No one's actively studying it anymore. It's officially closed."

"Oh, dear. I promised my boy pictures of the excavation for his class."

"If Jack is with you, it should be okay. It's the least we can do for you. And Jack knows better than anyone what's off limits. Just don't touch anything in the burial site itself. That's our agreement with the First Nations."

"Who were the most recent visitors to the excavation itself? Do you know?"

"Recent? None. The main archaeological work was completed some time ago, and then Aboriginal Legal Services, acting on behalf of the First Nations, enjoined our studying the interred remains further." Mackenzie stretched out his legs. "How concerned should we be about a recurrence?"

"No way to say, but everything is pointing to the work site at the polynya as the point of contact. At the moment, I don't think it's wise for anyone to do field research until I can pin down where this infectious organism is hiding."

"Right now everyone's much too scared to venture outside the station. Our major funders have started grumbling pretty loudly. If this goes on much longer, I'm afraid they'll start to pull out of Trudeau altogether. I don't know how long we could continue without them." Mackenzie's voice was strained.

"I wish I could be more reassuring, Dr. Mackenzie, but this is the most devastating infection I've ever seen."

"Well," said Dr. Mackenzie. "I know you'll take every precaution."

On the wall of Jack's bedroom, a modern steel hoop held an antique opalescent window of seal gut. A musk ox hide, splayed on the wall, was shockingly large. Two posters adorned the backs of doors: one for COPE, the Committee for Original Peoples' Entitlement, the other celebrating the birth of the vast northern territory of Nunavut, returned by the Canadian government to the Inuit. The posters were in English, French, and a language that looked to Hanley like a cross between stick figure ciphers and computer hieroglyphics. A flyer calling for action on behalf of First Nations was pinned alongside it.

Hanley examined a photograph of a younger Nimit with another man. She stared at the jet-black hair framing the dark, high-cheekboned face, his white teeth bared in a shout or a laugh. Alongside the picture was a sculpture made of primitive materials: sinew, fur, a contorted body carved out of antler, a hideous face with a gaping mouth and two fangs made of animal teeth, at once ugly and completely beautiful. A white card bore the object's title and maker: *Human Turning into Evil Spirit,* Nick Sikkuark.

She picked up a book lying on the narrow, curved counter that bulged out along the interior wall, and flipped through chapters on the matriarchal society of the Inuit, their blurred concept of time. She got engrossed in the illustrations of women's tattoos and lip piercings, and didn't hear Nimit arrive.

"Doc?"

"Hi," Hanley said. She put back the book and embraced him.

"I tried to find you after we shut down the lab for the day. You weren't here."

"Haven't been sleeping well. But I've managed to tune the engine of every damn vehicle in Trudeau."

"I'm glad you've got the vehicles in good shape. I need to get out to the work site," she said, stroking his forearms. "Somewhere around there is almost certainly the place of their exposure. Mac said you'd arrange it."

"You ready to go today?"

"The sooner the better. And I'd appreciate a look at the archaeological dig on the way, if you don't mind."

"Little Trudeau?" Nimit hesitated for a moment. "Sure, easy enough. It's nearby. The weather's not great right now, but we could probably set out this evening. We'll take a wanigan. It's a lot bigger and more comfortable than the cat: six balloon tires and room inside to stretch out. Even has a commode and a kitchen pod. Before you can go anywhere outside, though, you'll need a survival demonstration."

"I already got the basic course from Mr. Stevenson on the way up here. Green light, yellow light, red light, make a shelter out of snow, avoid open water. I get the picture. I don't think I have time for the advanced course. I need to get out there."

"You're not going anywhere before you get a survival demonstration." Jack's face was unsmiling.

"I guess I'll be having a survival demonstration before I go outside then."

"Right."

"Right." He kissed her and she felt herself surrendering to him. He stripped off their clothing and took her. The pleasure was nearly painful. She wished she could see more, see everything, every particle of their coupling. If she could have jumped into his hairless skin, she would have.

"Not rising to the challenge, eh?" she said afterward, when she couldn't arouse him again. Looking at him closely, she said, "Are you worried about something?"

"Exhausted," he said, "that's all."

She kissed his eyelids. "Then sleep for a bit. I'll wake you in a while."

He pulled her close. She rested her cheek on his smooth chest and listened to the sound of his heart.

# 31

Using the list Munson had handed him, Ishikawa traced Trudeau alumni to the National Institute of Polar Research in Tokyo, the Stefanson Arctic Institute in Iceland, the Institute of Arctic and Alpine Research in Boulder, the Alfred Wegener Institute for Polar and Marine Research in Bremerhaven, the Danish Polar Center in Copenhagen, and the Swiss Committee on Polar Research in Bern. Finding someone who would talk candidly about their deceased former colleagues had proved hard.

Then things had gotten interesting. Dr. Akimitsu Nura responded to the contact by asking for a face-to-face meeting. A cautious academic, he had insisted on no notes, no tape, no permanent record of the meeting. Those were his conditions.

Ishikawa drove immediately to LAX and got on the next non-stop to Tokyo. Eighteen hours later he arrived in Japan with only the clothes on his back and taxied directly to a bullet train that propelled him south at over a hundred miles per hour. Ishikawa slept as he sped through a world of terraced fields, across unimaginable bridges, eventually finding himself on a ferry and then on a chilly beach on Japan's southernmost island.

A nearby volcano spewed smoke and gray soot so fine it seemed like mist. An old woman—carrying an odd broom and openly scornful of his sansei schoolbook Japanese—pointed down the shore to a lettuce patch being tended by a group of stooped women.

Ishikawa's shoes slowed him down. He stopped to take them off, tying them together to make them easier to carry. Although the air was cool, to his surprise the sand underfoot felt warm. As he drew closer to the garden, he realized the five heads of lettuce protruding from the sand were chatting with each other. One was especially gregarious and apparently also amusing, judging from how much the ladies in attendance were laughing demurely behind their callused palms. The other heads, quieter and less animated, were relaxing in the soothing volcanic sand in which their bodies had been buried by the women whom he had mistaken for gardeners. Ishikawa approached and introduced himself. The chatty head turned out to belong to Dr. Nura, whose tone turned sober. The ladies quickly helped to exhume the other four men, leaving Dr. Nura alone with Ishikawa. Seeing that Ishikawa had not followed the rapid Japanese, Dr. Nura switched to English.

"I told them not to bother with me, that you will dig me out later," Nura announced.

Ishikawa felt awkward talking to a head at his feet. Swinging his shoes off his shoulder, he sat down cross-legged beside Dr. Nura.

"You indicated you wished to tell me something about your friend Annie Bascomb. Anything you might share will be in the strictest confidence."

Nura stared up at him. "It has been several years since I finished my work at the station."

"You were her close associate, I understand."

"I am honored to have you think so. If I may say, I believe that is correct. She . . . was a unique person, truly. Her passing is premature, and upsetting." He raised his chin at Ishikawa. "This is not the proper place for such a conversation. Can you extract me?" He indicated a spade lying beside him on the sand.

"Of course," Ishikawa said, and dexterously dug around Dr. Nura's shoulders, loosening the sand sufficiently to free his hands and arms. Nura pulled himself out.

"Ah," he said, "that was refreshing, but now I feel chilly." He retrieved a robe and indicated that they should walk. Ishikawa planted the spade upright in the sand and fell into step.

"Can you say what your work consisted of?" he said, catching up.

"Certainly. She is—was—with the Canadian environmental group at Trudeau. She was an environmental biochemist. As am I. I teach now at Tokyo University. We collaborated on studies of the impact upon the Barents Sea and on the Arctic as a whole of a half-century's industrial intrusion and pollution caused by negligent practices: effluents, accidental spills, and the like. And a second study in conjunction with the Canadian Atmospheric Environment Service on the effect of changes in thermohaline circulation upon ocean ecosystems and weather brought about by the melting of the Arctic. We modeled contingencies. The effects were most disturbing." He bowed his head. "She was completely dedicated. An inspired person."

"You had more recent contact?"

"Yes, we corresponded monthly by e-mail. Her last two were troubling. In the first she said she was deeply affected by something and that she was thinking about what she should do. In the second—which was her last—she intimated that she was weighing the consequences of making public her concerns."

"Did she say what they were? Could you tell what she might be referring to?"

"No," said Nura. "She was guarded, not entirely trusting the security of e-mail communications. It must have been serious. She implied she was considering actions that would risk her career and standing, and certainly could make her unwelcome at the station."

"Would you be willing to share these communiqués with us, sir?"

"I didn't retain them, I am sorry to say, as I also had to tell her friend Dr. Kruger. She seemed hungry for any reminiscence of Annie. But I assure you, my recollection is accurate. Perhaps Mr. Stevenson might be able to tell you more. He was on the station's governing board and kept abreast of Annie's work." He walked with his hands behind his back, tranquil and composed, although his mourning for Annie Bascomb was palpable. "I cannot believe she is dead."

The volcano's craw glowed faintly against the approaching darkness. Plumes of ash rose from it like bats. The two men walked in leisurely fashion across the warm sand, enjoying the cool evening breeze.

"My spa is providing a tour into the hills for those interested in the pleasures of firefly watching. It is a popular diversion here. Perhaps you care to join me?"

Ishikawa regretfully declined.

They strolled on. Ishikawa listened respectfully to Dr. Nura reminisce some more about his beloved colleague, and calculated time zones.

# 32

Nimit took her out to the large dome where the transports were garaged and serviced. In the changing room, he turned his back to her and started stripping. She found her equipment hook and did likewise. She couldn't resist a quick peek over her shoulder. The glance at his powerfully built body sent a tremor of longing through her.

She talcumed herself and struggled with the thin innermost layer. She remembered her college roommate trying to teach her how to put stockings on straight, which she never quite mastered. When forced to wear them to a formal occasion, she would periodically have to excuse herself to straighten them. The rest of the polar suit went on easily. Hanley carefully donned her helmet for the first time since arriving and checked its operating status. Nimit led the way into the foyer, carrying an exaggeratedly large glassware thermometer full of sloshing mercury.

"I hope that's not rectal," Hanley said. Nimit didn't laugh. Okay, she thought. Stick to business.

Just off the apron was a ledge about the size of a balcony, perched on the edge of the rock face. Before leading the way out, Nimit turned to her.

"Here's my speech. From here it looks okay out there, just a cold version of planet Earth. It's not. It's something else. I explain this once because that's all you get in this environment." He paused. "Any questions so far?"

"How thick is the ice? We can't fall through, can we?"

"Hardly. It's about seven feet on average. But leads and lanes do open from time to time. You've got to stay alert."

He waited to see if she had other questions; she didn't. "Okay, the nos. No earrings, no glasses other than propylene, no contact lenses, no regular cameras, no field glasses, no test tubes, no pens. They'll freeze to you, then they'll crumble."

"I think I've heard this song."

"You don't want fingers falling off or your nose turning black, or your tongue freezing to metal or your eyelashes to a viewfinder. Don't touch anything with a bare hand. If you do, your only chance to save some skin is to pee on it. The heat of the urine will release you, and then you must dry it immediately before the liquid freezes."

"I think that one's got to be easier for a guy."

"Probably. So don't chance it. No bare hands. Questions?"

"Anybody ever freeze to another person?"

"Not that they've admitted," he said.

"I guess they'd have to find someone to pee on them to set them free," she said.

"Sounds kinky."

"You think? So what's the moral of your story?"

"Don't run naked in the Arctic. Keep your flesh covered. Stay with your suit," Nimit said. "It's a frozen desert out there. Remember? Hell with the fires out."

"Is that how you see it?"

He eyed her as he tugged at her polar suit, checking the seals. "No."

"What's it like for you?"

"Peaceful. Quiet. Not crowded, like in here."

"Jack, before we go out there, I think you need to hear *my* speech on survival. You said the Arctic only gives you one chance. The bug I'm after is a hell of a lot more dangerous than ice and wind and water. If we come into contact with it, we may have no chance. So far, this infection hasn't spared anyone. Mackenzie asked you to take me out there, but you don't have to go. My job is to take these risks—yours isn't."

"I know. But I like the company."

"Me too. And I'm willing to follow your instructions about wind, snow, ice, whatever. But when we're out at the polynya, you have to follow mine. We can't fit hazmat gear under this getup, so whatever samples need to be collected, I'll do it. If we trap any animals, let me handle the traps. I don't want you touching anything that looks unfamiliar, any animal that appears ill. If we see any dead creatures, particularly birds, you don't touch them. That's my job. Okay?"

Nimit nodded. He gestured toward the ledge beyond the sliding hatch. "We finish my lesson outside." He led her onto the walkway. "Keep your visor open. Careful, there's no railing. It's a long slide down." He slid open the portal. They were forty meters up.

The air was exhilarating for a second, then devastating, as though oxygen were being torn from her chest a molecule at a time. She could only manage tiny sips. Each was a stab. "It's like breathing razors," Hanley croaked. "Geez."

Ice was forming at the corners of her mouth and the tip of her nose. Nimit seemed unaffected, barely squinting against the wind. Granules they had disturbed with their feet, billowed out from the ledge. His eyebrows turned white, her nose numb.

Nimit retrieved the glass tube of mercury from his cardboard box and plinked the glass with his gloved hand. It crumbled to grains and blew away. The mercury was a solid rod in his hand.

"I get the point," Hanley croaked, one eye frosted shut. Her lungs were burning, her status light flashing red. "My car alarm's going off."

"Close your visor."

Hanley complied instantly. The right eye saw everything in white. Her face grew moist as the ice melted. Her vision normalized. Her nose dripped. She sneezed. In a moment the faceplate cleared, and the light in her helmet went green.

"Okay," Nimit said, his faceplate close to hers. "There's only one prevailing truth about the Arctic you have to remember. It's an Inuit expression: *ajaqnak*."

"What does that mean?"

His black eyes fixed on her. "Shit happens."

## 33

**N**imit had insisted that she consume as many calories as she could before they set out. Hanley, in slacks and a dark-blue sweater, ran her fingers through her hair to comb it, and set off dutifully for the larger dining hall.

As she made her way through the dinner line, she saw Felix Mackenzie in his customary spot on the far side of the dining hall, beyond the huge cherry tree. He was framed by the imposing vertical window just behind him, an odd rhomboid portal that stuck out of the dome, creating the illusion that Mackenzie was actually sitting outside, oblivious to the elements.

One of the Russians was talking to him and gesticulating; a German, sitting opposite Mackenzie with arms crossed, was shaking his head slowly, disagreeing. Emile Verneau, seated alongside, followed the conversation without participating, occasionally pausing to note something in a small notebook. Senior staff drifted past, some pausing to whisper in Mackenzie's ear, exchange a word or two, others just acknowledging him with nods on their way to their labs or to bed after their shifts. Hanley smiled to see Jack Nimit stop by to talk, placing his hand on the older man's shoulder. Mackenzie put his hand atop Nimit's for a moment before the younger man left. Simon King entered, took in the scene, turned on his heel and walked away. Does not play well with others, Hanley thought.

Mackenzie waved her over and asked the others to excuse them. They exchanged pleasantries as he poured her coffee, then he asked,

"Have you everything you need for your trip? Is Jack behaving himself?"

"Absolutely," she said, a little taken aback. "Everyone has been generous and selfless. I can't believe the hours Dee and the others are putting in."

Mackenzie gave a slight nod. "Good. Good. And how are things with you and Jack? I hear you're romancing."

Hanley was chagrined. "I suppose privacy is too much to expect in circumstances like these."

"Useless to even think about," he said. "He seems to be serious about you." Hanley sipped her cup and stared out at the beautiful desolation illuminated by the exterior lights. The wind roared: a rare sound. Billowing snow and ice obscured the wind turbines on the ridge above, spinning like airplane propellers.

His demeanor became serious. "He means a lot to me, to all of us here. We don't want to lose him to a casual romance." He examined his palm for a moment. "Being at Trudeau is a bit like being on a ship or a transcontinental train. You're removed from the rest of the world. When spring comes and we're reconnected to the outside, things may seem different to you. Few relationships that start here survive, to be perfectly honest. Few marriages either."

"Are you speaking from experience?" Stung by his dismissal of her as a "casual romance," she was willing to inflict a little pain in return.

"By the time I was prepared to live a normal life, my wife had passed. So I stayed. There wasn't anywhere else for me by then."

"I'm sorry." His melancholy made her regret her earlier bitterness. Maybe he was genuinely trying to protect her—and Jack.

"Don't be. I loved it here. I only wish I had shared it with her. I was always away."

"I know what you're saying. My son lives with his father, hundreds of miles from me. I rarely see him. I'm beginning to realize I need to be with him much more than on school holidays."

"He's ten, you said?"

"Yes."

"Then you found out in time."

"And you, Dr. Mackenzie? Will you stay at Trudeau?" she said. "I understand many people are thinking of leaving after this season, after . . ."

He looked wounded at the idea of his colleagues' abandoning the ship he had so lovingly created. He shook his head. "I am among them. But perhaps not for the same reason. I have been offered the directorship of the Arctic National Preserve, but I doubt I will accept. I don't think I can bear witness to any more changes in the High Arctic."

"You mean the polar cap melting, the oceans rising?"

Mackenzie sighed. "If only it were that simple." He touched a napkin to his lips. "If it all melts, fifty-eight thousand cubic kilometers of fresh, cold Arctic water will flow into the Atlantic. Being cold, it should slip under the warmer water of the Gulf Stream. But because it's fresh water, it's lighter; so it will sit on top and it will snuff out the prevailing current. In the models, the Gulf Stream stops flowing."

"Just like that? Without warning?"

He shook his head. "We're getting our warnings. Bizarre weather. Floods. Droughts. Fires. The environment is out of kilter. No one's listening. They chatter endlessly, but they listen not a whit." He raised his eyes, cold with anger. "Once upon a time, at the end of the Cretaceous period, the carbon dioxide levels rose to seven times what they are now and the dinosaurs mysteriously disappeared. We're recreating that experiment."

He turned his gaze up at the roof. "Each season I go out later to greet our returning birds because each year they return a little later. Every year there is less winter, fewer migrating birds. The pack ice is half as thick as when Alex Kossuth and Primakov and I first came to the High Arctic. By midcentury there won't be any ice at all during the summer months. Trudeau, if it's still here, will be resupplied by ship." He raked his hair with his hand. "Canada has had two decades of drought from insufficient snowfall. Two decades. And Ottawa is still calling for committees and wondering whether it has a problem."

"Yes, our government is a little slow on the uptake too."

"That's the one trouble with democracies. A problem isn't a problem until it's a hopeless crisis."

Uli appeared in his lab coat, anxiously summoning Hanley.

"Excuse me," she said to Mackenzie, and joined him in the corridor. He had both hands buried in the pockets of his smock.

"What is it?" Hanley said.

"I stopped by the horticultural lab you requisitioned for the Kossuth autopsy."

"And?"

"Dr. Kruger is there with Dee."

"Great."

"Not completely." Uli was agitated. "Dr. Kruger keeps stopping, like she can't bring herself to continue. I think you may have to take over."

"Shit. I've got my hands full getting ready to go out to the polynya. Okay, let's take a look."

They hurried to the lab, which was shut down for the winter. A glass window separated them from the procedure under way in the adjoining room, where Dee and Ingrid Kruger had cleaned a long, metal potting table and laid out the mottled body. Kruger was bent over her work, Dee holding the instruments.

Dee was wearing a full biohazard suit and respirator with independent air supply, but Dr. Kruger had apparently declined any special equipment. Her sole concessions to Hanley's orders were double gowns, a plastic face shield, and a double layer of polyvinyl gloves.

"Why the hell isn't she in a Casper suit?"

Uli shrugged. "She said she'd done two without wearing such a thing and didn't see the need."

Hanley donned the familiar, bulky biohazard suit that Kruger had rejected. She pulled it on with impressive ease and turned on the oxygen valve of her portable tank, took two breaths to check air flow, and stepped into the sanitizing tent temporarily rigged outside the door to the room where Dee and Ingrid Kruger were working. She pulled the cord on the bleach and was showered with the disinfectant, followed by distilled water. Shaking off as much of the liquid as she could, she passed through the door.

Dr. Kruger was dictating into a recorder hung just above her head. The spools turned slowly beside its tiny red eye. The surgeon seemed in complete control—confident, erect, businesslike. Kruger checked over her shoulder to see who had entered, and immediately returned to her task, noting the time and Hanley's arrival on the audiotape as she deposited another tissue sample into a stainless steel basin. Dee handed Kruger a curved blade and carried the basin to a scale. She read out the weight of the specimen in grams and slid it into a vial. Kruger repeated the figure into the recorder. Then she stood, unmoving.

Hanley watched from a short distance behind Kruger's shoulder. She made an exasperated gesture at Dee, motioning at Kruger then tapping her own biohazard suit. Dee rolled her eyes and shrugged helplessly as she marked the specimen vial and waited for Dr. Kruger's next request for instruments.

"Nice of you to join us," Kruger said, regaining her focus.

Beads of water trailed down Hanley's visor. "Can I persuade you to put on a biohazard suit, Doctor? You're exposing yourself unnecessarily."

Kruger kept working as she answered. "I'm sorry. That space-suit getup was too bulky for me. I've never worked in one before. Alex Kossuth clearly died of the elements, not anything else."

"Doctor—"

"Look, this is very hard for me. And I am not feeling a hundred percent."

"But he was with the others. He may have been exposed."

"In which case, the total cellular destruction in the body has wiped out any intruders as well."

"Doctor, I don't like playing any odds, no matter how good they are."

Kruger shot her a bemused glance. "Are you worried? You appear safe enough, Doctor."

She resumed dictating. Hanley shook her fists behind Kruger's back in a hopeless gesture only Dee could see. Then Kruger stopped. She stood poised over the cadaver, scalpel raised like a baton. Hanley had seen her measured style on the Bascomb autopsy DVD. Kruger had a sure touch. No hesitation, no wavering. But instead of a swift, definite cut, she plunged the scalpel downward in a jagged slash, cutting through flesh, striking the ribcage with force. The blade bounced off bone and cartilage, and she slashed downward again, actually gouging the corpse.

Dee's eyes went wide with horror. "Ingrid!" she yelled. "What on earth are you doing?"

Kruger went rigid and toppled straight back. She was on the floor, in spasm, her arms straight down and turned slightly in, as if she were playing at being a seal, slapping her fins together. But her body was in seizure and she shook and shuddered, her face distorted. A hideous low whine sounded in her throat as she flailed. Then her back arched impossibly, as if possessed, her mouth foamed, her eyes . . .

Dee dropped the instrument tray and rushed around the autopsy table. "Ingrid!"

Hanley grabbed Dee's shoulder and held her back. Dee tried to wrench free. "She's going to choke herself!"

Kruger bent backward, her body like a taut bow, her forehead banging against the floor. She quaked as if jolted with electric shocks.

"Let me go!" Dee screamed, straining to break loose from Hanley's grasp.

Hanley held fast, staring at Kruger's contortions. Kruger's body locked, the death throes over. Her eyes were seeping.

"Don't touch her," Hanley said.

"But—"

"Don't touch her. Don't touch anything."

"We've got to—"

"There's no helping her. Step outside. Right now. Get under the detox shower." Hanley pushed her toward the door—"Now!"—and shoved her out. She grabbed the audiotape and DVD, closed the lab door behind them and held Dee in the makeshift scrubber.

"Pull the cord!"

Dee doused herself with bleach.

"Turn all the way around. Get every surface."

Hanley counted off fifteen seconds. The bleach would kill most anything bacterial or viral. But if it was prion or mycoplasma, even the bleach wouldn't protect them. She suppressed the thought. "Okay, Dee, rinse off." A watery downpour followed.

Dee emerged, her suit dripping. She was weeping and coughing, her body trembling.

"Wait right there," Hanley said. "Don't move."

A hum rose from Dee's throat.

"Dee, do you understand?"

Dee nodded rapidly.

Hanley closed the flap of the scrub tent and pulled the cord on a second supply of Clorox, turning slowly, letting it cascade over her. When it stopped, she doused herself with water and stepped out. She took Dee by the wrist and led her away.

Though visibly shaken, Nimit welded two flat bars across the horticulture lab's door, then welded shut the fire door. They lowered the temperature in the lab to just above freezing, taped the thermostat in place, then shut and locked the box, enclosing it. Hanley shakily put up biohazard signs all over the outer door, all around the huge sign that read QUARANTINED—DO NOT ENTER.

Even before any official announcement, word shot around the station and an eerie quiet descended on Trudeau. Most people remained in their rooms or sat in small groups, talking in subdued tones about the killer that was now among them. No one spoke to her; many stepped aside quickly when she walked by. Everyone avoided eye contact, except King. He stared straight at her with loathing as she passed him.

"Brilliant work, Dr. Hanley. Simply brilliant."

# 34

Dee sprawled across Hanley's bed. "They don't blame you, Jess."

"You should have seen King."

"Simon King is an asshole. Please."

"But I agree with him. I blame me. If only—"

"'If only' nothing." Dee sat up. She had cried for an hour but was rallying herself. "Ingrid Kruger didn't do what she was supposed to do and put on the goddamn suit. The precautions were there. She ignored them. It's tragic; it's stupid. It's done. Over."

"Okay, but I thought the procedure would be routine too. I mean, I publicly assured people that I didn't think the bodies were contagious. Shit, I should have insisted."

"There's no use arguing about what's happened. It's not like she didn't know what she was doing. She was a physician, for goodness' sake. Ingrid got unlucky. That's all. So many of us had been exposed to the bodies with no effect. She didn't suspect anything; none of us did. It happened."

"But if I—"

"Jess, stop!" Dee exclaimed. "Ingrid wasn't a novice. She wouldn't have done the autopsy without more protection if she had had any inkling that Kossuth was a carrier. Hell, she and I did two autopsies on people who actually died of this thing, wearing only gowns, gloves, and masks. It was perfectly reasonable not to put on full gear for a body that was totally asymptomatic. Also wrong. You can't shoulder this as if you'd deliberately exposed her to high risk. She did it to herself by not bothering with the suit. If she had followed the procedure you laid out, she'd be with us now."

"Tell me again what you wore for the first two autopsies."

Dee ticked off the list: caps, gowns, surgical masks, faceplates, and gloves. "No respirators, obviously, because we didn't have any."

"Yet somehow those bodies were safe to handle. The lethal agent had burned itself out. Now Alex Kossuth's apparently asymptomatic body turns out to have been a time bomb." Hanley held her face in her hands. "Somehow the bug survives being frozen. Maybe Kossuth was infected along with the others, but abandoning his clothes and stepping out of his life put the bug on hold. Maybe that's why he stripped down—to stop it. Maybe unfreezing and opening the body reactivated it. How could that be? It feels . . . wrong."

"You think?"

"I don't know what I think. Hell, I just feel like crap."

"Fine," Dee said. "I'll give you an hour. Feel like shit for two if you have to. Then you've *got* to find this thing, or else none of us will be allowed home in March, assuming we make it to March. They'll cage us up somewhere and make lab rats of us if we're still upright. I don't mind telling you, I'm scared."

Hanley stood with hands to her brow. "Five dead. Five out of five. Nothing's that lethal except avian flu. There's something—"

There was a gentle knock at the open door. Hanley hoped it was Jack. A gaunt Mackenzie stepped in, followed by Emile Verneau.

Mackenzie said, "What happened?"

Hanley rubbed a hand across her forehead. "Dr. Kruger didn't accept the precaution of a biohazard suit. Three hours and forty-eight minutes into the autopsy she went rigid, then into a seizure that culminated moments later with her death."

"Ingrid dead," Verneau said. "But you said the corpses weren't contagious."

"I was wrong. Dee and I each had our own air supply, and we were fine. Ingrid Kruger . . . she must have inhaled it. How is the staff reacting?" Hanley said.

Mackenzie exhaled volubly. "Shock. Disbelief."

"And naked fear," Verneau added. "They are terrified the organism is in the station, contrary to your earlier assurances. Everyone is asking for masks and gloves. We just don't have those in supply. I don't know what to tell them."

Hanley nodded, resigned. The fear was real and well founded. "You need to circulate a bulletin explaining how secure we've made the area the bodies are in. Double seals, lowered temperature. And that Dee and I decontaminated thoroughly." She didn't point out that even double masks and gloves hadn't protected Ingrid Kruger.

"What will you do now?" Verneau said. "Perhaps you want to rethink your approach after this."

Hanley shook her head. "No. We keep going until we find it."

"What do we do about their bodies?" Verneau said. "Dr. Kruger and Alex?"

"Until we know more," Hanley said, "they stay where they are. No one goes near them."

Verneau nodded to Mackenzie. "All right," Mackenzie said, and ushered everyone out.

Hanley exhaled slowly to calm herself as she progressed through the labyrinth of passageways. She reported the fatality to Cybil online, then paced the outer lab, trying to push away the thick white fog that filled her brain. Next to her workstation, a floor-to-ceiling whiteboard on wheels was covered with scrawled notes from the first few days, full of crossed-out hypotheses. Now the whiteboard's main function was to allow Hanley to vent her frustration by propelling it across the room. She took the marker and drew a long diagonal slash through the list of eliminated possibilities, then spun the board around to the side where she had printed the last names of the victims in large block letters. She added KRUGER.

On the third lap around the lab, she saw the envelope taped to the overhead fluorescent above her workbench. She took it down and opened it. In a beautiful hand, she read: *Thank you for allowing me to return to Annie's lab. I found all I needed. Ingrid Kruger*

∎

Clutching the note, Hanley moved quietly along the corridors. When she reached Kruger's office, she let herself in and closed the door. Feeling along the wall, she turned on the lights in the foyer and stepped in farther.

Her breath caught in her throat. A figure sat at the bare desk. "Jack."

He glanced back over his shoulder. The place was empty, the shelves bare. A lone stack of papers sat on the desk.

"Correspondence, notes, addresses—all personal," he said.

Hanley recovered herself and said, "What about the computer?"

"See for yourself."

The computer screen glowed blue. No desktop, no icons. The cursor throbbed in the top left corner. The text read—C formatted.

"It's blank. All gone. Cleaned."

"What the hell is happening?" Hanley said. "What do I do now?"

"You get out of the station. We go to the polynya."

# 35

Nimit eased the machine carefully down the long ramp and out into the night. A high-chassied robot cart, called a slinky, ran ahead of them, tethered to their vehicle by a coiled yellow wire. Checked for unanticipated openings in the ice.

At twenty-five minutes after eight P.M., the edge of the moon peeped above the flat, perfect blackness of the horizon and began its climb. By nine o'clock the cobalt-blue moon was so bright their vehicle actually cast a distinct shadow as it whined across the ghostly expanse of the slope. The ridged terrain was a moonscape, half illuminated, the other half shadowed so totally there seemed to be nothing beyond it, just emptiness. The edge of the world.

The clarity was breathtaking, the sky studded with stars, so dazzlingly bright Hanley had no sense of distance, no reference points. It took her a long time to adjust to this landscape without proportion or dimension. Some moments the immensity seemed to her actually a miniature, like a tabletop model. Other times the vastness of the desolation dwarfed her spirit.

"I wish I could relax and take it all in," she said.

"You haven't had much downtime since you arrived, have you?"

"Only with you. Everyone wants me working on the case around the clock. Who can blame them? They want to feel protected. And now, after Ingrid, it's clear to them—and to me—I'm not doing a very good job of it. I know it's cowardly, but I'm not sorry to be out of the station right now. It's hard to be on the receiving end of all that anger. I wouldn't blame you if you were pissed off at me too, you know."

"I'm not. I'd be lying if I said I wasn't scared. Everybody is. But we know science takes time."

"Sure, but this isn't some abstract piece of polar research. Your friends are dying. Nobody could have prevented the first exposure, but I was responsible for your safety after I arrived, and now another one of your colleagues is dead. And she didn't have to die."

"Nothing pointed to Alex being contagious."

"It's totally illogical. Yet I shouldn't have ruled out the possibility. I should never have let anyone else handle the body." She slapped her thigh in frustration. Nimit reached over and held her hand steady.

"Hey, hang in there. Don't all your cases take patience?"

"Sure, except right now who at Trudeau wants to hear that it took months to figure out the cause of Ebola or Legionnaire's? Or that they took four thousand samples from sixty different species in the markets in southern China, trying to find the source of SARS? I'm not going to inspire anyone's confidence by reminding people that Lyme disease took four years to identify."

"Well, I'd keep that part from Simon King if I were you. But don't be so hard on yourself. All those outbreaks had teams of people working on them."

"It's not just that I'm working virtually solo. I've been there before. This isn't like any organism I've ever worked with."

"How come?"

"Speed. Slow viruses can incubate longer than someone's life. The fastest I've seen are like floods. Organs and veins aren't solid, you know. They're permeable. If some organism destroys the film that keeps the blood in the veins and organs, the liquid seeps right out. The person drowns. Literally. But even that takes days. In this case, the growth was explosive. Yet it also had the capacity to lie dormant in Alex Kossuth's frozen flesh. It doesn't make sense. When the body thawed out," said Hanley, "could it have become viremic?"

She was quiet for a few minutes, brooding over the most recent death.

A man-made berm appeared among the ridges of ice. Nimit maneuvered their vehicle expertly up the incline leading to the top of the wall and onto a perfectly flat field.

"My guys built and maintain this landing strip. Most icy surfaces are pretty grumbly. You'll notice this one is completely smooth." He smiled, and Hanley could see the pride he took in his work. She was grateful too, for his obvious attempt to distract her from her self-recrimination.

"You could skate out here," Hanley said.

Half a mile farther on, he pointed to a knoll; at the top, the rise leveled out onto a plateau.

"There's a lake basin at the center," he told her. "That's where we scooped out the hydrohole."

"I'll have to take your word for it." The plateau with the frozen lake was indistinguishable from the rest of the ice, and became completely invisible as the wind picked up, blowing loose particles upward. Their headlights shone into a sheet of white, then blurred as the windshield went black. Nimit switched on an interior light.

"What's happening?" Hanley said.

"The wind's kicked up. We've been whited out."

"How long will it last?"

"You never know for sure, but it shouldn't be long. There were no severe weather cells when I checked before we came out. It should only be a few minutes. Don't worry. We've got rations, survival gear. I brought the chemical potty."

"Oh, swell."

"Try to relax. We just have to wait it out."

Hanley checked her equipment. Nimit had weeded out the items that couldn't withstand the severity of the elements they were likely to encounter, tossing aside all the zippered nylon packets, the plastic vials and syringes, the tubes and glass jars for collecting specimens. He substituted a box full of special temperature-resistant bottles with orange caps, and polyethylene bags that were good to a hundred below. She'd added a few small animal traps in the event they came across any likely viral hosts.

They sat silent for a while. Nimit seemed not to mind, but Hanley found it taxing. She needed to be moving, to feel that she was doing something useful. Her mind circled back to Kossuth's body on the autopsy table.

"What do you think Kossuth's last moments were like?"

He paused, reflecting. "Unpleasant. With no clothing, the temperature at thirty below and, say, a thirty-mile-an-hour wind, he would have been dead in half a minute. But he wasn't so lucky. It was fifty below that afternoon, but there was practically no wind. I would guess he lasted ten or twelve minutes."

"You found him out in this, naked?"

"Yes."

"How far was he from the others?"

"I don't know—far—out of their sight."

"Did he know what happened to them?"

"He could have heard something on the local channel before he tossed his suit."

"Did the station hear them too?"

"No. They wouldn't have been on the intercom channels. Teddy and his people monitor the long-range frequencies, not local VHF chatter. Do you know what happened to him?"

Hanley shook her head. "Not yet."

He poured her coffee from the insulated thermos, and she removed her gloves to take the cup. She sipped slowly, staring at the white wall in the headlights. Somewhere, far out beyond the light, was the horizon and the curve of the earth, and beyond that the sun and home. She exhaled and held the palms of her hands over her coffee.

"Rub your hands together, like this," said Nimit, demonstrating, "and then hold them against your eyes." He raised his hands, palms out, and cupped her eyes. She murmured with pleasure: the heat of his hands was soothing. She wished he'd place them elsewhere.

The headlights glowed against the blowing snow, which thinned and vanished. Hanley could see the top of a man-made structure up on the plateau.

"What did Minskov find up there," Hanley said, "below the lake ice?"

"Mostly a lot of algal mats."

"Doesn't sound all that exciting."

"Oh, you should've been here when we popped that baby. We treated it like a time capsule."

"What do you mean?"

"The glaciologists figured out that the surface had been sealed for maybe a few million years."

"Whoa," Hanley said. "Now that's old."

"Nah." Nimit turned toward her. "Our lake's a baby compared to ones they've found buried down in Antarctica. They've plotted seventy-six buried freshwater lakes under the ice. One's about the size of Lake Ontario."

"Under the ice? You're serious."

"Completely. And in ice that's two miles thick. Ready? Here we go," he said, and they resumed the journey, maneuvering carefully.

"Time for the tourist attraction?"

Nimit turned to her, face like a sledgehammer. "It's not a tourist attraction. It's a tomb."

Chastised, Hanley just nodded.

# 36

Nimit veered off toward the odd structure she had first seen from the air. What had looked like a bunker in the unsteady light of flares was in fact a huge covered trench easily four cars wide. The corrugated metal roof was trussed underneath and covered with snow.

A long ramp led down into it from one end. Nimit stopped at the top and eased the wanigan into the darkness.

"We scooped it all out with an eight-bladed rotor—the kind used to open alpine passes. Took a hundred fifty-three hours to carve this out."

Fifty-five-gallon fuel drums lined the wall of the entrance ramp.

"Decoration?" Hanley said.

"No. Empties. Too expensive to get rid of," Nimit said. "Costs two hundred dollars American to airlift one out of here. My budget won't take it at the moment."

"If I guaranteed their eventual removal, could you bring some to the hot lab for me? I could use a half dozen for lab runoff and contaminants, if you could rig them up to our detox shower and hazardous wastes chute."

"Sure, anything to help," Nimit said, and stopped the wanigan.

Carrying powerful lamps, they made their way into the darkness. Wooden planks creaked underfoot. A dozen eyes glowed. Nimit flashed his light in their direction and they scattered. Hanley started, and felt something run across her foot.

"Rats?"

"Don't be scared," he said.

"Me? I slow-pitched for the L.A. Lab Rats. We had a few experiment rejects as mascots. Not to mention my personal collection back in my salad days."

"They're lemmings. Not rats. Rats don't like the Arctic."

"I can understand why," Hanley said. He turned on her abruptly. She raised her hands defensively. "Didn't mean it, didn't mean it." She used her headlamp to scan the tunnel. She unwrapped one of the animal traps. "I'm going to try to bag a couple for testing. Rodents are notorious viral hosts," she said, and set the trap on the ground. "I don't care how healthy they seem—once they're in the trap, keep your distance. And if you see any dead lemmings, give a shout."

In the light of their headlamps, Hanley could see other passages radiating from the main tunnel at right angles. Quonsets, painted yellow and red, occupied the side corridors Nimit called *allées*. These were carved out perpendicular to the main street they were following. A Toronto street sign on one read *YONGE*; the adjoining panel read *BLOOR*. Farther on was a pair of ornamental pink flamingos, a patch of artificial green turf, and an assemblage of twisted copper piping and kettles.

"What's that?" Hanley pointed at the odd contraption with the beam of her light.

"A still," Nimit answered. "Fueled a lot of parties when it was the only hooch around. One of the engineers made a coil out of bull kelp. Ever see it? Thick as your fist and looks like long hollow tubing. They froze it into the looped shape they wanted, packed it in ice and began distilling. Eventually I replaced the kelp with that metal coil."

"You know how to brew?"

"Sure. It's easy. You don't have to be a chemistry major to make beer."

*Or bioweapons,* thought Hanley, but she brushed the thought aside.

He removed his helmet and signaled it was all right to follow suit. She eased hers off cautiously.

"Hey," she said, "feels warm."

"It is. Relatively. It's always twenty degrees Fahrenheit down here." His breath smoked. "In summer the snow cools the air. Keeps the mosquitoes out."

They hiked on into the gloom. Nimit was leading her into one of the *allées* without a Quonset hut. The passage canted downward.

"What if we trip over a hibernating bear?"

"Run," Nimit said. "But we're more likely to bump into a *tupilat*."

"What's that?"

"A ghost."

The passage grew narrower, the snow walls undulating unevenly.

"They're shifting," Nimit observed. "We'll have to do some milling soon. The permafrost expands and contracts and makes the walls wiggle like this."

"Mackenzie told me you guys maintain this place in case of fire. It must take a lot of work to keep up."

"Well, we worry a lot about fire. You've seen what it can do."

They reached a smaller opening, no longer ice, but a hole cut into stone. Nimit undid a fine netting strung across it. "To keep the lemmings out," he said without pausing, then bent down and entered the dark mouth of the rock tunnel. Hanley followed. The space had an entirely different odor from the snow passage: musty, almost sweet, like her grandmother's Empire couch. The shaft continued to narrow until they were crawling on hands and knees. Nimit signaled for her to duck her head, and they were both crawling on their bellies into a modest cave, Hanley protecting her insulated camera case.

Nimit rose to his feet, helped her up and drew closed more netting across the tunnel mouth. He collapsed the reflector of his lamp to illuminate the whole room.

They were not alone. Two dozen figures sat in the middle of a black circle on the stone floor, legs crossed, hands clasped just beneath their chins, their faces parched. Their leathery skin was black in spots but otherwise perfectly preserved, sinewy muscles sculpting their features. Tatters of animal hide hanging from crossed arches of whale ribs overhead indicated what had been some kind of cupola.

"Whoa!" Hanley exclaimed. "Incredible." She turned in a circle, taking it all in. Then, a little hesitantly, she said. "Is it okay to take flash pictures for my son?"

Nimit made a be-my-guest gesture. She joined her lamp to Nimit's and more figures became visible, arranged on tiers that rose up from the floor of the cave.

Males were in the front row, then the women and several children, the flesh surprisingly intact, many with eyes open and staring. Almost all had been preserved by the cold, except for two mummified figures at the farther side of the cave who were so severely decomposed they looked like primates, their jawbones and teeth exposed, as if snarling. Yet even their hands and fingers and nails were startlingly preserved and unnervingly expressive, held against their chests in supplication.

"The bodies are wrapped in animal skins," Nimit said. "Otter and sea lion. You see how the men's backs are braced against war shields? Most Inuit don't have a word for war, but these are Aleuts. Unlike most northern peoples, Aleuts were warriors."

"How were they prepared?"

"The corpses were eviscerated and stuffed with elymus—wild rye. The perfectly dry atmosphere and the cold will preserve them forever. The oldest remains I've seen were sixteen hundred years. These are much newer—late nineteenth century. The island was a summer campsite for the Aleuts. That's what brought Mac and everyone here to begin with. But even before that, archaeologists had found artifacts of stone-tool ancestors, layers and layers of animal bones. The bottommost were from extinct creatures. They even found fingerprints."

"Fingerprints?"

"Mmm. In the fat and soot of the firepits they cooked over. The prints got baked into the clay." Nimit turned slowly, taking in the room. "The Aleut came much later. Nomads too, of course."

Hanley gazed at the still forms. Still kicking herself for having called it a tourist attraction, she hesitated before asking, "Are these your ancestors?"

"No. Mine are probably on display at the Smithsonian or the Field Museum in Chicago, or stuffed and standing in a diorama at the Museum of Natural History in New York. These tribespeople were concentrated around the Aleutian Islands chain. Kurlak was their most remote camp. Trudeau was their refuge rock—a high ground for them to run to if enemies or strangers appeared while the men were away. But the island was so far east and north, our archaeologists doubt the Aleut were ever threatened."

"Must have been a harsh existence," Hanley said, scanning the faces.

"Yes, but probably better than where they came from in the west."

"How do you mean?"

"Fur traders wiped out their food sources in the mid 1700s and nearly destroyed their civilization. Their culture had lasted nine thousand years and then was almost extinguished in a season by a small number of Alaskan Russians who imported new diseases. Attacked the Aleuts too. Used rifles, cannons . . . nearly exterminated the survivors. Whoever could, fled. That's probably what brought them here originally."

"I don't see any old people," Hanley said, taking in the individual faces through her camera's viewfinder.

"Oh, they had them. But if you were unlucky enough to reach old age and became a burden, they'd stop feeding you. They'd also shift camp real fast. Leave their old behind."

"Not exactly a welfare state."

"No," Nimit said. "Not a society for the fainthearted."

"Why do you think these people stopped coming here?"

Nimit shrugged. "Died out, is my guess. There was a little ice age around 1840, we know that. Communities were small, vulnerable. And outsiders—Europeans—were generous with measles, smallpox, influenza, TB, alcohol. At one time, eighty percent of Inuit tested positive for tuberculosis. You Europeans almost wiped us all out. But hey, we got a written language out of the deal."

"That hieroglyphic writing? Like on your Nunavut poster?"

"You're very observant. Yeah."

"Wild looking, if you don't mind my saying. Like runes. Or code. Very . . . exotic."

Nimit smiled. "You think? It was foisted on us by a missionary who was into Gregg's shorthand. That's why the letters look like stick figures. A rare gift to the Inuit from the business world," he said, ruefully.

"Like the Aleuts getting their alphabet from the Russians?"

"Exactly. Other than that, they don't have much to thank the Russians for."

Hanley pointed at one of the males. "This guy could have used craniosacral treatment. His spine's way out of alignment, not to mention he's missing his mandible and his upper vertebrae."

Nimit nodded. "They were a little sloppy. He was decapitated, then the head was put back on."

"Whatever for?" Hanley said.

"He was *angakoq,* the shaman. A shaman could take a life and bring that person back from the dead. He himself can return to life as needed. The only wound that will kill him is to the throat."

Hanley frowned. "Why would they kill a holy man?"

"I can only guess," Nimit said, squatting beside the remains. "The shaman was usually the most difficult and asocial member of the tribe. Introverted, disturbed by hallucinations and dreams, maybe neurotic, even a little schizoid. Frail, a poor hunter. Might've been prone to fainting spells. You know, a nervous person— agitated. Still, he knew things they didn't. He had powers."

"Such as?"

"He could vomit up objects, tie knots in string in his mouth, make voices come out of his body, drive a knife into his flesh and not bleed. He could fly, swallow fire, transform into an animal, suck illness out of someone who was sick. He could predict the future. He could put himself into a trance and travel to the moon or the bottom of the sea, sink into the ground, conjure demons, talk to the dead."

"Did the tribe think the shaman was mentally ill? Or retarded?"

"Definitely not retarded. Simpletons were thought to be clairvoyant and benign, and were treated well." Nimit took in the cadaver. "The shaman was something else."

"What?"

"Trouble. When a shaman accepted his mystic gift, from that moment on he resigned himself to being the outsider. His job was to wrestle with the supernatural. Most important, he could kill the dead."

"Kill the dead?"

Nimit's dark eyes turned on her. "Yeah. His most important job was interceding with the dead." He looked at her closely. "Whites aren't that bothered by the dead, but you *are* afraid of dying. Inuit aren't afraid of dying, but they're terrified of the dead. It's important to treat the dead with respect and generosity. Otherwise they become jealous and wicked and vengeful toward the living, bringing on starvation and storms. The shaman was expected to appease them. Or kill them in a séance. The shaman was the intermediary between the living world and the darkness. But he was at risk. Evil could take hold of him—make him savage, half animal, a soul robber. When evil spirits—*ilisiitsogs*—when they take hold of someone, he writhes, tortured by the evil tearing at him. In the case of a shaman, the village would have put him out to live in the earth and ice like a beast. It didn't always work. To be completely rid of him, they'd have to kill him in this very specific way."

"By cutting off his head?"

"Otherwise he'd be reborn in an animal, and any hunter who trapped him would fall ill and become paralyzed."

"Scary."

"Yeah. The shaman was very powerful. The tribe must have been terrified to do this to him."

"So they killed him to end the threat," Hanley said, kneeling down alongside the body.

"Most likely." Nimit's black eyes took her in. "Then they buried him as an honored member of the community. He was a great force in their lives. Feared. Revered."

"How can you tell?"

Nimit pointed. "His jacket is made of bearskin. The hood is trimmed with blue fox. Those are rare pelts. His eyes are covered with light blue shells, the rarest commodity on the island. The iridescent beadwork on his hat is abalone, probably from trade with Pacific peoples, and the ones on the shaman's pouch are Venetian beads. Today you can buy stuff like that at any dime store, but back then one of those large blue beads could get you a sled, a pack of dogs, and half a dozen fox skins. And see how his hat is half light, half dark? That's because he's half in this world, half in the spirit world."

She leaned in closer to the cadaver. She felt Nimit's gaze on her and wished the dark semicircles weren't there under her eyes. She lifted up her camera and took a few pictures of the shaman. She zoomed in for a close-up.

"That tiny writing on the pouch—that's Cyrillic?"

"Yep."

"People still use it?"

"It's like Inuktitut. Dying out, mostly. Kids have to read and write English. They don't want to be bothered with the old stuff on top of it. Or there's no one left to teach them."

"What's inside the pouch?"

"Probably bones, for divining. Like cosmic dice."

"His clothes, they're . . ." She paused, her head cocked at an angle. "The trim, the necklace, the shells—almost feminine. Or is it my imagination?"

"No. Your intuition's correct."

"What does the outfit mean?"

"That he was probably homosexual. Maybe a transvestite."

"Gay?"

"Many shamans were. The shaman didn't completely fit into the community. This is how they could participate—by taking on the role of medicine man, difficult as it was. The necklace adorning the breastbone is made of red thorny oyster shells. Oysters are hermaphrodites. Male one year, female the next. Shape-shifters, like the shaman."

Hanley reached out to touch the shaman's face.

"Don't," Nimit said, grabbing her hand to stop her. He held her wrist, the skin of his palm oddly soft for someone who worked so much with his hands.

"Are you afraid of the shaman?"

"Hell, yes. And the Aboriginal Grave Preservation Act, which forbids it."

"Sorry." Hanley gently tugged her hand free. "Please don't hold this against me, but I have to see," she said. "The contortion of the spine, the muscles . . ." She reached out to the left eye socket and lifted away the blue shell.

Nimit flinched.

Hanley carefully lifted away the other shell and brought her lamp close to the shaman's face. Even in a room filled with the dead, the sight was chilling. The ruined eyes were identical to those of the three dead scientists.

# 37

"Our heritage people won't be happy about your disturbing the remains," Mackenzie said over the radio. Hanley nervously fingered the shaman's pouch, which she had hastily cut from its thong, slipped into a polyethylene specimen bag and into her pocket as soon as Nimit had turned to lead the way back out of the burial cave. If lifting the shells pissed them off, she could imagine what they'd have to say about this.

"*But under the circumstances, you're to be commended, Jessie,*" interjected Verneau. "Bien fait. *Well done.*"

Mackenzie sounded less convinced. "*You work with a good deal of intuition, Dr. Hanley. Perhaps you rely a little too heavily on such conjecture. We're going to be hearing about this from the commissioners. You will please proceed discreetly from here on.*"

"I plan to," said Hanley, stung by the rebuke. "Sorry."

"*Of course you will,*" Verneau added, obviously trying to shift the mood of the conversation. "*Where do we go from here? What can we tell our people about your progress?*"

"There's some good news. Whatever this is, it isn't a synthesized twenty-first-century superbug. We can rule out a bioengineered microbe because we know it dropped by here a century ago and annihilated the local shaman. It wasn't heard from again until your colleagues bumped into it in the course of their work."

"*That doesn't seem possible,*" Mackenzie said, sounding upset.

"The Aleut community isolated itself. The bug wouldn't have

traveled far if they were its only host. I think it may have just lingered in some other species, waiting for more human company. It's happened before. Like Ebola in the Congo."

"*Jesus,*" Verneau said.

"Whatever it is, it's biological and long established. It's got to be colonized in something out there on the ice."

"*Yes,*" Verneau said, "*and you may be heading straight for it. Please be careful, ma chere.*"

"Will do," Hanley said and signed off.

Hanley arched her back and glanced over at Nimit driving. She powered on the laptop poised on the flat dashboard in front of her. The satellite window was open; she was linked to the world. She logged onto a search engine to research Antarctica and the sub-ice lakes Nimit had told her about.

There they were, all right: subsurface lakes beneath an impossible thickness of ice and snow. Samples of ice, brought up from a depth of two miles, had revealed something unexpected—microbes. Microbes that survived in frozen states.


An unearthly screech, like elephants trumpeting, grew into an amplified pneumatic tapping—like a giant woodpecker—and finished with the groaning of enormous floorboards. Hanley jumped and quickly checked the light inside her helmet. It shone a comforting green. Nimit laughed.

"Just ice floes," he said. "They creak and sing, and break and raft. Wedge atop each other"—Nimit took his hands off the wheel for a moment to demonstrate the motion—"and press the broken sections upward in jagged ridges. Like tectonic plates."

An instant message flashed onto her screen. Joey.

> *MOM!*
> baby.
> *What's up?*
> I'm out on the ice floes, in a vehicle with a lot of fat
>   wheels

*How big?*
looks like your monster truck when you were 3
*Is it scary out there?*
it's beautiful—like you.
*Oh MOM. Hey, wait. Dad wants to talk.*

"Oh, shit," Hanley said under her breath.

*Jessie? I had two reporters parked on the lawn today ask-*
*ing where you were and what you were up to. What the*
*hell am I supposed to say?*
Tell them you and I don't speak.
*Not far from the truth.*
If that doesn't hold them, tell them I'm bound by medical
confidentiality. Send them to Munson. Let him fend
them off.
*I'll try, but if they start pestering Joey, fuck the First*
*Amendment—I'm going to punch their lights out.*
Right. Kiss Joey goodnight for me.

Teddy Zale radioed them to monitor their progress. Jack adjusted their course to align with the GPS signal emitted by the AR-
GOS site marker. The expanse across which they were traveling was
immense, but the marker and the positioning system would deliver
them to within a meter of their goal—the last campsite of the scientists. A transmitter in the wanigan conveyed their automated signal
back to Teddy Zale and was their second radio. A third was aboard
for backup, but it wasn't on. The transceivers they used the most
were in their helmets; their communications were relayed by the
second radio link aboard the wanigan.

"I hope we don't run into a pressure ridge," Hanley said, following the slinky skittering ahead of them on its yellow tether like a ro-
botic pet.

"There are worse places they could pop up," Nimit replied.

"Oh, yeah? Like where?"

"Behind us."

In the distance, a black slope bulged out of the flat white field of ice. Hanley recognized it from their charts as Mackenzie's Mount: a bald escarpment protruding from the frozen ocean. With no frame of reference, she couldn't judge how high or large it might be, or how far away. After a few minutes, Nimit cut the power to the slinky and parked their wanigan alongside the six chartreuse markers that indicated the perimeter of the scientists' shelter. He switched off the four-stroke engine, leaving the generator on.

"So where the hell are we," said Hanley, "relatively speaking?"

"In the middle of absolutely nowhere. Utterly alone, standing in the middle of an empty ocean two thousand miles across."

"How far from L.A.?"

He thought for a moment. "Maybe four thousand miles. You're about as far from L.A. as L.A. is from the Amazon."

"God, what I'd give for a latte. How far do you reckon we'd have to drive for one?"

"Angsta, Sweden, is probably your best bet. Or Murmansk. But I can't vouch for the java in either."

"This is the exact spot of the work site, I take it," Hanley said, gesturing at the markers with her thickly gloved hand.

"Yes. This ice around the promontory is pretty steady. It hasn't moved."

"I thought all ice moved."

"Sea ice is constantly moving, but we're on shore ice here. Land fast. Where it presses up against the moving ice floes is where it's least stable. Research stations out on the sea ice can drift nine miles in a day. The currents up here are peculiar."

"It must be weird to be in constant motion like that," said Hanley.

"Back in the nineties a Chinese vessel out of Hong Kong lost its cargo in a storm. Little yellow toy duckies. They went overboard in the Pacific. Seven years later they were turning up on beaches in the Atlantic, carried from one ocean to the other by these floes."

"Joey and I will have to keep our eyes peeled at the beach." Nimit smiled. "Does the ice always move in the same pattern?" she said.

"It gyrates counterclockwise, but in unpredictable zigs. Expedition ships used to get frozen in at one place and, slowly, over the course of years, they'd be shifted hundreds or thousands of miles from where they had entered the field. Depending on the design of their hulls, some were crushed—never seen again. Some remained intact. And are still out there, sailing."

Like the shaman's killer, Hanley thought. Perhaps preserved in the ice like the ships. Waiting to come ashore.

She climbed down from the wanigan, stood by the markers, and turned slowly in a circle. Nimit followed, rifle in hand. She took some ice samples from the immediate campsite. Back hunched, she searched the area with an electric torch, sweeping the ice in widening arcs.

"You're searching for something," he said.

"Cadavers."

"What?"

"Animals, birds, anything that could have been a carrier. Some creature the shaman could have encountered too. I'm trying to narrow it down. Infected birds often harbor viruses. Any birds here this late in the year?"

"Some winter over every year, yeah. Black guillemots. They're Arctic birds. Don't migrate to temperate climates. Occasionally a Glaucous gull or two will stay behind. But fewer pairs every year. Mac's got the head counts."

"What do they live on, the ones that stay behind?"

"Most shrimp and crustaceans descend to lower depths come winter, but there are just enough near the surface to sustain the stragglers."

"If they're eating crustaceans, that could account for the kainic acid we found in the bodies. Do you ever find dead birds at the polynya?"

"Sometimes."

"Recently? Would the scientists have recorded it if they came across any?"

"Probably not, unless they noticed something really unusual."

"Were any of them studying bird deaths? Annie?"

"Not that I know of. No."

She paced the area around the markers. "The carrier doesn't have to die to be infectious. They could be passing virus in their breath, or to insects feeding on their blood, or shedding it in their feces. Which leaves me hunting for bird shit, would you believe?"

"Any luck?"

"No. No spoor at all." Straightening up, she caught sight of him and laughed.

"What's so funny?"

"I've never seen an armed bird before. You sure that gun won't freeze shut out here?"

"Sprayed it with Teflon lubricant." Nimit pointed into the dark. "The opening's that way." They walked for several minutes until they reached the edge of the dark plain that was the polynya. Despite the moonlight, they could neither see the water nor hear it. The span was perfectly still, wholly black except for the stripe of moon melted across it. The primeval odor of the sea wafted up, pungent with kelp and algae.

"That machine in the water—the one they came to check—does it scare off wildlife?"

"It's a standard submersible research drone. Automated. Like a giant cigar—about ten feet long, maybe four hundred and ten kilos. Nine hundred pounds dripping wet. But it's very slow. Bumps into anything, it stops and backs off, goes around—like a bumper car. Marine life ignores it."

"There wasn't anything like that on the list of equipment brought back."

"No," Nimit said, "it stays down there. Operates pretty much on its own under the ice. With a low-yield engine, it can chug forever. It has a homing system that returns it to the launch hole when summoned. Otherwise, it just goes around and around in circles at four knots."

"And what does it do?"

"Takes a thousand readings. It can make a profile across the Arctic Basin with continuously recorded echoes. The field teams come out every three months to harvest its output and check its vital signs."

"Listen," she said. "I heard something."

They peered into the black. He picked up a chunk of ice and chucked it. It clunked into the water, followed by a second sound, something plopping.

"What the—" Hanley exclaimed. The moonlight flashed across the black waves.

"Seal most likely. They puff up their gullets and throats with air and sleep upright in the water, bobbing like corks."

"Isn't it too cold?"

"Not when there's no wind. If there is, they sleep under the ice, by their blowholes. They wake up, draw a breath through the hole, and go back to napping. They're remarkably efficient at conserving heat. You couldn't even find them with infrared sensors because they give off so little body warmth."

He pointed his light at a barely perceptible indentation in the ice and held up a hand to keep her silent, holding the beam on the hole. A minute passed. Then a jet of water squirted up from the opening. Nimit shushed her again. The air was perfectly still. A whooshing sound came from the hole.

She jumped back.

"Seal inhaling," he said, peering into the small opening.

"What was the little geyser about?"

"The seal pushed itself up into the funnel beneath the opening to force water out so it could take a breath."

"What do the seals eat?" she said.

"They're bottom-feeders. Algae and seaweed . . . mussels, whatever dead matter has settled to the seabed. The water under the ice is much less cold than the ice, or water exposed to the air. Tiny fissures in the ice contain pockets of seawater. Algae live in the brine inside the ice, form colonies. Some of the algae fronds are quite large and hang down in the water. Sea animals graze there."

"And they don't freeze."

"Not at all, the birds either." He lifted his arms to indicate his own feathery outfit. "Nature's insulated them."

"And there's been no rash of seal or walrus deaths?"

"No. But they've been abandoning the Arctic by the thousands."

"Why? Where are they going?"

"No one's had the chance to question them closely. My guess is, they sense some kind of great change and they're bailing out. In 1988 about two hundred thousand of them showed up on the northern coast of Norway."

"Like storks taking wing before volcanic eruptions and earthquakes."

"Something like that I suppose, yeah. Just a slower flight."

"Okay, I'm ruling the seals out for now—if they're carriers, most likely there's some intermediate vector. In summer I'd suspect insects, but not this time of year."

She followed a shooting star's slide across the sky. "What else did Ogata, Bascomb, and Minskov do out here?"

"Took ice samples with a Sipre ice corer. Annie was particularly interested in how far the pollution from the south was traveling, and what it was doing to the ecosystem."

"Yeah," Hanley said, "we tested the samples they took. It seemed the most likely place for a bug they might have bumped into. I was certainly hoping. But nothing's there." She walked ahead; he followed. The ice creaked underfoot as they trudged. "Not as lifeless out here as it appears."

"No," Nimit said.

She stopped and slowly arched her back.

Nimit said, "You feeling okay?"

"I'm fine. Just sore from sitting. Tired too."

Hanley tried to shake loose some of the tension in her neck by rotating her shoulders, then bent over, slowly lowering her arms down toward her toes. Without warning, the snowdrift beside her reared up, twelve feet high, and opened its mouth, showing off huge white fangs and claws as big as rake tines, and it roared.

Part of her brain knew its maw would be pink in the light, but out here it was dark as death and totally paralyzing. Her limbs were liquid; she could barely stand. The bear hissed. Even through the visor, his hot breath smelled meaty.

"Jack." She thought she'd screamed, but as in a nightmare, what emerged was barely a breathless whisper. "Jack."

Nimit was beside her, sighting on the creature with his rifle. The bear snorted. She could have sworn he looked puzzled, wondering why they weren't fleeing. Hanley wondered herself. Nimit fired past the bear to scare it off; Hanley jumped. The bear eased down to all fours, then turned his back on them, took two loping strides and launched into the black water of the polynya. There was barely a splash. The enormous hulk was gone in an instant.

"Oh, my God," she said, feeling the adrenaline recede with a hot rush. "Oh, my God."

"Take a deep breath."

"I'm shaking. I feel like I've been in a car wreck." She bent to rest her hands on her knees. "I can't believe how it just appeared like that."

"They hide in snow banks sometimes when they're hunting seals. They know seals like to burrow into drifted snow to keep warm."

"They're that smart, they camouflage?"

"Sure," Nimit said, laughing, the happy thrill of being alive after a close brush. "They'll even cover their black noses with their paws so their faces don't give them away."

She thought she was going to be sick. "I'd love to pop this lid." She tapped her faceplate.

"In there," he said, and indicated the wanigan.

He went first up the side of the machine, and she followed on watery legs, using the column of stirrups leading up to the cab. When they had been inside for a few minutes, they undid their ruffs and helmets and stripped off the outer suits, pushing them down around their waists. She was still trembling.

The cab was chilly. He pulled open the sliding door of a small re-frigerator and took out a block of something. The blade of his ice ax pinged open at a touch, and with its sharp blade he shaved off a wedge, handing it to her. She sniffed it and watched him saw off a piece for himself.

"What's this?" she said.

"To calm your nerves."

She chewed a piece and howled. "Whiskey!" She made a face as it melted and delivered its punch. She bussed him on the cheek. He laughed. She snapped off another piece and melted it in her mouth. Nimit crunched his as he busied himself preparing dinner from the various frozen items in the tiny galley. He offered her bittersweet chocolate and pulled out a frozen wheel of something.

"What the hell is that," she said, "a frozen pizza?"

"Nope. Beans."

"No can?"

"An old trick. Eliminates containers and trash. You break off however much you want and heat 'em up in the microwave, or over a fire if you're cooking out. We use cotton soaked in petroleum jelly for fuel. Burns steady and hot, kind of homemade Sterno. Or we crack open an emergency gas hydrate pack and make a cooking fire of it."

"It sounds like camping." She scrunched up her face. "I grew up in the woods. I hate camping. Indoor plumbing for me." Nimit chuckled at her expression. "I'm still quaking," she said, holding out a trembling hand and taking another piece of frozen whiskey. "I guess if you run into a bear and don't have Dr. Bach's Rescue Remedy handy, whiskey's a pretty good substitute."

"Dr. Bach, huh? How do you reconcile the lab coat and the homeopathy?"

"I don't. I don't like to admit it, certainly not to my colleagues, but my job has made me a bit of a hypochondriac. Every day I see what happens to a body attacked by some poison or disease. We all go into a . . . kind of denial that it could happen to us. The Flower Remedies is my approach. The idea is that you're addressing the mental process behind the physical ailment. There's something appealing about the idea that if you just get your mind straight, your body will follow."

"I can see that. Our shamans definitely work more on the mind than the body. They know their herbs and poultices, but that's not where their real work happens. That's in some other realm."

When the food was assembled, he put it in two small bowls and slid them into the microwave. The temperature in the cabin rose noticeably when he opened the door and took out their dishes. A cloud formed momentarily along the ceiling.

"God, I'm actually hot," she said.

"Slide off more of your outer layers and sit down. It's only warm on top—up here." He indicated the upper half of the space.

"I can't sit anymore," she said. "I've gotta stretch out."

"Sure." He pointed to the back of the vehicle. "Complete with potty and two bunks. They fold up into seats but I leave 'em down all the time."

She made her way back and sat down on the edge of a bunk. He followed, carrying their bowls, a spoon in each.

"Nothing to write home about," he said, "but this will jolt up your caloric intake. We have to keep it high."

She touched his smooth cheek and accepted the food gratefully: beans, instant mashed potatoes, pasta, jerked chicken cubes, and corn. She was famished and exhausted. They ate as if it were work—without speaking or stopping. When she was finished, she touched his hand lightly. "I need to turn in, soonest."

"Go," he said. "Keep two layers on, and the thermal blanket." He slipped his last few spoonfuls of food into the trap for the lemmings she had brought out of Little Trudeau.

"Thanks for saving me from Papa Bear." She swigged water from her canteen.

He smiled and kissed her. "I hate to tell you what my grandma would do when a bear came around."

"What?"

"She'd swipe at it with a wooden coat hanger and drive it off."

"Quite a gal, your granny."

"Yeah. Nobody else dared. The bears were dangerous as hell, but my grandma just shooed them away like they were pesky."

"Way to go, Grandma!" Hanley yawned. She squeezed past him and into bed. She had barely enough energy to get the outermost layer off before she collapsed onto her pallet. The roof over the rear area was transparent.

Jack made his way back to her, eased out of his outer layers and lay down next to her. Their metallic skins shone brightly in the starlight.

"Can you sleep?" she said.

"Yeah, in a while. I'm cranked. Also generally turned around."

"Sleep disorder?"

"More like my ancestral clock. Inuit stay up very late. In summer especially, we'd stay up all night, then sleep till noon."

"Why?"

"Don't know. Just did. We socialized so much in the summers, we stopped going to bed. Anyway, kids stayed up too. We didn't have bedtimes. We'd hang with the adults and go to sleep when they did."

"But you had to get up for school."

"Sure. It drove the school authorities crazy. We'd either be home snoring or passing out in class. A lot of kids just stayed out and played bingo. This went on all summer long. I got back into the habit here—switched midnight for noon. I'll turn around gradually over the winter."

"No bedtime. My son would love that. No one insisted?"

"No. We weren't reprimanded or controlled that way in the community, except maybe by white teachers. We made our own decisions. You can't order Inuit children around. Everyone had to respect the adult in us."

"The adult?"

"Sure. All kids have their *atiq*, the spirit of the family ancestor they've received."

"I don't follow."

"Inuit believe humans have two souls."

"Two?"

"Yes. One is the body's and stays with it. The other, the higher soul, moves out at death and starts its immortal journey. It's kinder. That's the one given to a new person—that eternal soul. That's *atiq*."

"So you get reincarnated as a family member. Your soul stays related."

"Right. The *atiq*, the spirit, is taken up by a newborn in the family and gets the same name."

"No wonder you seem older than your years," she said, smiling. "Who were you named for?"

Nimit chewed on a piece of dried beef. "My grandfather's brother on my mother's side. A noted hunter. My grandmother and mother would both call me Old Uncle sometimes."

"Did you know all your grandparents?"

"Yes. Especially my mom's mother, of coat hanger fame. And her husband, Lightstone, who taught me to hunt. He was an old-fashioned Inuk. Hunted until his last day. Even when he stopped in the winter months, he kept at it in summer. And he would fish, always. When he couldn't do either anymore, he loaded up all his gear and took his boat out. He never came back. I watched him go."

"You didn't try to stop him?"

He shook his head. "No. I had no right. And his wife had passed by then. My mom was sad. And pissed."

"She was angry at him? For dying?"

"We lost his social welfare check." He shrugged with resignation. "All the families tried to keep their elders around as long as possible because we were all hungry, all on the dole. A far cry from when the old-timers were burdens the village would try to abandon."

"Excuse me," she said, yawning. "It's not you. I'm so tired my skin hurts, but I can't fall asleep."

"But you can relax a little. You're making progress."

"Yeah, the fact the shaman died of it means it's out here somewhere, but 'out here' is enormous." She closed her eyes.

"Easy to see why you're having trouble sleeping." Jack sat up and retrieved something from a sack. "Here."

She reached for what he was offering. "All right!" she exclaimed. "A joint!" She smelled the crude cigarette. "How did you find dope out in the middle of nowhere?"

He chuckled and snapped a lighter open to light it for her. "Arctic High, the guy calls it. He grows it hydroponically in the horticulture lab. He's a serious huffer. Works in the dining hall. You've probably seen him—the Aleut with the T-shirt that reads REHAB IS FOR QUITTERS."

She inhaled deeply and held her breath, cheeks puffed. "You most certainly had a wayward youth," she said, exhaling. She giggled, pushing the hair back from her eyes. "Wow. Wow!"

Nimit laughed. "I guess it passes the California taste test."

Hanley's muscles melted. She inhaled again and passed him the cigarette, then eased down onto the pallet, the stars overhead ablaze. The cab was all black and white and silver, except for the one orange spot that turned hearth red as Jack drew in the smoke and held the stub aloft among the cold points of light that filled the black sky.

"Tell me," she said, closing her eyes.

"Tell you what?"

"What Inuit see out there."

Nimit pushed the coverlet higher on her shoulder. "Fellow creatures. They're our only food in the Arctic. But otherwise they're like us: they have souls, they speak."

"Yeah?"

"They come from us. That seal today? He comes from the arms of a girl, cut off by her own father."

"Ouch. Tough love." Hanley lifted her head from the bedding and made a face. "Why'd he cut off her arms?"

"She wouldn't marry the one he wanted her to marry. That's one version. They're on a boat in a huge storm, and the father puts the daughter overboard. She's hanging on for dear life and he cuts off her fingers, and they became seals; then her hands, and they became walruses; her forearms, whales. She finally sank to the bottom of the ocean and became our sea goddess. Sedna. If you disrespect a mammal you've hunted, its soul won't pass to the next life and will remain to haunt you. It turns into a monster. And Sedna won't send any more seals up to feed you."

"But if you respect the animal you hunt?"

"If you honor the animal's spirit, it agrees to be reborn to be hunted again. In a way you spend your life hunting the same animal, the same spirit in different bodies. Our local shaman used to say that we lived on a diet of souls."

"That's pretty wild." She yawned. "What else?"

"Once upon a time we thought there were just a few white people in the world." He curled up behind her, his arm around her. "We thought the earth was a flat disk and the stars were moving spirits. Our word for soul, *anerca*—the breath of life—is also our word for poetry. Poems weren't memorized, carvings weren't kept, we made no maps, we had no permanent address." Her breathing was steady and deep. He lifted a loose strand from her face and tucked it behind her ear. "We thought death made storms, that killing a spider would cause rain, that Pierre Trudeau was a shit."

# 38

When she awoke some time later, Nimit was warm beside her. The only light came from the thousand stars ablaze overhead, like microscopic particles in a black field. Despite her body's exhaustion, she clung to wakefulness as her mind spiraled like the great pack ice, her thoughts slowly, inexorably carrying her into a strange twilight.

Most bacteria and viruses coexist with us, she thought. They set up housekeeping in a host and settle down. Neither is interested in destroying or even dislodging the other. Normally neither party deviated from the long-standing arrangement. When they did, it was often disastrous. Polio in the intestine, harmless to the host; relocated to the nerves and spine, the host is paralyzed or dies. Meningitis in the nose and throat, nothing; in the brain, catastrophic. When microbes stayed put and the balance was maintained, large and small organisms coexisted in peace.

Not this thing. Its intent from the first was to kill the host, destroy it in as short a time as possible. Colonize and kill. What in the host was so threatening?

The microbe eradicated bacteria. Bacteria being what? A concentrated protein. The eyes too. Lungs? A different story. There it created some kind of toxic fiber that destroyed the elasticity and turned tissue to stone. What in the lung field triggered the microbe this way? What was it trying to do? And why go after the red blood cells and eye tissue?

She imagined herself inside her body, her cells a dynamic process, open, exchanging materials. Cells were replicating, dying, being renewed. They would be replenished about forty times in her life before they were exhausted altogether and her body called it a day. By comparison, a virus was inert. No skin, no nerves, no brain. Life at its minimum. Unable to metabolize nutrients, to reproduce, even to move. Its sole function was to create more of itself, endlessly. And prions were even worse—inert, yet nearly indestructible.

Her eyes opened momentarily and a terrible panic passed through her.

Reaching out to Jack, she touched his arm and thought she actually experienced loving him as a feeling of comfort. The fact of it settled inside her physically. It didn't matter that he was younger, that he was from another world. She pulled the covers to her chin and closed her eyes and let herself float down.


The strident beeping of the alarm roused them both. Nimit squinted at the digital time and date indicator. They had slept six hours. He microwaved two coffee packets in water and broke open an aluminum bag of dehydrated rations without even bothering to read what it claimed to be. The microwave clock ticked off the seconds; the aroma of coffee filled the compartment. He brought it back to Hanley, who was almost fully dressed in her full suit of layers. The quilled outermost layer was halfway up, bunched at her waist.

"Thanks," she said, accepting the coffee and frowning at the dehydrated food. But he insisted and she relented, munching unhappily on what were supposed to be eggs and buttered toast.

Jack was having only black coffee and cereal moistened with water. Hanley expressed her surprise at the Spartan meal.

"I thought we were supposed to be calorie loading. You should pour on the milk, get the extra protein."

"Inuit can't do milk. We don't have the enzymes to process it."

"Sorry to hear that," said Hanley. "More ice cream for me, I guess. So what else is unusual about Inuit physiology, besides no body hair?"

"An extra artery near the heart. Supposed to keep us warm. We're mostly right-handed, rarely left. And we have small hands." He held his palm against hers; her fingers were a full joint longer. "Extraordinarily iron-rich blood, and—sadly—very high dioxin levels. As Annie liked to point out."

"From U.S. industrial pollutants," Hanley said. "I heard."

"Every step up the food chain concentrates the chemicals. And we're the top of the chain. People with high-fat diets—like us—accumulate high levels of dioxins. Inuit breast milk has the highest level of PCBs anywhere on earth. Not to mention assorted pesticides, solvents, mercury from power plants. When they first started testing the breast milk, the results actually overloaded the lab's equipment. The stuff rates as toxic waste."

"Jesus."

"Cancer rate's high," Nimit said, staring back at her, "and our kids' immune systems and IQ levels aren't doing so well, but at least we're easy to find in the dark."

"Radioactive, huh?"

"You got it."

"Small hands, eh?" Hanley said, raising an eyebrow. "Is it true what they say?"

"No truth at all," Nimit retorted. "Inuit are among the most endowed males of the species."

"I've heard that." Hanley nodded, deadpan. "I don't imagine there's firsthand . . . data."

"Only anecdotal, but I'll be happy to volunteer for an experiment." He bent and kissed her. Concern came into his eyes.

"You worried?" she said.

"For you, yes."

"Don't be."

"I don't want you to get hurt. I don't want to lose you."

She hugged him. "I'll see that you don't. I really do know how to protect myself, Jack. I've been at this a long time. Since you were a teenager." He had to laugh.

After breakfast, Nimit radioed Trudeau to report they were exiting the vehicle and would monitor the station's frequency for weather warnings but transmit only to one another locally. They donned their headgear and carefully climbed down the thin ladder of steps fixed onto the side of the wanigan.

The stars cast an odd light. A boulder in their path might be yards or miles away. There was no frame of reference.

Nimit pointed in the direction they would be traveling and they set off, Hanley carrying the sample bags. Nimit pulled back the bolt of the composite rifle he carried and let it spring forward, chambering a round.

"In case we run into Mr. Bear." He clicked on the safety.

"Is it as lifeless as it feels?" she said, as they walked through the eerie moonlit landscape.

"No." He motioned vaguely. "Just sparse. Life goes on. You just can't see what's there. Creatures large and small."

"Large I've seen enough of, thank you. Small?"

"Small." He shone his light on a cross section of buckled ice stippled with dots. "To start with, lichen and fungi."

"In the ice."

"Yeah. And in rocks, like on the outcropping there." Hanley removed samples and placed them in vials. "What else?"

"At the polynya, carnivorous amphipods. They hang under the ice, feed on dead crustaceans, larvae, whatever they can snag. They're like piranha. They'll strip the flesh from a carcass in a day or two. The biologists at Trudeau sometimes use them to clean off a specimen: just dangle it in the water. I've seen these tiny guys turn a dead bear into a skeleton in forty-eight hours."

"Lovely. Sounds like they're smack in the middle of the food chain. I'll need to test them to see if they're carrying anything."

Nimit led the way across the barren plain. A dense curve in the blackness suggested the promontory that housed the bird population in summer. He slipped on the ice and his arms flew out from his body as he balanced himself.

"Careful with that rifle," Hanley said.

"Safety's on. Don't worry. I've never shot anyone. Accidentally."

"Any suggestions for how we collect some of those underwater carnivores without losing our fingers in the process?"

"They don't like live flesh."

"That's a consolation. But how am I going to lure these guys out from under the ice?"

"If you're willing to sacrifice lunch . . ." Nimit reached into the bag on her shoulder and removed a clear polyethylene bag. He took out a fist-sized ball of beef jerky, which he secured with plastic fishing line. At the water's edge, he lowered the ball of meat into the sea.

"Anything?" Hanley said, shining her light on the surface.

Nimit scooped some seawater into the bag. "Agitate this so the saltwater doesn't freeze." He waited some moments and slowly pulled up the line. The wad of meat came out encrusted with writhing creatures.

"Whoa," she said, amazed. They were the size of shrimp. He lowered them into the bag and sealed it.

"What else is living under the ice that I have to worry about?" she said. She knelt at the edge of the opening and peered down.

Nimit bent over her. "This particular polynya remains open year-round, but it hasn't behaved normally for a couple of years. This winter it's contracted to a fraction of its usual size. Changing along with everything else, I suppose. Part of the warming."

"A major concern for all of you, I take it."

"The Arctic is where the planet vents heat. If the temperatures here rise radically and the Arctic melts away, that vent closes, and you've got problems worldwide."

"Right now my problem is samples. Are you going to help or just stand there?"

"I've been ordered not to touch anything. But I'll be happy to hold the flashlight."

"Thanks. That'll be a big help."

She stood up and carefully pocketed the container of deadly amphipods. "Right," she said. "So we're down to the birds."

She scanned the terrain with her lamp. "Jesus—I said I was looking for bird droppings," she muttered. "Be careful what you wish for."

"Mackenzie's Mount is pure bird shit, as far as I can tell." He pointed his lamp in the direction of the bulge of rock they could barely discern. "It's a rookery, after all. Swarming with birds and chicks all summer."

"Is that one season's worth?"

"More like thirty years' worth. Nothing to wash it away. The cold dryness preserves everything."

"If the bug is in that guano heap, how the hell am I ever supposed to find it?"

He shrugged. "I told you shit happens in the Arctic." She groaned.

He led the way to Mackenzie's Mount, where she took a deep breath and started to scale the hill of frozen guano, her awkwardness a combination of the bulk of the extreme environment suit and the inner discomfort of being this close to a potential source of lethal infection with none of her usual protective gear. She worked her way methodically across the surface, doing the best she could to scrape samples from different sections of the frozen top layer into the containers Nimit handed her.

When she reached the far end, she took a deep breath and half slid, half ran down the hill. "We could be here a month," she said, panting from the exertion. "These couple dozen samples will have to do for now." She stood with her hands on her knees, catching her breath, peering into the dark, across the icy expanse. "If I find it here and it's in the migratory birds, the people to the south are in trouble."

Ice floes ground against one another with an unnerving low screech: *raaaaaah*.

"God," she said, "I hope that's somebody's mating call."

Nimit smiled. He obviously wasn't alarmed, so Hanley tried to match his composure. Another slow groan followed, like unimaginably huge elephants rubbing giant balloons along their flanks, and occasionally trumpeting.

"My granny used to say it was God cracking his knuckles."

The sounds stopped. Hanley breathed a sigh of relief at the sudden quiet and took in the expanse of the sky, glittering with stars.

"God's dust," Nimit said, as they stood staring at the sparkling heavens.

"Granny was a poet."

"No," Nimit answered, "Not Grandma. Jorge Luis Borges."

"You're full of surprises."

"Hope so."

"Jack, you've seen the work notes from the site?"

"Yes."

"You know that notation about the *ignis fatuus*? Turns out it means swamp gas, which seems crazy. There isn't some kind of gas out here, is there?"

He thought for a moment. "Actually, sort of, yeah. I'll show you."

He motioned for her to follow him, and started over a hummock and around a small pressure ridge, his lamp beam igniting the white surface, making it glisten blue and green, like bottle glass. A misting of ice crystals drifted past on a gust of wind. Nimit switched his handheld lantern to its widest beam and revealed a collection of circular mounds two feet across and a foot high.

"They're fairly common in the High Arctic. We called them pongos when I was a kid. Maybe two dozen of them here." Nimit pointed out a few more with the beam, then knelt by the closest one. He brushed aside particles of snow, which arced away in wisps, lifted by the slight breeze. The ice beneath was as transparent as the finest glass, with something dark at the bottom of the globe.

"I've never seen anything like them," Hanley said, impressed by their crystal clarity.

"They're algal pits." Nimit sat back on his haunches. "Gas bubbles carry pieces of green algae up from the seabed to the underside of the ice we're standing on. The algae cling to the underside, grow, and work their way up."

"Through six feet of ice?"

"Seven feet, ten . . . more even. All the way up to here." He pointed at the pongo. "Starting in spring, the dark layers of algae absorb sunlight through the ice casing."

"Easy, since it's so clear."

"Yes," he said, stroking the flawless ball. "The constant light and the glassy ice promote rapid photosynthesis."

"I can see that. The dome is a perfect natural greenhouse."

"As the algae grow toward the light, the oxygen the algae

produce pushes upward, creating the dome over the colony." He looked at her face framed by the helmet. "You with me?"

"So far."

"That's in spring. In summer, the ice dome melts open, so it fills with fresh, clear ice water. The sun's out round the clock and the algae flourish. The green algae are darker than the ice around them, of course, so they retain the sun's heat. That keeps the top of the dome open and enlarges the pit. The colony grows, merges with other colonies, and grows even wider." He pointed with his light. "Two, three feet across. The max the sunlight penetrates is maybe nine inches into the ice, so the pits stay fairly shallow. At the end of summer, the sun fades."

"Making the pit freeze over."

"Yeah, quickly. The algae's oxygen output has dissolved in the pit water, so it's trapped at the center. The water, expanding as it turns hard, presses on the oxygen and creates the hump."

"The ice doesn't kill the algae?"

"No. It spends the winter frozen into the ice at maybe minus thirty degrees centigrade. The globe actually shields it from the lower air temperatures outside, and from the wind."

"Great trick. But where's the swamp gas?"

Nimit rose to his feet and motioned for her to back away. "We're not supposed to do this, but anything for science." He took a loose brick of ice and threw it overhand. The dome exploded with a pop. Fine particles of crystals and algae burst into the air in a ghostly shimmer.

"Swamp gas!" Hanley exclaimed, startled and momentarily frightened.

"Yeah," Nimit said. "The oxygen is under pressure. Makes quite a cloud."

"You're right," she said, trying to calm herself. "It looks absolutely gaseous."

Had the three scientists been standing like this around an algal pit when it burst? Or the shaman, a hundred years before? Had they inhaled the particles that flew up in a mist around them?

"What's wrong?" he said. "You don't look well."

"How many of these have you broken open in your time, Jack?"

"Dozens when I was a kid. They made great targets. Lately not so many. We try to avoid them. The Polar Commission wouldn't be pleased to hear it, but we drive over them sometimes before we realize we're in a patch."

"Any ill effects?"

"On us? No, never."

But who's to say all the pongos contain the same species, she thought. Ninety-nine could be benign, and the hundredth, deadly. In the rain forest, one tree could be home to dozens of insect species that existed nowhere else—not even on the neighboring tree. Why couldn't the same be true here? Hanley drew a plastic vial from a pocket on her thigh and bent over the broken dome. Careful not to get fragments on her gloved hands or the fibers of her polar suit, she scraped several samples of the algae and capped the tube. "I'm afraid I'm going to need to break a few more pongos," she said.

"Can't be," she heard Nimit say, as a vibration rippled through the ice they were standing on.

"Shake and bake," Hanley said without thinking—California slang for earthquake. But that was impossible.

The creaking noise was horrible. Huge black gaps appeared in the ice around them, sloshing with seawater, gagging Hanley with trapped odors of primordial brine. The breath of the Reaper, she thought. She thought of every warning she'd heard since flying out with Stevenson: *Avoid water. Everyone's careful around water in the Arctic.*

They turned toward the source of the terrifying sound. The snout of a huge fish filled the polynya's opening, hung suspended for a moment, and crashed down, smashing great slabs of ice as it fell forward. Geysers flew into the air, obscuring everything. Molten with iridescent microbial life streaming down its flanks, the creature floated higher, a Leviathan, a narwhal's unicorn horn rising from its hump. Ice slabs slid off its enormous girth like scales, plummeting noisily along the bulkhead.

The ice around them started fracturing in all directions, opening fissures. If a loose section tipped and plunged them into the water, they were as good as dead.

"Run," Nimit said, pushing her, and the two of them turned and ran.

A lead opened right in front of Hanley. Her arms shot out from her sides and she rotated them like wings, trying to regain her balance. She teetered on the brink, about to topple, when she felt Nimit grab her by the seat and pull her back.

The terrible sounds diminished.

"What the fuck was that?" she panted.

"Jessie," Nimit said, "put out your light," and Hanley did. He pulled her down behind an ice boulder. Her visor was completely fogged.

Filling the entire polynya and beyond, was the longest, tallest, blackest beast ever risen from hell, a monster from the netherworld ferrying evil to the surface, towering over them, luminescent plankton streaking its great sides.

Along with the groans of the ice came metallic clanks as hatches opened and black creatures crawled out, stood on the giant's spine, hoisted shapes from within, and painstakingly lowered them down to the ice, followed by black figures who shouldered weapons and rappelled downward along invisible lines. Reaching the surface, they struggled over to the descending equipment and helped land it right side up. Bulky tracked sleds the size of snowmobiles clanked along the metal and onto the ice.

There were shouts. One of the figures slipped and slid down too quickly, crashing onto the hard blocks of broken ice below, still clutching his line. He landed badly. Others rushed to him, shouting. Several figures, black as their shadows, convened near the first vehicle. Hanley could smell gasoline as engines coughed into life, died, sputtered, started again, and finally quit altogether.

The wind picked up only slightly, but the figures bent against it. They slowed perceptibly and hunched, some turning their backs to it, evidently suffering its bite. Human after all, Hanley thought.

The creature had vanquished the ice, but it wouldn't be long before the floe retaliated, freezing it in place like an insect. They must realize that. Hanley glanced at Nimit, who was staring at the shapes as if at visitors from another planet. How long would it be before they saw the wanigan fifty yards off?

An engine turned over, faltered, and revved into a sustained growl. Smoke chuffed from the exhaust. A large headlight switched on, catching Hanley and Nimit squarely in its huge beam. In the black-and-white polar landscape, their brilliant coloration startled the armed men alongside the sub.

An unmistakable chorus of weapons being loaded and shouldered echoed across the stillness. Hanley squinted against the glare, able to make out the black maws of gun barrels trained on them.

Instinctively Nimit raised his arms straight out to the sides, and Hanley followed suit.

"Are you American?" Nimit shouted through the faceplate. *"Parlez-vous Français? Deutsch?"* Could they even hear him over the wind and with the visor?

"Forward!" called a tremulous and heavily accented voice. "Now be forward. Step, step!"

They complied, walking slowly toward the giant hull that loomed above the ice, steady as a building and long as a city block.

"What are they so anxious about?" Nimit said.

"Maybe they've never seen an armed bird before either."

"Discharge weapon," the sailor called to them.

"What?" said Nimit, bewildered.

"Discharge weapon!" The voice was insistent, painfully shouting. The sailors advanced toward them, rifles raised.

"Maybe he means discard," Hanley suggested.

Nimit let the rifle sling slide down his arm, barrel down. It clattered onto the ice. "Let's hope," he said.

Hanley lowered her arms completely as she approached the first armed man, who was grimacing in excruciating pain, teeth visible.

"Oh, damn," Nimit said softly, hurrying forward. The sentry's bare cheek had frozen to the stock.

# 39

**N**imit showed them how to help the sailor who was frozen to his weapon, while Hanley pointed at herself and repeated "Doctor" until they allowed her to tend to the man who had fallen along the bulkhead. Someone in authority emerged, clad like the rest in a black hooded parka and face mask. Ice was frozen around the openings for his mouth, his nostrils, and his eyes.

"I am Pushkin, second captain. Admiral Rudenko is injured. We have corpsman but not doctor on board. First Captain Nemerov will transport him to your base, yes? That was destination. And Mister Koyt. He wish to be accompanied, four sailor. Seven together. Is possible?"

Nimit held up a palm to signal the officer to wait as he switched to his radio link to Teddy Zale. He had to repeat the story twice before the extern tower fully grasped what was happening.

*"Okay, Jack, wait one. I've got to check."*

No doubt Teddy had to wake Verneau or Mackenzie for approval. A few minutes passed; the sailors grew even more ice encrusted. Zale came back on with instructions: to pass along invitations for three Russians. *"But Jack, try and talk them out of bringing armed sailors. No escort."*

Nimit conveyed the message: "The invitation stands for three of you. You've got to act quickly, or you'll all become guests of the station. The polynya is especially small this year. Your vessel is freezing into the ice fast. It's going to be spending the winter there soon if the ice pack doesn't crush and sink it first."

The elderly Russian admiral, now leaning on two young sailors, nodded. "We know. We gratefully accept your hospitality. No need for an escort." He switched to Russian, arguing with Captain Nemerov, apparently trying to countermand Nemerov's insistence on accompanying him to Trudeau. Nemerov was having none of it; he was going with the admiral.

Rudenko, squinting against the wind, eyes and mouth frosting over, was in no shape to insist, and relented. Nemerov gave his second officer orders to assume command of the ship and submerge. From his gestures, they gathered he wanted the ship to remain on station and wait in the polynya.

The Russian called Koyt paid close heed. Pushkin stood to attention and saluted. Nemerov barely returned the salute.

"This cold is sharper than needles," Rudenko said in a raspy voice, and closed his eyes.

Hanley was on him instantly. "No, Admiral. Keep your eyes open."

The sailors propped the admiral atop the hood of a vehicle. Hanley rechecked the ankle, which jutted off at an impossible angle, clearly broken. The old man gave no sign of the pain he must have been in, but he was terribly pale. She immobilized the break and pantomimed lifting him up.

Nimit suggested to the Russians that their small gasoline-powered engines would prove inadequate to the terrain and weather, that the wanigan could accommodate another three people, even with the admiral reclining.

Hanley strapped the admiral's ankle in a temporary splint to relieve the pressure of the break but the foot was swelling rapidly. She packed snow into a fabric sack and applied it to the ankle. Nimit went to retrieve the wanigan. The Russian sailors kept a respectful distance from the slinky, shining their lights on it to keep it under surveillance.

Nemerov and two sailors hoisted Rudenko into the wanigan,

then he and Koyt boarded. Koyt sat beside Nimit, half turned in his seat toward the three on the bench just behind him, scanning the tools of Hanley's trade arrayed around them, the cooler of labeled specimen vials and the lemmings squirming in their trap.

Nimit turned the vehicle toward Trudeau. Over her shoulder Hanley watched the sailors climb single file back up the flank of their enormous vessel and disappear quickly below decks, out of the punishing wind. The officer of the watch was the last to vanish as the great black vessel sank straight down into the polynya like an elevator. Hanley sat beside Rudenko and busied herself cutting away the admiral's boot and further immobilizing the ankle. He gratefully accepted the rest of the frozen whiskey, the closest thing they had on board to an anesthetic.

When she glanced back again, the submarine was nearly gone, the moon above it luminous and white.


Riding up the empty tunnel of the ramp, the wanigan rolled out onto an apron crowded with staff who, despite the early hour, were standing and staring as if at a holiday parade. They broke into applause as the Russians descended from the vehicle, excited by the novelty of yet more midwinter guests, and the illusion the visit gave after the terrifying deaths of their colleagues that they were not entirely alone and cut off from the world.

No one yet had the slightest idea what had brought the Russians to Trudeau. That was the first question Mackenzie intended to put to them in his office, where all the senior scientists had crowded in, chief among them Vadim Primakov. Finally there were too many to fit and the answer had to wait until they'd moved the group to the auditorium. Dee and Uli maneuvered the admiral onto a gurney, and Dee wheeled him in while Uli ran for the painkillers in his medic's kit.

Verneau said, "Would you mind relinquishing your weapons while at Trudeau? We have never had assault weapons actually on the premises, other than hunting rifles we employ to secure the entryways from marauding bears and protect our ice vehicles."

Nemerov handed over his rifle, which Verneau passed to Teddy Zale. He opened his hand and waited for Koyt to surrender his too.

"Certainly there's no danger in the station itself that would require a firearm," said Simon King, impatiently. "Your automatic rifles are too lethal to have around so many civilians, and your pistols would be useless against a bear. If you are to be our guests for a time, we must insist—"

Hanley was fascinated to see King this angry at someone else. Raising himself from his gurney, Admiral Rudenko spoke for the first time, looking directly at Koyt: "If I were armed, sir, I would be delighted to surrender my weapon while under your roof." Rudenko had learned his English on the pillow of the assistant to the British cultural attaché when he was stationed in Rome, and he retained a baroque command of the language. "And I thank you for taking such exquisite care with my injury," he finished, wincing as Hanley reset the bone.

"Your pistol wouldn't even fire in this climate," King said to Koyt.

"As it happens, these bullets are tungsten base. The gun, it is graphite and plastic. No metal. This gun will fire under water, and it will fire here," Koyt said. "I assure you." He smiled genially, like a salesman convinced of the superiority of his wares. "But our assault rifles are of course unnecessary." Koyt unslung the semiautomatic rifle with its folding stock and long magazine.

"As to your principal question," said Koyt, snapping the holster of his pistol, "we have come to inquire into the death of Dr. Minskov and to bring his body home. We are to ensure the safety of our nationals, and anyone else who wants our protection. Our government is very concerned about what is transpiring at your facility. They insist on knowing what killed Minskov and the others."

"Funny, we've been wondering about that ourselves," Simon King said, pointedly looking at Hanley. "Although, you do realize, do you not, that technically you have no jurisdiction on Kurlak? This is Canadian territory, a Canadian matter."

"Technically, sir," said Koyt, "our countryman died at sea.

Therefore Canada has no primacy in the matter of the late Dr. Minskov. I have authority from my government to investigate and to take charge of the murderous thing that killed them." He patted a long aluminum tube.

"What is that?" King said.

"A safe conveyance."

Mackenzie swiveled toward him. He seemed nervous. "I believe you have met Dr. Hanley, of Los Angeles, who is heading our examination of the events."

Koyt followed his gaze. Hanley waved wanly. Primakov said something in Russian. Koyt listened, his eyes never leaving the American woman.

"*Nu*, a Canadian from California. Interesting," he said, glancing at Simon King, then back to Hanley. "How do you come to be involved in this Canadian matter? Am I misinformed; were Americans in party of those who died?"

"North Americans, yes," Hanley said. "Which is why I was invited."

"How neighborly," said Koyt. "So you are a medical investigator. Somewhat like me. I will report for duty in the morning. I will do my best not to get beneath your foot. We both want the same result: to find the culprit and end the danger for everyone. We could be of use to one another. I could help keep you and your staff safe."

Hanley pointed to the large thermoslike object. "You've brought along a biocontainment chamber, so clearly you think the culprit's biological. How exactly do you think you or your pistol can protect us from Nature?"

"Well, this is Nature scything people. I worry it will turn on you. As you get closer to it, it gets closer . . . to you."

"Thanks, but I've got all the manpower I can handle at the moment." Hanley muttered to Uli, "Who exactly is this asshole who thinks he's going to barge in on my investigation?" Rudenko, who understood perfectly, suppressed a smile.

Mackenzie raised a hand. "You are all welcome for as long you need to be here. Shall we call it a night?"

Mackenzie was putting a good face on it, but no one believed for an instant that Moscow, with its depleted resources, had risked sending a submarine to investigate the death of an obscure glaciologist in the middle of an Arctic winter, or to recover a body that would easily keep until the following spring.

# 40

The aide opened the great windows in Chernavin's Moscow office and instantly the chill afternoon air rushed in with a vengeance. He shivered and hurried away. The commander did not so much as look up from his desk. A few minutes later the aide was back.

"We have had calls from the president's office. American and Canadian ambassadors, sir, have requested an appointment with you for a Dr. Ishikawa."

"Fine. See what I have open on my calendar next week."

"He is here now, sir."

"Here?"

"Yes, sir. In the anteroom."

Chernavin weighed whether to see him immediately or have him wait, then said, "Bring him in. And send for a translator."

The aide marched off. A few minutes later Kim Ishikawa appeared, his hand outstretched. The admiral rose to take it, displaying the casual charm that always worked so well on westerners.

Ishikawa thanked the admiral profusely for seeing him on such short notice. Chernavin only nodded, smiling at everything as the translator relayed it. Laid backward, he thought the Americans called it. He offered Ishikawa a dish of his snack of Baltic sprats, cucumbers sprinkled with dill, horseradish, garlic slices, and salt. Ishikawa eyed the boxes of papers being packed for the archives and accepted the offered treat.

"Admiral Chernavin, I work for a research facility in the United States and I need to know the whereabouts of Dr. Tarakanova, who was evacuated by submarine from an Arctic research station at the very end of October. I need to see her, urgently."

*Ahhh.* Chernavin nodded vigorously. He summoned a subordinate and gave terse instructions. The captain nodded at each item and picked up the telephone. He stylishly recited an order, listened for a moment, and hung up. He stiffened and related something to Chernavin, who waved him out.

Chernavin turned his attention to Ishikawa, who had been watching closely. He spoke slowly, waiting for the translator.

"The navy only provided transportation, you understand," the translator explained very sincerely. "We have no official word on the doctor's whereabouts. She is a civilian and, unlike the admiral, free to do as she pleases. He suggests you speak to her employers, Shirshov Institute of Oceanography. He will call ahead if you wish."

"Yes, please," said Ishikawa.

The translator placed the call, then handed the phone to Chernavin, who rose, speaking in a nasal tone as he paced back and forth, one hand casually in his trouser pocket. He seemed to be examining the high luster of his shoes as he listened, then said, *"Da, konyechno,"* and rang off. In English, he said to Ishikawa, "Shirshov Institute vill see you at once."

Back on the street, Ishikawa stuck out a hand to hail a taxi, but the car that stopped was a civilian sedan, one of the many that rented itself out for cash. The Shirshov Institute wasn't far. Its director was not nearly as pleasant as the admiral, nor as cooperative. His translator struggled to convey his words to Ishikawa in inoffensive English.

"Dr. Tarakanova visited friends in Moscow after returning, and has been reassigned to sensitive post on Caspian Sea. She is not expected back for eight months and cannot receive visitors where she is. Communications with region are notoriously unreliable, not that Moscow telephones are much better. The director appreciates your interest but wishes to assure you Dr. Tarakanova is fine."

Just then an assistant interrupted to report a phone call. The director answered. Ishikawa stood up to leave, but the man waved him back into his seat. By coincidence Tarakanova was calling to upbraid them about some omission in supplies. He passed the receiver to Ishikawa, who asked if she could tell him anything unusual she had seen before her departure from the field site. Her answer was emphatically negative.

Ishikawa put a hand over his other ear to hear her better. "Was anything delivered by the sub left by the crew at the work site?"

A curt no. He tried a few more specific queries about the scientists' activities in the hours before her departure, but she deflected all of them. Ishikawa apologized for intruding upon her work and hung up.

Ishikawa thanked the officious man and left. At the airport he cleared customs and queued for the phones. He reached Munson at home. Was it what they had feared, Munson wanted to know. Ishikawa thought yes. Perhaps worse.

# 41

The Trudeau board of governors, reached in conference call, were not pleased to learn of the surprise visit by the Russians but agreed to grant Koyt as much access as he wanted to conduct his inquiry. There was, after all, a Russian national in the makeshift morgue.

For his part, Koyt did his best to ingratiate himself with everyone he came in contact with, and they were many (although these didn't include any of his fellow Russians, from whom he kept his distance). Even Simon King came around, flattered by Koyt's requests for information about all aspects of the installation and advice in interpreting Bascomb's field logs and Minskov's elaborate graphs. King's customary grimace took on the resemblance of a pained smile. "That or gas," Dee said under her breath.

Hanley managed to duck Koyt whenever possible; she gave her staff clear instructions that this was her lab, and he was not welcome.

Admiral Rudenko got around quite well on his crutches and asked Emile Verneau if he would mind showing him around the facility. The admiral was an appreciative visitor, taking in each invention and convenience with appropriate awe. Nemerov accompanied him and was equally childlike in his delight.

Finally, Nemerov insisted that in spite of their shared desire to see every last nook and cranny, the admiral must stop to rest his foot. They retired to the main dining hall, where they were greeted like celebrities and seated with Mackenzie and a dozen staff members at a large oval table.

Emile Verneau formally welcomed them to "*notre modeste repas*—our humble repast."

Nemerov looked quizzically at the admiral, who whispered, "Food."

"Ah," Nemerov replied.

Mackenzie looked worn. Rudenko said, "How is your health?"

"Recent events," Mackenzie said, "have taken their toll on my concentration."

"Drink," Nemerov urged, lifting a bottle to pour. "To replenish blood," but Mackenzie covered his glass and stuck with water, pleading work he had to do before bed.

Koyt appeared and slipped into a vacant seat. He had augmented the station's quilted cotton jacket with a green silk cravat.

"May I buy the next round?" Koyt said, and pulled out several notes.

"*Mais non*, no," said Verneau. "Nothing is for sale here, and you are our guest."

"Then allow me to propose a toast. To our gracious hosts," Koyt said. They all lifted their glasses and drank, except Nimit, who picked up a ruble and examined it.

"How do you say money in your language?" Rudenko asked, setting down his glass.

"*Kenouyiat,*" Nimit said.

"*Kenouyiat,*" Rudenko repeated. "Does it have a meaning?"

"Paper with a face on it."

"How very sensible." Rudenko's face crinkled in amusement.

"Is it true," Uli said, "that in your language you refer to us as 'long noses'?"

"Yeah," said Nimit, "but more often we call you *qaablunaat*—'people with bushy eyebrows.'"

"Admiral." Mackenzie turned to Rudenko. "Perhaps our guest of honor would like to propose a toast?"

He raised his glass and said something in Russian. Koyt's face flushed briefly. Everyone looked at Rudenko, waiting for the English, then to Nemerov.

" 'To those still at sea,' " Nemerov translated.

"To those still at sea," they repeated happily, except Koyt, who remained silent and didn't clink his glass or drink.

Hanley leaned in toward Nemerov. "Mr. Koyt wasn't entirely happy with that toast. Has he got something against the navy?"

"Oh, no,"—Nemerov said in a low voice—"is because toast refers to gulag and its passengers. A toast made for too long in honor of friends . . . and family. Mr. Koyt is annoyed hearing this, he is accompanied man."

"Company man?" Hanley said.

"Company man," Nemerov corrected himself, nodding.

"So you twit him," Hanley said.

"Twit?" Nemerov looked puzzled.

"Tease."

"Ah. Tease. Yes, tease." His eyes darted mischievously.

Mackenzie tapped a spoon against the stem of his goblet. The diners grew quiet and gave him their attention.

"In case anyone needs an excuse to hold a party, I am taking this occasion to announce my long-postponed retirement." An *ahhh* went up, more regretful than happy sounding. "Emile Verneau will be succeeding me. We'll announce it officially at the next sunrise reception in March, when the commissioners fly in."

Everyone applauded. Dee, sitting at the end of the table, grew teary and next to her Ned Gibson, the psychologist, looked glum. His face was turned to the large window behind Mackenzie and the illuminated terrain just beyond.

Mackenzie toasted Verneau and all raised their glasses. Rudenko raised his and said, "*Udachi*. Best of luck."

"*Merci*," Verneau said, and stood to receive the good wishes and applause of the room. The staff working in the serving line whirled dishtowels and clattered silverware containers, generally doing their best to greet the news with levity.

Rudenko recognized the false bravado of the group. Like sailors in dangerous seas, they were trying to gloss over an undercurrent of fear. These people lived their work. The life here had always been fulfilling. Now it was endangered; they were endangered, and they knew it. And like sailors, they were on their own. It was the gusto seamen exhibited before an oncoming storm.

The admiral said to Mackenzie, "You're certain?"

"Yes. I am mostly just underfoot. I get rolled out for dignitaries, but any real work was finished long ago. Nostalgia isn't a good enough reason anymore. It's time. This tragedy with my colleagues has affected me deeply. I can't quite recover my momentum. Emile must guide the station from here on."


Hanley showered in the locker area by the extern after the party and headed back to the lab. She returned to her desk to find an encrypted message from Cybil reporting Ishi's suspicion about Tarakanova's demise. Hanley tapped Dee on the shoulder and indicated the screen.

"Wow," Dee said under her breath. As soon as Dee had read it, Hanley deleted the file.

Hanley left Dee examining specimens from Mackenzie's Mount, looking for signs of microbial life in the guano, and took the shaman's pouch into the hot lab. If what she was doing was desecration, she didn't want witnesses. She carefully emptied its contents onto the lab bench. Just as Nimit had said, the bones were ordinary, mammalian, worn by years of use, but showed no signs of disease. She took some scrapings from the inner side of the hide pouch and examined them under the microscope, but again, they seemed to be perfectly unexceptional, if well-preserved, animal hairs.

Someone knocked on the outer wall of the lab, and Koyt came in without waiting for a response. Hanley quickly gathered up the bones, dropped them back into the hide pouch, pocketed it, and stepped into the outer lab.

"I tried to catch your eye at party, but without luck. Would it be a convenient moment to speak with me?" he said to Hanley, eyes mirthful.

"It'll cost you a cigarette," she said.

"Two," said Dee.

Koyt offered his pack. They were English.

"Pull up a chair," Hanley said, sliding out a cigarette. "What's on your mind?"

He sat down and held a light out to each of them in turn. "Annihilation."

Dee's gaze flitted to Hanley. "Excuse me?"

"Of the three scientists."

"Three?" Hanley said.

"And Dr. Kruger and Kossuth too, of course. I am wondering how you are understanding what happened. My English is clear?"

"Clear enough." Hanley rubbed her temples. "But nothing else is. When were you planning to add Dr. Tarakanova to your list? My English is clear?"

If the question surprised him, he gave no indication. "You know then," he said.

"Everyone seems to." She arched an eyebrow. "And what do *you* know?"

Koyt wrinkled his nose for a moment. "Her condition did not match anything our experts had ever seen."

"Could I get autopsy results? Did they interview the crew about the course of the illness once she boarded?"

"I'm sure the results of her autopsy would match your victims' here; any interviews would be a matter to take up with the naval authorities. I am authorized to tell you that, based on observations of her remains, my facility delegated a team of medical historians to search our archives for a similar event."

"And?" In spite of herself, Hanley was curious to know whether the Russians might have a useful lead.

"Closest they came was an odd occurrence during the First World War. A German aristocrat was detained by authorities in Norway. Among his belongings were a few lumps of sugar pierced by small holes. Several cubes had a peculiar coloration in the center. One opening held a tiny sealed glass tube. The authorities thought it might hold anthrax. The nobleman's itinerary had included travel in a part of Norway where horses and other drayage animals had mysteriously perished, among them reindeer used to haul war matériel. Lung tissue of the deer had atrophied in a very short time, turned hard and dry and inflexible, like your victims here."

"Which is not anthrax."

"No. They haven't the faintest clue what it is," he said, as though it were some delightful academic puzzle, and not a lethal microbe. "And they are none too happy about it."

"Thanks. You've confirmed it's not anthrax, which we knew from day one. That's a big help."

Koyt chose to ignore her sarcasm. "They must have put three dozen people on the case. My hat goes off to you, laboring here alone. I wonder which of you will reach the solution first?"

"I am not alone, as you can see," Hanley said.

"Yes, of course, but no one else at Trudeau has relevant training, no one with experience comparable to your own. Except for me."

"What exactly is your area of expertise?"

"Solutions," he said. "Like yourself. Since my offer of help has not yet interested you, I have been conducting my own investigation into fieldwork logs, marine data from the polynya, and Minskov's ice core studies. Like you, I am looking for a design, or a disruption."

Uli, in his rumpled lab coat, took him in and said very coolly, "What sort of help do you offer?" Hanley shot him a dirty look.

Koyt shrugged. "Whatever you need. I know something of what you are after." He looked about and stepped over to a shelf of lichens being prepped for testing. Picking up one of the specimens Hanley had collected at the polynya, he said, "This, for instance. Wolf lichen, yes?"

"Yes," said Dee, "quite harmless. "Native peoples here in the Arctic use it to dye ceremonial blankets."

"How useful. In Russia we extract vulpinic acid from it and use it as a poison"—he stared into Uli—"to kill wolves." He put the cutting down.

Hanley looked from the delicate strands of lichen back at Koyt. "We're well staffed at the moment, but we'll let you know."

"Please do. I'm intrigued by what you are doing here. How often do we get to hunt in unknown territory like this? I would like to contribute something of real use. I wouldn't mind being part of the team that bests the combined energies of my country's finest minds. But this is your lab, of course, Dr. Hanley. I only hope that when you find the solution, you will alert me."

"Believe me, everybody in Trudeau will hear when we find it."

"Then I will make sure to stay close, so that I hear you first," said Koyt. "Good night."

The two women stared as he walked away into the short connecting tunnel that led back to the rest of the station.

"Well," Uli said, dryly. "He's what you would call a piece of work."

Hanley said, "Good of you not to start an international incident, Dr. Steensma."

"You have no idea how badly I wanted to put this cigarette out on his forehead. How dare he not mention Tarakanova!"

"Yeah," Hanley said. "But damn, he does seem to know what he's talking about." She handed the container of wolf lichen to Uli. "Better move this one to the top of the list."

Hanley spent the rest of the day with Dee in the lab, testing the algae samples she had collected near the polynya. During a late lunch break, Dee lay across Hanley's bed, staring at the soft hues of the rounded ceiling. Hanley was slumped in a bentwood armchair nearby, feet flat on the bed, knees raised, with a mirror propped on them. "Ow!"

Dee raised herself up on an elbow. "What the hell are you doing to yourself?"

"Ow! Plucking my eyebrows."

Dee laughed so hard she snorted. " 'People with bushy eyebrows,' eh?"

"Ow!"

"What are you plucking them with?"

Hanley examined the object in her hand, as if for the first time. "Pliers."

"Pliers?"

"Yeah. Mini pliers from my pathology kit, if you must know."

"Yikes." Dee made a pained face as she watched Hanley. "Would you like to borrow my tweezers?"

"No. Thanks. These are okay. You do know he's eight years younger than I am?"

"Yes. So what?"

"You don't think it's . . . inappropriate?"

"What if he were eight years older? Would you think that was inappropriate?"

"No."

"I rest my case."

"Do you think people think—?"

"Hey. People don't think anything. Certainly not here. If you two are okay with it, no one at Trudeau is not okay with it. Stop worrying."

"Uh, this is uncivilized," Hanley said, tossing the pliers aside and rubbing her brow. "I think I'm bleeding."

"Are you getting serious about him?"

"Enough to go through this to beautify myself. God, what women do." She held out a length of hair, examining it critically. "I can't believe I might be falling for somebody so young. Plus, I'm weird."

"So is he. You're both obsessed with your work, both obsessed with solving problems. You're hardly incompatible."

Hanley smiled to herself. "Aside from my being taller, we're almost too compatible. We put the lab rabbits to shame."

"See, you don't seem to have a problem keeping up with a younger lover," Dee said, teasing, then minced: "Oh, Jack, darling. Tell me again about how you drove those long, hot steel pilings into the earth."

A pillow struck Dee in the forehead. "Hey!"

Hanley resumed plucking. "Ouch. Waxing couldn't be worse than this."

"It is, take my word for it," Dee said. "I don't know. I think Jack's as solid as they come. I've never heard that he was a womanizer or anything. He's always been the solitary soul, as far as I can tell."

"Probably why he feels so familiar."

Dee smiled sympathetically. "It has a way of happening. Just let it. You're both totally dedicated to your work, nearly to the exclusion of everything else. As different as you two are, you're twins on that score. It's kind of great that you should find each other."

"I hope you're right. Are you seeing anyone?"

"I wish. Since my boyfriend decamped, I've made do with the occasional Aussie or German, and there was a Japanese botanist, but he went home at the end of the summer. That Captain Nemerov is pretty cute."

"So you like a man in uniform, do you?" Hanley said.

"Yeah, but I think there's a Mrs. Nemerov."

"That's too bad."

"Yeah."

"And you would never . . . ?"

Dee shook her head. "No."

Hanley leaned back on her palms, her straight arms and torso outlining a triangle.

"You're a good girl, Dee Steensma."

"Yeah. Ask me if I'm happy about it."

# 42

Nimit herded Hanley into his bedroom and started to undress her.

"You think this will last beyond the winter?" she asked.

"Are you referring to us or your great bug hunt?"

"Us."

"Hard to tell. I can only hope."

She gazed up at him. "You're not the easiest person to fathom."

Nimit nodded, having heard it before. "*You* could get to know me. When you're less preoccupied, let's talk."

"You talk," she said, "I'll listen."

"Okay, I'll talk." He slipped off his baggy trousers. "See, I'm talking."

"Yeah," she said, reaching out and touching him shamelessly.

"I would chain you to a radiator," he said, "if we had any here."

"Promises, promises," she said and pulled him close. "We want to know your innermost desires, everything naked and open."

"Naked and open could definitely be arranged."

"And maybe a back rub?"

"I'll see what I can do."

"Wait one. Let's resume this under the covers. Last one turns out the light," she said, peeling off her boots.

"We should sleep," he said, sliding in beside her, and kissed her platonically on the forehead, which made her laugh given the location of her hand and the effect it was having.

She sat up and kissed the top of his head. "Hmmm," she said. "Have you considered hair restorer?"

"What!" Nimit exclaimed, clamping a hand over his crown.

"Just kidding," Hanley said, giggling.

He pulled her close and they kissed languidly.

"The call of the wild," he said, clutching her and kissing the nape of her neck.

"Okay, okay, a quickie."

"We have all night. What do you mean?"

"Baby, I'll be asleep in seven minutes. You think you can handle that?"

He frowned.

"Come on, take me or leave me." She tickled him.

"Hey."

"You're wasting precious seconds."

"Why me?" he said, grabbing her wrists.

"What?"

"Why me?"

"I guess I admire technical ingenuity," she said, and shifted him around. "Did you ever try it in one of those Kama Sutra bridge positions?"

"Not since engineering school."

Hanley shivered. "It's chilly." She pulled the coverlet over them and jabbed him lightly.

"Stop," Nimit ordered.

"Sorry," she said, with utter insincerity, and poked him again. "Six minutes and counting." She poked him again. "Let's concentrate here."

"Hey!" he protested, laughing. He suddenly clutched her and kissed her passionately, and they fell back onto the pillows, heady with desire.

Outside the window, it sounded like a herd of elephants braying, followed by a churning screech and a huge *kraaak*.

"What the hell?" Hanley said. "Ice slabs rafting?"

"Shh. It's nothing," Jack said to her cheek, "just the earth moving."

Hanley sat up and swung her feet out of bed. She mashed her face in her hands and slumped forward, exhausted. Nimit rose up an elbow just behind her and touched her.

"You rock, girl."

"Please. You make me feel old talking like that."

"Why?"

"Never mind." She eyed him over her shoulder, nearly laughing. *You rock.* He sounded like her son. Hanley started putting on her clothes.

"Are you leaving?" he said, sounding hurt.

"Seduced and abandoned, yes. I've got to go save the world."

"At three in the morning? It's the middle of the night."

"It's always the middle of the night here." She sighed, and slipped her one-piece bra over her head and under her breasts, aware of their weight, worrying momentarily about their sagging. The worry had become ritual. She groped around in the bedding for her underwear and noted his demeanor. "Hey," she said, "don't take it personally. This was great."

"Glad to oblige. God, you make it sound like a superior work-out."

"No, Jack Nimit, that was fucking, pure and sensational."

"You don't mince words, Doc."

"I haven't the luxury. What you see is what you've got. I loved it." She reached back for him and touched his chest. Loved it more than she wanted to even think about at this moment. "Come on. You're a great lover. You hear?" She brushed his arm. "But one of these days we've got to think seriously about where all this is headed."

"What's to think about?"

She brushed her hair in place with her hand. "On my side, there's my age, my line of work, my life back in Los Angeles. My son." She pulled on a sock. "Mackenzie's sure it's just a fling."

Nimit darkened. "You talked to him . . . about us?"

"It was more like he talked to me."

"Where? When did you see him?"

"The other day, before we went to the polynya. I was summoned."

"If he asks to see you again, I want to be there."

She took him in. "Sure."

"You promise?"

"Yes." She kissed his eyelid. "Think about us, Jack. Carefully."

He raised up higher and kissed her chastely on the nose. "I have."


It was an ungodly hour, even for a facility that operated round the clock. The last shift was more than halfway through, and there was almost no one else abroad in the dining hall except, Hanley noticed, the Russian admiral.

"Sir," she said in greeting. "How is my favorite patient?"

"Dr. Hanley." His face came alive. "Please." He indicated a chair opposite.

"You're sure?"

"Yes, yes. Please, sit."

She did. "I don't even know why I'm here," she said. "I'm not hungry."

"Good," he said, and leaned closer, whispering: "The cook is not the best." Hanley smiled, recognizing the "serious huffer" idly stirring what looked like scrambled eggs.

Rudenko tested the heat of the pot in front of him. "Coffee?"

She nodded. "Thanks. How is your ankle? I hope the pain isn't keeping you up?"

"No, your handiwork is fine. It's stronger." He sat back. "No, I was thinking about the past," he said. "At my age, that is more sensible than the other. And what has you up at this hour?"

"I snuck away to think about my dilemma."

"Microbes?"

"Boys."

"Ah. Complicated organisms too."

"Jack Nimit and I . . . we've become involved."

Rudenko nodded. "Love. It's a good thing. But, yes, it will keep you awake worrying."

"I hope it's good," she said. "We're from such different worlds."

Rudenko poured her a cup and refilled his. "I was in love with an English woman—a culture and a country far from mine. And we met in a third country yet. The differences didn't seem to matter."

"You didn't stay together?"

"No." He sipped and cleared his throat. "She was married. Her husband was chronically ill. She returned with him to England eventually, to look after him."

"How did you cope?"

"I was heartbroken, of course. But I was proud of her too. She had such . . ." He groped for the right word.

"Character?"

"Exactly, yes. Such courage and dedication. It pained me to see it, and yet I would have been disappointed in her if she had not stood by him. She had such conviction. She lived the way she loved." His eyes found hers. "We were fortunate. However brief the time we had, it filled us."

"Did you ever see her again?"

"She sent me a postcard one spring. The address was a place called Gordon Place, in London. Years later, I went there. An exquisite, tiny cul-de-sac off a small street near a Carmelite church she had told me about. The walk was completely overgrown with flowering vines and roses. Like a fairy-tale arbor."

"You saw her again."

"I didn't. I wasn't even sure she was there anymore."

"Why didn't you knock on her door?"

"We had had our moment, our chance. Life is rarely so kind twice. I didn't want to spoil what we'd had. I kept it as it was."

She laughed with incredulity. "How . . . Russian."

"Oh," he exclaimed, "and what would an American do in such circumstance?"

"Set off fireworks. Blare music up the street. Yell. Wake the neighborhood. Flush her out."

"Ahhh."

"An American wouldn't suffer silently," she said.

He wagged a finger at her. "It's not suffering."

"No?"

"It is living. Living hurts. It is unavoidable."

"Only death and taxes are unavoidable, Admiral."

"Death and taxes," he repeated slowly. "This is very American. In Russia many of us manage to avoid taxes altogether. And I wonder if the tax cheats will become so rich they will come up with a way to cheat death as well." She laughed.

He said, "You gleam when you laugh, and you look so young."

"Thank you," she said. "Admiral, may I ask you a favor?"

"Of course."

Hanley drew the shaman's pouch from her pocket and showed him the Cyrillic characters.

"This is not Russian," he said, puzzled.

"No, it's an Arctic language, using your characters. Could you sound it out to the Aleut cook? I need to find out what it says."

He asked no questions, and immediately stood to walk with her to the serving line, where she explained to the cook what she needed. Rudenko read the words slowly, in rounded Russian tones, and then the Aleut repeated them with his own emphasis, full of catches deep in the throat.

"Does it mean something?"

"Sure, Doc. It's about a what-do-you-call-it—a poultice made from a 'ghost plant.' I can't tell if it's a prescription or a warning. But he's saying it's very strong medicine."

"Thanks," she said to the cook, and then walked with Rudenko to the door.

"Was that useful to you?"

She stood thinking. Where would Annie and the others have

encountered a plant this time of year, ghost or otherwise, except the pongos? Would the shaman have thought of the shimmering mist as a trapped spirit? A ghostly plant?

"I think so. I'm not sure. But thank you, Admiral, for all your help. In both departments."

"Entirely my pleasure, Doctor," he said. "As we say in my business, good hunting."

# 43

shikawa dozed most of the way to Ottawa, never fully unconscious, always hovering just above sleep. Before he left, Petterson had lent him an overcoat, but when he deplaned at Macdonald-Cartier International, it turned out what he needed most were sunglasses. The weather was certainly cold in Ottawa, but the November sky was brilliant and filled with white feathery clouds. He bought a pair at a kiosk and queued for a taxi.

The road into town wound along a wide canal and scenic parkland. Everyone along the way was wearing a poppy in his lapel. The flowers appeared almost orange against the scarlet tunics of the mounted police in their dress uniforms.

"Remembrance Day," the cab driver volunteered. "You know, commemoration of the First World War dead."

The parkway ended in an off-ramp that curled onto an elevated boulevard that passed his hotel, the magnificent Chateau Laurier. The canal crossed under the boulevard and continued past the formidable building and into a narrow gorge that disappeared into a limestone bluff.

Dead on his feet, Ishi opened the western window in his room and thrust his head out into the bracing cold. Straight ahead sat the ornate Parliament Building, sitting on a high cliff over the Ottawa River with French Quebec on the far side. Beneath his window, stone locks stepped the canal down to the level of the river. Back along its banks, in the direction he had come from, a restaurant nestled in the depression of the canal.

Like Washington, Ottawa was a company town whose business was the nation's governance. Martial music wafted from the direction of the Parliament grounds, where crowds of celebrants milled about: bureaucrats in overcoats bundled against the cold, Royal Canadian Mounted Police, soldiers flooding out onto the esplanades and boulevards, ceremonies concluded. Like the civilians, they all sported poppies at their breasts.

Revived, Ishi called to confirm his appointment and asked if they could meet for brunch in an hour at the restaurant by the canal, then collapsed on the bed fully clothed, just barely rousing himself in time.

He followed along the canal to the restaurant, where he was escorted to a window table. Stevenson was already seated.

"Welcome to Ottawa," Stevenson said, "not too rough a flight, I hope."

"A little bumpy. I'm still light-headed."

Stevenson sympathized. "There can be a lot of turbulence this time of year. I'm logging a lot of miles myself."

"Who do you work for, now that you're not with the Trudeau oversight board?"

"Actually, I was just on loan to Trudeau. I'm back warming a government cubicle."

"Oh," Ishikawa said, "and what do you do for the government?"

Stevenson sampled his Canadian bacon and said, "At the moment we're doing the security arrangements for the importation of surplus plutonium bought from the Russians. It's being tried as reactor fuel to make electricity."

"Weapons-grade plutonium?"

"Warheads. I wish we could buy them all and get 'em in safe hands where we can keep an eye on them. Every day more turn out to be unaccounted for. It's not certain they'll work in our reactors. Green groups are hysterical about subjecting the country to the danger of accidental contamination, even detonation. You can't believe the stir this has caused. God, if Annie were around, I'd be getting an earful daily. Russians. They've been dumping radioactive waste into the Arctic Sea from their coasts for years. Liquid nuclear waste. They load it onto ships and scuttle them, or simply pump the stuff overboard. They sink their worn-out submarines without bothering to remove the nuclear fuel first."

"Doesn't their press raise hell?"

"Any journalists brave enough to report on it have been rewarded with prison sentences for treason and espionage. And all this goes on even as the Russian Federation collects millions from England and us and the U.S. to decommission subs and dispose of their reactors safely. The foreign money rarely reaches farther than pockets in Moscow. Or Switzerland. Russia is Russia, no matter who's in the Kremlin."

Ishikawa tried to quiz Stevenson about Annie Bascomb, but Stevenson pointedly changed the subject.

"How's Jessie Hanley progressing?"

"Hard to say." Ishikawa buttered his toast. "It's sort of all or nothing in our line of work. Until you've got something, you've often got nothing. Or that's how it feels. We can hit a lot of dead ends along the way."

"How can I help?" Stevenson appeared somber and sincere.

"I'm hoping for a little candor. We're worried that we've sent Jessie into a situation more dangerous than we'd anticipated. We have concerns about her safety and what is happening at Trudeau."

"Concerns. Such as?"

"Dr. Lidiya Tarakanova is apparently deceased. Like her Trudeau colleagues. We don't want to see Jessie Hanley added to that list. We want to know what she's up against and what we need to do to help her."

Stevenson lifted his water glass. "Yes," he said, "I see," and sipped. "I wish I could help you."

"Mr. Stevenson, you may not like my questions, but I doubt very much that you want to hear them asked on the floor of your parliament."

Stevenson put down his glass and met Ishikawa's gaze. "I have to make a call," he said, and excused himself.

Ishikawa ordered coffee. Stevenson returned and took his seat.

"I'm afraid all I can tell you is that we have misgivings too, and we're monitoring the situation closely. That's on the record. Off the record, we think Dr. Tarakanova was a Russian agent. You've seen Admiral Chernavin?"

Ishikawa was startled. No one but Munson knew his travel agenda. "In Moscow, yes. Why would the Russians need an agent in the middle of the Arctic? Mr. Stevenson, what is this all about?"

"What it was always about—advantage. The Russians have had agents at Trudeau from the first."

"Why? If they're up there doing bioterror research, and you let us send Jessie Hanley into the middle of it without any warning . . ."

"God, no. Not bioterror." Stevenson sighed. "I suppose it had to come out sometime," he said as if to himself. "The Russians have a vested interest in the Arctic." Stevenson put aside his cutlery and leaned on his elbows, arms crossed, voice low. "Years ago, Washington committed to developing unimaginably costly defenses to detect Russian submersibles and neutralize their power. Before long, American equipment could detect the whole Soviet submarine force, even boats under the Arctic ice. Your undersea surveillance was nearly omnipotent. To drive the point home, every American sub that was secretly shadowing a Soviet sub somewhere on the planet, simultaneously activated its sonar against its unwary communist counterpart."

"They pinged the other boat."

"Yes. And at exactly the same second. This demonstration of complete supremacy was synchronized worldwide."

"That was bad?"

"It sent the Russians an unmistakable message about their slipping prowess, and created near-panic in Moscow. American arms superiority was nearly total, they realized. The last possible moment to confront the West was facing them: it was now or never."

"And they chose now."

"You might say that. First-strike scenarios were brought out, sabres drawn. Amid the hullabaloo, Chernavin came up with a scheme that quelled the hysteria. He said their missiles needed an undetectable place from which to launch. Somewhere impervious to radar, sonar, satellite surveillance."

"Even though the Americans had demonstrated their superiority in sub detection?"

"Yes. But how? There could be no motion, no motor signature, no noise, no telltale sonar shadow."

"That would be impossible," Ishikawa said, "unless—"

"Unless what?"

"There was no sub."

"Very good." Stevenson scratched his cheek. "Stationary unmanned platforms under the ice. Additional problem: static launching points required unimpeded trajectory: openings in the ice. Reliable openings, never frozen shut."

"Polynyas."

"Trudeau—the old Trudeau—was coordinating the mapping of polynyas in the Canadian archipelago and the rest of the Arctic Ocean. The Soviets had a man there and availed themselves of the data. The polynyas provided the missiles with foolproof positions undetectable by the new technologies."

"What an idea—missiles on the seafloor. And in the Western Hemisphere." Ishikawa was incredulous. "How long were they there?"

Stevenson sat silent.

"They weren't removed?"

"As far as we know—no."

"Where? How many?"

"We don't know. One? A dozen? They're not easily detected, which was the whole point, I suppose. Most definitely there's one in the polynya by Mackenzie's mount."

"Where the trio died." Ishikawa felt light-headed. "What is your government doing about this?"

"Isn't much we can do. Our territorial claims in the Arctic have been systematically ignored by the Russians—and you—for years. Foreign planes and boats move through our territory at will."

"You don't object?"

"Ottawa's ignored the incursions. We pretend they haven't

occurred so our sovereignty remains intact. There's little choice, I suppose, when you're a tenth the power of the intruder. Challenging the Soviet military about their errant missile was out of the question."

"You never notified Washington."

"Officially involving the Americans back then would have put us in the middle of a global confrontation." He shook his head. "We did nothing. The missile languished down there for decades. We're pretty sure Tarakanova was the latest minder for this orphan."

"And now she's dead?" Ishi said.

Stevenson's eyes stared into his. "Apparently."

Ishi braced his arms stiffly against the banquette seat on either side of him. "This is more than we bargained for when your government enlisted our help. What can we do for Dr. Hanley?"

"I wish I knew," Stevenson said. "Have your people contacted your federal officials about all this?"

"Not yet," Ishikawa answered. "No."

"You should eat—your food's getting cold."

"I've lost my appetite." Ishi straightened his utensils on the plate.

Stevenson waved for the waiter and mouthed *bill*. He said, "Let's walk by the canal. It may afford us more privacy."

"What do you mean?"

"The gentleman over your shoulder, in the corner—Armani sport coat, sunglasses—has been very interested in our conversation."

Ishikawa snuck a quick glance, and felt dizzy.

"Know him?"

Ishikawa nodded, remembering the feel of the embossed card the man had handed him in the Center's parking lot. Christ, could the guy have actually been following him since L.A.? Ishikawa hastily tried to remember if he had seen him in Moscow or Tokyo.

"He's press. L.A. *Times*. Payne, I think."

"Right," said Stevenson, leaving money on the table and standing. "Shall we?"

Outside, the water changed from blue to black to blue again as a white cloud's shadow sailed past. They strolled along the canal, lapels upturned, and climbed stone stairs to street level, then strolled through well-attired crowds up to the Parliament and around behind it. In the back, they paused at a spot overlooking the frozen river.

"This was built in the 1860s," Stevenson said, indicating the waterway and the locks farther on. "A major piece of engineering. Cut by hand out of sheer rock. Just recreational these days, but its original purpose was strategic. After an earlier war, Canada realized its vulnerability to renewed attack and set out to build the canal as a defensive precaution, so we could move troops and supplies inland in a hurry."

Ishikawa said, "Who were you fighting back then?"

"You. The United States." He held his coat closed. "History is fickle. Allies become enemies, enemies allies. If you had bested us back then, we'd be having this conversation in American Ottawa." Stevenson tipped his chin toward the canal. "In time, one regime's Herculean labor becomes another's walk in the park. Mortal enemies mellow, and open mutual animosity becomes one-sided resentment." He smiled wistfully. "Battlefields are out; markets, in."

"Who exactly do you work for?" Ishikawa said.

"C-SIS."

Ishikawa glanced at him. "What's that?"

Stevenson shielded his eyes with a gloved hand to stare at the far shore. "Canadian Security Intelligence Service."

Ishikawa took in Stevenson, appraising him anew. "What can you tell me about the Russians who have arrived at Trudeau?"

"Rudenko and Nemerov are career military."

"And Koyt?"

"He has a degree in biochemistry and a degree from the London School of Economics."

"Is he a spook?"

"Yes. Like me." Stevenson eyed the American. "You seem agitated by what I've told you."

"You could say that."

"Why? Have I said something to give offense?"

"You knew what the Russians had installed there, and the

dilemma Trudeau Station would face at some point. You put Hanley in there anyway, and precisely because she's not Canadian. That's what I'm beginning to realize, and, yes, it's upsetting."

"She was the most qualified."

"Oh, I know, I know. That was convenient, wasn't it? It let you drop an American into the middle of your conundrum instead of a Canadian."

Stevenson didn't protest his organization's innocence.

"If it was a Canadian health worker, you couldn't have kept the lid on this long. Health Canada wouldn't have put up with cloaking the situation. An American was far easier to control. She's a guest, after all. And our own interest in keeping a missile's presence quiet would eventually suit your needs too. It gave you a shot at keeping it all from going public." Ishi paused.

Stevenson offered no challenge. "We saw a possibility of keeping Trudeau going, yes."

"Yeah. So I'm pissed. You put my friend in there knowing it was more dangerous and complicated than any of us realized."

Stevenson squinted at him in the bright sunlight. "Safe home," he said, and walked away without offering his hand.

# 44

Notification came from Moscow over the shortwave. It wasn't encoded—just a simple voice message in Russian. Teddy Zale summoned Koyt, Rudenko, and Nemerov to the extern to receive the news that Admiral Chernavin had resigned his post upon being named first deputy of the armed services, following a cabinet shuffle. The delegation at Trudeau was no longer operative.

Koyt was furious. "This is unacceptable. He can't just walk away at such a moment."

Nemerov made a hapless gesture. "A promotion. What's to be done?"

Koyt exhaled slowly through pursed lips, trying to calm himself.

Zale made discreet noises that suggested they should probably hold their conversation elsewhere, so they departed for the admiral's *couchette*.

"Do you think," Nemerov said, as they walked along, "that it would be proper to convey our congratulations to the new first deputy before we plan our retirements?"

"For myself," said Rudenko, "I have a beach in mind, on a warm sea." He leaned against a wall for a moment to take the weight off his ankle. "And you, dear boy, will be able to command unarmed ships that adhere to schedules. Your wife will be relieved, and how happy your girls will be. My goddaughters will come to visit their *papachik* in summers and on school holidays when their father is away on shipping business."

Koyt said, "Chernavin's removal is not anything to be light-hearted about."

Nemerov couldn't contain himself. "Well," he said as they reached the admiral's door, "if you are mobile, we'd best speak to Verneau. We will need an escort back to the ship."

Rudenko entered his quarters and eased down into an armchair. Immediately he began scratching what skin he could reach of his immobilized ankle. Nemerov poured drinks from a bottle of cognac Verneau had presented them. Koyt waved his away.

"We are not leaving," Koyt said.

Rudenko accepted the glass and said, "Mr. Koyt, I understood that the mission was under my command, not yours."

"Don't be coy. My orders supersede yours, as you well know."

Rudenko assumed a puzzled expression. "What orders? Admiral Chernavin's authority is no more."

Koyt smirked. "There is always a successor. In the interim, it is not our place to deviate from prior instructions, or to compromise national interests unilaterally."

Nemerov bristled at the younger man's lack of respect for Admiral Rudenko. "Exactly how long do you expect my ship to wait?" he said.

"Until I am ready to leave." Koyt stalked out.

Nemerov turned to the huge windows and the constant darkness beyond. "What to do?"

Rudenko sipped his drink. "Whatever Koyt is involved in here, stay out of it. Take cover in my wake. If there's trouble, it will be harder to level accusations at me. No reason for two of us to risk official displeasure. You have far more to lose." The admiral savored the bouquet of his cognac.

"What are you thinking," Nemerov said, "with that long face?"

"About the newly minted First Deputy Chernavin." He rubbed his eyes. "Poor Panov."

"Poor Russia."

Nemerov raised his face to the black sky outside. Rudenko put down his glass and lifted his injured foot onto the footrest.

"This place is wondrous," Nemerov said, tapping the window with his finger. "The technology, the concept."

Rudenko nodded. "Yes. I'm not sure they fully realize. Maybe they're just too scared by what has been happening here. Or perhaps they've gotten used to it all and aren't affected anymore."

"How could you not be?" Nemerov said.

There was a knock at the door. Both turned at the sound.

"Come," the admiral said.

"Gentlemen," Jessie Hanley said, standing on the threshold. Nemerov rose to greet her.

"How is your ankle progressing?" she asked Rudenko. "Is the cast itching?" she said, seeing the reddened skin around the top of it.

"Very much. But I am healing. It doesn't hurt. That's all I seem to care about at the moment." He lifted a crutch. "I will soon graduate to a cane. Excellent for sympathy. Have you come to check up on my progress?"

"Not really. I've come to interrogate you."

"What about?" Rudenko said. He raised his eyes to Nemerov.

"Please, Dr. Hanley," said Nemerov, hand extended toward the empty modern armchair. "Sit."

Hanley drew the chair closer and eased herself down. The admiral was perfectly still, his foot propped up on a stool. Nemerov remained on his feet, leaning a hand upward against the curvature of the cupola rising up over them. Hanley realized he must be used to such walls from his years in submarines.

"I've had disturbing news from my colleagues in Los Angeles," she said. "It's pretty clear Lidiya Tarakanova is no longer alive. They also tell me—just by the way—that we're sitting on a junked nuclear device—possibly Russian made—that's been parked under the polar ice cap for, oh, twenty or thirty years. A big deal, I'm sure. But frankly not of much interest to me at the moment. I'm a lot more worried about how far our mysterious contagion may have spread than this overlooked . . . device. On that subject, Mr. Koyt has been singularly unhelpful. So I'm turning to you. Do you know anything about what happened to Dr. Tarakanova? Did you talk to the crew? Can you tell me what happened between the time she boarded the sub and the time she died?"

Nemerov and Rudenko exchanged glances. Nemerov put his hands in his pockets. "We know things, yes. However, if we share information with you, it can have serious repercussions for us."

"If you are not discreet," the admiral said, "we could be accused of treason."

"Treason?" She half laughed. "You're serious," she said, swiveling toward the admiral.

"I could not be more serious. But you are right. That abandoned device isn't your problem. The Russian sailors, who died like your scientists, are."

Hanley said, "Sailors? Members of the crew that came to pick your scientist up at the polynya?"

"Dr. Tarakanova was not a scientist. Or rather not just a scientist," Rudenko said. "An agent . . ." He half turned to Nemerov, motioning for the right English word while saying it in Russian: *"Nyanka."*

" 'Babysitter?' " Nemerov suggested, then to Hanley: "Is like child chaperone."

"Yes, yes." Rudenko nodded. "She was here to protect the secret, and keep Moscow informed, as I recently learned." He glanced at Nemerov, giving the younger man a chance to stop him, but Nemerov remained silent.

"Secret?" she said.

"This nuclear device, as you call it, is a missile not intended to strike anything. It was designed to blow up overhead so as to propagate an artificial aurora across two thousand miles of the Arctic, emanating from where the lines of magnetic force fan out. Here, near the pole. A 'shell of intensity': a burst of high-energy electrons, flowing in a thin spray around the earth, following the lines of the field."

"What the hell for?" Hanley said.

"To feed its radiation into the earth's magnetic field," Nemerov said, "and blind you."

"How do you mean, Captain?" she asked, afraid to hear the answer.

"Location is critical. Detonation in atmosphere over Arctic would affect the entire magnetic field for forty-eight seconds. It would scramble American radar."

"It was meant to cloak an attack," Rudenko explained. "To be the opening shot."

"Detonated *over* the Arctic? My God." Hanley clasped her hands over her head, unable to sit still.

"But then," the admiral said, "the Soviet Union dissolved, history's wheel turned. Our armories shut down, our stock markets opened. Enmity gave way to deals. This strategy was quietly abandoned, replaced by *bizness*."

"Holy hell," Hanley said. "It's even worse than my people suspect. If word of this got out, Trudeau would instantly be the biggest political hot potato on the planet. Can't your government just remove it?"

Rudenko set aside his glass. "The possibility that it would remain idle for so many years was not something anyone foresaw. There is neither method nor money in my homeland to even contemplate raising it. No capacity. No political will. What is one little rocket in the Arctic Ocean? Cold temperatures preserve man-made things in the sea, after all—that is their simplistic attitude, as if it were produce in the vegetable compartment of a refrigerator. They are more worried about the American reaction than about the device itself. We recovered Lidiya Tarakanova's report. She was notifying her superiors about the victim named Bascomb. I believe Annie Bascomb had discovered what was in the polynya."

"Annie knew? Maybe that's what she was obsessing about. Talk about the mother of all pollutants!"

"Pardon?"

"Nothing—please, go on. What exactly happened to Tarakanova? How long did she survive after leaving the polynya?"

"She died on the submarine," Nemerov said quietly.

"Yes," Rudenko said. "With our sailors."

"She was contagious? How many others were affected?"

Nemerov gazed sadly at her. "Everyone. All."

"All?" Hanley said, hoarsely. "The entire crew?" The information tumbled in her gut. "Any survivors?"

"None," said Rudenko.

"You look white, Doctor," Nemerov said, worried.

"I'm having sort of a bad day." Hanley massaged her forehead. "Or is it night? How many in the crew?" She rose and walked a little, circling nervously, hands on her waist.

"Ninety-four men aboard."

"And Tarakanova makes ninety-five," Hanley said slowly, wrapping her arms tight around herself, taking it in. "Ninety-five. Lungs solid, eyes gone—all the same symptoms?"

Nemerov nodded.

Hanley raised her hands to her cheeks. "So the bug replicated," she said, thinking aloud. "It's definitely cellular. Viral or smaller. A contagious microorganism the submarine's crew was exposed to, like the scientists on the ice."

"So it would seem," the admiral said.

"Did they actually set foot on the ice when they came to get her—the crewmen, I mean?"

"No," said Rudenko.

"This is important. You're sure?"

"Yes."

Hanley nervously tapped her clavicle with the flat of her hand. "It kills three. It lies dormant in Alex Kossuth; it doesn't kill him, but it kills Dr. Kruger when she opens him up. Tarakanova's exposed with the others, but it kills her and the sub's entire company much later and farther away. What are we up to?"

"Ninety-nine," Nemerov said.

"God, this bug is virile—not that we didn't suspect it. We've been lucky so far that it hasn't spread at the station, but who knows what's stopping it?" She stood silent in front of the Russians. "Do you know any more details?"

They shook their heads. "The postmortem on the one recovered body yielded nothing," said Rudenko.

"Your scientist—agent—Tarakanova, she didn't die on the ice with the three others. Why not? How did the bug get aboard the ship with her? Carried in her system? Her luggage?"

Nemerov shrugged. "Perhaps special mixture and pressurized atmosphere of submarine did something to accelerate whatever killed sailors. Maybe this is just most deadly microbe ever. We have no facts. Just theory and fear."

# 45

I don't know which I find more shocking." Dee slumped on her couch, weighed down by Hanley's news. "You're sure?"

Hanley nodded.

Dee sat up and hugged herself as if to ward off cold, her chin resting on her knees. "It's surreal. Intended to explode in the atmosphere? Over the ice pack?"

"Yes."

"Are they insane? The Arctic is such a vulnerable ecosystem. It would never recover." She fell silent, rocking, thinking. "This could be the end of the station. The Americans will go after this missile in an instant once they know about it. How could they not? The sponsors will freak. God, which is worse: the Russians abandoning the thing or the Americans going in after it?"

"Hey," said Hanley, on her knees in front of her friend, "at least we didn't do a one-way installation of a thermonuclear device under your butts, say sayonara, and leave it to the mercies of the ocean. They let you amble in here and build Trudeau without the slightest warning. But Dee, honestly, we don't have time to get worked up about some Cold War cocktail shaker."

"Which Ottawa just pretends isn't there. Why suffer embarrassment when the only downside is possible Armageddon? Fuck." She hurled a shoe; it bounced off the wall. "We're always so damn sensible." Dee's tears were cascading.

"Dee, listen to me, stay with me here. You've got to calm down.

I have to be able to talk to you. What we're searching for is far more immediate and a bigger danger than that atomic trash under the ice. Ninety-five people died on that sub. Ninety-five out of ninety-five. You've got to help me find this bug's whereabouts and contain it. Trudeau has barely recovered from the deaths here. If they now learn of ninety-five more, there's going to be pandemonium. Health Canada will seal this place off. Nobody is going to take the chance of that organism's getting out into the general population. Not your government, not mine. We'll be headlines. And they won't be letting us disperse and go back to our home countries, no way. You mustn't repeat this to anyone, but this bug makes Ebola look like a picnic."

Hanley sat down heavily. "We can't focus on this junked war toy. It's been down there a few dozen years. We have to trust it'll behave itself for a few more weeks. That's all."

"Jessie?"

"Yeah."

"I'm really scared. Between the bug and now this . . ."

Hanley put her arms around Dee. "Scared is normal. Means you're in touch with reality. That's healthy: like quitting smoking."

"*You're* still smoking." She sniffled.

"I just quit again. Great timing, huh? I'm trying not to taste like an ashtray, if you know what I mean."

Dee laughed and sniffled. "Okay, we'll do it together. I'll bring you some fresh patches."

"Thanks, Dee," she said, gently rocking her friend.

"You're welcome. Jess?"

"Yes."

"Aren't you scared? This feels like the end of our world."

"Scared doesn't come close. If you're okay, I'm going next door. I need to think."

"I'm okay. I'll just sit here for a few minutes and then get back to work."

"I'll be right next door if you need me."

Hanley suited up in Tyvek, donned her respirator, and unlocked the adjacent room. She stared at the piles of gear and goods from the work site, neatly laid out in a grid of numbered squares. She was back at square one, literally, and feeling totally spent.

They had painstakingly cataloged each of the deceased's belongings and equipment. Hanley examined the objects and the corresponding graphed lists in her hand. Tarakanova's few items were allocated the least space and consisted mostly of layers of her polar suit. Hanley went methodically around and picked up every single object, contemplated it, put it back in the correct spot. It took her two hours to accomplish exactly nothing. If it was in the pongo, and they all inhaled it, then how the hell did it get on the ship and kill the rest of them? Was there a brief period before death when the person was highly contagious?

Dee came in, pushed the protective lab glasses to the top of her head and sat down on a folding chair behind Hanley. Uli followed right behind her.

Dee said, "Snowball fight at the bottom of the ramp at three P.M. The Germans against everybody else."

"*Ja.* What else is new," Uli said. He handed Hanley the report on the algae samples she'd taken from the pongo. "*Nichts,*" he said. Hanley nodded and passed it back to Dee. The sample was benign. Uli gave a wan smile and left.

Dee was exhausted. "So, wrong pongo? Or wrong suspect altogether? I wish you'd hurry up being a genius and crack this."

Hanley offered cigarettes and Dee took one. They lit up and stared at each other through the haze of cigarette smoke.

"We're quitting now, right?" Dee said, French-inhaling a gray ribbon of smoke. "Last drags?" She unbolted a small baffle in the cavity of the dome and the smoke whooshed out as if vacuumed. "I'll close up the lab."

"Good. I gotta face the music with my boss."


L.A. came online at 4:00 P.M. West Coast time. She couldn't hold off any longer. Hanley made sure the Zero encryption program was engaged before she typed.

## INCIDENT REPORT

| | |
|---|---|
| Location: | ARS Trudeau |
| Agent: | Organic |
| Toxicity: | Level 4 |
| Victims: | 100 worldwide (4 confirmed deaths, 96 more are probable) |
| Mortality | 100% |
| Portal of Entry: | Aerosol (hypothesized) |
| Vector: | Unknown |

The tally of victims would shake them. A hundred victims of a Level 4 bug would set off worldwide alarms. It didn't get any nastier than this; there was no Level 5. The bug was officially a hot virus. Munson would be required to notify an epidemic intelligence officer for North America at the CDC in Atlanta, and apprise them of the outbreak. Their Canadian counterparts would be called in immediately, albeit confidentially. All information would be restricted.

Munson answered formally at 4:46 P.M., saying he understood. He passed along the Center's pro forma cautions about dealing with so dangerous a bug. A list of mandatory procedures followed that everyone knew Hanley would never comply with. She couldn't, given the need for haste and where she was. L.A. was simply establishing a record in case it all went south.

Dee came in and fell across Hanley's bed. "Lab's almost shut down for the night." Hanley plopped on the floor, her back braced against the side of the bed. It had been a long shift. Dee picked up one boot and tried to find the other.

"Where are you going?"

"I need a reality check. I'm supposed to be taking a moonlight spin with that cute Kjell Eliasson who works for Verneau in astronomy. He says we may see a celestial event." She chuckled with derision. "If that Russian missile decides to wake itself, we will certainly witness an event."

"Unlikely," Hanley said. "It's behaved for decades. I'm sure it will last the night. Go. Get outside for a bit."

"I'm too wrung out," Dee said, giving up on finding the second boot. "And too distracted." She slumped back and kicked off the other. "I could fall asleep right here."

"Why don't you then?"

"Maybe I will." Dee slipped out of her beige overshirt. "I want sleep so badly it hurts."

"Crash. I'm going over to Jack's for the night after I lock the lab. I'll tell your Swede you're not going to make it."

Dee had already stripped and fallen asleep. Hanley was reminded of Joey as she tucked her friend in.

# 46

**W**hile Jack slept, Hanley hunched over her laptop, teleconferencing with Cybil.

*"What the hell is going on up there, girl? A hundred dead? Level 4? Where are you heading with this one?"*

"I've got a strong feeling about the pongos, Cyb. It's gotta get into their systems at exactly the same moment. What would do that except something nearly gaseous?"

*"That's certainly where we started: positing they inhaled the stuff,"* Cybil said.

"I know the algae I brought back came up negative, but these algal pits fit that scenario perfectly. It's the only real aerosol out there." She told Cybil about the Aleut on the shaman's pouch. "Cyb, those pongos really do look like ghosts when you break them. Are they really all going to inhale some dessicated guano at the same moment? I don't think so. But a pongo breaks, they're all right there, breathing it in."

*"Remember when Ebola first showed up? It didn't seem like anything we'd seen before, except for plant viruses."*

"Man, how terrified we were about what that would mean." Hanley rocked dangerously on the back legs of her chair. "If Ebola was a plant virus that had jumped not just species but kingdoms . . . You think that's what we've got here—a plant virus that's taken the giant step?"

*"Could be. I don't know,"* Cybil said. *"I'm just saying it's weird*

how similar the structure of chlorophyll is to hemoglobin. And you've got something that's gone after the hemoglobin. But does it jump directly, or is there an intermediate vector?"

"It bothers me that there's nothing in their work notes or journals to indicate they were anywhere near a pongo, except for that vague thing about will-o'-the-wisp. Wouldn't they record it if three of them—four of them, with Tarakanova—got dusted with algae particles?"

"*Not if they didn't think it was noteworthy, Jess. No. Not if they'd done it so many times before.*"

"Or maybe they didn't enter it in their data because they didn't want to catch hell from Environment Canada for injuring the delicate ecosystem."

"*That too.*" Cybil didn't sound convinced. "*But before you run out too far on this particular limb, from what you've told me about Jack Nimit's experience, the pongos really are harmless. If he's been popping them all his life, isn't that a valid statistical sample? They'd have to've stumbled onto the one pit that no one had encountered before, except the shaman.*"

"Yeah, and if the one they broke open just happened to contain something that rare and lethal, how am I ever going to find it? I've put a close watch on the sample, but the odds are slim to none that it's the same kind. What then?"

"*Are the pongos all in one spot out there at the site?*" Cybil said.

"No." Hanley examined the tiny image of Cybil in the corner of her screen. "They're all over." Hanley watched Cybil light another cigarette and lit one too. Cybil said, "*Look at this database, girl: thirty thousand species of algae. You better find out which ones are local.*"

Teddy Zale hailed Hanley on the intercom and said she had an Imersat call on the phone.

"Cybil, Joey's trying to get through."

"*Later, Mama Bear,*" Cybil said and coughed.

Zale patched the call through.

"Honey, what time is it where you are? What's going on?"

"They're going to leave me back, Mom," said Joey, tragedy welling in his voice.

"Oh, honey."

"All my friends are going on next semester. Except for math, I've gotta do reading and everything all over again. You said the laptop would fix it, but it didn't. I still wasn't good enough. I messed up the reading part on the state test."

"Darling, it's just one semester. It won't be so bad," she said, not knowing whether that was true or not. "And you'll come out confident and well grounded when you finish."

"And what if I don't?" he sobbed. "What if I flunk the test again?"

"Oh, baby. You won't."

"You don't know that! You don't know anything! You're not even here!"

"Sweetheart. Joey." The line erupted in static. "Joey?" She rang the extern station.

"He hung up," Zale said. "Should I try to get him back?"

She thought for a moment.

"Dr. Hanley?"

"No," she said, finally. "No, he needs some time to calm down." The truth was, she didn't know what to say to him. He had tried so hard and in the end it hadn't mattered. She was trying so hard too, she thought, and it didn't matter either. Trying wasn't always enough.

She slipped in beside Jack and tried to sleep. It was completely dark, she was exhausted, and yet her brain was wide awake and refusing to shut off. Giving up, Hanley slipped out of bed without waking Jack, retrieved her soft outfit and boots, and let herself out quietly.

"Thanks for meeting me on such short notice, Dr. Skudra. I'm trying to narrow down the types of algae that might be in the pongos. I need to see as many local species as you've got."

"Actually, algae are Simon King's purview, but he begged off, given the hour. As I am a night owl, it has permitted me the pleasure of being your host once again."

"I appreciate it." Hanley crossed her arms across her chest. "Simon King. Now there is someone who could use a little self-actualization. What is King's problem?"

Skudra shrugged. "Simon dislikes American culture, thinks it's morally bankrupt. Truth be told, he's not unduly fond of me or my work either." Skudra glanced sideways and said in a conspiratorial voice, "Simon saw himself as the heir apparent to Dr. Mackenzie. He became especially difficult after it became clear Emile Verneau would succeed Mac, when he moves on to direct the Arctic Preserve.

"So, let me show you our algae collection. It's quite extensive. Did you know algae have circadian rhythms built into their DNA—they can distinguish day from night? We have been investigating how the polar environment affects those rhythms."

Skudra ushered Hanley over to three sealed saltwater tanks, the glass streaked white with trails of salt. The algae in the first tank were green; in the second, red; the third, brown. The temperature was tropical in the first tank and temperate in the other two. Minuscule tapers of algae lay woven together in their brine at the bottoms, like discarded doormats.

"Our everyday algae," Skudra said. "Green." He bent to inspect the contents of the first container. "The oldest life form. They once dominated the earth. Hardly changed at all in their three and a half billion years on the planet. I'll be happy to harvest samples of all the local species we have."

"Thanks." Hanley pointed at the adjacent tank. "Looks like bloom. We call it red tide when it shows up off the coast of California and kills all the fish. Sometimes even large mammals like dolphins."

"It *is* red tide, and does precisely that. Exhausts the oxygen. Shuts it out."

"What's the exact effect of the red algae on other organisms?"

"Narcosis. Although there's an even deadlier variety that starts out as a plant and then, when it reaches critical mass, becomes an animal. Then it swarms—attacks. Of course, as a sociobiologist, that's what fascinates me: a plant crossing that indefinite line and exhibiting animal behaviors."

"Attacks?"

"Yes. It goes after tissue, after blood cells. Killed the first two scientists who studied it with microscopes. Bored in through their eyes, then into their skin, their muscles."

"Eyes?"

"Yes."

"And this deadlier variety you're describing lives in the lake, here?"

"Oh, no, no, no."

"Damn. Hates blood, goes for the eyes . . ."

"Yes, I can see why it would intrigue you. Come," he said, "I'll show you the native lake specimens."

He handed Hanley a pair of goggles and led her to a circular door at the back of the lab. He pushed the right side, and the round door pivoted open on its axis. They proceeded into an insulated corridor; the door revolved to close behind them.

Instantly, cold numbed Hanley's cheeks and pained her hands.

The room smelled brackish but not salty. The water in the cylindrical tank was lake water—fresh—although hardly clear. A thin sheet of ice covered the surface. The algae suspended beneath it were transparent—as colorless as an X-ray—almost entirely woven into a single mat of tiny, pale strands.

"Almost every creature on earth has a transparent cousin under water," said Skudra. "Crustaceans, snails, worms. Invisibility is a great defense."

"Smells like the worms you sent me," Hanley said, making a face. "Rotten eggs."

"They metabolize sulfur."

"What do they eat"—she bent from the waist and peered at the specimens—"if they have mouths?"

"Manna from heaven," Skudra said with delight. "Ion particles. The odd configuration of magnetic field lines here, near the Pole, permits subatomic particles to rain down in extraordinary numbers. This bombardment of ions and electrons produces the auroras in the sky, also the nitrates that feed the colonies of algae and fungi." Skudra bent closer to the tank.

"This specimen was taken from our lake through the hydro-hole," Skudra said. "Very different from the varieties I've shown you so far. Those others come from different depths and waters and grow in different levels of light, but most are oxygen friendly, or at least tolerant. Not this fellow. The algae here"—he pointed to the colorless mat—"these straddle the evolutionary ladder between bacteria and higher algae. They harken back to the earth when there was no oxygen. And plenty of radiation."

"The Creature from the White Lagoon," said Hanley. She was reminded of the mysterious, nearly transparent jellyfish Joey loved to visit at the aquarium in Monterey.

"'I can call spirits from the vasty deep,'" said Skudra.

"Inuit legend?"

"Shakespeare."

Hanley, fixed on the tank, said, "Shines like a five-dollar toupee. I wonder what all the radiation did to the toupee's DNA. I'm surprised it didn't grow eyeballs and fangs. What was the atmosphere like then," Hanley asked, "before oxygen?"

"Think volcanoes. Carbon dioxide; nitrogen; formaldehyde, would you believe; ammonia; hydrogen sulfide; methane; and even hydrogen cyanide, best known for its prominent use in the gas chamber. Hardly friendly, but these fellows," he held out his hand toward the algae, "they liked it. They and the early bacteria subsisted on hydrogen. Lots of it around all those volcanoes. Early life forms abhorred oxygen. The oxygen was toxic; it oxidized everything, including cells. But every critter used hydrogen, and there wasn't enough to go around. Primeval bacteria and most algae didn't like the oxygen. Some fought back. They developed ways to get rid of the oxygen, such as combining it with hydrogen to form . . . ?" Skudra waited expectantly like a high school teacher.

"Water?"

"$H_2O$. Exactly right! But the hostile algae split the water molecules into its component parts to extract the hydrogen, and it just freed up even more oxygen. The oceans became saturated with the gas, and it began to escape, to spill over into the atmosphere. More complex organisms finally developed, so these algae and their symbionts withdrew. They have clung to undersea volcanoes and the poles ever since, shunning light, still shunning oxygen. This particular variety went deep. Down into the cold. No sunlight for months was ideal, because it meant there would be no photosynthesis to produce oxygen."

"That frozen lake must be quite a cauldron, sealed for what, a few million years? Aren't there other living things in the lake beneath the hydrohole?"

Skudra shook his head. "The algae pretty much make the lake uninhabitable for oxygen-dependent life. Not surprisingly, there aren't any true oxygen zones in the lake. And no light. Very little penetrates below eighty feet or so, even with the sun out round the clock at the height of summer. This alga uses a tenth of a percent of what manages to reach that far down. It simply does not live by photosynthesis. We have replicated its natural habitat here: no light, no oxygen, secure beneath a layer of ice. We even transported it from the hydrohole that way so as not to disturb it."

Skudra contemplated the specimens serenely. He indicated the tanks. "This is what the world was like before there was a breathable atmosphere."

"Before there was a breathable atmosphere," Hanley repeated. She felt her pulse quickening. "Dr. Skudra, what would happen if these algae woke up in an oxygenated world?"

"What would happen to the algae?"

"No," she said, as much to herself as to him, "what would happen to the oxygen?" She didn't wait to hear his answer. She didn't need to.

# 47

Hanley shot off a message to Los Angeles and ran to share the news with Dee. If she was right, she needed help to work out the next steps carefully: how to secure the algae and how to test it without risking the lives of her lab techs.

Hanley found Dee where she had left her, still in bed in Hanley's quarters. She hadn't had a good night. The bedding was a mess. Hanley picked up a pillow from the floor and threw it at the lump under the blankets.

"Rise and shine, Dr. Steensma. Have I got news for you! Hey, Dee, you wanted a genius, you got one!" But Dee wouldn't budge.

"Hey, lazy bones. It's wakey-wakey time," Hanley said. "You're not going to believe what's happened. I cracked it!" She pulled back the blanket, laughing at the resistance from Dee. The laugh froze in her throat.

Dee was bent backward, nearly in half, ankles practically on her shoulders, terror—or realization—frozen on her face. And pain. Unimaginable pain. Dee lay with mouth agape, neck muscles rigid, body contorted hard by paroxysm. Eyes . . . Hanley couldn't fully engage them, what was left of them.

Hanley backed out of the room and nudged the door closed. Her back to the wall, she slid down to a sitting position, where Uli found her.

"Jessie," Uli said. "Are you okay?"

"Stop!" Hanley shouted. "Don't come any closer. I'm all right for the moment. We'll know for sure in a few hours. In the meantime, get me a walkie-talkie or something—and keep away. Keep everyone else away." She slipped off her watch and laid it flat on the floor next to her. "Four hours. No one comes near me. Close off the dome. I've been exposed."

Uli backed away. "What's happened?" he said. "Where's Dee?"

"In my quarters."

"Shouldn't we get her out before we close off the dome?"

"No. Get out of here. Go."

"But she's in danger."

"No," Hanley said, voice wavering. "She's not," and he finally understood.


No point in checking her pulse or her temperature. Both were wildly elevated, the adrenaline was doing its job. Her heart was racing, her body shaking and sweating.

Jack talked to her by walkie-talkie. He kept repeating one thought, like a chorus: she hadn't caused this.

"Jessie? You have to hold on to that."

"I'm trying."

He pitched her a fresh pack of cigarettes. "You ever been quarantined before?"

"Twice. Once in the field, in Africa, during an Ebola epidemic. Once in Atlanta when I was exposed in a lab. That was pretty damn scary."

"What happened?"

"Like being locked in a bank vault. You're isolated, underground. They minister to you in Casper suits, covered from head to toe, not even breathing the air you breathe. I saw my kid once, on a screen through a protective window."

"You and he are close, huh?"

"I miss him all the time. My ex-husband says I'm not really mom material—obsessed with my work, more comfortable with dead people than live ones. He may have a point. Sometimes I think I could be a bad influence on my kid. What if he picks up my interests?"

"That's bad?"

"My ex thinks so. He thinks they're unnatural."

"What do you think?"

"I worry that he's right. I don't want Joey to be the freaky kid I was. I was pretty weird when I was his age. My ex started worrying when I was pregnant. He thought what he called my clinical interest in the whole process wasn't normal."

"What do you mean?"

"He claimed I was treating our unborn child like a guinea pig. I wanted to examine the placenta. Make sure the umbilical blood was harvested for stem cell propagation. My ex made a major scene." Hanley paused. "I don't know. I know I love my kid."

"Do you want me to get your laptop? Or get Teddy to contact Joey on the sat phone?"

"No, it's too dangerous for anyone to come near me. Besides, I don't think I could fake it that well. I don't want to terrify him. We each prepare a videotape for our families ahead of time. You can't really . . . you wouldn't want your kid to see you symptomatic— suffering."

"You sound so matter-of-fact about it."

"Comes with the territory. We go through the same routine each time we're sent into the field. If you can't approach it as a normal part of the work, you couldn't go. It would be paralyzing." She grew quiet. "I can't get Dee's face out of my mind, Jack. She was in so much pain. She was so scared."

Jack could hear her teeth chattering. "Shh. It's going to be okay."

"I can't die this way. I refuse to give my ex the satisfaction of being right—that this isn't an appropriate job for a mom." She gasped, thinking of Joey orphaned at ten.

To distract her, he told her stories from his childhood, Inuit legends, how to build a snow bridge—anything. Sometimes she just cried, and he listened and waited. After four hours, when she was still asymptomatic, he fetched her, covered her shoulders with a blanket, and held her. Hanley was cried out, but she couldn't stop shuddering. She had never reacted to a dead body this way. Her head spun, unable to fasten on what she'd seen. Her mind kept flitting, refusing to alight on anything for more than a second. Her hands, she noticed, were still trembling. She was nearly hallucinating from the shock. She knew she had to pull herself together, get back to work.

"I think I found the ghost plant, Jack." She said it without a trace of the triumph she usually felt at such a moment, when weeks or months of frustration gave way to a solution.

"Ghost plant?"

"Oh, shit, Jack, I never told you. Please don't hate me, but I took the shaman's pouch from Little Trudeau. I had to know if there was anything there that would help me figure out how he'd died."

"Well, did it help?" His voice was cool, level. She couldn't tell what he was thinking.

"I'm sorry about doing it, Jack—it's my job. But yes, I think it did help. The Aleut in the cafeteria line translated it for me. The shaman was talking about a 'ghost plant' he'd used to make a poultice. I think I found his ghost plant."

"Where?"

"It's the clear algae from the hydrohole."

"Whatever killed them is in the hydrohole?" Nimit said.

"Yeah. Hiding inside the transparent algae."

"But we brought up a whole tankful of it from the lake. No one got sick or anything."

"That's because you were keeping it happy—away from light, away from oxygen. No need to attack. Dormant."

"So it wasn't in a pongo?"

"No. The clear algae would never survive so close to the surface, to sunlight and oxygen."

Nimit was quiet for a minute. "Then they'd have to have come into contact with it at the hydrohole or in the lab. Dee hasn't been near the hydrohole in months. Could she have been exposed in the specimen dome?"

"No. She had to have been exposed after I left her last night."

"How?"

"I've been thinking about what Koyt said when he first got here—do you remember? Something about the closer I got to it, the closer it was getting to me? This was deliberate. Dee's death was premeditated. Dee didn't get close to this. Someone brought this close to Dee."

"God, no."

"What I need to figure out, and fast, is how. I've got to go back to the lab, Jack. I'll need help getting . . . getting Dee . . . onto a gurney. I'll show you how to suit up."

"Of course. I'm not leaving you alone."

As they donned the full hazmat gear, Hanley tried to keep her thoughts on what she was doing that instant, but they kept skipping away from her, taunting her with flashing slivers she'd recall involuntarily. When she came face to face with Dee's body, her mind seemed to stop, and she had to stand for several minutes and still her brain so she could see what lay before her. Hanley had never felt this in the presence of a corpse: desolation. No scientific excitement or majestic sense of absence, just devastating loss. Nothing relieved it. It just was.

By the time they had lifted Dee's body onto the gurney, Hanley realized she was fully attentive and engaged. Her mind flooded with questions even as she finished the painstaking procedure of securing the quarantine bag around the body of her broken friend.

Together they rolled the gurney with Dee to the makeshift morgue, and afterward stripped out of the hazmat suits. Jack walked her to Mackenzie's office. Verneau, Rudenko, and Nemerov were sitting quietly with Mackenzie, brought together more for the solace of one another's presence than to actually do anything. What could they do?

"Why her?" Hanley said, falling onto the couch, clutching her back where it was in spasm from the tension and odd angle it had been in while she'd sat on the floor in the corridor. They all looked at her with concern and, except for the imperturbable Koyt, who hovered in the doorway, they were grim.

Nimit sat down beside her. He tried to knead the tender muscles in her shoulders. It was an intimate gesture, but she was beyond caring what anyone thought or knew.

Verneau attempted to comfort her. "You can't blame yourself. We all know how cautious you've been. This isn't your fault."

Hanley shook her head. "It never would have happened if I hadn't . . ."

Rudenko started to say something to reassure Hanley but couldn't seem to find the words.

"Dr. Hanley is right," said Koyt from the doorway.

Verneau turned on him. "What a cruel thing to say. Do not listen to him, Jessie."

Koyt remained aloof, unmoved by the others' expressions of grief and bewilderment. "This was not accidental," he said.

Hanley looked up at him, startled. "No, I don't think it was. But how could anyone do that to her?"

"Anyone didn't," Koyt said. "This is a dangerous environment. Perhaps you will now take extra precautions?" he said. "As I offered you before?"

"Do you mind?" Mackenzie nearly shouted.

"Precaution would be advisable," Koyt persisted.

"Who would want to kill Dee Steensma?" Verneau said.

"No one," Koyt said.

"Now you're not making sense," said Verneau. "You say no one wanted to kill her, and yet you're flashing your pistol around, offering protection?"

"No," Hanley rasped, pressed against Nimit. "He means she wasn't the intended victim. I was."

# 48

"My God," Mackenzie said after Hanley had reviewed her conclusions concerning the deaths at Trudeau. "We must make arrangements for your safety."

"No," said Jack, loudly. Everyone turned toward him. "I'll take care of it. Nothing is going to happen to Dr. Hanley. I guarantee it."

"Of course," Mackenzie said shakily. "Nothing will happen to Dr. Hanley. We can't let it."

"Thank you, Jack," she said. "Could you walk me back to the lab?"

They slowly made their way across the complex. Hanley stopped outside the walkway to the laboratory and took a deep breath, steeling herself to go in.

"You okay?" Jack said.

"Not really. You don't seem okay either. Where will you be later?"

"I've got something I need to do. I'll come find you as soon as I'm done." He held her close, kissed her eyelids gently. "I'm so sorry, Jessie. Sorrier than you can know. But nothing will happen to you. I promise."

Hanley reported her suspicions to Los Angeles: the origin of the bug was biological, and almost certainly identified; the method of transmission was man-made, and still unknown.

Munson didn't take the news well. He kept shouting over Ishi on the hookup back to California, so she and Ishikawa had trouble hearing one another. "This was not part of the deal," Munson kept saying adamantly. The more impotent he felt, she knew, the louder he got, and he was in full cry. Utterly annoyed, she typed a message Munson wouldn't see, as he was too busy gesticulating.

> *Ishi, this isn't helping at all. I'm logging off until he cools down or leaves.*

Hanley paced in the lab. She spread a sleeping bag on the floor next to her place at the lab bench and curled up in it. How could she be so tired?

A few hours later she came awake, feeling rested and refreshed for a moment. Then she remembered, and the stone moved back onto her heart. The lab was quiet but she wasn't alone.

"Good afternoon, Dr. Hanley," Nemerov said.

"What are you doing here?" she mumbled.

"I am of your new bodyguard." He squatted down next to her, holding the gun in its shoulder holster out of the way.

"Who installed the guard?" she said.

"Your boss man."

"Dr. Mackenzie?"

"Jack Nimit. He asks us to move into empty quarters across from yours, and we must take turns protecting you."

She rubbed her face. "Probably a good idea."

"Any orders?"

She just shivered.

"There, there," he said, stroking her hair as though she were one of his young daughters.


Uli and Kiyomi reported for work. They had taken extra precautions, wearing double gloves, respirators, and Tyvek suits, but she was so moved that they had come back to work at all that she started to cry again. By unspoken agreement, they would pay tribute to Dee by finding the bug that had taken her life.

She briefed them on what she'd figured out in Dr. Skudra's lab.

"Guys, I think the culprit's been right here at Trudeau all along. The transparent freshwater algae from the hydrohole. I think it's the shaman's ghost plant."

"So why does it attack what it attacks?" Uli asked.

"Because it can't tolerate oxygen. Yet it finds itself in an oxygenated world—blood, lungs—that it's got to shut out if it wants to survive."

"*Ja,*" Uli agreed. "So it attacks the oxygen that it cannot abide in the lungs and blood cells."

"Maybe fibers in lung are bug making protection?" Kiyomi wondered.

"Yes! Why didn't I look at the algae sooner?" Hanley's voice rose, the excitement of piecing together the puzzle temporarily getting the better of her anguish over Dee. "The kainic acid. Cybil told me it was close to domoic acid, which causes shellfish poisoning. When we eliminated the whelks the scientists had eaten, I started to look for vectors *up* the food chain—at birds and mammals and the like. I wasn't thinking about where the shellfish get the toxin *from*: the algae."

"Or where *they* get it from," said Uli.

"Right," said Hanley. "The algae could be a reservoir for a symbiotic virus that decomposes sulfate from the water . . . and releases hydrogen sulfide."

"Like our specimens in the lake," said Kiyomi.

"Poison for most organisms," Uli said.

Hanley raised a finger. "But not for our nasty bug. The microbes in the algae make the bottom of the lake uninhabitable for most other forms of life, except the algae. Cybil said something about that: whatever in the algae chokes off photosynthesis, whatever in it hates chlorophyll, also hates hemoglobin. It wants to be in a world without oxygen. Damn. That's another confirmation: the hydrogen sulfide in the lung field."

"You are convinced?" Uli asked.

"Yes. We still don't know why whatever is in the algae attacks specific proteins. But so far, out of ten, the algae's at least a seven or an eight, and in my business, that's all you need. But now we have a much harder task," she said to the earnest faces around the table. "We have to figure out how the algae got into the three scientists at the field camp, and Dr. Kruger, and Dee. If it was just the three out on the ice, I'd say okay, somehow they bumped into this algae out at the polynya, and chalk it up to a terrible accident, a chance exposure in the wild. But Dee had to have been infected last night. If Dee's death was deliberate, what about the others?"

"But why?" Uli's open face registered genuine bafflement.

"I have no idea. But I know we need to find the *how* if we want to prevent it from happening again. Kiyomi, I want you in full hazmat suit with air supply. Go to Dee's room and catalogue everything in it. Everything gets a separate container and log number. Uli, I want you to put together a complete list of the effects of the bug on the body so we can begin to analyze its mechanism and compare it to everything we can find about the clear algae."

Subdued, Kiyomi went off to inventory Dee's belongings. Hanley took a deep breath. How had the algae gotten to the scientists on the ice? Or to Dr. Kruger? What had happened at Kossuth's autopsy? She and Dee had had their own air supplies, so Kruger must have inhaled the algae. But how? What was present at Kossuth's autopsies and not in the others?

Hanley put the DVD of the Bascomb and Ogata autopsies in her laptop, the Kossuth DVD in the computer at Dee's workstation, and ran them side by side. Looking back and forth between the screens, she compared the array of bone cutters, scalpels, scissors, hammers, handsaws, and probes of various lengths and sizes—instruments tempered to be harder than the bones and joints they would expose. For all intents and purposes, the equipment was the same in both procedures. Where was the broken pattern?

Hanley watched the screens intently. On the left, Ingrid Kruger opened the membrane enclosing the heart and other vital organs. She sliced a section from each lung and weighed the specimens. The normally spongy tissue was stiff. The bubbly sacs where the body traded oxygen for carbon dioxide thousands of times a day had been destroyed, leaving the victim only minutes of consciousness. Kruger probed further, separating skin from tissue, and commented on her findings.

*"The turbinate bones in the nasal passage did nothing to prevent intrusion; likewise the cilia in the bronchial tubes. The passages, ducts, and alveoli are actually brittle. The mucous glands and respiratory muscles seem atrophied."*

She removed the lungs and weighed them individually. They were each close to one kilogram—three times normal. As Ingrid Kruger's must be now. And Dee's.

Hanley looked away. On the other monitor, Dr. Kruger was preparing to peel back a section of Alex Kossuth's black skin. Hanley froze the frame, wondering whether she just wasn't seeing what she was looking for, or whether it was somewhere outside the frame.

Hanley started the first autopsy DVD from the beginning. On screen the hands of Dr. Kruger once again reached into the chest cavity of Annie Bascomb. Her eyes drifted to the other screen, then froze. Hurriedly, she hit pause on both computers. On the laptop's screen, Ingrid Kruger's hands held a slice of her lover's flesh, and Hanley's heart raced. She looked back and forth between the two images.

"Violet," she said. "Violet." There it was: the broken pattern. Not what was different from one autopsy to another—what was different about Kruger.

## 49

"Uli!"

He spun on his stool at his workbench. "*Ja,* what is wrong?"

"Come."

She led him to the area next door housing the meticulously cataloged items brought back from the doomed expedition.

"What is the matter?" Uli said.

"I think we've got it—the portal of entry." Unlocking the door, they went in. She was flushed with excitement.

"*Ja?*" He was incredulous and becoming excited too. "You are certain."

"Think of the things we all have in common. Head, hands—"

"*Ja.* But all those differ."

"What *doesn't* differ in three people? What's the same, person to person?"

Uli screwed up his face. "I don't know. Blood? No, no. Too many types."

"Exactly, it varies."

"Lungs?"

She shook her head. "Lungs vary with age, smoking—"

"Temperature!" he exclaimed. "*Ja,* temperature."

Hanley's eyes smiled. "*Yes!* What else?"

Uli rubbed his cheeks. "I am with you incompletely."

"If we were terrorists, manufacturing a biological weapon in a frozen desert, what would we be doing?"

"Cooking up batches of the bad stuff and freeze-drying it. Easy here, in the Arctic. Then we reduce the microbial matter to granules. Maybe we coat the particles for smoother sailing so as to make them easily drift. Then we spray it in the air over our targets so they breathe it in."

"Right," she said, softly, her brain racing. "And if I had that here—the bug iced and hibernating, and reduced to particles—but I had no means of getting it into anybody's lungs, how do I introduce the microbe into four people out on an ice floe?"

Uli screwed up his face. "Sorry. *Nichts.*"

"Think about the timing again. We've said it ourselves. The three died too close together for anything ingested to have done it. It had to be inhaled. Yet there's no sign of an aerosol, other than the pongos, which they'd broken open dozens of times. And this bug wouldn't live in a pongo."

"I cannot imagine what may be left," he said.

"Why did Dr. Kruger wear violet gloves?"

"I suppose she was allergic to the latex, so she used polyvinyl gloves."

"Right."

"You're not suggesting allergic reaction killed them."

"No."

"So . . . I am still not with you. What is it then that we all have? Hands, fingers?"

"Skin."

"Skin," Uli repeated, pondering.

"Yes, Uli. The largest single organ in the human body."

"Skin would absorb at a uniform rate, and body temperature in everyone would be practically identical to activate it. *Ja.*"

"Yeah, it's in some dormant form, dry, then comes in contact with tiny amounts of moisture and warmth. It comes to life, is absorbed through the skin, bypassing all the usual alarms and countermeasures in the gut. It quickly deceives cells into accepting it, then explodes with growth, replicating, breeding like a reactor in heat. At some biochemical signal the virus, or whatever the agent is in the algae, is expressed simultaneously by the cells, and all at once it attacks like nothing we've ever seen."

"*Ja,*" he said, "I see, but they were in polar suits. How could it get to their skin?"

"You tell me."

Uli stared off. "You must do it when they are outside their polar suits. When they are out of the suits," Uli said, thinking aloud. "Naked."

"Exactly."

They turned to the array of objects spread across the floor, each in its proper location, neatly numbered, tagged, prioritized for testing.

Hanley clasped her hands atop her head as she walked carefully through the assembled articles, scanning them.

"It's here, I know it's here," she muttered as she walked slowly down an aisle, feeling the adrenaline suffuse her system, her heart banging in her chest.

Uli trailed behind.

"What goes inside all surgical gloves?" she said. "What do we all do before we get in the suits?"

Hanley stopped and stood stock-still, eyeing the mounds of belongings and equipment, tagged and cataloged in their chalked squares.

"*Ja.* We put on talcum."

# 50

Hanley and Uli checked through the log, but could only find one can of talcum. Not the station's generic powder, bought in quantity in anonymous white cans, but a commercially produced powder. One.

The broken pattern.

Based on where it had been found, Dee had logged it in as Annie Bascomb's. The can was the three hundred twenty-ninth inventoried item awaiting examination. They would have arrived at it eventually, perhaps disastrously if someone had mishandled it. Hanley walked carefully between the items on the floor until they found the square it had been assigned. SAFE ENOUGH FOR BABY, it read on the can.

Wearing respirators with independent air supplies, full hazmat suits and gloves, she and Uli commandeered the lab crew's beverage cooler, the closest container at hand. She rifled through the drawers hunting for tongs, tossing the contents impatiently on the floor as she went. Uli quietly improvised a pair out of two of her hangers and handed it to her. Finally, painstakingly, she pincered the can and placed it inside the Styrofoam, then Uli duct-taped the lid shut.

Hanley sighed, sweat beading on her chin under the respirator. "Man, what's the temperature in here?"

"I do not know this," Uli said. "Not ninety-eight point six. Maybe sixty Fahrenheit."

"We don't really know at what temp the bug gets excited," Hanley said. "Let's lock it up somewhere really cold."

"*Ja, ja.*" Uli nodded and took charge of the box, sealing it with a large biohazard sticker.

"For the next few steps, we must be really careful. We don't want to cause more panic," she said.

"What do you mean?" Uli blinked.

Hanley paced and spoke. Her thoughts and intuitions were coming in a rush.

"I think the odds are that somebody removed the algae from the lake, or maybe even the tank right here, easily freeze-dried it just by taking it outside, sending the bug into dormancy, then crumpled the mat to a powder and spiked the talcum. So horribly simple. The stuff is incredibly lethal." She clutched her forehead. "Then the powder takes out Tarakanova and the whole sub with her."

"Something else happened in the undersea boat, no? To kill so many?"

Hanley surveyed the inventoried items. "Wait. Tarakanova left her polar suit at the camp. The outer layers, they're here. I saw them on the inventory list."

"What are you saying?" Uli was puzzled.

"She left her polar suit and helmet at the work site before she sailed away. After all, the suits are expensive. They're Trudeau's property. Her suit was brought back and tagged with the rest of her things, but not all of it. Not the innermost layer. She wore the body-stocking layer onto the sub."

"She uses the powder too," Uli said, "along with the others."

"Yes, but she must have taken off the body stocking on the boat. Maybe before her temperature and perspiration had a chance to activate the microbe and make her body absorb it."

"Yes!"

Hanley was fully alert. "Captain Nemerov says the amount of oxygen is greater in a submersible than on the surface. I think the Russian's suspicion might be right. The artificially enriched atmosphere was like an accelerant. She—somebody—got the powder on themselves or put the spores into the confined air."

"And the oxygen regenerating system spread the virus particles uniformly," Uli said, "right through their air recirculation system and throughout the boat. What do you think?"

"Yes, I think so. In the even more oxygenated world in a submarine, it goes ballistic—no pun intended." Hanley touched Uli's elbow. "Yeah. I'll buy it."

He beamed. "Okay. Me too."

"Uli, we have to very quietly quarantine the aquarium that the lake algae is in. Even if we destroy the talcum, if someone is determined to repeat the experiment . . ."

"They would just need to visit the specimen dome."

"Right. We'll have to make an airtight seal eventually, maybe with paraffin. I can't think that far ahead right now. For the moment we'll just make sure it's taped shut and secured. Tyvek suits, gloves, and respirators again."

"Good."

"We talk to Verneau and Mackenzie first thing in the morning. They'll have to keep the hydrohole under guard as well. I'll get Jack to help me seal that opening. Meanwhile, we say nothing to anyone."

"Will do."

"Okay. Let's cage it."


Hanley called to Nemerov, who was standing guard outside the lab, and explained that she would need him and the admiral to stand watch over the lake algae until she could think of some more permanent solution.

"But what about you?" Nemerov asked. "Should I leave weapon with Uli to protect you?"

She nearly laughed. Men. If someone was determined to get to her, no gun was going to help. They'd have to act as tasters and babysitters and test everything coming into contact with her skin— from clothes to soap to perfume—to keep the killing agent from its work. At least she didn't have any makeup to worry about. She smiled, remembering Dee trying to bum a lipstick.

The smile faded as she realized that if she had been the intended target, then whatever had killed Dee must have been something they shared. Could they have spiked her cigarettes? No, not the cigarettes . . . She reached for her neck and tore at the rectangular patch sticking to her skin. Her logical brain told her it couldn't possibly be contaminated, but she couldn't get if off fast enough.

"Sonovabitch!" she screamed.

"What's wrong?" Uli said, concerned.

"I know how Dee was killed."

"How? She has no need of talcum inside Trudeau."

"The nicotine patch. It's an incredibly effective drug-delivery system. I'm sure it's contaminated. I bet they all are in my medicine cabinet. Dee must have used one of mine."

Kiyomi came in from dinner. Hanley asked her to bag the nicotine patches in her quarters, using full protective gear. "Uli will help. I don't want either of you doing it alone."

Kiyomi bowed and retreated.

A few minutes later, Uli appeared and stood in the archway leading in from the tunnel. He didn't say anything, just stood. Hanley finally took notice and walked up to him.

"What's wrong?"

"Jack. He's in the yard area—where we sun ourselves in the summer. You know, where he gives his Arctic crash course, just off the extern driveway."

"Is he all right?"

"I think so. You need to see."

He led her out of the lab, to a niche off one of the corridors that passed the yard. From there they could see Jack Nimit, wearing his native furs. The thick fur hood covered his head and a balaclava was pulled up over his nose to protect against the punishing cold. He had piled up rocks, almost boulders, in two columns and joined them together with a slab, bridging the two. Now he was starting a pile of smaller rocks atop the connecting span. Nimit's cheeks were mask white with frost, as were his eyebrows.

"How long has he been out there?" Hanley said. "What's he doing?"

"Building an *inuksuk*."

"What's that?"

Nimit struggled to lift a large stone atop the slab. The stone figure began to take on human shape. "I think it's a kind of memorial."

"For Dee."

"I'd say so." Nimit lifted another large rock in place. A cloud of steam enveloped him.

"He must be exhausted," Hanley said.

"He's expending himself," Uli said.

Hanley asked to borrow his down jacket. Uli helped her into it and deployed the hood hidden in the collar. He pulled his insulated gloves out of the pockets and insisted she put them on.

"You've only got about five minutes dressed so," he said.

She nodded and ran outside. The cold struck instantly. Instinctively, she lowered her head. No wind, thank God. When she reached him, he was putting a last, square stone atop the figure. He wrestled it into place and half collapsed against the sculpture, lungs heaving. Hanley put her face close to his.

"Honey, you need to come inside."

He nodded, unable to speak.

"Now," she said, and took his arm, steadying him as they made their way back to the door and the extern courtyard, and then into the station proper.

She walked him back to the niche where Uli stood, staring at the stone. Jack's hands were bruised from working the large rocks into place, and his face had a gray splotch.

"Frostbite," Uli said, touching the skin on his cheek.

In the faint light from the station, the *inuksuk* took on a life of its own. It had a crude magnificence. Which, Hanley supposed, was the idea. This was a monument to Dee's spirit, so others would remember and honor her as he just had.

She leaned against him, feeling his exhaustion. "It's beautiful, Jack. It's beautiful."

"I feel so bad, Jess."

"We all do, baby," she said and drew him close.

# 51

Nimit loaded an insulated water tank into the wanigan. Hanley helped him hoist the heavy canister into the high cab. Then they donned their polar suits in the locker area. Hanley struggled getting into the skintight layer because she couldn't bring herself to use any talcum.

Zale radioed from the extern tower: *"Uli has sealed the tank of algae. Admiral Rudenko will guard it until you're back."*

"Great," said Hanley. "Look, it's imperative no one follows us or interferes with what we're about to do. Captain, you and Teddy mustn't allow anyone to log out for the hydrohole."

*"Understood,"* said Zale.

At 5:31 they were under way, waving to the extern tower, then easing down the ramp.

The sky was beautiful and moonless, but bright with stars by the million.

"You think the same algae killed the shaman."

"Yes, I think so. The shaman wouldn't have known how to concentrate it," Hanley said. "He probably made a poultice by laying it on his patient wet. It wouldn't have been as potent that way. Nothing like the concentrated form, which spreads like wildfire. As long as you didn't touch it, you were probably safe. Handling it eventually killed the shaman, but apparently not as fast."

"So once we seal the hydrohole it's over?"

"Not quite. I understand how they died. Someone will have to untangle the why."

Nimit handed her a thermos of coffee. Hanley looked back. The station was entirely lit up. Everyone was awake: word was getting around.

The wanigan droned up the incline to the top, where the ridge leveled off. Nimit's construction revealed itself to be a very large hill of ice sitting on the plane, flattened on top and capped with a prefabricated dome like those at Trudeau but not at all insulated, not even closed. A violently yellow staircase led six feet up to a platform that wrapped the shelter like a porch. Nimit parked and helped her down onto the frozen surface and unloaded the insulated canister. They hauled it up the stairs, onto the ice platform, and into the dome shelter, where he engaged the lights. It took a moment for the batteries to work and the lights to come on.

Bright yellow scaffolding surrounded them, anchored to the exposed ribs. A dozen beach chairs were scattered about. Lines hung down from a large winch over the middle. In the center of the floor was a metal grating about six feet across and, below it, a metal hatch the size of a manhole covering the opening bored into the hummock of ice. Nimit collapsed into one of the beach chairs, toes pointed up clownishly. Hanley eased down on all fours beside him, breathing hard. She scanned the interior.

"Rest a minute," Nimit said. "I'll cart the tank over to the hatch. Then we can spray it shut. It'll freeze over instantly. We've got to be careful not to get any on us or we'll freeze over too. Don't think of it as water. Think fast-setting concrete."

"Right," Hanley said, crawling into the beach chair as Nimit surrendered it.

Nimit stood poised over the hatch. He attached a hose to the nozzle of the tank. "Stand away," he said, and sprayed the metal gate at an angle, holding the plastic hose close to the hatch so the water wouldn't freeze as quickly as it would if he stood farther back. It also wouldn't splash as much as it rushed out under pressure. Even so, some water escaped and instantly turned to mist, producing a thick fog inside the dome. The fog momentarily impeded the lights; their white and orange suits went black and their visors looked like opaque shells. Then the fog turned to frost and fell like tiny snowflakes, clearing the air.

"Okay," Nimit said, holding the hose. "We'll let it set for a few minutes and see if it needs a second layer."

The drips had frozen back up to the hose, forming an icicle. He broke it off, removed the rigid nozzle, which was stiff as a baton, and banged it against a railing. Ice spilled out. When it was flexible again, he reattached it and checked the hatch. "No second coat necessary," he said, examining his work. "We're done."


Uli secured the top of the algae tank in the dark room and taped it shut, then carefully dated and initialed the tape in four strategic places. He handed Admiral Rudenko quarantine tape to string across the doorway and slapped biohazard signs on the door itself. Uli lowered the temperature in the room for good measure, left the admiral his down vest and went off to check with Kiyomi.

Shortly afterward, the door opened and, ducking under the tape, Koyt slipped in, barely a shadow in the purplish light.

"Greetings, my admiral."

"Mr. Koyt," Rudenko said warily.

"She has isolated the vector."

"Yes," Rudenko said. Why bother dissembling, he thought. It was obvious.

"Good. I should take charge of it now."

"Excuse me?" Rudenko stood in his way, between Koyt and the sealed tank. Biohazard warnings stuck to it like road signs. "Dr. Hanley doesn't want the specimens tampered with. There's far too much danger to us all if you disturb them. You've seen the consequences firsthand."

"I have the authority to confiscate all of this material."

"All of it?" Rudenko retorted. "You must be joking. How do you plan to move that tank?"

"All I need is a cutting. I can easily carry what I need back to the boat."

"This monster has already killed the entire crew of one submarine. I can't allow it to endanger another."

Koyt stepped nearer, eyeing the admiral closely. "Chernavin thought your loyalties might be a problem."

"Did he?"

"Yes. But I assured him they wouldn't."

"How not?"

"They would be addressed. You are just taking up space in the new Russia, old man."

Koyt's stubby silenced pistol sounded like a pencil snapping in half. Rudenko flew backward from the velocity and down, crashing into the leg of one of the tank's supports, blood gushing, running into the cast on his foot, pooling on the floor.

Koyt donned the heavy maintenance gloves Uli had draped on a nearby faucet and grabbed up a scoop. A knife dangled from his wrist by a short cord. He yo-yoed it into his hand expertly and released the spring-loaded blade, which shot straight out of the handle. Walking around the tank, he slit the seals one by one, slicing open the panel like an envelope. That done, he retracted the blade and let the knife dangle again. He opened the biocontainment receptacle he'd brought from Moscow, took up the scoop, broke the sheet of ice across the top of the tank and eased it carefully into the saltwater and down to the pale algal mat at the bottom. A chunk floated off in the disturbed water, which he netted with the scoop. He captured more of the algae from the sunken colony, then brought it gently to the surface and ladled it into the container.

Fingers trembling, Rudenko pinched off the artery in his arm, slippery with blood, sticky and slick. His fingers shook but he managed it. Now if only he didn't pass out.

Koyt released the scoop into the water, and screwed the lid tight on the specimen bottle. He stepped over the admiral's grunting form, bleeding on the floor, and turned, squatting down beside him.

"I won't forget this," Rudenko hissed, teeth gritted.

"I should think not," Koyt said. "And in case your aging memory fails you, a reminder." The gun snapped again.

Rudenko writhed and cried out. The brutal hole, punched into his knee, radiated a nauseating rush of excruciating new pain. Bloody sinew and bone stuck out from the dark wound. He moaned in short gasps, like heartbeats, desperately holding the artery in his arm closed.

"That's good," Koyt said. "Keep it pinched shut as best you can. You wouldn't want to empty out." Koyt rose. "*Das vedanya*, Admiral," he said, and eased out the door, closing it behind him.

Rudenko's vision glazed. He was glassy eyed, growing faint as his blood pressure plunged, marring his vision. A falling sensation passed through him like a wave, lifting him, dropping him. He was in free fall.

Suddenly his vision tunneled, the light at the other end receding. Nemerov's voice was speaking but he couldn't make out what. The light at the end turned green as the sea, and finally black.

# 52

Hanley helped carry the canister back down to the wanigan. As they paused to catch their breath before hoisting it up into the high cab, they both stopped and glanced at Trudeau.

"What the hell?" said Nimit. "Everyone in the station is awake."

"They know we've found it," Hanley said.

"Yeah. Seems that way."

In addition to all the blazing windows, a single headlamp was moving away from the station.

Nimit clicked on the long-range radio in his helmet. "Extern. Niner at the hydrohole. Who's running full out on the ice?"

No response. Nimit repeated the call. Still no answer. He looked at Hanley, puzzled, and climbed up into the cab. He raked a knob on the radio, changing frequencies. "Teddy," he said into the mike.

"Sorry, Jack," Teddy Zale answered, breathing heavily.

"You okay, Teddy?"

"Just bruised. Jack, Koyt disabled the primary radio. He's shot Admiral Rudenko."

"What happened?"

"Damned if I know. Except Uli says to tell you Koyt's got it."

"How is Rudenko?" Nimit said.

"Bad."

"Shit."

"Koyt took a polecat," Zale said. "I can see his lights, and his GPS is on. He's heading toward the polynya."

Hanley was wrestling the water canister up into the cabin of the wanigan.

"You heard?" Nimit said.

"Yes," she panted. "Poor Rudenko. Where the hell is Koyt going with the algae?"

"To the sub, I think. He knows how to use the positioning system to find the polynya. The sub left an antenna trailing. He'll summon his comrades by radio and order them to sail him out of here."

"Can the captain tell the sub not to pick him up, to stay put?"

"I don't know. Come on." Nimit helped her with the canister and started the wanigan. "Hurry."

Hanley climbed in.

"Put on your harness."

The wanigan lurched forward and sped to the lip of the plateau and caromed over the ridge, slaloming down the incline on its giant tires.

"Can we catch him?"

"Hang on."

They bounced onto the sea ice at the bottom; Hanley ducked as equipment and provisions flew out of the cupboards. The engine whined. The blip of light ahead grew slightly larger.

Nimit said, "We're gaining."

Hanley braced herself. The engine's pitch increased. The wanigan was bigger and faster, and it closed the distance. Hanley glanced back. Dots of other vehicles' headlights were following. In front of them, Koyt's polecat veered left.

"What's he doing?" she said.

"He must have come up on an obstacle—a pressure ridge—and he's running alongside it, trying to find a way through."

Nimit aimed at a spot in front of Koyt's cat to intercept him, and kept the joystick pulled all the way back for maximum acceleration.

"If he finds a way through, we're in trouble."

"Why?"

"We may be too wide to fit if he locates a narrow opening."

"No way," she said. "We have to catch him. If he gets out with that specimen—"

The wanigan drew closer. The polecat reversed, running the other way, then turned completely again.

Koyt was desperate to find an opening, but the wall was unbreached: a jagged escarpment of ice, ten, eight, fifteen feet high. Nimit slowed as they approached. Koyt steered away from the ridge and toward them. Nimit bore down, headlights growing brighter as the beams combined.

Koyt aimed his vehicle straight at them. It rushed forward, whining like an electric saw. Nimit turned the yoke at the last moment and the wanigan's huge tires ran over the polecat's left front. It crunched. Nimit spun the wanigan around and chased after the crippled cat. He knew just where it was vulnerable and how to damage it. He ran over the cat's back and rammed it again.

Koyt was only able to turn a small circle now, his steering compromised. Nimit bashed into it methodically until it couldn't move at all and rammed it against the wall of the pressure ridge. The wanigan wedged the polecat into the ice.

Koyt bounded out of the cockpit and ran at them, gun out. He was clearly practiced with it. The trigger housing, Hanley noticed, was exaggerated in size to accommodate gloved fingers.

He leaped onto the side of the wanigan and scrambled up to the door. Nimit kicked it open, knocking Koyt off, then hurled the water canister after him, just missing as the Russian rolled aside and leaped to his feet.

"Out," he ordered, pointing the maw of his machine pistol at them. Nimit raised a hand and climbed down, using the other to grip the handholds. Hanley glanced toward Trudeau. The others were far back.

"You also," Koyt screamed at her, and she climbed out too, and down the side of the vehicle, hand over hand, to the ice field below.

"Jack Nimit," Koyt said. "Dr. Hanley. I need you both to cooperate. If you do, we can part amicably. If not—" He leveled the gun at them. "I need your vehicle. Step aside."

"Get bent," Nimit said.

The biocontainment canister was secured to Koyt's waist. He raised it for emphasis. "This must be kept from injuring others. There is really no room for debate on this point."

"I see," said Hanley. "You'll take it back to your superiors and trade it for quick promotion. Or maybe freelance it to the highest bidder, once you've demonstrated its value."

"You misjudge me, Doctor," Koyt said. "I am a servant of the Russian people. That is all."

"And so diligent," said Hanley.

"We all have our roles, Doctor. I am not a good person, but I am a good hunter, don't you think?"

"And what was I?" said Hanley. "The hound you used to flush out the fox?"

"I would never compare you to a dog, Dr. Hanley. No, you were the lure," he said. "Bait."

"We won't help you," Nimit said.

Koyt turned to Hanley. "Complete foolishness." He stepped to the side to go around them. Nimit moved with him, blocking the way.

"Koyt," she said, "do you really have any idea what this bug does to people?"

"The total effect is devastating, I believe," he said.

"You neglected to mention that it killed a shipful of those fellow citizens you're so concerned about."

"A pity, yes. But compelling evidence of the effectiveness of the microbe," he said pleasantly.

Jack said, "What the hell makes you think we'd risk that happening to anyone else?" and took a step toward him. The muzzle came up slightly and Hanley cried out involuntarily. She doubted Koyt was a bad shot.

Koyt looked past them at the slowly approaching headlights and cocked the pistol. "I'm running out of time. You are young, Mr. Nimit. Death would be regrettable. And completely avoidable. Ridiculous."

Hanley said, "You make it sound like we're going to shoot ourselves."

Koyt eyed the American. "It is tantamount to suicide, not cooperating."

"Maybe you have license to brutalize other Russians," said Hanley. "But shooting an American and a Canadian, that wouldn't be without consequences."

"My God," Koyt said with disbelief. "You two are mad."

Nimit lunged for him. A shot popped. Nimit's arm blossomed crimson, and he fell to the side.

Hanley bent down and grabbed the canister nozzle, and sprayed Koyt with the pressurized hot water. The gun retorted; water steamed. Drenched, the pistol stopped firing, its mechanism frozen.

Koyt held a hand up against the spray. Hanley doused him from head to foot until the liquid stopped. The lip of the hose had frozen shut. Realizing it was only water, Koyt assumed an exasperated tone and began to lecture her in a chiding voice. As he started to sense the effects, his tone changed, rising an octave.

"*Bozhe moi!* What the hell?" The light in his helmet shone red.

Hanley couldn't believe how fast Koyt's suit was freezing solid. His chest was a deformed rock; his legs had stopped moving. The biocontainment canister dropped from him and rolled away. Koyt stood rooted, a glistening, man-sized matrioshka doll, beseeching: "Help me, damn it. Help me!"

"Jack!" Hanley yelled.

Nimit came around behind Koyt, brandishing his ice ax. He'd stanched the bleeding with snow that froze the wound closed the instant it touched his arm. Nimit pushed a button and the blades of his ice ax deployed with a *ching*. He toppled Koyt over like a statue and raised the ax one-handed. Koyt was screaming hysterically, but the ice muffled his pleas.

His face contorted with effort, Nimit struck with all his might, driving the point deep. Hanley screamed. Koyt cried out in pain. The ax came out streaked with blood.

"Jack!" she yelled.

"Idiot," Nimit cursed, and leaned down on Koyt's chest with the blade. "Don't move."

Jack stood up again and hammered with a vengeance until the

blade caught on the fifth blow. He braced his foot on Koyt and twisted away a chunk. He punctured the hardened garment again and again, and bent back the front like a lid. It peeled away, rigid, exposing flesh. Hanley retrieved a fiberglass-handled hammer from the wanigan but the handle disintegrated in the cold after a few blows. Desperate, she tore at wedges of ice with her hands as Nimit broke the slab into scales.

Koyt was finally upright, shaking uncontrollably and changing color, his body smoking in the cold. His mucous was frozen, his voice tracheal and hoarse, the silvery under-layer marred and ripped. Hanley worked feverishly to pull away the shattered outer suit.

"Get the emergency blanket from the wanigan," Nimit ordered and Hanley rushed to obey. By the time she returned, Koyt was standing in nothing but the body stocking and *gilet,* two cuffs of ice around his ankles like shackles. Nimit wrapped him in the metallic blanket.

Nimit said, "This won't be very comfortable. Get over it. Your core temperature should recover once you're in your vehicle."

Koyt gave a staccato nod and tried to lurch away, but Nimit held fast. "If you threaten her again, they'll be shipping you home in an ice cube tray."

Koyt eyed him warily but said nothing. He turned toward his polecat, teeth clacking, grunting his distress. "Everything was negotiable," he yelled hoarsely, over his shoulder, his head steaming, an icy sheen forming on his hair. "There was no need for this. None. You are savages." Livid, he turned and hurled a final epithet in Russian and growled hoarsely, "If you and Bascomb hadn't found our discarded weapon under the ice, none of this would have happened, damn you."

Nimit shook his head.

"Jack?" Hanley said, looking at him closely. "What's he saying?"

Teeth chattering, body quaking, Koyt answered for him. "Simple. Jack Nimit was there when Annie Bascomb found the rocket."

"You know about the missile?" Hanley said to Nimit.

Koyt scurried back, a foot closer to them. "Well? Are you going to lie to her?"

Nimit stood alongside Hanley. "Annie and I," he said, "we found the thing in the water. Last summer."

"Excellent!" Koyt spat and resumed his awkward trot toward the polecat, teeth clattering like castinets. "Confession is so good for the soul."

The lights of the first vehicle racing out from Trudeau were growing larger.

Nimit glanced at her and turned away. He walked to the wanigan, climbed up the ladder to the driver's side. Hanley followed, clambering up into the passenger seat. He removed his helmet; she did as well.

"Let me see your arm, Jack." He mutely held it out for her inspection.

"You're lucky. A surface wound." She reached for the wanigan's first-aid kit and tore open a pack of gauze.

"Talk to me," Hanley said. "You have to tell me."

"Koyt's been nosing around everywhere in the station. He must have figured it out from the field records. I was assisting Annie with the drone last summer."

"What happened?" she said.

"We were at the polynya, taking readings. The drone was circling deeper than it was supposed to and picked up something odd on its sonar and laser video. Its compass went nuts from the mass of metal. Annie saw what it was in a heartbeat. She marched up and down the beach ice, raging. She was livid. 'No imperialist Yankees are going to compromise the Arctic!'"

"Yankees?"

"She assumed it was American, like the rest of the marine pollution she was tracking. She said, 'This thing makes their hideous toxics look harmless!' I barely kept her from calling Mackenzie and Verneau, and putting the story out to the world that afternoon. The session was under way, new people arriving every day. If she revealed what we'd found, there'd be panic, the season would be lost, Trudeau closed for our own safety, maybe never reopened."

"So what did you do?" Hanley wasn't sure she wanted to hear the answer.

"Me? Nothing."

"And Annie?" She started to shiver.

"When we got back to Trudeau, she started digging on the Internet. A couple of days later, she dragged me out on the permanent shore ice where it was beautiful and peaceful, and she screamed at me, pumping herself up to take on everybody. 'Did you know seawater mixed with rocket fuel produces sulfuric acid? Only a matter of time before that fucking thing starts to leak! Nothing can withstand the sea forever. The whole Arctic ecosystem will become radioactive.' She was right. It was unthinkable." He bit his lip as she tightened the bandage.

"She said the device had to be exposed even if it meant Trudeau had to shut down. Whoever had put it there had to come and remove it, immediately. She prepared a public statement."

"What did you do about Annie wanting to go public?"

"I begged her not to. A media storm would wreck the place. Sponsorships would dry up, staff would flee. I know it was selfish, but I built this place. I didn't want to see it destroyed. She wouldn't listen. She lectured me on Canadian denial." He paused. "I thought Alex might talk some sense into her."

"Why Alex?"

"They went way back. She respected him. So I risked it: asked him to help persuade her to keep it quiet. He saw the danger to Trudeau instantly. He pleaded with her not to go public, said that we could handle it ourselves. She said it was a global disgrace. Once it began to leak, the Arctic would become a dead zone."

"A shore of corpses."

Nimit gave her an odd look.

"Go on." She'd finished patching him and started patching the suit.

"Alex kept her talking. It went on for days. She quieted down, then flared up again. Kossuth had brought her to Trudeau. If she was going to tear it down by going public . . . He felt responsible.

He stopped sleeping, started drinking, and muttering to himself all the time. Just before their last field assignment at the polynya, she told him she was going to send the drone down to get video of it and release it over the Internet—just raise holy hell."

"What did Kossuth do?"

"He was beside himself. This place was his life. He called her a self-righteous bitch, said she would destroy everything we all had worked for. He threatened her. She just laughed."

"She didn't take the threat seriously?"

"She told him he was being ridiculous. At least that's what he said. He asked me to help him shut her up."

"Did you?"

"No. No."

"Thank God."

"But I didn't stop him either."

"You knew this, about Kossuth, and you didn't tell me."

Nimit couldn't meet her eyes. "I couldn't believe he'd done it. I knew he wanted to silence her, but I couldn't believe he'd kill her. When you arrived, I kept hoping you'd find some natural explanation. I didn't think he could have killed them all like that."

"Jack, who knew what was on the shaman's pouch?"

Nimit was silent.

"Little Trudeau was an archaeological dig, right? Must have been an expert around who could read Aleut. Someone must have translated it and talked about what it meant with the rest of the people on the dig. That's the thing about Trudeau, right, you all share your findings? So all of you who were here back then would have known—including Alex Kossuth."

"Yeah, we all knew what it said."

"So why the hell didn't you tell me?"

" 'Ghost plant' didn't sound like anything local. The consensus between the archaeologists and the botanists was that it was probably some plant he'd brought here with him. And nobody got sick or anything handling the pouch. How could the plant that killed him have killed Annie and the others?"

"Kossuth freeze-dried the algae and put it in her talcum. Why he killed Ogata and Minskov, I don't know."

"I can't think he meant to. It had to be unintentional. Maybe they all shared her talc and he wasn't expecting that, or the devastating effect of the stuff."

"That would explain his remorse—and suicide."

"He must have listened on the local channel for the others to summon help for Annie. When he heard what was happening, I think he lost his mind. That he'd killed himself didn't surprise me." Nimit hunched. "I felt bad enough to contemplate it myself."

"Jack, you didn't kill them. Alex did."

"I couldn't believe I hadn't warned anyone about his threats. I still can't believe he meant to cause lasting harm. I really think he just wanted to put Annie out of commission for a while." Nimit bit his lip. "It's a miracle Alex didn't wipe us all out."

"Why didn't you tell me? I would have been looking for something manufactured, not something out in the wild. And you're still not telling me everything. What about Dee? Kossuth didn't kill Dee."

Nimit was ashen.

"Or Ingrid Kruger." She was exasperated. "His body wasn't contaminated. He didn't kill her either."

He made no response.

"Jack? Listen to me—"

Nimit gestured over his shoulder. "I've got an inflatable sea kayak in back, extra electrical drivers and hydrogen cells, food, a wind-turbine rig that could power it in a pinch."

"Oh, no. No. You don't have to go. You didn't do anything. You didn't cause it."

"That's just it. I didn't do *anything*. I knew Alex intended to shut Annie up however he could. I did nothing to stop him. I couldn't face everything coming out about what she'd found, seeing Trudeau shut down, all our work—all my work—shot to hell. I let him go out on the ice with her. I am guilty. And I didn't tell you in time to save Ingrid. Or Dee."

"If you leave now, where can you possibly go?"

"South."

"South? Everywhere from here is south."

"To Nunavut, to Inuit territory."

"But there's nothing there—wilderness."

"There's nothing here," he said. "I can't stay at Trudeau. It's finished for me." He was in despair.

Hanley put her hand on his shoulder. "Please, Jack. Stay. Your involvement may not even come out."

"Everything's going to come out. You can't silence two hundred people. I can't face that. My punishment is having to leave. I *belong* here. You can't imagine."

"Jack!"

"There's no way around it for me. I have nowhere to go, but also no choice. If I hadn't asked Alex to talk her out of it . . . I'm sorry, more than you can know. I was never happier, never more useful than here. It will stay the best part of my life. I . . . I fell in love here."

"Please, Jack. Darling, you can't—"

Nimit started up the engine. The approaching lights were close now. "I've gotta go."

Hanley wanted to say something to stop him, but couldn't. She opened the passenger door to climb down. Jack pulled her back.

"Shut the door, Jessie! Now!" She did, and saw through the windshield that Koyt was making his way toward the wanigan. He had fashioned an outer layer from the polecat's emergency blankets, and makeshift boots from the stuffing in the seat cushions. He was shouldering a large rifle—the bear gun from the vehicle. He shuffled toward them, eyes fixed on the biocontainment canister lying by the wanigan. Hanley saw what he was after and quickly exited the cab to get to it first. The air seized her lungs; she'd left her helmet. She ran toward the canister.

A shot cracked.

The sound stopped her cold. She spun around. Nemerov was walking forward into the light, dressed in his heavy black naval gear, eyes narrowed against the cold, arm straight out, accusingly, gloved hand closed over a small pistol, pointed at Koyt. In spite of the fur-lined hood of his parka, the cold had already frosted his mouth, his eyes. Behind him bobbed more vehicle lights.

Koyt leaned heavily on the butt of the rifle he'd stuck barrel first into the ice. With his free hand, he felt around his torso. His hand came away red, steaming. The blood froze in the open air. He eyed it, squinting against frost.

Nemerov advanced steadily, gun still outstretched.

"You and the admiral will pay for this," Koyt said, face gray with cold, coughing. He leaned forward on the rifle butt for support.

The bullet punched a small hole in Koyt's throat. He straightened for a second, eyes wide, then toppled backward.

Nemerov lowered his arm, the pistol at his side. He made sure Koyt was finished, then walked past her to retrieve the canister. He brought it to her. "The admiral he . . . he's dead," he said.

Hands buried deep in his pockets, he hunched against the alarming cold and walked back toward his polecat.

The bulbous wheels of Nimit's vehicle churned as it moved off. Hanley saw her helmet on the ice, tossed out for her. She put it on and climbed an ice boulder, and watched the wanigan's lights cut the dark, the beams growing ever narrower and shorter as it bucked across the floe. They were mere flickers by the time the others reached her.

# 53

It was hard to have to peer at Dee through the thick plastic quarantine covering, harder not to touch her. Hanley and Uli stood silently for some minutes. Finally, Hanley undid one of the ports on the side of the container.

"Doctor Hanley!" Uli exclaimed. "You are not worried about contamination?"

Hanley sadly shook her head no, and reached in to put a tiny sprig of white Arctic poppies on Dee's shoulder. She still looked contorted and anguished, Hanley thought, and would forever. The thought of remembering her like this was awful.

She bent close to Dee and remained that way for several moments, rocking. "I don't know," she said, emitting a deep sigh and swaying back and forth. "I don't know." She was bereft. Then she stopped.

"What is it?" Uli said.

"Her lips."

"What about them?"

Hanley was distracted. "They're dry."

She recovered herself, brushed her own cheek and reached in through the port again to touch the tear to Dee's lips.

Uli shuddered. "It's cold. I am having chills."

She nodded, absently, and closed the port. "Yeah. We've said good-bye. Let's go."

■

Mackenzie surprised everyone by announcing that his retirement was effective immediately. His office was being cleared to facilitate Emile Verneau's succession.

"I hope I'm not interrupting," Hanley said to his secretary, stepping into the space that, oddly, seemed less spacious and smaller empty. The windows, however, appeared bigger, taking in the radiance of the starry sky.

"Not at all," the young man responded. "I'm nearly done. Just the art and plaques left to take down. I don't know why he's doing this now. We have months to go before the winter session is over and planes can get in. Oh, please forgive me, Dr. Hanley. Can I get you tea, coffee?"

She shook her head. "I'm fine, thank you. Is he around?"

"He went down to the herbarium."

Hanley thanked him and wended through the now-familiar corridors to the dome that housed the plants Dee had loved. Entering through the round valve door, she found the herbarium empty except for Mackenzie, who was sitting with his back against a rock outcropping, feeding the atrium's tiny finches by hand. Amazingly, they alit on his palm and pecked at the particles of food. Their song was the only sound. The room couldn't have been more peaceful.

He raised his free hand in greeting, moving slowly so as not to disturb the birds. She walked up the flat paving stones along the room's edge, trying not to spook them.

"If you keep your distance and sit down very carefully, they'll stay," he said softly, his eyes on the birds.

Hanley approached cautiously and sat down on a step a few yards from where he was communing with the tiny creatures. All but one took wing. The lone maverick remained, feasting.

He said, "There's one in every crowd." His voice was light, but his face seemed pinched. "I gather your encounter on the ice with Mr. Koyt was quite intense."

"You could say that. He was pretty insistent on getting his hands on the infective agent. I'm not sure what would have happened if Captain Nemerov hadn't arrived."

"Thank God for that. If it ever enters a biological arsenal—anyone's . . . What am I saying?" He sighed. "It has to now, I suppose. The Americans' for sure, perhaps Canada's too, if we've got such a capability."

"Yes," she said, "most likely."

"But that has to be the concern of others. I've done my work. And you've done yours."

"Not completely," she said. "Questions remain. I haven't cleared up Dee's death."

Mackenzie glanced up from the bird. "You're right."

"Or Ingrid Kruger's, for that matter. I'm trying not to blame myself. Ned Gibson says I mustn't. He says it's natural to feel that way. Survivor's guilt."

"I imagine he would know," Mackenzie said. The tiny bird hopped off his hand for a moment, then right back on. "Greedy beggar," Mackenzie said. "How did you know I was here?"

"I stopped by your office."

Mackenzie nodded. "Has my secretary finished packing up? Emile needs to get in there."

"Almost. Just the plaques and photographs left, including that one I like so much."

"Which is that?" he said.

"The Inuit hunter in furs. He's lying alongside a seal, almost like he's kissing it."

"Like it, do you?"

"It intrigues me," Hanley said. She hugged her knees and rested her chin against them. "It's a powerful image, the man being so intimate with the animal."

"Do you recognize the subject?"

"I didn't when I first saw it." Hanley pictured the seal reclining in death. The man heavily clad in furs, lying next to it like a lover, arm across the carcass. "It's Jack, isn't it?"

"Yes, taken years ago, when he was in his teens. You should have it. I would be happy if you accepted."

"I do accept. What's he doing?" she said. "In the photograph?"

"When an Inuit hunter kills an animal, he thanks it for its life by melting snow in his mouth and giving it water. That's what Jack is doing with the seal he's killed."

"Giving it water?"

"Yes, from his mouth."

Hanley nodded thoughtfully. "Say more."

"A spiritual gesture. A kindness to the animal's soul. An intimacy. The belief is that the seal, who comes on land and allows itself to be killed, is thirsty, and the hunter must reciprocate by slaking its thirst. So it's a ritual expression of regret—and thanks."

"A sort of apology." Water, she thought, full of benign bacteria, not from the victims' mouths.

"And a redemption," Mackenzie said.

"Will the Canadian authorities pursue him?"

He seemed reluctant to answer. "Most probably, yes. They're duty bound. Whether they'll find him is another matter. It's awfully big country he's headed toward. And they're not even certain what they're after him for. Eventually, they'll relent."

"You know," she said, dabbing at her eyes, "his feelings for you, Dr. Mackenzie . . . It actually made me jealous to think how much he cared for you, and how much your mentoring affected him."

Mackenzie nodded, gravely.

"He loves you," she said. "Unconditionally."

"He's a fine young man."

"Were you surprised he could keep silent about what Alex had done to Annie? And his other colleagues?"

"No."

"How not?"

"Because of what the station means to him."

"As it does to you."

"Yes, to many of us. Also, given what's at stake—or was."

"How do you mean?"

"Geothermally speaking, things are desperate. The changes in the Arctic are ominous. Whatever the planet is in for from greenhouse gases, it will affect us here first. That's how the global atmosphere works. Little stands in the way of warming except research done at rare outposts like Trudeau. Jack was well aware of that. I think he was trying to protect us, protect the Arctic."

"Even at the cost of human life?"

"So it turned out," Mackenzie said, "awful though that was." He sounded anguished.

"What is making you step down now?" she asked, her voice vibrating slightly, but otherwise calm.

He shrugged. "I . . . it was time. My colleagues are gone. Our Russians are resigning to a man. Maybe the Japanese too. We're losing sponsors. Primakov, Ned Gibson, going. Jack already gone. It's not the same. And when news of what the Russians have left down there gets out . . . They will surely shut the station when they come to deal with the missile."

"Close Trudeau?"

"For the summer season at least. If there's no way to remove the monstrosity safely, they could close it forever. No one knows." He shook his head. "The research here at Trudeau is vital to the survival of the Arctic. Perhaps of the entire planet. Without Trudeau . . ." He tilted his head back. "We dreamed the dream here, quite a number of us. It demanded many sacrifices to make this place a reality." He sounded bitter.

"Perhaps you blame yourself also."

"I can't help it," he said.

"What will you do? Where will you go?"

"I haven't thought it through. To be quite honest, it's been dispiriting this winter. I'm feeling somewhat used up."

She bit her lip. "I think others would share that sentiment, if they could."

"Others?"

She counted them off on her fingers. "Junzo Ogata, Minskov, Annie Bascomb, Tarakanova, Dr. Kruger, Alex Kossuth. All those young sailors. Dee."

Mackenzie stared straight ahead, his face exhausted, eyes empty. His features took on the aspect of the mineral samples that had littered his desk: hard, ruched.

Hanley shifted. "If you don't mind my saying so, you seem like you could use some time away. I was thinking you might revisit Little Trudeau, take a sentimental journey back to the early days, when everything was clearer." He watched her intently. "Leave high tech behind. Wear furs. Do some basic archaeological work."

"I'm not sure I'm up to making nostalgic day trips."

"For the rest of this season, I meant. Camp out at Little Trudeau."

"You're talking months."

"Perhaps do a small dig."

"A dig?"

"Yes," she said. "A contemplative venture to get back in touch. I mean, you have gasoline cached there, rations, a generator."

"I'll give it some consideration."

"Good." She glanced at her watch. "Uli and Captain Nemerov are ready to take you. Everything's there. You won't need much."

Mackenzie appraised her with concern. "Are you all right?"

Hanley shook her head. "Mostly not. Dee meant a lot to me." She fixed him with her eyes. "What *about* that sentimental journey?"

"I . . . I don't think fussing with gasoline generators and oil heaters would offer much respite."

"You realize," she said, "Ottawa knew about the abandoned missile all along. Annie Bascomb and the others, they died for nothing. All that's going to come out, unless something is done."

He eyed her for a moment before speaking: "I don't follow."

Hanley picked up a twig of scrub and twirled it in her fingers, remembering how much Dee had loved this spot.

"I didn't either," she said. "Then I thought over what Jack had told me about Inuit souls. That they have two. An eternal one that goes on, and a baser one that doesn't. I think you have two souls, Dr. Mackenzie. One quite splendid. The other . . . compromised."

"Please explain yourself," he said, his expression strained.

"There's no one else Jack would have sacrificed himself for. Certainly not Alex Kossuth. Jack would only have turned himself into a scapegoat for you. He tried to take all your sins away with him into the wilderness. Draw suspicion away from you and onto himself. I'd like to think that's what he's doing. I can't bear to think you ruined him and drove him away. I wonder if you understand the depth of his loyalty. Even with me, he pretended that he and Alex were the only ones who'd tried to keep Annie quiet. Perhaps he left because he couldn't bear to be here anymore, near you, knowing what he knew."

She paused to see if he was going to protest. He sat silent, unmoving. She went on.

"Jack told me that he went to Alex Kossuth to talk Annie out of going public. But he wouldn't have gone to Alex. He would have come to you, his mentor, the man for whom he built this place. *You* went to Alex, your oldest friend at Trudeau. You convinced him Annie Bascomb was endangering everything both of you had worked for. Somebody had to shut her up. And Alex did—for you. But Alex was practically cracking. I very much doubt he was in any shape to figure out the identity of the shaman's ghost plant, much less handle making the ghost plant powder out of the algae that had come from the hydrohole. You did it for him, and sent him on his errand. With him and Annie dead, you thought the station was safe again. Jack would never speak of the rocket under the ice, would never do anything to harm you or this place. Then Ingrid Kruger became determined to know everything about her lover's last weeks, so you had to deal with her too."

He covered his eyes. He could barely stand to hear it. She didn't stop.

"You had waited to silence Annie until it was too late in the year for anyone to get here, anyone who might eventually realize it wasn't an accidental exposure out on the ice. Then I appeared. And you would have contaminated me as well. Is that why you were so eager to convince yourself I meant nothing to Jack?" Her face shriveled.

"Jack left only on the condition that you would be safe." He reached for her, to touch her. She drew back, crying out involuntarily. "You have to understand," he said, bringing a hand to his face in a fist. "I couldn't face what that device meant for us all, what it dashed." He turned away. "I did a terrible thing."

"Many terrible things, actually. You unleashed this indiscriminate horror on everyone." She looked away for a moment. "You didn't kill Ingrid Kruger and Dee to save Trudeau. You did it to protect yourself."

"I was afraid." Tears filled his eyes. "I was afraid a lifetime's work would be undone by my unpardonable act."

"Well put, Dr. Mackenzie. You have a gift for synthesis, for inspiring and leading others. A great gift." She hugged herself to stop her shivering. "You acted to protect your creation. But if Trudeau doesn't survive, it won't be because of Annie. It will be because of you. You've brought ruin. You're the station's greatest liability. You. And you'll have to erase that if the unblemished legacy of the great Felix Mackenzie is to be preserved."

"I . . ."

"You need to complete your dark work. If you do, your complicity will be kept secret." There was a slight tremor at her center that shook her body. "Trudeau will be spared that, whatever else may befall it."

Mackenzie's eyes welled up. He sighed.

"You have a little time to make it right."

"How?" he said.

"The dig."

"Are you imprisoning me there? Punishing me? You don't think it would be dangerous?"

"I'm sure it will be. Exceedingly. Especially with gasoline generators underground. One needs to be careful with ventilation."

"Jessie. You can't be asking—"

"Who's asking?" She wanted to look away but kept him in sight. "Do you suppose I could sleep knowing the man who'd hunted us like animals, who destroyed Dee in my place, was under the same roof"—she glared at him—"enjoying the heather? You've killed nearly one hundred people. What are we supposed to do, sing 'Auld Lang Syne' and move on?"

He sat quiet for a moment, then pulled his knees to his chest. "You don't understand. They made utter fools of us, a mockery of this place that is a gift, and mortally endangered it."

"I don't care. I do not care! Dee's life was a gift. Annie's life was a gift. Ingrid Kruger's . . . all the rest. I'm a doctor. I can't kill you. But, God, I wish you dead."

He was bewildered, distraught. "How . . . how much time do I have, to put my affairs in order?"

"At Trudeau? None. On the planet? That's your decision. But if you are still . . . with us at noon tomorrow, everything about what's happened here will be made public. If you attempt to come back to the station beforehand, the arrangement is likewise void."

"Is there—?"

"No."

"Dr. Hanley—"

She rose in a fluid motion. "I will be sorry to hear of your accident," she said, and left without looking back.


Nemerov and Uli stopped her as she came out of the herbarium. She took the captain's black pistol from her pocket and handed it back to him. He tucked it into the admiral's sealskin jacket, so old and polished with wear that it shone.

"How did he take it?" Nemerov said.

"He's resigned to doing the honorable thing, I think."

"We will escort him," Nemerov said.

Uli touched her forearm with concern. "You were brave to face him alone. Listen, we have found some suspicious powder in his quarters. Kiyomi is searching to make sure we have found it all."

Nemerov said, "Teddy Zale wants to see you in extern immediately." He offered his handkerchief. Hanley hadn't realized until then that she was weeping. She thanked him.

"Would you like to leave with us?" he said. "We are taking the admiral. We will bury him at sea."

The idea of home was overwhelming, but she shook her head. "I've volunteered to provide basic medical care until they can get a replacement in here. Practice on the living for a change. That'll keep me busy, so I won't have to think too much. When I can face it, I'll go back to the lab and try to learn whatever I can about the toxic microbe in the algae. I figure I've only got a slim head start before somebody out there tries to put it to use. I might as well take advantage of that and see if we can figure out a way to protect against it. My techs have agreed to help." She dabbed at her eyes with the handkerchief. "I'm also going to spend at least a part of every day with my son. Electronic visits for the moment, but that's better than nothing, which is what he's gotten from me lately. Are my eyes red?"

"You can't see in this light," Nemerov said, and touched her cheek with his palm.

Hanley sniffled and headed for the extern tower alone. She paused by windows along the way, staring over the crackled ice at a nightscape without color: black and bone white. She felt the Arctic's enormity and loneliness and peace.

When she got to the extern, the lights were dim.

"Eventually," Teddy said, "a dull smudge of pink will appear along the horizon at midday. It'll last maybe a quarter of an hour and turn oxblood red. People here will gather every day to see it, as if it were sunrise on Mars."

"What's up, Teddy? You wanted me?"

Zale led her under the dome of the communications center and pointed up at a large map of the Arctic projected on the curved ceiling. "AVHRR thermal infrared satellite images."

Unlike most atlases, proportions on this map were true, and Hanley felt the full immensity of their distance from anywhere. The polar region was like another continent, with Trudeau an infinitesimal orange dot near the center. Teddy pointed to a quadrant almost directly overhead: a live satellite image, he said, of the highest resolution. He enlarged it.

Hanley had been at Trudeau long enough now to recognize the demarcation between sea ice and land-fast ice. A tiny point of warmth on the sea ice was advancing incrementally toward the field of white that was the land. A dot in the dark void, moving steadily. Nothing chasing him but ghosts.

"That's the new Inuit territory," he said. "It's huge, Doc. He gets there, they'll never see him again."

Nor will we, Hanley thought, tears silently rolling. Nor will we.

"But if a friend were to show up in a year or so," Teddy said, gazing up, "I'm sure he would know and come find that friend."

"You think?"

Teddy nodded. "I gotta go," he said, jabbing a thumb vaguely over his shoulder, and left Hanley alone with the speck moving slowly across the vastness toward home.

# ACKNOWLEDGMENTS

My eternal gratitude to Bella Pomer, my dear friend. Thank you for your kindness and help. I shall always remember you there with us, in the icy snows.

And many thanks to the inimitable Kim McArthur and her gang: Janet Harron, Ann Ledden, Taryn Manias, Jim Palmieri, and Thea Kooy. Nunavut rocks! And so does McArthur & Company.